THE SILVER MAGE

Katharine Kerr was born in Ohio in 1944 and now lives in San Francisco. Her extensive reading in the fields of classical archaeology and medieval and Dark Ages history and literature has had a clear influence on her work. Her novels have been published around the world and she is a bestseller on both sides of the Atlantic.

By Katharine Kerr

The Deverry Series:
DAGGERSPELL
DARKSPELL
DAWNSPELL
DRAGONSPELL

A TIME OF EXLIE
A TIME OF OMENS
A TIME OF WAR
A TIME OF JUSTICE

THE RED WYVERN
THE BLACK RAVEN
THE FIRE DRAGON
THE GOLD FALCON
THE SPIRIT STONE
THE SHADOW ISLE

Other Fiction:
POLAR CITY BLUES
FREEZEFRAMES
SNARE

With Mark Kreighbaum:
PALACE

THE
SILVER MAGE

BOOK SEVEN OF
THE DRAGON MAGE

KATHARINE KERR

HARPER
Voyager

HarperCollins*Publishers*
77–85 Fulham Palace Road,
Hammersmith, London w6 8jb

www.harpercollins.co.uk

Published by Harper*Voyager*
An imprint of HarperCollins*Publishers* 2009

I

A catalogue record for this book
is available from the British Library

ISBN: 978-0-00-728736-9

This novel is entirely a work of fiction.
The names, characters and incidents portrayed in it are
the work of the author's imagination. Any resemblance to
actual persons, living or dead, events or localities is
entirely coincidental.

Set in Fairfield Light by
Palimpsest Book Production Limited,
Grangemouth, Stirlingshire

Printed and bound in Great Britain by
Clays Ltd, St Ives plc

Mixed Sources
Product group from well-managed
forests and other controlled sources
www.fsc.org Cert no. SW-COC-1806
© 1996 Forest Stewardship Council

FSC

FSC is a non-profit international organisation established
to promote the responsible management of the world's forests.
Products carrying the FSC label are independently certified
to assure consumers that they come from forests that are managed
to meet the social, economic and ecological needs
of present and future generations.

Find out more about HarperCollins and the environment at
www.harpercollins.co.uk/green

For Howard
First, Last, and Always

PROLOGUE

The Northlands
Summer, 1160

The serpent of Time winds itself about the cross of Matter. Some say it has seven heads, some only three, but the difference counts for little. It is the body of the serpent, not the head, that crushes its prey.

The Secret Book of Cadwallon the Druid

D eath had turned Dougie's hair white and his flesh translucent. In the darkness he glowed with a faint silvery light as he stood smiling at Berwynna.

'Remember me, lass,' he said in the language of Alban, 'but live your life, too. I loved you enough to wish you every happiness. Find a new man.'

'I don't want to,' Berwynna said. 'The only thing I want is for you to come back to me.'

'This is as far back as I can come, just up to this side of dying. Wynni, live your life!'

He vanished.

Berwynna screamed and sat up, scattering blankets. She found herself in a round tent so unfamiliar that for a moment she thought she still dreamt. *The Ancients*, she reminded herself. *I'm safe among the Ancients, but Dougie's dead.* The first light of dawn fell like a grey pillar through the smoke hole in the centre of the roof. Across from her, on the far side of the tent, a bundle of blankets stirred and yawned. Uncle Mic sat up and peered at her through the uncertain light.

'Are you all right?' he said in Dwarvish. 'Did you make some sort of a sound just now?'

'I was dreaming,' she said. 'In the dream I saw Dougie, and when he disappeared, I screamed.'

'Ai, my poor little niece!' Mic paused to rub his face with both hands and yawn prodigiously. 'It sounded like a moan, here in the waking world.'

'That would fit, too.'

Mic let his hands fall into his lap. From outside came the noises of a camp stirring awake – dogs barking, people talking in an unfamiliar language, occasionally a child crying or calling out. Distantly a horse whinnied, and mules brayed in answer.

'We might as well get up,' Berwynna said.

'Indeed, and I wouldn't mind a bit of breakfast, either.'

They'd both slept dressed. Mic pulled on his boots, then got up and left the tent. Berwynna busied herself with rolling up their bedrolls.

'Berwynna?' Dallandra pulled back the tent flap and came in. 'You're awake, then?'

'I am, my lady.'

'There's no need to call me lady,' Dallandra said with a smile. 'I wanted to tell you that your father's flown off to scout the Northlands. He asked me to give you his love and to tell you he'll be back again as soon as he can.'

'My thanks.' Berwynna bit her lip in disappointment. 'I'd wanted to say farewell.'

'Dragons come and go as they please, not as we want, I'm afraid. He also told me about the lost dragon book.'

Berwynna winced. Dallandra sat down opposite her. In the pale light from the rising dawn, she seemed made of silver, with her ash blonde hair, steel grey eyes, and her pale skin, so unexpected in a person who lived most of her life out of doors. *Silver or mayhap steel*, Berwynna thought, *like the pictures on the doors of Lin Serr*.

'In a moment I'll have to go tend the wounded men,' Dallandra said. 'But I wanted to ask you about the book. You've seen it, I take it.'

'I have,' Berwynna said. 'Not that I were able to read a word of it, mind. Laz, he did say that it be written in the language of the Ancients, your language, that be.'

'It was written, then, in letters?'

'Be not all books written so?'

'They are, truly.' Dallandra smiled at her. 'But some also have pictures in them.'

'I never did see such, but then, my sister wouldn't be allowing me to turn its pages, and no doubt she were right about that, too. What little I did see did look to me much like the carvings on our walls.'

'The what?'

'Forgive me.' Berwynna smiled briefly. 'I do forget you've not seen Haen Marn. In the great hall, the walls, they be of wood, and there be carvings all over them, letters and such, I do suppose them to be. Laz, he did call some of them sigils, whatever those may be.'

'They're a particular type of sign, a mark that stands for the name of a thing or a place or suchlike.' Dallandra paused. 'Well, that will do as an explanation, though it's not a very good one.'

''Twill do for me, truly. But the book, it were such a magical thing. It does ache my heart that I had somewhat to do with the losing of it.'

'No one's blaming you, Wynni. Try not to blame yourself. You're exhausted, you're mourning your betrothed, and every little thing's going to weigh upon you now. One of these days your mind will be clearer, and you'll be better able to judge what happened.'

'I'll hope that be true.'

'It *is* true. I lost a man I loved very much, and I thought at the time that I'd mourn him all my life. In time, I laid my mourning aside and found another love. So I know how you must feel.'

'You must, truly.' For the first time since Dougie's death, Berwynna felt – not hope, precisely, but a rational thought, that one day hope would come. 'My thanks for the telling of this.'

'You're most welcome.' Dallandra reached over and patted her on the shoulder. 'Now, about the book, though, I'd like to know how large it was, how thick, how many pages.'

'As to the pages, well, now, I be not sure of that. It were a great heavy thing –' Berwynna stopped, struck by a sudden realization. 'At least, it were at first, when Dougie did bring it to Haen Marn. But it did shrink.'

'It what?'

'I did carry it once on Haen Marn, and it were so heavy that there were a need on me to clasp it in both arms.' Berwynna demonstrated by holding her empty arms out in front of her. 'But when I did take it from the island, it did fit most haply in one of my saddlebags.'

'That's extremely interesting.'

'Laz did talk of guardian spirits. Think you they do have the power to change it – oh, that sounds so daft!'

'Not daft at all. That's exactly what I think must have happened. A person with very powerful dweomer made that book.' Dallandra got up, stretching her back as if it pained her. 'My apologies, but I truly do have to go now. Your uncle should be here with your breakfast in a moment, but please, feel free to leave this tent. Come out whenever you're ready. This will be your first day in a Westfolk alar, so everything's going to seem strange to you, but your other uncle – Ebañy, his name is – will be glad to introduce you around.'

'My thanks.' Berwynna rose and joined her. 'Be there any help I may give you?'

'Not needed. I have apprentices.' Dallandra cocked her head to one side to listen. 'Ah, here's Mic now.' She strode over and held the tent flap open.

'My thanks,' Mic said as he ducked inside. He was carrying a basket in one hand and a pottery bowl in the other. 'Bread and soft cheese, Wynni.'

Berwynna took the bowl from him. When she glanced around, Dallandra had already gone, slipping out in silence.

Dallandra found Neb and Ranadario at work in the big tent that the alar had allocated to its healers. Ranadario was explaining how to bandage a bad wound on the upper arm of one of the Cerr Cawnen men while Neb listened, his head cocked a little to one side as if he were afraid that her words would evade him. Their patient, a beefy blond fellow with the odd name of Hound, kept his eyes shut tight and panted in pain. The wound had cut deep into the side of his upper arm, missing the largest blood vessels but severing muscles and tendons. Dallandra doubted that he'd ever be able to use the arm properly again.

'Ranadario,' Dallandra said in Deverrian. 'Did you give him willow water to drink?'

'I did, Wise One,' Ranadario said. 'This cut is healing so slowly, though.'

Hound opened his eyes and stared at her. His breathing turned ragged, and Neb laid a hand on his unwounded shoulder to steady him.

'Not slowly for a child of Aethyr.' Dalla paused for a quick smile to reassure him. 'It's doing as well as we can expect. Don't you worry, now. It'll heal up soon.'

Hound returned the smile, then shut his eyes again.

With her apprentices to help her, Dallandra tended the wounds of the two Cerr Cawnen men and did what she hoped was right for the wounds of the others, four of them Horsekin and one a half-blood fellow. Since those who'd sustained the worst cuts in the fight to save the caravan had all died during their journey south, she could be fairly confident that those who'd lived to reach her would recover.

When she left the tent, Neb followed her with his fat-bellied yellow gnome trailing after. For a moment he merely looked up at the sky as if he were expecting rain. The gnome kicked him hard in the nearer shin.

'Dalla,' Neb said, 'I owe you an apology.'

The gnome grinned and vanished.

'You do, truly.' She kept her voice gentle. 'I wondered when it would come.'

'Pride's an infection in itself.' He was studying the ground between them. 'I should have spoken before this. I never should have tried to ride away like that.'

'Well, it's not like you're the only man or woman either to kick like a balky horse during training. It's a common enough stage in the apprenticeship, especially among the lads.'

Neb winced, his shoulders a little high, as if he expected a blow. 'Common, is it?' His voice choked on the words.

'Very, actually.' Dallandra felt genuinely sorry for his humiliation, but he'd earned every moment of it. 'I take it you're no longer so confused. Your decision about becoming a healer who incorporates dweomer into his work is a truly good one.'

At that he looked up again.

'Now, I'm a healer, certainly,' Dallandra continued, 'but it's only a craft for me. You're hoping to try somewhat new.'

'Hoping is about right. I don't know if I can or not.'

'No more do I, but I wager you'll succeed. At this stage you've got to learn both crafts down to the last jot.'

'I know that now.' Neb's voice rang with sincerity. 'And I promise you that I'll gather every scrap of knowledge that I possibly can.'

'Good! That's all anyone can ask of you. Now we'd both best clean up. I've got gore all over my hands, and your tunic is a fearsome sight.'

Dallandra had just finished washing her blood-stained hands in a bucket of water when one of the Cerr Cawnen men walked over, another beefy blond with narrow blue eyes, a common type among the Rhiddaer men, who were descended from the northern tribes of 'Old Ones', as the original inhabitants of the Deverrian lands used to be known. This particular fellow introduced himself as Richt, the caravan master.

'You do have all my thanks, Wise One,' he said, 'for the aid you and your people do give me and my men. I would gift you with somewhat of dwarven work. It be a trinket I did trade for in Lin Serr.' From the pocket of his brigga he brought out a leather pouch.

'I don't need any payment, truly,' Dallandra began, then stopped when he shook a pendant out of the pouch onto his broad palm. 'That's very beautiful.'

'As you are, and I would beg you to take it.'

The pendant hung by a loop from a fine silver chain. Two silver dragons twined around a circle of gems, set in silver. The jeweller had arranged three petal-shaped slices of moonstone and three of turquoise around a central sapphire.

'Are you sure you want to part with this?' Dallandra said.

'I be sure that I wish you to have it.' Richt smiled, a little shyly.

'Then you have my profound thanks.'

When Dallandra held out her hand, he passed the pendant over, then bobbed his head in respect and walked away. The more she studied the pendant, the happier she was that she'd accepted the gift. Rarely did she like jewellery enough to wear any of it, but this particular piece made her think of the moon and its magical tides. A bevy of sprites materialized in the air and hovered close to look at it. She could hear their little cries of delight, a sound much like the rustling of fine silks.

'Who gave you that?' a normal elven voice said.

Dallandra looked up to see Calonderiel watching her with his arms crossed over his chest.

'The caravan master,' she said. 'In thanks for tending his wounded men. He told me it's dwarven work.'

'Oh.' Cal relaxed with a smile. 'It's beautiful, isn't it? Thus, it suits you.'

'Shall I put it on?'

'Please do.'

The pendant hung just below Dallandra's collarbone. As it touched the magical nexus at that spot, she felt emanations.

'There's dweomer on this piece,' she said to Cal. 'I'm not sure what, though. I'll have to show it to Val later.'

'Maybe you'd better show it to her now. Are you sure it's safe to wear it?'

'Yes, actually. Cal, you sound so worried.'

'I keep thinking about the spell over Rori.' He paused, glancing away, biting his lower lip. 'And how dangerous it's going to be to lift. I've got suspicious of everything dweomer, I guess.'

'Reversing the spell may not be dangerous at all. We don't know that.'

Cal did his best to smile. 'If it turns out to be dangerous, then,' he said, 'warn me.'

'I will, I promise. I've been thinking about what happened to Evandar. He wasn't incarnate, don't forget, which meant there was nothing truly solid about him. He could appear to have a body, but at root he was nothing but pure spirit, pure vital force. After he drained himself of most of that power, there was nothing left for him to fall back on, as it were.'

'Ah.' Cal paused, visibly thinking this through. 'I do see what you mean. But I've heard you talk of the – what did you call that? the rule of compensation or suchlike.'

'The law of compensation, yes. Any great pouring out of dweomer force is going to have an equal reaction of some kind. The problem is knowing what it will be.' Dallandra smiled briefly. 'I may never be able to fly in my own bird form again. That's my best guess.'

'You're willing to do that?'

'Flying comes in handy, but it doesn't mean a great deal to me any more. I have you, I have our child, and the ground seems like a very pleasant place to be.'

He smiled so softly, so warmly, that she felt as if she'd worked some mighty act of magic.

'I do love you,' he said. 'I'm terrified of losing you.'

'Don't worry, and don't forget, I'll have a great deal of help – Val, Grallezar, Branna, and for all I know, the lass on Haen Marn knows enough to take part in whatever the ritual is.'

'That's right! I tend to forget about them. It's not like you'll be fighting this battle by yourself.'

Dallandra smiled and said nothing more. At the very beginning of a ritual she always asked that any harm it might evoke would fall upon her alone, but that Cal didn't need to know.

'I'm not just worrying for my own sake and for Dari's,' Cal went on. 'If you –' he hesitated briefly '– went away, what would happen to the changelings?'

'There are other dweomer workers. Look at Sidro. She's amazingly patient with those poor little souls, much more than I can be.'

'True.' He suddenly smiled. 'Oh very well, I'm truly worried if I can forget things like that. I'll do my best to stop, but I make no promises.'

Richt and his gift reminded Dallandra that she had an extremely unpleasant task ahead of her, telling her fellow dweomermaster in Cerr Cawnen about the fate of the caravan. As she went to her tent for privacy, she wondered if Niffa might already know, since Niffa had lost a great-nephew in that attack. The plight of bloodkin had a way of reaching a dweomermaster's mind. Indeed, as soon as Dallandra contacted her, she could feel Niffa's grief, as strong as a drench of sudden rain.

'My heart aches for your loss,' Dallandra said.

'My thanks,' Niffa said. 'Jahdo's the one who's suffering the more, alas. Aethel was always his favourite grandchild.'

Dallandra let a wordless sympathy flood out from her mind. Niffa's image, floating in a shaft of dusty sunlight, displayed tears in her dark eyes. Her pale silver hair hung dishevelled around her face, a sign of mourning.

'The men who've survived this long are likely to live,' Dallandra said. 'I just tended them and spoke with Richt. They won't be able to get back on the road for some while, though.'

'My thanks for the telling. With my mind so troubled, it's been a hard task to focus upon their images and read such things from them.'

'No doubt! Here, I'll let you go now. I'll contact you again to let you know how they're faring.'

Niffa managed a faint smile, then broke the link between them.

Just as Dallandra got up to leave, Sidro brought her the baby to nurse. They sat together, discussing the changeling children, until little Dari fell asleep. Dallandra settled the baby in the leather sling-cradle hanging in the curve of the tent wall. Westfolk infants sleep more or less upright, settled on beds of fresh-pulled grass, rather than wearing swaddling bands as we Deverry folk wrap our babies.

'I was just going to talk with Valandario,' Dallandra said. 'Do you think you could watch the baby for me?'

'Gladly, Wise One,' Sidro said. 'I'll take her with me to my tent, if that pleases you.'

'It does, and my thanks. Ah, here's Val now! I thought she might have heard me thinking about her.'

Val had, indeed. After Sidro left them, they spoke in Elvish. Valandario exclaimed over the pendant when Dallandra handed it to her, rubbed it between her fingers, and pronounced the dweomer upon it safe enough to wear.

'Someone's turned it into a talisman to attract good health, is all.' Val handed it back. 'Huh, and the dwarves claim they don't believe in dweomer!'

'Probably one of the women did the enchanting.'

'I suppose so.' Valandario settled herself on a leather cushion. 'I've been thinking about the dragon book, and I don't understand how Evandar could have written it. He couldn't read and write, could he?'

'I honestly don't know.'

'What? The subject never came up in all those hundreds of years?'

'There's something you don't understand. Hundreds of years passed in this world, yes. For me it was only a couple of long summers with barely a winter in between. That first time when I went to Evandar's country, I thought I'd spent perhaps a fortnight away.'

Valandario pursed her lips as if she were clamping them shut.

'Don't you believe me?' Dallandra went on.

'Of course I do.' Val stayed silent for a moment more, then let the words burst out. 'But how could you love a man who'd trick you that way? He trapped you in his little world, and by the Star Goddesses themselves, the grief he caused in this one!'

'Tricked me?' Dallandra found that words had deserted her. She sat down opposite Val, who apparently mistook her silence.

'I'm sorry,' Val said. 'A thousand apologies.'

'No, no, no need.' Dallandra managed to find a few words. 'I'd never – I don't think I ever thought of it – of him – that way before.'

'As what? A trickster? He had to be the consummate trickster, the absolute king of them all, from everything I know about him. This book – it's another of his tricks, isn't it? Like the rose ring and the black crystal. I hope it's the last of the bad lot.'

'Well, so do I.'

The silence hung there, icy in the pale silver light. Abruptly Val flung one hand in the air. The dweomer light above them changed to a warmer gold.

'About the book,' Val said. 'So Evandar could have written it.'

'Yes, perhaps he might have.' Dallandra let out her breath in a long sigh. 'Though it seems like it would have taken a long time, just from its size, I mean, and he had so little patience.'

Valandario quirked an eyebrow. Dallandra kept silent.

'What about the archives in the Southern Isles?' Val went on. 'Could it be a copy of something there?'

'I had hopes that way, but no,' Dallandra said. 'Meranaldar was a librarian there, you know, and he knew every single volume that survived the Great Burning. Before he left last autumn, I asked him about the book that Ebañy saw in the crystal. He didn't recognize it, and yes, he remembered all the covers of the books, too.'

'He would.' Valandario grinned at her. 'But boring or not, he was a useful sort of man to know. You were already wondering, last summer, if the book contained dragon lore, too.'

'So I was. He told me that the only dragon lore they had was the occasional comment or passage in books about other things.'

'Didn't you say that Jill had books from the Southern Isles?'

'Yes, and when she died, Evandar reclaimed them. Meranaldar told me that he brought them back to the archive. I've got her other books, and the only dragon lore in them is what she wrote in the margins.'

'So much for that, then. Now, what about Laz's book, his copy of the *Pseudo-Iamblichos Scroll*? It has such a similar cover. Sidro told me that he bought it already bound but with blank pages up in Taenbalapan. Do you suppose the dragon book came from there, too?'

'A very good point.' Dallandra rose and began to pace back and forth in the tent. 'I wonder if Evandar saw the other one there and acquired it somehow.'

'Stole it, you mean.' Valandario got up and joined her.

Dallandra swirled around to face her and set her hands on her hips. Val's expression revealed only a studied neutrality. *She's right*, Dallandra thought. *He really was an awful thief.* She wasn't quite ready to admit it aloud.

'Anyway, to return to the book.' Val's expression changed to narrow-eyed disgust. 'I suppose we'd better talk with Laz Moj about it.'

'You suppose? Val, you look like you just bit into turned meat.'

'He's someone else I have to forgive.' Valandario forced out a brittle little smile. 'After Jav's murder, Aderyn and Nevyn spent a long time trying to piece together what had happened. A very long time, truly. Things didn't fall into place till after the war where Loddlaen died.'

I was still gone then, Dallandra thought. The guilt bit deep. If she'd not gone off with Evandar, how different things might have been!

'It wasn't till then,' Val continued, 'that they realized Alastyr lay behind the murder and the war both.'

'Rori told me that Laz was once Alastyr.'

'Exactly, and I actually saw him when he was only a lad, a nasty little bit of work named Tirro. He grew up to be a merchant, and it was his ship that carried –' She paused briefly '– the crystal away, which is why no one could scry for it. They would have been out on the open sea by the time I tried to find them.'

She means the crystal and Loddlaen, Dallandra thought. Aloud, she said, 'I'll go speak with Laz, but there's no reason you need to come along.'

'Thank you. I was hoping you'd say that.' She hesitated again, then glanced away as if she'd decided not to say some painful thing.

'What is it, Val? You might as well say it.'

'Why couldn't Evandar have just told you about the book on Haen Marn?' Val's words floated on a bitter tide. 'Why all this secrecy and glittering crystals and the like? If that wretched crystal hadn't existed, Loddlaen wouldn't have coveted it. Yes, I know that sounds stupid, but he wanted it enough to kill for it. Why all the –' She stopped, breathing hard. 'My apologies.'

Dallandra could think of a dozen reasons why, but faced with Val's undying grief, she found them shallow, stupid, pointless – rationalizations, not reasons. She sighed and said the simple truth, 'I don't know why, Val. I truly don't.'

'Oh.' Val paused for a long cold moment. 'Yes, I suppose you don't.' She got up and left the tent.

Dallandra followed her, but she left Val her privacy, and instead went looking for Grallezar. The royal alar spread out along a sizeable stream, tents on one bank, horse herds and sheep flocks on the other. Against the rich green of the grass, the freshly painted designs on the tents gleamed in the summer sun as if the dull leather had been beaded and bejewelled. Children and puppies chased each other among the tents, followed by swarms of Wildfolk, crystalline sprites in the air, warty grey and green gnomes on the ground. Now and then this crazed parade ran into an adult who, nearly toppled, yelled imprecations upon them all as they raced on past.

Dallandra found her fellow dweomermaster standing on the edge of the camp well away from the children's chaos. She was talking with a Gel da'Thae man who wore a filthy grey shirt and trousers, the remnants of a regimental uniform, Dallandra assumed. Indeed, Grallezar introduced him as Drav, an officer in one of Braemel's old cavalry troops.

'He does want to take his men away from Laz and join us,' Grallezar said. 'I did tell him that only the prince could decide such a thing.'

'That's very true,' Dallandra said. 'How many men are there?'

'But four, and one of them wounded. Two others did die in the rescuing of that caravan.'

'I can't see, then, why Dar wouldn't agree. By all means, take Drav to him. I think Cal's over there, too. Could you ask Drav if Laz is going to come tell us about that crystal?'

The two Gel da'Thae conferred briefly. Drav rolled his dark eyes and swung one hand through the air, a gesture that Grallezar had often used when dismissing someone as a fool.

'He tells me,' Grallezar said in her dialect of Deverrian, 'that Laz be in a fair foul mood over Sidro. He does walk around swearing and kicking at things that be in his way. So he knows not what Laz might or might not do.'

'I see. Thank him for the information, will you? Then we can go talk with Dar.'

By then the royal alar had grown used to travelling with individuals of the race they'd always called Meradan, demons, now that they knew that these 'demons' were real flesh and blood, not some faceless horde but individuals who were capable of changing their minds and their allegiances. The prince was glad enough to have more highly trained warriors in his warband, even if these were Gel da'Thae.

'Besides,' Dar told Dallandra in Elvish, 'they understand the Horsekin, and they despise them even more than we do.' He rubbed his hands together. 'Drav has some solid information about their forces.'

Drav returned to his former camp to collect his men, but not long after he sent a messenger. Grallezar brought him and his news to Dallandra: Laz and those of his men who were unwounded were striking camp and planning on riding out.

'What?' Dalla snapped. 'He's leaving his wounded behind?'

The messenger spoke; Grallezar translated, telling her that the wounded men had asked to change their loyalties and stay with the alar. They would ride under Drav's orders, or so they'd sworn on the names of the old Gel da'Thae gods.

'Good riddance to the rest of them,' Grallezar said, 'or truly, it would be good riddance if we needed not to know what Laz knows.'

'But we do need to,' Dalla said. 'I'll go talk with him.'

'Might that not be dangerous?'

'It might, but I doubt it, not with his band so badly outnumbered, and Drav and his men right there.' Dallandra considered briefly. 'On the other hand, you might collect a few archers and come – oh say, about half-way to his camp.'

Grallezar grinned with a flash of needle-sharp teeth.

In the midst of a welter of half-struck tents and bedrolls, Laz's remaining men hurried back and forth, saddling horses and gathering gear. Dallandra found Laz standing by his saddled and bridled horse, a stocky chestnut that bore a Gel da'Thae cavalry brand. The bright sun picked out the pink scars on his face and those cutting into his short brown hair. *He's got a face like a knife edge*, Dallandra thought, *all sharp angles and bone and that beaky nose. He looks half-starved, too.* His smile did nothing to soften the impression.

'Welcome,' Laz called out. He spoke surprisingly good Deverrian. 'Or perhaps I should say farewell. Alas, fair lady, I feel the need to take leave of you and yours, before the rest of my men decide they'd rather join you than stay with me.'

'Well, I can understand that,' Dallandra said. 'It's too bad, though. I was going to offer to trade you dweomer lore in return for some information.'

'Oh?' Laz glanced away, entirely too casually. 'What kind of lore?'

'What are you most interested in?'

'At the moment, the burning questions in my mind concern those wretched crystals.' He looked at her again. 'Who, by the way, was Evandar?'

'I can tell you a great deal about Evandar. The black crystal, it's largely a mystery to me, though I do know somewhat that might interest you.' She paused to glance around them, saw some of his men standing nearby, and dropped her voice to a whisper. 'You owned it in a former life. In fact, I know somewhat about two of your former lives.' She raised her voice to a normal level. 'It won't make pleasant hearing, though, so no doubt you're wise to leave now.'

Laz's eyes went wide, and he whistled under his breath. He gaped at her, as well and truly hooked as a caught trout, gaping at the end of a fisherman's line. His horse stamped and tossed its head at the sudden slacking of its reins. At last Laz sighed and turned away to speak to his men in the Gel da'Thae language. Some of them shrugged, some of them raised eyebrows, others glanced skyward in disgust, but they all stopped work on striking the camp and began, instead, to restore it.

'We need to find a place to talk,' Laz said to Dallandra. 'We can meet between the camps.'

'Very well. You're welcome in our camp, for that matter. The Westfolk will never eavesdrop on a Wise One.'

'I will not set foot over there.' Laz's voice turned hard. 'I see no reason to let Pir gloat over me.'

'Oh come now, you know Pir better than I do! Would he truly gloat?'

'I never thought he'd steal my woman, either.' Laz hesitated, then shrugged. 'That's unfair of me. No one stole her. She's not a horse.' Laz seemed to be choking back either tears or anger, but he arranged a brittle smile.

He's trying, Dallandra thought. *Desperately trying to be fair, to do the right thing.* She regretted her slip, mentioning that she had information about two of his past lives. Discussing Lord Tren was doubtless safe enough, but Alastyr? She found herself loath to speak of dark dweomer. What if it awakened Laz's memories and, worse yet, his desire to use it? Worst of all, what if he already remembered and was hoping to get more information? Sidro had often warned her that Laz lied as cheerfully as most men jest.

'Well, it was her right to choose.' His voice sounded as tight as a drawn bowstring. 'Alas. Let me hand my horse over to Faharn, and then we shall go to neutral ground and talk.' Laz shaded his eyes and looked in the direction of Grallezar and the archers. 'Ah, I see you prudently stationed a few guards out there.'

'I'll dismiss them.'

He grinned again, bowed, and led his horse away.

*   *   *

Laz handed his horse over to Faharn, then gave his apprentice a few quick instructions about setting up the camp. By the time he returned to Dallandra, the archers had gone back to the Westfolk tents. Dalla had picked out a spot midway between their two camps and trampled down the grass in a small circle. When they sat down, he felt oddly private despite the blue sky above them, as if they sat in a tiny chamber curtained all round with fine green lace.

'Would you tell me what you know about the dragon book?' Dallandra began.

'The dragon book?' Laz said. 'Ah, there was a dragon on the cover, indeed. I held it in my hands and turned the pages, but I can't truly read your beautiful language, so I have no idea of what was written in it.'

'Berwynna told me that you thought the text had somewhat to do with dragons.'

'Somewhat. For one thing, there was the image on the cover.'

'I wanted to ask you about that. You have a book that's decorated with the reverse colours but the same outline of a dragon. Did you buy that in a marketplace?'

'I didn't. My sisters had it made specially for me as a coming of age present. I saved it for years until I had somewhat important to write in it. You look surprised.'

'I am. I suppose Evandar might have scried it somehow. He did see bits and pieces of future events, and if he saw you and the book, he might well have decided to make one much like it.'

'I truly want to learn more about this fellow.'

'I'll tell you, fear not! But about the book –'

'Well, beyond the cover, I could pick out a word here and there, and "drahkonnen" was one of them.' Laz paused to summon his memories. He could see the pages of the book clearly in his mind. 'Odd, now that I think of it! That word seemed to recur in the same place on every page. Indeed, about half-way down and to the right of the line, and on every page that I saw.'

'How very strange!'

Laz nodded his agreement. 'Did Wynni tell you about the spirits?'

'She mentioned that you'd said some were attached to the book, but no more than that. She apparently can't see the Wildfolk.'

'She can't, truly, but I did. They were spirits of Aethyr. They appeared once as flames, icy white with strangely coloured tips. Another time I saw them as a lozenge, floating just over the book. They can move it, by the by, and they must have some way of influencing people's minds. Somehow they tricked Wynni into taking it from the island.'

'That's fascinating! I can see Evandar's hand in this, all right.'

'Have you ever heard of anything like this?'

'Once.' Dallandra hesitated, then spoke carefully. 'It reminds me of a tale I heard a long time ago. Have you ever heard of the Great Stone of the West?'

'I've not.'

Yet Laz felt an odd touch on his mind, not a memory, more a feeling of danger attached to the name. Dallandra was watching him, not precisely studying his face, but certainly more than usually alert.

'What is this fabled stone, if I may ask?' Laz said.

'An opal that one of the Lijik Ganda enchanted – oh, a long time ago. Ebañy told me about it. It had spirits guarding it, too, you see, which is why it came to mind.'

'Ah, I do see. Ebañy's Evan the gerthddyn?'

'He is. My apologies, I forgot you wouldn't know his Elvish name. He's Wynni's uncle, by the way.'

'And a mazrak, I gather.'

'He is that. He's not the dweomerman who enchanted the opal, though. Nevyn, his name was, and I know it means "no one", but it truly was his name.'

The danger pricked him again. Laz felt as if he'd run his hand through the silken grass only to thrust a finger against a thorn. Dallandra was smiling, but only faintly, pleasantly. He wondered why he was so sure she was weaving a trap around him.

'Can you scry for the book?' Her abrupt change of subject made him even more suspicious. 'You've actually seen it, and I never have.'

'I've been doing so to no avail, alas.' Laz decided that talking about the book was safe enough. 'When Wynni took it, she put it into a leather sack, then wrapped the sack in some of her clothing. The bundle's still in her lost saddlebags, or at least, I'm assuming that. All I get is an impression of a crowded darkness.'

'Well, that's unfortunate!'

'If I ever see anything more clearly, I'll tell you, though. Does the book belong to you?'

'In a way, I suppose it does. I think – I'm hoping – that it contains the spells I need to turn Rori back into human form. The being who wrote the book is the same one who dragonified him, you see.'

'So Enj told us. Um, the "being"? This Evandar wasn't an ordinary man of your people, I take it.'

'He wasn't, but one of the Guardians, their leader, as much as they had one, anyway.'

'Ye gods, then he's the one the Alshandra people call Vandar!'

'Just that. He'd never been incarnate, so he could command the astral forces – or play with them, would be a better way of putting it. He never took anything very seriously.'

Laz looked away slack-mouthed for a moment, then regained control of his voice. 'Well,' he said, 'I don't know why I'm so surprised. It would take someone that powerful to work the dweomers we're discussing.'

'Indeed. And I have no idea how to unwork it, as it were.'

'You said you knew him well?'

'I did. He was my lover, in fact, for some while.'

Laz felt himself staring at her like a half-wit. A hundred questions crowded into his mind, most indelicate at best and outright indecent at worst. A beautiful woman like this, and a man who wasn't really a man, but some alien creature in man-like form – the idea touched him with sexual warmth. He could smell the change in his scent, but fortunately she seemed oblivious to it.

'Working the transformation killed him – well, I don't know if killed is the right word,' Dallandra went on. 'It drained him of the powers that were keeping him from incarnating. That would be a better way of putting it.'

'I'm not sure I understand.'

'I'm not sure I do, either.' Dallandra smiled at him. 'He had no physical body, only an etheric form that he'd ensouled. To be born, he had to remove that form, but he'd woven it so well, and he had so much power at his disposal, that it refused to unwind, as it were. Turning Rhodry into a dragon left him absolutely helpless, all that power spent, his own form destroyed. He could go on at last to cross the white river.'

'I see.' Laz turned his mind firmly back to questions of dweomer. 'Speaking of incarnations, you mentioned having somewhat to tell me about mine.'

'I certainly do, thanks to Rori. It turns out that dragons have a certain amount of instinctive dweomer. He remembers you quite clearly from the days when he was human, and in dragon form, he can recognize you.'

'I'd suspected as much, but I'm glad to have the suspicion confirmed. What does he remember that's so distressing? Distressing to me, I mean.'

'Do you remember aught about your last life?'

'Only a bit, that last battle in front of Cengarn, where Alshandra – well, died, or whatever it is Guardians do when they cease to exist. It's all cloudy, but I think I was a Horsekin officer.'

'You were there, certainly, but you were a Deverry lord with an isolated demesne just north of Cengarn. You'd gone over to the Horsekin side. They probably treated you like one of their officers.'

Laz winced. 'Oh splendid! A traitor to my kind, was I? No wonder I've ended up a half-breed in this life! You're quite right. That does distress me.'

'Well, Rhodry thought it was your devotion to Alshandra that drove you to it.'

'Worse and worse!' He forced out a difficult smile. 'Mayhap it's just as well that Sidro left me. She'd gloat if she knew that.'

Dallandra nodded, and her expression turned sympathetic.

'I have a vague memory of dying in battle,' Laz went on, 'so I suppose I got what I deserved.'

'Your last fight was with Rhodry Aberwyn, a silver dagger. Um, here's the odd part. Rhodry's the man whom Evandar turned into the dragon.'

'He killed me?' Laz tossed his head back and laughed aloud. 'No wonder he remembered me, eh? And wanted to do it again.'

It was Dallandra's turn for the puzzled stare. The Ancients, Laz decided, weren't as morbid as Deverry men and Gel da'Thae if she couldn't see the humour in the situation.

'Your name was Tren,' Dallandra went on. 'Another tale I heard has you killing a Gel da'Thae bard.'

Laz winced again. 'That's a heinous thing among my people,' he said. 'And among the Deverry folk, too, I think.'

'One of the worst crimes under their laws, truly. I don't know much else, because you were part of the Horsekin besiegers, and I was inside the city walls, so –' Dalla paused abruptly. 'Now, who's that?'

Someone was calling her name as he came walking through the rustling long grass. Dallandra rose to her feet, and Laz followed, glancing around him. A man of the Westfolk was striding toward them; he paused, waved to Dallandra, and hurried over with the long grass rustling around him. Tall, slender, pale-haired and impossibly handsome like all the Westfolk men, he had cat-slit eyes of a deep purple, narrowing as he looked Laz over. *Ah,* Laz thought, *the lover or husband, no doubt!*

'This is Calonderiel,' Dallandra said, 'our banadar, that is, our warleader.'

'How do you do?' Laz made him a small bow.

'Well, my thanks.' Calonderiel held out his hand to Dallandra. 'Our daughter's awake.' The emphasis on the word "our" was unmistakable.

'You'll forgive me, Laz,' Dalla said, 'but I've got to go. We'll continue this discussion later. I'd like to know what you think of Haen Marn, among other things.'

'Therein is a tale and half, indeed. One quick thing, though,' Laz said. 'Little Wynni, is she well? As well as she can be, I mean.'

'She's deep in her mourning, but she's young, and she'll recover, sooner or later. Evan's doing his best to cheer her a bit.'

'He told me,' Calonderiel put in, 'that he was going to take her to meet her step-mother today.'

'Step-mother?' Laz hesitated, thinking, then grinned. 'The black dragon, you mean?'

'Just that.'

'Well, I've heard women describe their step-mothers as dragons before, but this is the first time I've ever known it to be true.'

Calonderiel laughed, but Dallandra spun around to look back at the elven camp.

'That could be dangerous,' she said, then took off running, ploughing through the tall grass.

'What?' Laz said.

'I don't know.' Calonderiel shrugged, then turned and trotted after Dallandra.

Laz set his hands on his hips and stood watching them go, cursing silently to himself in a mixture of Gel da'Thae and Deverrian. *Warleader, is he? Doubtless he could slit my throat without half-thinking about it, and no one would say him nay.*

All his life he'd heard about the fabled Ancients, but he'd never met any until the previous evening. Somehow he'd not expected them all to look so strange and yet so handsome at the same time. Despite her peculiar eyes and ears, Dallandra struck him as more beautiful than any woman he'd ever seen, certainly more glamorous than Sidro. *Delicate yet powerful,* he thought, *that's Dalla.* And dangerous – the scent of dangerous knowledge hung about her like a perfume, or so he decided to think of it, the best perfume of all. What was that powerful opal, and who was this Nevyn? She'd been hinting about something. That he knew.

Laz walked back to his camp, which had returned to what semblance of order it had, the shabby, rectangular tents set up randomly, the men lounging on the ground or wandering aimlessly through scattered gear and unopened pack saddles. Beyond the camp their ungroomed horses grazed at tether. One of the men, one of Faharn's recent recruits, laying snoring on his blankets. Laz kicked him awake.

'Ye gods!' Laz snarled. 'Where's Faharn? You lazy pack of dogs, this place looks like a farmyard, not a proper camp.'

'Indeed?' Krask scrambled up to face him. 'Who do you think you are, a rakzan?'

Laz raised one hand and summoned blue fire. It gathered around his fingers and blazed, bright even in the sunlight. Krask stepped back fast.

'No,' Laz said. 'Not a rakzan. Something much much worse.'

He flung the illusionary flames straight at Krask's face. With a squall Krask ducked and went running. The other men watching burst out laughing. A few called insults after Krask's retreating back, but they got to their feet fast enough when Laz turned toward them.

'Get this place in order,' Laz said. 'Now!'

They hurried off to follow his command. Grumbling to himself, Laz ducked into the tent he shared with Faharn and which, apparently, his second-in-command had already organized. Their bedrolls were spread out on either side; their spare clothing, saddles, and the like were neatly stacked at the foot of each. Faharn himself, however, was elsewhere. Laz sat down on his own blankets and considered the problem of Sidro in the light of what he now knew about his last life.

She was a half-breed, just as he was, an object of scorn among the pure-blooded Gel da'Thae and their human slaves both, no matter how powerful the half-breed mach-fala and how weak the slave. Had she too betrayed her own kind, whichever kind that may have been, back in that other life? *We must have been together*, he thought. *We must have some connection.* It occurred to him that Dallandra might know. *She might have told me if that lout hadn't interrupted!*

Although he'd not meant to scry, his longing brought him Sidro's image, so clear that he knew it to be true vision and not a memory. She was kneeling beside a stream in the company of Westfolk women, laughing together, chatting as they washed clothes, their arms up to their elbows in soap and white linen. It suited her, this slave work, or so he tried to tell himself, with her plain face, so different from the elegant Dallandra's, with those round little eyes and scruffy dark hair. She'd done him a favour, he decided, by leaving him. *What would I want with her, anyway? An ugly mutt without any true power for sorcery!*

Still, something seemed to have got into his eyes, dust from the camp, maybe, or smoke. Although he managed to stop himself from sobbing aloud, the traitor tears spilled and ran.

Toward noon Berwynna finally overcame her weariness enough to leave the refuge of the tent she shared with Uncle Mic. She emptied their chamber-pot into the latrine ditch at the edge of the encampment, rinsed it downstream, then returned it to the tent. For a few moments she stood just outside the entrance and looked around her. Talking among themselves the strangely long-eared Westfolk passed by. Many of them looked her way, smiled or ducked their heads in acknowledgment, but she could understand none of their words, leaving her no choice but to smile in return, then stay where she was.

Eventually someone she recognized came up to her, Ebañy the gerthddyn. When he hailed her in Deverrian, she could have wept for the relief of hearing something she could understand.

'Good morrow, Uncle Ebañy,' Berwynna said. 'May I call you that?'

'By all means, though most people in Deverry call me Salamander.'

'I do like the fancy of calling you Uncle Salamander.'

'Then please do so.' He made her a bow. 'My full name is Ebañy Salamonderiel tran Devaberiel, but I'm your uncle, sure enough.'

'My father's brother. Right?'

'Right again, though we had different mothers. But can I turn myself into a dragon? Alas, I cannot.'

'Mayhap that be just as well. No doubt one dragon be more than enough for a family.'

'You have my heart-felt agreement on that. I can, however, turn myself into a magpie.' The beginnings of a smile twitched at his mouth.

'Be you teasing me?' Berwynna crossed her arms over her chest.

'Not in the least.'

'Ah, then you be like Laz and the raven. A mazrak.'

'Just so.' Yet he looked disappointed, as if perhaps he'd expected her to be shocked or amazed.

'That be a wonderful thing, truly,' Berwynna went on. 'Better than being stuck, like, in one shape or another, such as that sorcerer did to my da. Or be it so that a man can get himself trapped in some other form, all by himself, I do mean?'

'He can, indeed, and frankly, I worry about Laz. Sidro's mentioned that he often flies for days at a time.'

'I ken not the truth of that, but I did see him fly every day, twice at times, when we were travelling.'

'That's far too often. Huh, I should have a word with him about it, a warning, like.'

'Think you he'll listen?'

'Alas, I do not. Now, speaking of dragons, did you know that you have a step-mother and a step-sister of that scaly tribe?'

'I didn't! Ye gods, here I did think that dragons be only the fancies of priests and story-tellers, and now I do find that my own clan be full of them.'

'Priests?'

'Father Colm, the priest we did know back in Alban, did tell me once an old tale, that a dragon did eat a bishop – that be somewhat like a head priest, you see – but she did eat a bishop some miles to the south of where we did dwell. But I believed him not.'

'I have the horrid feeling that this Colm might have been right.' With a slight frown Salamander considered something for a moment, then shrugged the problem away. 'Ah well, the dragons are sleeping the morning away in the sun, but when they wake, I'll introduce you. In the meantime, Wynni, come with me, and let's meet some of the ordinary folk.'

'Ordinary' was not a word that Berwynna would have applied to the Westfolk. With their cat-slit eyes and long, furled ears, they fitted Father Colm's descriptions of devils, yet she saw them doing the same daily things that the people of her old world did: cooking food, mending clothes, tending their children. They greeted her pleasantly, and some even spoke the language she now knew as Deverrian. Several woman told her how sorry they were that she'd lost her betrothed. *Not devils at all*, she thought. *Most likely Father Colm never actually knew any of them.*

One odd thing, though, did give her pause. Now and then she saw a person talking to what appeared to be empty air. Once a woman carrying a jug of water tripped, spilling the lot. After she picked herself up, she set her hands on her hips and swore at nothing, or at least, at a spot on the ground that seemed to contain nothing. Another person, a young man, suddenly burst out of a tent and chased – something. Berwynna got a glimpse of an arrow travelling through the air, but close to the ground and oddly slowly. With what sounded like mighty oaths, the man caught up, snatched it from the air, and aimed a kick at an empty spot near where he'd claimed the arrow.

'Uncle Salamander?' she said, pointing. 'What does he talk to?'

'Hmm? Just one of the Wildfolk.'

'Oh, now you be teasing me.'

'You don't see the Wildfolk?' Salamander spoke in a perfectly serious tone. 'I would have thought you could.'

Wynni hesitated on the edge of annoyance. With a smile he patted her on the arm.

'Don't let it trouble your heart,' Salamander said. 'Ah, there's Branna. Let me introduce you.'

Branna turned out to be a human lass, blonde, pretty, and about Wynni's own age – a relief, she realized, after all the strange-looking folk she'd seen and met. She also spoke the language that Wynni had come to think of as Deverrian, another relief.

'Dalla told me that you'd lost your man,' Branna said. 'My heart aches for you.'

'My thanks.' Wynni managed to keep her voice steady. 'I'll be missing him always.'

'Well, now,' Salamander said. 'I have hopes that in a while you'll –'

'Oh, please don't try to make light of it,' Branna interrupted him. 'It sounds so condescending.'

Salamander winced and muttered an apology. Wynni decided that she liked Branna immensely, even though it surprised her to see her uncle defer to one so young.

Branna accompanied them as they continued their stroll through the camp. As they walked between a pair of tents, they came face-to-face with a small child, perhaps four years old, who held a small green snake in both hands. The child ignored them, and Branna and Salamander turned to go back the way they'd come. Wynni lingered, watching the child, who had eyes as green as the snake and slit the same vertical way. She was assuming that the snake was a pet, but the little lad calmly pinched its head between thumb and forefinger of one hand, then twisted the creature's body so sharply with the other that it broke the snake's neck and killed it. Wynni yelped and stepped back as the child bit into the snake's body. Blood ran down his chin as he spat out bits of green skin.

Salamander touched Wynni's arm from behind. 'Come back this way,' he said. 'That's one of our changelings, and he won't move for you.'

A changeling, Wynni assumed, must be the same thing as a half-wit. She followed Salamander out of the narrow passage, but she glanced back to see the child still eating the snake raw.

'My apologies,' she said. 'He just took me by surprise.'

'No doubt,' Branna said. 'We never know what they'll do.'

When they reached the last tent, Berwynna looked out into the open country and saw dragons lounging in the grass. She stopped with a little gasp and stared at them, the enormous black dragon, her glimmering scales touched here and there with copper and a coppery green, and the smaller wyrm, her scales the dark green of pine needles, glinting with gold along her jaw and underbelly.

'They be so beautiful,' Berwynna said. 'How I wish my sister Avain were here to see them! She does love all things dragonish so deeply.'

'Well, if the gods allow,' Salamander said, 'mayhap one day she will. Now, the black dragon is Arzosah, your father's second, well, wife I suppose she is. The smaller is Medea, a step-sister.'

As the three of them started toward the dragons, Wynni heard Dallandra calling from behind them, though she couldn't understand her words. She glanced back to see the dweomermaster running after them, waving her arms.

'She wants us to stop,' Branna said.

The three of them waited for Dallandra to catch up.

'Let me go ahead,' Dalla told them. 'I want to make sure that Arzosah's in a good mood. One never knows with dragons, and she's very jealous of your mother, Wynni.'

Dallandra strode off through the grass to join the dragons. Arzosah lifted her massive head, and Medea sat up, curling her long green and gold tail around her front paws like a giant cat. Although they were too far away for Berwynna to hear their conversation, she could see the results. At first Arzosah listened carefully, then suddenly threw back her head and roared. Dallandra set her hands on her hips and yelled right back.

'Oh joy,' Salamander said. 'It's a good thing Dalla did go ahead, it seems.'

While the black dragon and the dweomermaster argued, the green and gold dragon waddled toward Berwynna and Salamander. Although Father Colm had always said that dragons were the absolute peak and zenith of evil, Berwynna had lost her faith in the priest's sayings, but she had to admit that her heart began to beat faster and harder. Salamander went tense, then stepped in front of Berwynna, but the dragon ducked her head and let out a quiet rumbling sound, a dragonish equivalent of a smile.

'Greetings, step-sister!' she said. 'My for-sharing name is Medea, and I assure you that I don't bear you the least ill will.'

'My thanks.' Berwynna curtsied to her. 'I do feel a great fear upon me of your mother.'

'No need.' The dragon rumbled a bit more loudly. 'She agreed right away to never harm you. They're arguing about somewhat else, the spirit named Evandar.'

'Ah.' Salamander sounded greatly relieved. 'They argue about him constantly, so we may rest assured that all is normal and summery in life.'

'Very true.' The dragon paused for a yawn that revealed teeth like long dagger blades. 'My apologies. These warm days make me sleepy. Anyway, so you're my step-father's hatchling?'

'I am, and I do have a twin sister back home. Her name be Mara.'

'So I have two step-sisters.' Medea seemed honestly delighted with the news. 'And you have another step-sister and a brother back home in our fire mountain.'

'Oh, that be splendid!' Berwynna said. 'We were so lonely, you see, on our island, but now we do have a clan. What be your father like?'

'Alas, he's no longer with us. The wretched Horsekin slew him.'

'That aches my heart. They did kill my betrothed as well.'

Medea stretched out her neck and gave Berwynna a gentle nudge of sympathy. 'So sad!' the dragon said. 'To lose someone so young! Now, our father was old and ill. That's the only reason those horrible bastards of Horsekin could capture him.'

'Were your da a fair bit older than your mam, then?'

'Truly he was. At least a thousand years older, maybe more.'

'Ai! You live so long a time!'

'We do, at that. But Papa was so ill that he wanted to bathe in a hot spring near our lair. When he didn't come home, Mama left me to watch my younger hatchling while she went off to find him.' Medea hissed as if she were remembering the day. 'Papa never came home. The Horsekin slew him while he tried to get free of the spring, and then they gloated about it.'

'Did your mother kill them for it?'

'As many as she could catch, truly. They couldn't harm her. I can't imagine anyone capturing Mama.'

'No more can I. She be magnificent.'

'I'll tell her you said so. She'll like that.'

Medea turned around and waddled off, heading back to her mother, who was still in full argument with a furious Dallandra. Salamander sighed and shook his head.

'They can go on like that for half a day.' He waved a hand toward the pair.

'Truly,' Branna said. 'I think we'd best go back to camp.'

'Indeed,' Salamander said. 'Wynni, I'll introduce you later.'

*   *   *

By the time she finished talking with Arzosah, Dallandra's mood had turned foul. It seemed to her that all of her female friends, whether Westfolk or Wyrmish, were taking entirely too much pleasure in telling her their low opinions of Evandar. She stalked back to camp to find Calonderiel waiting for her.

'Where's Dari?' she snapped.

'Sidro put her down for a nap in our tent,' Cal said. 'I want to talk with you, beloved. I don't want you going off alone with that Laz fellow. If you don't want me to go with you, take some of the men. He's not trustworthy.'

Dallandra sighed, considering him as he stood with his arms crossed over his chest, his eyes narrow. Arguing with him in one of his jealous moods would only waste a long valuable part of the day.

'Very well,' she said, 'I'll ask Ebañy to go over and finish our talk.' She glanced around and saw him standing nearby with Branna and Berwynna. 'Ah, there he is now.'

'That'll be much better.' Cal grinned at her. 'And my thanks.'

Salamander left Berwynna in Branna's care, then went to his tent with Dallandra. She stood watching while he took the black crystal from his saddlebags, then repeated his instructions all over again.

'But don't talk to him about Alastyr,' Dallandra finished up. 'I don't want to awaken any memories of dark dweomer.'

'The temptation to use it might be too great, you mean?'

'Just that. Sidro told me about their teacher back in Taenbalapan. Ych! A truly loathsome dark dweomer refugee from Bardek, back when the cities were breaking the power of the dark guilds. Apparently he escaped the archon who was trying to hang him and managed to take ship for Cerrmor. How he made his way north Sidro didn't know. I'll wager that Laz learned plenty of dubious things from him.'

'Very well, then.' Salamander made her a bob of a bow. 'My lips are sealed with the wax of circumspection and the signet of prudence.'

As he walked over to Laz's camp, Salamander called up from his memory what he knew about Alastyr, whom he'd seen in the flesh only briefly, when he was a very young child and Alastyr a young lad who went by the nick-name of Tirro. Salamander had been gone from the camp when a fully-grown Alastyr had helped Loddlaen murder Valandario's lover, but he'd of course heard the tale. Many years later he'd helped Nevyn track down an utterly corrupt Alastyr, who preyed upon young children of both sexes not merely for pleasure but also to drain their life force for his evil dweomer workings. Although

Salamander had never actually seen the dark dweomermaster Tirro had become, Nevyn had told him the tale in some detail. *A thoroughly loathsome soul, that Alastyr,* Salamander thought.

And yet, when he sat down with Laz to discuss the black crystal, Salamander found him no fiend. Berwynna had told him how Laz had risked his own life to save the caravan. Laz seemed concerned about her, asking Salamander how she and her uncle fared, expressing sincere sorrow over the death of her betrothed and the deaths of the other men as well.

'But in the end,' Laz said at last, 'death takes us all, and life on the caravan road is generally short.'

'True enough, and alas,' Salamander said.

They shared a brief silence in the memory of the slain. Salamander took the chance to study Laz's aura, a strangely mottled swirl of purple and green. Laz, he supposed, was doing the same to his.

'I see you've brought that black crystal with you,' Laz said eventually. 'Do you know somewhat about it? Dalla mentioned that I'd owned it in a former life.'

Salamander had sudden thoughts of doing Dallandra bodily harm. How was he supposed to gain Laz's trust by telling him the truth but never mention Alastyr? Fortunately Laz misread his silence.

'I take it you don't know,' Laz said.

'Well,' Salamander found a dodge just true enough to pass muster. 'Dallandra doesn't like to tell tales of other people's past incarnations unless they've told her she may.'

'Very honourable of her, then.'

'I do know a bit about the crystal, though. Whenever I look into it, I see the same vision, of Evandar standing on the pier at Haen Marn.'

Laz mugged shock. 'Evandar again? Very strange!'

'Even stranger,' Salamander went on, 'is this. I've never been to Haen Marn, and yet in the crystal, I'm apparently scrying it out. What have you seen in it?'

'Only the location of the white crystal, which is, unfortunately, now at the bottom of Haen Marn's lake. They're linked in some way, but I have no idea of how.'

'Have you ever thought of using it to scry for the dragon book?'

'I haven't, but that's a good idea.'

When Salamander held out the crystal, Laz took it in both of his maimed hands, using them like a pair of tongs to set it down on the ground in front of him. He leaned over and stared down through the squarecut tip. After some little while he swore with a shake of his head.

'When I think of the book,' Laz said, 'the interior of the crystal changes to a thick black darkness. I suspect I'm seeing the inside of Wynni's saddlebags.'

'Not very helpful, then.'

'Maybe, maybe not. I felt my mind touch those spirits attached to the book. I have no idea, though, if they knew it did.'

'They might have. If they're spirits of Aethyr, they're more highly developed than most. I suspect that this crystal and its brother are attuned to Aethyr, too. May I ask you where you came upon the white one?'

'In the ruins of Rinbaladelan.' Laz grinned, a gesture sharp as a knife-edge, as if he were expecting a reaction.

Salamander saw no reason to deny him. He whistled under his breath in sheer surprise.

'I went there on a whim,' Laz continued, 'just to see what I could see, which wasn't much. The city's been taken back by the forest. The walls are split, the streets crumbled, the towers fallen, and over everything grows trees and ivy and the like. I was poking around, pulling off a vine here, a cluster of weeds there, and along one wall I poked too hard. It started to collapse, and when the dust cleared, lo! I saw the remains of a wooden casket. Inside was the white crystal.'

'You found it just like that?' Salamander said. 'By chance?'

'Not chance.' Laz frowned, remembering. 'Someone or something had left a trail. Some of the underbrush was cleared away or trampled down, so it was easier to walk up to that particular wall. And the casket itself looked big enough to hold a pair of crystals, but only one remained.'

'I think we can guess who made that trail.'

'Evandar?'

'So I suspect. Very well, you found the crystal he left for you –'

'Oh ye gods!' Laz stared, the grin gone. 'How would he have known I was going to go there?'

'From what Dalla's told me,' Salamander said, 'Evandar knew a great many things about the future. Unfortunately, they were all small details, mere glances, glimpses, and flashes of things to come, like lines snatched randomly from a long poem. So he saw naught wrong with trying to arrange those fragments into the tale he wanted told. I'd wager high that he saw someone finding that crystal. Whether or not he saw you in particular, who knows?'

'Very well, then.' Laz's grin came back, but as brittle as glass. 'And here I thought I was being so clever!'

'Evandar played a great many tricks on a great many clever people. Don't let it trouble your heart.'

For some while they discussed the crystal and the dragon book, until Salamander felt he knew everything Laz had learned about them – not that such amounted to a great deal. Laz, however, seemed pleased with their talk. When Salamander stood up to leave, Laz joined him and invited him to come back whenever he wanted.

'It's a relief to find people who'll talk openly of dweomer matters,' Laz told him.

'No doubt, after being surrounded by Alshandra's believers.'

Laz laughed and agreed.

When Salamander left the camp, two of the men followed him, both pure Gel da'Thae from the look of their long black hair, braided with charms, and the brightly coloured tattoos on their milk-white skin. His heart pounded briefly in fear, but they bowed to him, then knelt at his feet.

'Big sir,' one of them said in a language that was more or less Deverrian. 'I speak little words, but we –' he paused to gesture at the other man' – now want leave Laz. Go with Drav. We ask, safe?'

'It is. The prince has taken Drav into his service.'

The man stared at him in desperation. Salamander tried again.

'Safe,' he said. 'Come see Drav with me.'

At that they both smiled.

As they followed him back to the Westfolk tents, Salamander saw Grallezar and hailed her. She took these new recruits to Drav while Salamander sought out Dallandra to give her his report.

'Laz thinks the spirits of the book may be aware of his mind trying to reach them, but he couldn't be sure,' Salamander finished up. 'And they wouldn't know if he were a friend or an enemy.'

'That's very much too bad,' Dallandra said. 'I keep wishing I'd seen the wretched thing myself.'

'Me, too. You know, it's an odd thing about Laz. Is Rori truly sure he knew this soul as Alastyr?'

'Well, he's told me so a couple of times now. Why?'

'He doesn't seem as horrible as he should.' Salamander shrugged with an embarrassed laugh. 'I suppose that's what I mean.'

'You know, some people do learn from their lives. It's one of the things that keeps my faith in the Light strong, actually, that some people really do see the evil they've done and do their best to redeem themselves. The opportunity's offered to every soul in the Halls of Light.'

'Of course.'

'You sound doubtful.' Dallandra cocked her head to one side and considered him.

'In a way I suppose I am. I've never had grand memories of my past lives, you know. I assume I must have had some, but without actual memories, the assumption's – well – bloodless.'

'You should talk less and meditate more.'

'Why am I not surprised you said that?'

When he grinned at her, she scowled at him, then softened and returned the smile. *Still*, he told himself, *she's right, you know – you should*.

'Besides,' Dallandra continued, 'Laz also had that miserable life without a shred of dweomer in it, where he was nothing but a rene-gade Deverry lordling, and I think he truly learned something from that, too.'

'Which reminds me. Laz said you told him that he owned the crystal in a former life. He certainly did – as Alastyr.'

'Yes, I know, that was a nasty slip on my part. I'll have to think of a way to tell him without evoking that life in his mind.'

'Good luck! Better you than I.' Salamander hefted the crystal. 'Shall I give this to Valandario?'

'By all means. It rightfully belongs to her.'

Valandario was sitting in her tent, studying an array of her scrying gems, when Salamander called to her from outside.

'Oh esteemed teacher, may I enter?'

'Yes, certainly.'

Salamander ducked under the tent flap and came in, carrying some-thing wrapped in what looked like an old shirt. Val smiled at him, then began picking up the gems and putting them back into their pouch. He hunkered down and waited until she'd finished.

'I brought this back to you.' Salamander laid the bundle down in front of her. 'It's the black crystal. I know you asked me to smash it, but it occurred to me that you might enjoy doing it yourself.'

'Most likely I will,' Val said. 'My thanks.'

She unrolled the wrapping – indeed, an old shirt – and set the crystal down on the tent cloth between them. At the moment it appeared so ordinary, just a carved bit of obsidian, that she wondered if it were the correct crystal. Salamander supplied the evidence without being asked.

'Every time I look into it,' he said, 'I see Haen Marn and Evandar.'

'That seems to be its one power,' Val said. 'I wonder why Loddlaen wanted it so badly.'

'Doubtless he didn't know how limited it is, and besides, he was fetching it for the man called Alastyr.'

Val nodded. She was remembering Jav, laughing at some jest as they walked together down by the ocean. With a shake of her head, she banished the memory.

'Well, what to do with it?' Val said briskly. 'I'd enjoy smashing it to bits, certainly, but since we don't truly understand this bit of work, I'm hesitant. Besides, it doesn't seem evil to me, now that I look at it.'

'Was the crystal evil, or was it the lust for the crystal that brought the evil?'

'A very good point.' With a sigh Val wrapped the black stone up again in the shirt. 'Well, I'll keep it for a few days at least, to study its emanations. Evandar's little gifts – by the Black Sun, how much trouble they've caused! The rose ring, this crystal, and now that wretched book.'

Some words they had, for dealing with those, either spiritfolk or flesh-folk, who knew Elvish words, but among themselves, the spirits of the dragon book used shape and colour to convey what thoughts they needed to share. Some leapt up in long iceblue lines, others agreed in a dim blue glow: danger, terrible danger, despite the smothering dark around the book they guarded.

Evandar, where is Evandar? They asked each other repeatedly by creating images of his various shapes, flashing like lightning in the dark. They summoned their lords and petitioned them. They brazenly asked their king, when at last he deigned to notice them. *Where is the spirit known as Evandar?*

Answers never came. No one knew.

'You know, it's odd,' Branna said, 'but I keep thinking about the dragon book. I wonder if we'll ever find it?'

'I do hope so,' Grallezar said. 'Without it, I doubt me we can ever turn the silver wyrm back into his true form.'

'I've been thinking about that, too. Since dragons have some kind of instinct for dweomer, couldn't we just teach him how to transform himself?'

'After many a long year, mayhap. And mayhap the turning would fail and kill him, too.' Grallezar sucked a thoughtful fang. 'Did Dalla ever tell you how Evandar worked the dweomer?'

'She did. He made some kind of dragon-shaped mould out of astral substance and wound it round Rhodry. Then the physical matter poured into it.'

'Just so. And here be the crux of the thing. The turning itself may well be simple enough, once we find the key. But what then do we do with the astral substance that did make the mould? It be heavily charged with dweomer – twice so charged, once we free it from the man inside. I doubt me if a simple touch of a pentagram will turn it harmless and send it on its way.'

'Oh. I'd not thought of that.'

'The problem be a bit much for an apprentice, truly. I know you be eager to help with this working, but dealing with that dragon simulacrum had best be left to me and Dalla. Other work will come your way.'

'Very well, then. Of course I'll do as you say.'

Grallezar smiled briefly. 'It gladdens my heart to see you listen to your master in the craft.'

'Well, after what nearly happened to Neb –'

'Indeed. At least some good did come of it, since you did take the lesson to heart.'

'I have. I promise. But it's a bit more than just my wanting to help with the working when it comes. I feel like I have to do this for some reason I don't understand. I mean, I know Jill wanted to spare him this wyrd, but it seems like there's more to it than that.'

'Indeed?' Grallezar paused to study her face for a moment. 'That be a good theme for your meditations, then. See what symbols rise around your thoughts, and we shall discuss them.'

'Well and good. I'll do that.' She paused, glancing to one side, where she'd seen a flash of movement. Her grey gnome had appeared. He sat down cross-legged, imitating her, and began picking his nose. When she shook a finger at him, he vanished. Grallezar rolled her eyes at his antics, but she was smiling.

'Now it be time to stop thinking of dragons and the like,' Grallezar said. 'Let me hear you recite the true names of the spirit lords of each sphere.'

With a sigh, Branna began the lesson. Thinking about the silver wyrm held a great deal more interest than all the memorization that dweomer entails, but she knew that the one was the key to the other.

Dallandra, however, cut that particular lesson short. Branna heard

her calling Grallezar's name in a voice brimming with excitement.
With a sigh Grallezar got up and stuck her head out.

'I don't mean to interrupt,' Dallandra was saying, 'but —'

'Do come in,' Grallezar said. 'Being as you've interrupted already.'

When Dallandra ducked under the tent flap and came in, she was
smiling, her eyes gleaming with delight.

'And what be all this?' Grallezar said.

'I've just had a talk with Laz,' Dallandra said. 'He's told me about
the true nature of Haen Marn, so my apologies —'

'The interruption, it be as naught.' Grallezar pointed at a cushion.
'Sit you down and tell.'

'I shall do exactly that.' Dallandra flung her arms into the air and
danced a few steps. 'It bears on the dragon book, too. Neither of them
really exist.'

'Hah!' Grallezar said. 'So we did wonder.' She glanced at Branna
and laughed. 'You do look dumbfounded utterly.'

'I am,' Branna said. 'Or do you mean, they don't exist on the physical plane like ordinary matter?'

'Just that.' Dallandra sat down on a cushion. 'You learn fast.'

After he spent some futile days searching for Berwynna's lost mule
and the book it carried, Rori took a round-about route back to the
royal alar. On his previous scouting trips, he'd seen parties of Horsekin
raiders on the move. Somewhere they had to have a central force,
most likely one that was travelling toward the new fort he'd seen
a-building. The logical starting point for this central army lay near
Taenbalapan and Braemel. Braemel, Bravelmelim as it was known in
the old days, lay more west than north. He passed over fields and
pastures tucked into the mountain valleys and terraces, green with
crops, that climbed the lower hills like steps. Now and then he saw
flocks of sheep as well as cows grazing in the mountain meadows.
That first night he picked off a cow, in fact, for his dinner and found
her fat and tasty.

In the morning he reached Braemel, a prosperous-looking place lying
in a broad valley, a semi-circle of houses set along straight streets, with
the river along one edge of the town and good stone walls surrounding
it on the other three sides. A straggle of huts stood outside the west
gate, but when he flew low enough, he could see that they were guard
stations and barracks. His shadow, vast in the morning sun, swept across
the road like an omen. Shouting, soldiers ran out to watch him as he
spiralled higher, well out of arrow range, and flew on.

Tanbalapalim, to give it its ancient name, lay spread across three hills. A river cut through the town, entering and leaving through breaches in the outer walls. In the old days, two graceful bridges made of stone overlaid with different colours of marble had arched over the smooth-flowing water like twin rainbows. Although stubby stone piers still jutted from the river banks, the bands of marble had been scavenged for other projects. The Gel da'Thae had built new bridges of wood reinforced here and there with plain stone.

When Rori flew over the town, he saw only one wooden bridge still whole and the other, burned down to the water line. Fire had swept through the eastern sectors, leaving nothing standing but the occasional blackened stone wall. Ashes covered the ground in sweeps of grey. Had there been riots, he wondered, when the Gel da'Thae realized that their new Horsekin neighbours had taken control of their city? The western half still stood, but as he circled far above it, he saw only a few people moving in the streets.

Not far south of Tanbalapalim, Rori found what he'd been looking for. An army marched down the road beside the river, several thousand men by his rough estimate, more than half of them riders, the rest spearmen. Behind them trailed a long supply train, and small boats glided beside them on the slow-flowing river. He circled them several times to study, then headed for the mountains to the west. At a mountain pass above Braemel lay another ancient site. On the off-chance that the Horsekin had decided to occupy it as well, Rori flew there, only to find it deserted.

As he drifted on the wind high above it, Rori saw why the ancestors of the Westfolk had named it Garanbeltangim, the 'Reaching Mountain'. Ancient layers and slabs of rock make up the Western Mountains, all twisted and folded, heaved out of the earth by some colossal cataclysm, perhaps, then washed bare by millennia of rain and snow. The old tales of giants may be true, that in their final war they threw huge rocks and slabs at one another and in the process built the peaks of the far west. Be that as it may, the highest peak of all is Garangvah, to give it its modern name. Like hands three huge slabs of sea-stone reach up to the sky and form a semi-circle around the high terraces that once held Ranadar's fortress.

The Hordes from the north never conquered Garangvah, though they did take over the lower slopes and the farms that had previously supported Ranadar and his men. For an entire year the fortress held out, living on its stores, until the last grain of wheat, the last fleck of cheese rind, and the last mouse and rat had been eaten. Just when starvation threatened the defeat that the Horsekin couldn't deliver, the Horde broke the siege and fled. Their look-outs had spotted a relieving force headed their way.

While the rescuers did bring food, they also brought the worst news of all, that Rinbaladelan had fallen, and the Vale of Roses lay destroyed, covered in ashes and cinders. Ranadar was king of precisely nothing worth ruling. Revenge alone remained to him. For its sake, he left the Reaching Mountain, and he never returned. The limestone slabs continued to cast their shadows over the palaces and walls, the store-houses and the towers, the outbuildings and alleyways. The roofs fell in with time and the snows. Mosses, the sparse mountain grass, and a scattering of twisted, stunted trees pried apart the fine paving stones of the courtyards.

By the time that Rori flew over Garangvah, the palaces and outbuild-ings had worn down to mere stubs of walls and heaps of rubble. The wind had blown soil over them, and grass had sprouted. A few small trees stood upon them. Doubtless their roots would soon destroy what-ever fragments of splendour still lay hidden.

The stone outer walls, however, stood strong. Although they'd been built without mortar, the masons had shaped and fitted each stone to those below and beside it so carefully, so tightly, that the walls had survived for a thousand years and more. Rori circled overhead, looking for Horsekin, but saw no sign of occupation except for some ancient nests, probably built by eagles, in the towers. A few foxes darted across the ruined courtyard to their burrows in the palace mound to hide from the silver apparition in their sky.

Since Rori had flown all day, he needed immediate rest. He found a place on the outer wall where the stonework looked as if it could support his weight. He landed cautiously, wings akimbo, ready to leap skyward should the wall crumble under him, then settled when it held. From his perch he could see down the slopes to the hazy land-scape below, a thing of patchy grass and tumbled rock where once had lain fertile terraces.

In his mind, however, his dragon mind with its long link into the past, he could see much further. He found himself remembering the long slope of another hill, covered with brush and boulders, choked with dust in the late summer heat. *That hill was far to the north,* he thought, *farther even than I realized at the time, not that the distance mattered, in the end.*

PART I

The Northlands
Autumn
Five Years Before the Founding of the Holy City

The Greggyn astrologers tell us that the end of a thing lies curled in its beginning like a tree inside an acorn.

The Secret Book of Cadwallon the Druid

'Y ou should leave me,' Gerontos said. 'Just leave me here and save yourselves.'

'Never!' Rhodorix laid a blood-stained hand on his brother's shoulder, then glanced at the druid, standing nearby. 'Think your god will intervene and save us?'

Galerinos merely shook his head, too exhausted to speak, and leaned, as bent as an old man, onto his heavy staff. Rhodorix considered his cousin's wounds, slight if Galerinos had been a warrior, but grave enough for a softer man. The young priest's arms, bare in his linen tunic, bled from a hundred scratches, the work of the thorny bushes and low-growing trees of this stretch of countryside. Blood stained the hem of his tunic as well from the cuts and scratches on his bare thighs.

All that hot autumn day the three of them had been scrambling through the underbrush in the rocky hills, trying to find a hiding place, taking turns supporting Gerontos, whose broken leg could bear no weight.

'No use in you dying with me, Rhoddo,' Gerontos said. 'Either of you.'

Rhodorix helped his brother sit down among the boulders. Gerontos's leg, snapped below the knee by a savage axe, had turned purplish-black; blood oozed from under the bandages Rhodorix had improvised from strips of their tunics. He helped Gerontos settle himself, then got up and looked down the long slope of the hill to the valley below. Somewhere among the tall grass and the patches of forest waited their clan and safety, somewhere too far to see. Unfortunately, he could all too clearly see a small mob of their enemies, still some distance below them, but coming inexorably up the hill.

Just after dawn that morning, Rhodorix, eldest son of the Dragon clan, and his warband had been guarding Galerinos as he dowsed for water. Instead of a spring they'd discovered a trap set by the white savages. All fourteen of his men lay dead down in the valley; only he himself, his brother Gerontos, and the druid had survived the attack. Unhorsed, desperate, they had taken too many wrong paths during their attempt to escape.

I made too many bad decisions, not anyone else but me, Rhodorix thought. 'The shame's mine,' he said aloud. 'Better I just die with you here. Even if we got back, what am I going to tell the vergobretes?'

Neither Galerinos nor his brother could look him in the face. Neither said a word.

'But Gallo, you can hide or suchlike,' Rhoddo went on. 'Get away after they kill us.'

'If Great Bel wants me to die, then die I will,' Galerinos said. 'There's no use in running.'

'Well, how by the hells do you know what he wants? You keep praying, and we keep getting more and more lost.'

'That's why I think he wants us to die. If he'd only led us to water right away –'

A cry drifted up on the hot and dusty air, a shriek of triumph, an answering howl from a band of men.

'They've spotted us,' Rhodorix said. 'Naught else matters now.'

'Help me up!' Gerontos said. 'Cursed if I'll die sitting down.'

Between them Rhodorix and Galerinos hauled him up and helped him prop himself against a boulder. Gerro's face had gone pale under the smears of dust. Sweat plastered his dark hair to his forehead. Had his leg been sound, Rhodorix knew, the two of them could have scored some kills before the superior numbers against them brought them down. As it was, they could no longer fight back to back. *Not long now*, he thought. *Soon we'll all be drinking in the Otherlands.*

Twelve men were making their way uphill through the rocks and the underbrush, twelve savages with manes of dark hair and milk-white skin, scored with the black lines and dots of tattoos. Ten of them carried spears; the others bore the heavy war-axes that had so efficiently shattered the Devetians' wooden shields that morning. Some hundred yards downhill they paused to argue among themselves, pushing each other in their eagerness to be the first to attack.

'Gallo, run!' Rhodorix snarled. 'Get out of here now!'

'I won't.' The young priest stepped forward and raised his staff to the sky. 'I'll beg Bel's help and try to curse them.'

'A load of horseshit would do us more good than that.'

Galerinos ignored him and took another step forward. He stared straight at the enemy and began to chant, a low rumble of sound at first, then louder and louder. His words came punctuated with deep breaths, and every breath seemed to draw power from the very air around him. Each curse vibrated like a swarm of angry wasps as it streamed toward the enemy below. Rhodorix had never heard such a sound out of any man's mouth. He felt himself turn cold as the chant rose and fell. More to the point, their enemies seemed as transfixed as he. They stood and listened, weapons slack in their hands as Galerinos cursed them, their women, their offspring, their clans, their future offspring, their crops, their herds, and anything else they might touch or cherish.

With one last bellow of sound, Galerinos cried out, 'Begone!' and swung his staff down to point straight at them. All of the ill luck of the curse sprang out at them – and a good deal more. With a hiss and crackle like lightning from a clear sky, blue fire leapt from the staff in a long sizzling bolt and struck among them. They screamed, began to back away, screamed again as a further shower of blue flames burst out of the staff and struck. One man fell backward, writhing and foaming at the mouth. Two others grabbed him, but he continued to twitch and foam. All at once the enemy band broke. They ran this way and that, for a brief moment hysterical and leaderless, then turned and began to race downhill, howling as they ran. A last bolt of blue fire followed them.

Galerinos stood staring, his mouth half-open, his eyes stunned.

'What did you do?' Rhodorix grabbed him by the shoulders. 'How did you do that?'

'I don't know.'

'What – you have to know!'

'The curse never worked like that before! Back in the homeland, I mean.' Galerinos paused to gasp for breath. 'You heard me. I asked the god to send ill-luck down upon them, and from the look of things, I'd say he did.'

Laughter sounded behind them, an odd laugh, more like the plucking of a cithara's strings than a sound made by a throat. Rhodorix spun around. The strangest man he'd ever seen stood leaning against a tree trunk and smiling at them. A slender fellow, he had yellow hair as bright as the paint on a Rhwmani standard, and his lips were a paint-pot red as well, while his eyes gleamed sky blue. His ears, however, were the strangest feature of all, long and furled like lily buds.

'I doubt if your god had anything to do with those bolts of fire,' the fellow said. 'You know sorcery, don't you?'

'What?' Gallo gaped at him like a dolt. 'But that's unclean!'

'Sorcery such as my friend Caswallinos studies is not unclean.' He pried himself off the tree trunk and walked over. 'My name, by the by, is Evandar.'

Rhodorix dropped to his knees. 'Forgive my brother, Mighty One,' he said. 'He can't kneel before you. He's badly hurt.'

'So I see,' Evandar said to him, then turned back to Galerinos. 'Your master, in fact, that very same Caswallinos, asked if I might find you for him. Come walk with me.'

Galerinos obeyed, striding uphill to join the being that everyone in the migration of the Devetii assumed was a god. Together they moved a few paces off. As Rhodorix got up to keep a watch downhill, he felt the air turn cool around him. He glanced up and saw a mist forming in the sky, a strange opalescent cloud shot through with pale lavender gleams and glints. The hairs on the back of his neck rose.

'Ye gods!' Gerontos said abruptly. 'They're gone!'

Rhodorix spun around to look where his brother pointed. Sure enough, Evandar and Galerinos both had vanished. As he watched, the cloud of peculiar mist began to shrink into a swirl of grey and lavender. In a heartbeat it had disappeared as well. Rhodorix tried to speak, then merely shook his head in bafflement.

'Do you think Gallo will bring us back some aid?' Gerontos said.

'I hope so,' Rhodorix said. 'I'd think so.' Yet he felt that he lied. Why would the clan care about two shamed men such as themselves? *Especially me*, he thought, *I'm the one who led us right into the trap.*

With a curse and a groan of pain, Gerontos let himself slide down against the boulder until he sat upon the ground. Rhodorix sat down next to him and prayed that the gods would allow his clan to take mercy on his brother.

To Galerinos it seemed as if he and Evandar had walked but a few feet away. The god, as he thought of the being next to him, paused and turned to face him.

'Your master worried when you lads didn't come back,' Evandar said. 'He and some of the other men found that battlefield, if you can call it that. A slaughter yard, more like.'

'So it was,' Galerinos said. 'I'm surprised that any of us got away.'

'They assumed you'd been taken prisoner, so I said I'd fetch you back.'

'You have my humble thanks.' Galerinos glanced around and saw nothing but mist all around them. 'Where are the other two?'

'Back where I left them. I told Casso that I'd bring you back. He said naught about your friends.'

'I can't desert them!'

'You already have.' Evandar grinned with the wide-eyed innocence of a small child and pointed off in the distance.

Galerinos spun around to look downhill. The mist was lifting, revealing a clear view of the camp, only some five hundred yards away.

Horses, wagons, people – they spread out in a dusty spiral on the plain, desolate except for grass, crisping in the autumn heat, and a few straggly trees. A faint umbrella of brown dust hung in the air above the conjoint tribes of the Devetii, refugees from the Rhwmani wars.

Out in the open grass stood Caswallinos, his hands on his hips, his staff caught between his side and the crook of his left elbow. For someone so blessed by divine power, he was an unprepossessing fellow, almost as skinny as his staff and bald except for a fuzz of grey stubble round the back of his skull. As they hurried down to join him, Galerinos was expecting his master to kneel before the god. Instead, the old man merely smiled and bobbed his head in Evandar's direction.

'My humble thanks for returning this stray colt to me,' Caswallinos said. 'I take it the other lads are all dead.'

'Two were still alive last I saw them,' Evandar said.

'Then where are they?'

'Still up on the mountain. They were wearing iron, and so I left them there.'

Caswallinos sighed and ran a hand over his face as if he were profoundly weary. 'What have I told you about wyrd?' he said. 'And how things undone redound upon you?'

'Do you think those two are part of my wyrd?' Evandar said.

'They are now, since you left them somewhere to die.'

'But they were wearing iron.' Evandar stamped his foot like an angry woman. 'Iron swords, iron shirts. It aches me.'

'I know that,' Caswallinos said. 'No one was asking you to touch them.'

The supposed god – Galerinos found his belief in Evandar's divinity crumbling – stared at the druid for a long moment, then turned away. He seemed to be watching the white clouds drifting in from the south.

'We need our two lads back,' Caswallinos said, 'and we need water.'

'You're not far from a big river.' Evandar kept his back to the druid. 'Head to where the sun rises. It won't take you long to reach it.'

'I wish you'd told me that this morning.'

Evandar merely shrugged.

'If you had,' Caswallinos went on, 'those lads wouldn't be dead, and the last two stranded on a mountainside.'

'Oh.' Evandar turned around to face him. 'Mayhap their wyrd is mine, then.'

'It is.'

Evandar pouted down at the ground for a long moment. 'I suppose you're right,' he said at last. 'But I shan't bring them here.'

'Why not?'

'Because you'll be leaving to find that river.'

'Will you bring them to me there?'

'I shan't.'

'Why not?'

'Because the river's too wide. Too much water!' He vanished, completely and suddenly gone without even a shred of the opalescent mist to cover his departure.

Caswallinos muttered a few words under his breath, something highly unpleasant from what Galerinos could hear of it.

'Master?' Galerinos said. 'Is Evandar truly a god?'

'Of course not! I'm not sure what he is, mind, but he's most assuredly not divine.'

'But he opened the sea road for our ships, and he comes and goes –'

'Just as the gods are supposed to come and go?' Caswallinos snorted profoundly. 'In the old tales, fancies of the bards, lad, fancies of the bards. I'll explain later. Come with me. We need to tell the vergobretes about this river.'

'True-spoken. We'd best get there today. The horses have to have water.'

'Indeed. My heart aches for your two friends, but I'm afraid we'll have to leave them to Evandar.' Caswallinos paused to look Galerinos over. 'Ye gods, your arms, lad! It looks like you've been fighting a few savages yourself. By the by, did Evandar drive your attackers off?'

'He didn't.' Galerinos paused, wondering if his master would believe his tale. 'I uh well er I did. Not that I know what I did. I mean –'

'What by all the hells do you mean?'

'I cursed them by the power of Great Belinos, just as you taught me. I pointed my staff at them, but then these long bolts of blue fire leapt out of it. Evandar called it sorcery.'

Caswallinos glared at him with narrow eyes. He opened his mouth to speak, seemed to think better of it, opened his eyes wider, then shrugged. 'He warned me, Evandar that is,' the old man said, 'that our magic would be a fair bit stronger here than in the homeland. I had no idea what he meant until this moment.'

'What did he mean?'

Caswallinos smiled. 'Let's find Adorix,' was all he said. He turned and strode away with Galerinos hurrying after him.

The tribesfolk stood beside their horses or sat on the ground in the little squares of shade cast by the loaded wagons. A fine film of brown dust covered everyone and everything. Children whined or wept while exhausted women tried to comfort them. The horses stood head-down;

the dogs were panting open-mouthed. As Caswallinos walked through, people turned to him and wordlessly held out desperate hands.

'There's a river ahead!' the elder druid called out repeatedly. 'The gods have promised us water. Not far now. Big river ahead!'

The news spread in ragged cheers. Even the slaves, white savages captured in one battle or another, managed tired smiles in their chains.

Eventually the two druids found Adorix in conference with the cadvridoc, Brennos, as well as Bercanos, head of the Boar clan, and Aivianna, the Hawk woman and moon-sworn warrior. Although none of them wore armour or carried shields, each had their long sword slung in a baldric across their chests, and all four of them had warriors' hair: bleached with lime until it stood out stiff and straight, as if a private wind had blown it back from their faces. The faces in question were all grim, tight-lipped, narrow-eyed, as they turned to the druid and his apprentice, though Avianna's was the grimmest of all, scarred as it was by the blue tattoo of the crescent moon on her left cheek.

'Water straight ahead to the east,' Caswallinos said. 'Evandar his very self told me that a big river lies nearby.'

Brennos smiled briefly. The others nodded.

'I don't suppose,' Adorix said, 'that he had any news of my two cubs.'

'He didn't.' Caswallinos lied smoothly. 'But Galerinos does. They're alive up on the mountain. He can lead some horsemen back to them.'

'There's no time for that now.' Bercanos stepped forward. 'If the savages attack us, our men and horses are barely fit to fight. We've got to reach that river.'

Adorix laid his hand on his sword hilt and turned toward him. Aivianna stepped in between them. She stayed silent, merely looked at each in turn, but Adorix took his hand away from the sword hilt and Bercanos moved a good pace away.

'There's no time for arguing amongst ourselves, either,' Brennos said.

The heads of the two clans agreed in sullen mutters. Aivianna's expression never changed as she returned to her place by the cadvridoc's side.

'Evandar brought my apprentice back but not the others,' Caswallinos said. 'I don't know why. The gods are like that, truly. But Gallo here can tell us what happened.' He cocked a thumb at Galerinos. 'Tell them the truth, lad.'

'Just at dawn we rode out to find water,' Galerinos began. 'I chanted the prayers and held out my staff, but we rode till the sun was half-way to zenith before my staff began to tremble. It seemed to be tugging toward the hills, so that's the way we went. We saw a little valley twixt two of the hills where the trees looked fresh and green. You couldn't see clearly into it, though, and our god sent me an omen about it. Just as we reached the trees a raven flew up, squawking and circling over the valley.'

'Here!' Brennos interrupted. 'Didn't Rhodorix realize you were riding for an ambush?'

Galerinos felt his stomach clench. He hated to betray his cousin, but Caswallinos was glaring at him, his arms crossed over his chest, in a way that brooked no argument.

'He didn't,' Galerinos said. 'He led us right into it. I tried to warn him, truly I did, but Rhoddo just spurred his horse forward, and everyone followed him.'

Adorix grunted once, then shook his head. 'Let them rot, then.' He held out his hand to Bercanos, who laid his own palm against it.

'Forgive me,' the Boar said. 'My foul temper –'

'Mine's no better,' Adorix said. 'We've got more to worry about at the moment than my stupid son. If he was coward enough to live when his men died, then he can freeze in the hells for all I care. I have other get to take his place.'

'But –' Gallo began, then swallowed his words. Arguing with Adorix was a good way to die young. 'As you wish, honoured one.'

'Well and good, then.' Brennos took command. 'We can't stand here jawing like a pack of old women. If there's a river ahead, let's get on the move. We can't risk losing our horses.'

'Let us hope that Belinos and Evandar lend us their aid,' Caswallinos said and folded his hands with a pious expression on his face, one that Galerinos had seen before, whenever his teacher was hiding something.

Shouting orders, the warleader strode away with the other warriors trotting after. Galerinos turned to Caswallinos. 'I thought you said Evandar wasn't a god.'

'He's not,' the old man said, grinning. 'But they don't need to know that, do they now? Keep silence, lad, whenever you can, and your life will be a fair bit easier. Now let's find you a new horse and move out with the wagons. Tonight, however, I want to hear more about this curse of yours.'

The sun crept down the western sky and shone full-strength onto the hillside. Gerontos's face had turned a dangerous shade of red. 'If only we had some water,' he whispered.

'True spoken,' Rhodorix said. 'This cursed stretch of country is all dust and thorns.'

'I wish we'd stayed by that harbour. We could have built a city there.'

'The omens weren't right.'

Gerro nodded, then closed his eyes.

'It'll be cooler when the sun goes down,' Rhodorix said.

Gerro never answered. *It'll be too cold, most likely*, Rhodorix thought, *and us with not one cloak between us.*

As if in answer to his thoughts, a shadow passed across the sun. He looked up to see a lavender cloud, a small smear of colour at first against the blue. The cloud grew larger, sank lower, and formed a perfect sphere of mist. Out of the mist swooped a hawk, an enormous red hawk, shrieking as it glided down toward them. For the briefest of moments it hovered a few feet from the ground, then with a shimmer of silver light Evandar dropped down lightly and stood, back in his more or less human form. The lavender sphere vanished.

'I'll take you somewhere safe,' Evandar said. 'Can you get your brother onto his feet?'

'He can't stand up,' Rhodorix said. 'Maybe I can carry him over my back.'

The god frowned, considering Gerontos, who had slumped down against the boulder. Rhodorix had a panicked moment of thinking him dead, but he opened his eyes with a groan.

'I'll bring help.' Evandar snapped his fingers and disappeared.

And how long will that take? Rhodorix wondered if Gerro would live long enough for this promised help to arrive. He scrambled up and stood between his brother and the sun to cast a little shade. He heard Gerontos mutter something and glanced back to see him trying to swat away the flies that were crawling on the blood-soaked bandage.

'Leave them be,' Rhoddo said. 'Save your strength.'

When he returned his gaze to the hillside he saw the lavender mist forming in mid-air. A vast cloud of it hovered in the form of an enormous ship under full if ragged sail, which first settled to the ground, then began to thin out, revealing Evandar and a tall man wearing what seemed to be a woman's dress, a long tunic, at any rate, with gold embroidery at the collar and hem. Around his waist he wore a belt from which hung a good many pouches. This fellow had the same peculiar ears as Evandar, and his hair was just as yellow, but his cat-slit eyes were a simple grey. He started to speak, saw Gerontos, and trotted forward, brushing past Rhodorix to kneel at the injured man's side.

The last of the mist-ship blew away. Four stout young men appeared, carrying a cloth litter slung from long poles. They wore plain tunics, belted with leather at the waist. From each belt dangled a long knife in a leather sheath.

'A healer,' Evandar said, 'and his guards.'

'You have my humble thanks, Holy One,' Rhodorix felt himself stammering on the edge of tears. 'My humble undying thanks! I'll worship you always for this. If I swear a vow, I'll seal it with your name.'

Evandar smiled in the arrogant way gods were supposed to smile, judging from their statues, and waved one hand in the air in blessing.

The healer pulled a glass vial filled with a golden liquid from one of the pouches at his belt. He slipped one arm under Gerontos's shoulders and helped him drink, one small sip at a time. Gerontos's mouth twitched as if he were trying to smile. The healer got to his feet and began barking orders in a language that Rhodorix had never heard before. With a surprising gentleness the guards lifted Gerontos onto the litter. The healer put the vial away, then from another pouch took out a peculiar piece of white stone – a crystal of some sort, Rhodorix realized, shaped into a pyramid. For a long moment the healer stared into it, then nodded as if pleased by something and put the pyramid away.

No time for a question – the lavender mist was forming around them with a blessed coolness. Everyone followed Evandar as he led them uphill, only a few yards, or so it seemed, but when the mist lifted, they were standing on a different mountain, and the sun was setting over its peak. Rhodorix felt as giddy and sick as if he were drunk.

He tipped his head back and stared uphill at a massive fortress above them, huge, far grander than anything the Rhwmanes had built in the homeland. To his exhausted eyes it seemed almost as big as an entire Rhwmani walled town. Over the stone walls he could see towers rising and the slate-covered roof of some long structure in their midst. Beyond, at the peak of the mountain, three huge slabs of stone loomed over the fortress, dwarfing it. The sun had just lowered itself between two of the slabs, so that a long sliver of light flared and gleamed like a knife-blade on the mountainside.

'Garangbeltangim,' Evandar said. 'And safety, at least for now.' He tipped back his head and laughed in a ringing peal. 'Indeed, at least for now.'

His laughter lingered, but the god had gone.

As they walked the last few yards, massive wooden gates bound with bronze bars swung open with barely a squeak or puff of dust. Rhodorix looked around him, gaping at everything, as he followed the

healer inside. Big slabs of grey and reddish slate covered the courtyard in a pattern of triangles that led to a long central building. Its
outer walls gleamed with tiny tiles of blue, white, and green, set in
a pattern of half-circles so that the enormous rectangular structure
seemed to be rising out of sea-foam. To either end stood towers, built
square like Rhwmani structures, but far grander, taller, and the top
of a third tower, standing behind the main building, was just visible.
Off to each side he could see various small huts and houses. Even
the lowliest shed bore a smooth coat of bright-coloured paint.

A number of people were standing around, watching their procession straggle into the courtyard. They all had the same furled ears
and cat-slit eyes as the healer; they all wore tunics and sandals like
his as well. Off to one side someone was leading a horse around
the end of the main building, a stocky warhorse whose coat shone
like gold and whose mane and tail flowed like silver. Rhodorix had
a brief moment of wondering if he'd died without noticing and now
walked in the Otherlands, but his thirst drove the fancy away. Dead
men didn't long for water.

Bells chimed over the courtyard, followed by the louder boom and
reverberation of huge metallic gongs. The sound came from the top
of the tower to his left. When he looked up, Rhodorix saw men on
the roofs, and the gleam of metal swinging as they struck the gongs.
Up on the mountain peak the sun slipped a little lower. The long
knife-blade of light disappeared. The gongs fell silent as the healer
urged his men forward again.

They entered the largest building by a narrow door at one end.
More colours, more mosaic walls – they turned down a corridor with
walls painted with images of trees and deer, then passed red-curtained
alcoves and went through a gilded room into a mostly blue corridor,
decorated with a long frieze of circles and triangles. Glowing cylinders topped with flame burned in little tiled alcoves on the walls. In
this maze of design and brightness, Rhodorix could barely distinguish
what he was seeing, nor could he tell in what direction they walked.

At last the healer ushered them into a small chamber with a narrow
plank bed, a round table, a scatter of chairs, and a window open to
the air. The men with the litter transferred Gerontos to the planks,
then pulled off his hauberk and his boots. They bowed to the healer
and left.

Rhodorix was just wondering how to ask for water when four cat-
eyed servants came trotting in. He assumed they were servants because
they carried plates of bread, silver pitchers, and a tray of golden cups.

One of them filled a cup with water and handed it to Rhodorix without being asked. Thirst and dust choked his mouth so badly that he could only smile for thanks. The fellow pointed to the food on the table with a sweep of his arm that seemed to mean 'help yourself'.

Other servants carried in big baskets and set them down beside the plank bed. The healer took out several sticks with spikes at one end and put them on the table. Onto the spikes he put thick cylinders of wax with a bit of thread coming out of their tops. When he snapped his fingers, the threads caught fire, and a soft glow of light spread through the shadowed room. Rhodorix took a fast couple of steps back. The healer smiled at his surprise, then pointed to the food and water before returning to Gerontos's side.

Rhodorix drank half a pitcher of water before his head cleared enough for him to consider food. He took a chunk of bread and stood eating it while he watched the healer and two of the servants washing Gerontos's broken leg. By then his brother had fainted. *And a good thing, too,* Rhodorix thought when the healer grabbed Gerontos's ankle with one hand and guided the leg straight with the other. Gerontos woke with the pain, groaned, and fainted again. A servant came forward with a bowl of some thick, reddish substance. At first Rhodorix thought it blood, but the smell told him that it was in fact honey mixed with red wine and some ingredient that made the liquid glisten.

The healer dipped strips of cloth into the mixture, then bound them round the break in the leg, over and over until he'd built up a thick layer. A servant came forward with a bowl of water and held it out while he washed his hands. Another slipped a pillow under Gerontos's head. At that Gerontos woke again, groaning repeatedly, turning his head this way and that. Rhodorix strode over to the opposite side of the bed from the healer and caught his brother's hand. Gerontos fell silent and tried to smile at him. His mouth contorted into a painful twist.

Two servants hurried over to help Gerontos drink from a cup of the yellow liquid. A third handed Rhodorix a cup of red wine, which he sipped, watching his brother's pain ease with every swallow of the yellow drink. The healer himself considered Rhodorix, seemed to be about to speak, then smiled, a little ruefully, as if perhaps remembering that Rhodorix wouldn't understand a word he said. He went to the doorway and spoke to someone standing just outside. A woman's voice answered him; then the woman herself strode into the chamber.

She stood by the bed and set her hands on her hips to look Gerontos over while the healer talked on. Now and then she nodded as if agreeing with something he said. Tall, nearly as tall as Rhodorix, she wore her

pale hair pulled back into a pair of braids. Under thin brows her eyes
were the blue of river ice and deep-set in a face that most likely became
lovely when she smiled. At the moment, frowning in thought as she
considered Gerontos's leg, she looked as grim as a druid at a sacrifice.
Gerontos looked at Rhodorix and quirked an eyebrow. Once, during
Vindex's ill-fated rebellion, they'd seen a contingent of Belgae warriors,
all of them as pale-haired and pale-eyed as this woman.

'She must be a Belgae woman,' Rhodorix said.

'Indeed,' Gerontos whispered. 'Unless she's from Germania.'

Neither the woman or the healer took any notice of their talk. She
wore a long tunic, belted at the waist like the healer's, pinned at one
shoulder with a gold brooch in the shape of a bird with outstretched
wings. Around her neck hung a cluster of what Rhodorix took to be
charms on leather thongs. One of the Belgae wise women, he assumed
– he'd heard about them back home in Gallia. Eventually she turned
to him and spoke. He understood nothing. All he could do was shake
his head and spread his hands to show confusion. Her eyes widened
in surprise.

The healer came over to him, made a questioning sort of face, and
pointed to his ear.

'I'm not deaf.' Rhodorix made a guess at the meaning. He pointed
to his own ear and smiled, nodding. 'I can hear you.'

The healer seemed to understand. He in turn nodded his agreement, then spoke to the woman. They left the chamber together.

'What was all that?' Gerontos said.

'I don't know for certain,' Rhodorix said. 'But I'd guess they were
expecting us to understand her talk. They were certainly surprised
about somewhat.' He paused to sip from the cup. 'This wine is very
good.' He pointed at a servant, then at his brother.

The fellow filled a second cup and brought it over. With Rhodorix's
help, Gerontos raised himself up enough to take a few sips. He sighed
and lay back down.

'Enough for now,' Gerontos whispered. 'Go eat. I have to sleep.'

The servants took themselves away. Rhodorix got up and returned
to the table, but even though he ate, he was considering suicide. He
could go outside to the courtyard, find a corner where no one would
see him, and fall upon his sword. Or, if the guards would let him, he
could climb one of the high towers and step off into death on the
stones below. Death seemed the only honourable act left to him after
his failure of the day, yet at the same time, how could he abandon his
brother here among these strange folk?

If only Galerinos were still with them, he could ask the young druid to cast omens or deliver some kind of opinion based on the holy laws, but Gallo was far away – safe, or so he hoped. He finished his wine, downed what Gerontos had left, then poured himself more. Lacking a holy man, he sought his answers in drink. After the fourth cupful, the room began dancing around him. Rhodorix lay down on the carpeted floor and slept.

'I don't understand,' Nallatanadario said. 'If they don't belong to your people, who are they?'

'I don't know,' Hwilli said. 'But they certainly didn't understand a word I said to them.'

The two apprentice healers, one human, one elven, were sitting in Hwilli's tiny chamber, Hwilli cross-legged on her bed, Nalla on a high stool beside Hwilli's slant-top lectern. On the walls, frescoes of rose gardens gave the small chamber illusory depth. Distant birds flew in the painted skies. While they discussed the two strangers, resting in a chamber just down the corridor, Nalla kept combing her silvery-pale hair. It tumbled in waves about her slender shoulders and down her back, so different from Hwilli's own fine, limp hair that would have hung in ugly tendrils, or so Hwilli felt, had she worn hers free like Nalla did.

'Could Master Jantalaber tell you anything more?' Nalla said.

'He thought perhaps they belonged to some northern tribe. With the Meradan on the move like this, their lands might have been attacked, too, and their tribe might have fled south.' Hwilli shrugged uneasily. 'If that's true, there must be thousands of Meradan out there. It makes my flesh crawl, thinking that.'

'Mine too.' Nalla looked down at the carved bone comb in her hand. Her fingers clenched tight around it. 'I wonder sometimes what's going to happen to us. I truly do.'

Hwilli turned and looked out of the small window, set into the frescoes at the chamber's end, that looked out to the actual sky. She could just see the tops of the fortress's towers, gleaming in moonlight. *We'll be safe here,* she thought. *Won't we?* Nalla shuddered, as if she were wondering the same. She resumed combing her hair, then paused, and with a quick frown shoved the comb into the pouch hanging from her belt.

'Anyway,' Hwilli said, 'the master's going to ask the Guardians for help. He thinks the crystals Evandar gave him might allow us to talk to the men, since they transfer thoughts and images. But he doesn't know how they could actually translate our speech.'

'No one's ever sure how Evandar does anything.'

'That's very true. And Evandar might not help with this, either. So I suppose there's nothing we can do but wait and see.'

'That's the Guardians for you.' Nalla slid off the stool and walked to the door. 'Are you coming to the refectory? The men will be waiting on table tonight in the great hall, so it'll be just us women.'

'Good. I don't want to sit in the hall with the prince and his warriors.' Hwilli got up to join her. 'All they talk about is the war.'

'What else is there to talk about?'

'You have a point, unfortunately. The master did say he was going to consult with the prince about the strangers. He was thinking that the prince might want send out a squadron to find the tribe they came from and see if they'd join the People.'

'Ah, to be allies, you mean.' Nalla frowned, considering something. 'I wonder where Evandar found them, though. They could have been up on the Roof of the World, for all we know.'

'Quite so. I'll wager that the prince realizes that. I doubt if he'll want to risk losing any of his men on a scouting expedition. The Guardians never seem to grasp the idea of distance.'

'That, alas, is very true. Or the idea of time, either.' Nalla abruptly shuddered with a little shake of her head.

'What?'

'I don't know, maybe an omen, maybe not. There's so much to be frightened of, these days.'

'Well, that's true.'

Yet Hwilli assumed that some long wisp of the cloud that covered future events had touched her. *Nalla's marked for the dweomer*, Hwilli thought, *while I'm only here to learn herbs and the like*. Master Jantalaber had made it clear to her from the beginning, that only the People could use dweomer, never the humble village folk that they treated like children at best and slaves at worst. As she and Nalla walked down the long corridor to the special dining area set aside for the healers in the fortress, Hwilli fought her endless battle between gratitude and envy.

Once they were sitting in the refectory with food spread on the table in front of them, gratitude won a temporary victory. Hwilli reminded herself, as she generally did, that she'd been lucky to be chosen to study with a master healer, to live here in the fortress and have plenty to eat. She'd been born and raised in huts that always smelled of the manure and mud that filled in the chinks in the walls. Her parents had worked so hard that their backs were permanently bent and aching. Her father had died, feverish and half-starved, long before he'd grown old. Her own life, even though brief compared to the spans allotted to the People, would be comfortable and respected because of her knowledge. *But so brief*, she thought. *Still so brief.*

Envy rose like bile in her throat. While the other women ate, chatting and laughing, she crumbled a bit of bread between her fingers and watched them. Despite their cat-like eyes and furled ears, they were beautiful, young and beautiful, and they would still be lovely hundreds of years on, when she'd been dead and forgotten for those same hundreds of years.

'Hwilli!' Nalla said. 'Try some of this roast partridge.' She leaned over and placed a choice slice onto Hwilli's plate. 'It's awfully good.'

'My thanks.' Hwilli managed to smile. 'I was just thinking.'

'About that handsome stranger?' Nalla said. 'And he is handsome, or he will be after a bath. His brother's good-looking, too. Now, don't deny it.'

'Oh yes, I suppose they are. For men of my kind.'

'Well.' Nalla paused for a grin. 'If you shut your eyes, you could ignore their ears.'

When the other women laughed, Hwilli decided that hatred tasted like sour wine. She gathered a few bitter remarks, but when she looked Nalla's way, Nalla rolled her eyes with a shrug toward the laughter, and Hwilli kept the remarks to herself.

Caswallinos, or so he'd often told his apprentice, had also realized that distance and time meant nothing to Evandar, but much to the elder druid's surprise and Galerinos's relief, the river did lie where that supposed god had told them. As they came down from the hills they could see the gleam of water far ahead, winding through a grassy plain scattered with huge boulders and dotted with the occasional copse. Laughter and cheers rippled up and down the line of wagons. The horses and cows raised their heads and sniffed the air, then walked a little faster.

As they hurried across the plain, Galerinos noticed several long and oddly straight lines of small stones. The savages had laid them out, he assumed, though the landscape made him think of old tales about the giants of olden times and their furious wars. Perhaps the Devetii had wandered into an armoury of sorts, with rocks laid ready for some battle that had never occurred.

Just at sunset they reached the river. The Devetian line of march spread out along its banks to allow their weary horses to drink. After them came the cattle and sheep. Only when the animals had drunk their fill, and the mud had had time to settle, did the humans wade into the river to drink and to collect the precious water in amphorae and waterskins. As priests, Galerinos and his master received their share first. After they slaked their thirst, they stood by their wagon and looked out across the stone-studded plain.

'This is a very strange place,' Caswallinos remarked.

'It certainly is, your holiness! All those rocks! Do you know why they're here?'

'The Wildfolk told me that a big sheet of ice crawled down from the north. When it melted, it dropped them.' Caswallinos shook his head sadly. 'The Wildfolk lack wits as we know wits.'

'So they must.'

'But rocks or no rocks, the land looks good enough to plant a crop in. We need to get the winter wheat in the ground.'

'Are we going to settle here for the winter?'

'We can't march in the snow, can we? Think! Besides, we're going to have to build a bridge to get the wagons across that river. It's far too deep to ford.'

'You're right, and my apologies, but it wearies my heart. This will be our second winter in Evandar's country. Do you think we'll ever stop wandering?'

'Eventually even our cadvridoc will grow tired of slaughtering the white savages. I've given him that omen to look for, one we can arrange when we find a suitable place.'

'Arrange? You mean you lied to him?'

'Let's just say I created a soothing truth.'

'But that's still lying –' Galerinos caught the grim look in his master's eyes and stopped talking in mid-sentence. 'Apologies.'

Caswallinos snorted with a twist of his mouth.

Cadvridoc Brennos had reached the same conclusion, that the Devetii would set up a temporary settlement near the river and plant their carefully hoarded seed grain. That night, in the midst of campfires he called a general council of the vergobretes, the clan heads, and every free man who wanted to attend. Once the crowd had gathered, he stood on one of the smaller boulders and raised his arms for silence. In the firelight his golden torque and arm bands winked and gleamed. His stiff limed hair gave him the look of a spirit from the Otherlands.

'You all know,' he began, 'that we travel east in search of the omen granted to us by the gods. By another river we'll find a white sow who's given birth, and there we'll found our city.'

The gathered men murmured their agreement.

'But the year turns toward the dark,' Brennos continued. 'According to the bronze marker of days that our druid carries, soon Samovantos will be upon us. We must plant our crops somewhere and build ourselves shelter. Now, right here the gods have given us plenty of stones to work with – an omen, or so I take it. I'd say that this is the place for our winter camp.'

More murmurs, a few cheers – as usual, Brennos had carried the day. Not even Bercanos of the Boar stepped forward to argue, an omen in itself, or so Galerinos thought of it.

'For the first days here,' Brennos began speaking again, 'we'll camp in our usual order, all together in case the savages attack us. After that, we can build farmsteads and walls to protect ourselves.'

More cheers, more murmurs of assent.

'While everyone was watering our stock,' Brennos continued, 'I rode a little ways south. I found a grand supply of stone, waiting for us right beside a spring. We can use that to build a dun that'll strike fear in the hearts of the savages. What say you?'

The entire assembly cheered him. The men of the council of vergobretes stood and threw a fist into the air to show their support. As the crowd scattered back to their various wagons and tents, Caswallinos and Galerinos left the camp to walk down by the river, rippled silver with moonlight.

'Now,' Caswallinos said. 'Tell me about that curse.'

In as much detail as he could remember, Galerinos described what had happened up on the hillside. Caswallinos listened, nodding now and then.

'I never dreamt you had this much of a gift,' he said at last. 'It's time to let you know a few secrets, lad. The first is very simple. The power behind that curse didn't come from the god. It came from your own soul.'

Galerinos stared at him with his mouth slack. *I must not have heard right*, was his first thought. Caswallinos laughed, just softly.

'Don't believe me, do you?' the druid said.

'Of course I believe you, but I'm just surprised.'

'There are bigger surprises ahead. This will do for tonight.' Caswallinos glanced at the sky, where the full moon hung like a beacon. 'I'd ask you to show me that blue fire, but I don't want you setting fire to the grass or boiling any undines out in the river, either. Huh. That reminds me.'

The elder druid frowned at the water and whispered a message to Evandar. Galerinos waited, unspeaking.

'There, I've told the Wildfolk,' Caswallinos said at last, 'though I've no idea if they'll find Evandar or not. I haven't forgotten your two cousins, lad. I know how close the three of you are, raised together like that.'

'They're more like brothers, master.' Galerinos's voice went unsteady with fear. 'I'll pray he brings them back to us.'

But Evandar never returned. Late that night Galerinos woke from an omen-dream of loss and realized, deep in his heart, that he'd never see his bloodkin again.

Rhodorix woke to the sound of the bronze gongs booming over the fortress. Dawnlight streamed through the window, touching the painted walls with silver. His back ached from his night's drunken sleep on a thin carpet over a stone floor. He sat up, yawning and stretching the pain away. The chamber door opened to admit the healer and the pale-haired woman. They ignored him and marched over to the plank bed where Gerontos was lying. The healer held a knife with a long, thin blade.

Rhodorix scrambled to his feet – what were they planning on doing to his brother? But as he watched, the healer deftly ran the blade under the cast around Gerontos's broken leg. The honey had stuck bandages and leg both to the planks as the cast had dried overnight.

With the leg free, the pale-haired woman helped Gerontos sit up, then slid him back to lean against the wall at the head of the bed. She turned away and called out. Servants hurried in, carrying food, fresh water, and an empty shallow pot covered by a cloth, which one of them handed to Rhodorix. Puzzled, he stared at it until the healer laughed and took it from him. With a few deft hand gestures he explained its use. The woman was grinning at him. Rhodorix felt his face turn hot with a blush, but he knew that he needed the thing after all that wine. The woman obligingly stepped out of the chamber.

Once he and Gerontos had relieved their aches, the servant whisked a cloth over the chamber pot and took it away. The woman came back in, carrying a basket.

'Ah gen Evandares,' she said.

She set the basket down on the table, then brought out a pair of crystal pyramids, one black, one white, glittering in the morning sunlight. She handed the black to Rhodorix but kept the white. When she gestured with her free hand, Rhodorix realized that she wanted him to hold the pyramid close to his face. She smiled when he did so, then spoke into her crystal.

'My name is Hwilli.' Her words seemed to come out of the black crystal, yet at the same time he heard in the normal way her speaking in her unfamiliar tongue. 'What's your name?'

'Rhodorix, and my brother is Gerontos.' He aped her mannerism and spoke directly into the crystal.

'What strange names!' Yet her smile made the comment pleasant. 'My master has asked me to talk to you and for you, because you and I are both children of Aethyr.'

'Children of what? My apologies, but I don't know that word.'

'The word doesn't matter.' She smiled again. 'Let's just say that you and I are more alike than we're like his people.'

That's as true as it can be! Rhodorix thought. Aloud, he said, 'Then my thanks. Can my brother's leg be saved?'

'It can, though I doubt me if it'll heal perfectly straight. Still, he should be able to walk without pain.'

Tears of relief welled up in Rhodorix's eyes. He brushed them away, then repeated the news to Gerontos. Gerro grinned so broadly that his smile was all the thanks that anyone needed. The healer patted him on the shoulder, then spoke to Hwilli, who in turn spoke to Rhodorix through the crystal.

'Your brother needs to rest. Give him plenty of water whenever he asks. And make sure he eats, too, will you?'

'I will, and gladly.'

'In a little while a servant will come to lead you to the bath house. Others will help your brother get clean here. Um, your people do bathe, don't they?'

'Whenever we can.' Rhodorix ran one hand over his stubbled face. 'We shave, too.'

'I'll tell the servant that. I'll leave this piece of stone with you. If you need something, give it to the servant and ask through the black one.'

'Very well. One last thing, though. What's in that stuff you smeared on his leg?'

'Wine, honey, and egg whites. It stiffens the linen as it dries.'

'So I see, and my thanks.'

Hwilli set the white crystal down upon the table. The healer and his retinue left, talking among themselves. Much to Rhodorix's surprise, he could pick out three words that he understood – heal, leg, and water – words Hwilli had used when she spoke to him through the pyramid.

A bath, a clean tunic, and a good bronze razor went a long way to making both Rhodorix and Gerontos feel like men again. Later that day Hwilli returned with a flock of servants and a litter. She put the crystals into their basket, then gave orders to the servants. Rhodorix followed as they carried Gerontos to another chamber, this one with a bed that sported a straw mattress and blankets, big enough for the two brothers to share. Once they'd got Gerontos settled, Hwilli dismissed the servants. She handed Rhodorix the black pyramid and took up the white.

'You're a fighting man?' she said.

'I am that.' He hesitated, then decided that she needn't know of his shame. 'So is my brother. We know swordcraft.'

'Good. Our rhix needs swordsmen. Will you fight for him?'

'It would gladden my heart to repay you for the aid you've given us, but truly, who is your rhix? Is he the head of your clan? I've never heard of him or this dunum until Evandar said its name.'

She stared at him slack-mouthed, then laughed. 'You must come from very far away.'

'We do. We were fleeing the Rhwmanes.'

'Ah, so that's what you call them! Master Jantalaber thought your tribe might have been trying to escape them. The master is the man who set your brother's leg, by the by. The rhix is Ranadar of the Vale of Roses, cadvridoc of the Seven Cities, Master of Garangbeltangim.'

'My thanks. I'd not heard of him before this day.'

'I see. Master Jantalaber mentioned that Evandar favoured you.'

'Well, he saved my brother and me from death.'

'A sign of favour, sure enough!'

For the first time it occurred to Rhodorix to wonder why the god had come to their aid. Perhaps he wanted them to join this clan's warband. Doing the will of the god, in that case, looked far better than either killing himself or returning to his own clan and facing his father's outrage at his blunder over the ambush.

'Is your rhix fighting those white-skinned savages?'

'He is.'

'Then it will gladden my heart to serve him.' He glanced at Gerontos, who was listening intently, at least to Rhodorix's half of the conversation. 'Evandar brought us here to help the rhix who's the master of this dunum. His name's Ranadar.'

'Then as soon as I can stand, I'll fight for him,' Gerontos said. 'I owe these people my life.'

'So do I.' Rhodorix returned to speaking into the crystal. 'It will gladden our hearts to swear loyalty to your cadvridoc.'

'Splendid!' Hwilli said. 'I'll tell the master of arms.'

Some of the words she spoke in her own language, those he heard as an echo to the words from the crystal, made sense to him, he realized. Somehow the crystal was teaching him her speech at the same time as it transformed it into his own. *I wish we'd had these in the homeland*, he thought. *It would have made learning that wretched Rhwman tongue easier.* As the eldest son of a clan head, he'd been expected to learn Latin in order to speak to the conquerors and a little Greek as well in order to bargain with merchants.

Rhodorix and Gerontos received their chance to swear to Ranadarix, as they called him, when the prince himself came to their chamber. His retinue, six men with spears, four with swords, marched in first. They all wore polished bronze breastplates, each inlaid with a red enamel rose, over their tunics.

The prince followed, unarmed, wearing no armour, though a glittering belt, inlaid with gems in a pattern of overlapping triangles and circles, clasped in his rich red tunic. Around his neck he wore an enormous sapphire, as blue as the winter sea, set into a gold pendant three fingers wide. He was a tall man, dark-haired, with lavender cat-slit eyes and the strange furled ears of his people. Behind him came a child, dressed in a simple white tunic, who looked so much like him that Rhodorix could assume him to be the prince's son.

A swordsman picked up the white crystal and handed it to the prince. Rhodorix took the black, then knelt on the floor in front of the cadvridoc.

'I understand that you've chosen to join my warband,' Ranadarix said.

'We have, honoured one,' Rhodorix said, 'in gratitude for the aid your people have given my brother. We both can fight on foot with swords or on horseback with javelins.'

'On horseback?' The prince suddenly grinned. 'Well, now, this is a welcome thing! None of my men can do that. Horses are new to me and my people.'

Rhodorix stared, his mouth slack, then remembered that he was talking to a cadvridoc and a rhix. 'Forgive me, honoured one. That surprised me, about the horses, I mean. We'll be glad to show you what we know.'

'Splendid! Then you shall be weaponmasters and serve me doubly.' He turned and beckoned one of the swordsmen forward, a pale-haired man with deep-set green eyes. 'This is Andariel, the leader of my personal guard. In the morning, he'll fetch you, and he'll show you what horses we have. Obviously your brother needs to rest.'

'So he does, honoured one. If Andariel approves of my skill, then I'll teach your men everything I know.'

Ranadarix repeated this to Andariel, who smiled and nodded Rhodorix's way. Ranadarix set the white crystal down, then turned and walked out with his son and the guard following. Rhodorix got up from his kneel and sat on the edge of the bed to talk with Gerontos.

'What's so surprising about the horses?' Gerontos said.

'He told me that they were new to his people.'

'New? That's cursed strange!'

'So I thought, too. Well, it's good luck for us, though. If we prove ourselves, we'll be weaponmasters and have some standing here.'

'Splendid.' Gerontos abruptly yawned. 'Ye gods, I tire so easily! But truly, Evandar's brought us good fortune. This Ranadarix must be as rich as a Rhwmani propraetor!'

'And a lot less corrupt.'

'Huh! Who isn't?'

They shared a laugh, interrupted by the boom and clang of gongs from the towers outside. When Rhodorix went to the window and looked out, he saw that the sun had reached zenith.

Servants appeared, carrying food, which they silently put on the table, then bowed their way out. While they ate, Rhodorix found himself thinking about Hwilli. If he and his brother became weaponmasters, he'd have the standing he needed to keep a woman. She appealed to him a great deal more than the longeared people who ruled this dun. When he considered their cat-slit eyes, he wondered if they were truly human. He doubted it, but as long as they treated him and his brother so well, he would serve them as faithfully as he could.

Since they kept the herbroom locked, the scent of the pharmacopeia lay heavy in the air. When Hwilli walked in, she could smell a hundred different tangs and spices. Master Jantalaber was standing by the marble-topped study table. He was turning the pages of a small leather-bound book, but when he glanced up and saw her, he shut the book and shoved it to one side. Hwilli glanced at it but saw no name on the plain brown cover. Beside it on the table sat a basket of dried plants.

'A good morrow to you, child,' he said.

'I am not a child.' Hwilli drew herself up to full height. 'By your own reckoning, I've seen seventeen winters.'

'That's true.' He smiled at her. 'I call you "child" out of affection, you see.'

'I –' Hwilli felt her anger spill and run like water from a broken glass vessel. 'I'm sorry.'

'Come now, I know it must be hard on you, living here, so far from your own kind. But you have a mind, Hwilli, true wits, something I've not noticed much among your people, and you belong with us.'

Who has the leisure to grow their wits? We work too hard growing crops for your kind to gobble up. Aloud, she said, 'Thank you. I know I'm lucky to be here.'

'And someday, after you've passed over the great river and seen the black sun rise in the otherworld, you'll be reborn as one of us. I know that deep in my heart.'

Tears filled her eyes, hot tears of rage at a promise, oft repeated, that seemed utterly empty to her, but she mumbled another thank you. When the master turned his back to arrange the dried plants on the study table, she wiped the tears away before he noticed them. He set the empty basket down on the floor.

'Before we start our lesson, I want to ask you about those strangers,' Jantalaber said. 'Have they ever told you where they came from?'

'Only that it's very far away. Their name for the Meradan is "Rhwmanes", though. Roseprince told me that much.'

'Roseprince? Is that truly his name?'

'Well, that's how the crystals translate it. It sounds like "Rhodorix" in his own tongue. His brother's name is Oldman, or Gerontos.'

'Ah, I see. The crystals find the root meaning of words.'

'Yes. The strangers' word for prince seems to be rhix, but I have the feeling it doesn't mean quite the same thing as our word.' Hwilli considered for a moment. 'The words that come from the crystals have odd echoes to them. I'm afraid I can't explain it any better than that.'

'The whole thing is very odd, but then what else would one expect from the Guardians?'

They shared a smile.

'Every now and then,' Hwilli continued, 'Rhodorix uses a word that sounds familiar to me, one that my own kind would use, I mean.'

'I see. No doubt his people are related to yours somehow, then. You see, that's what I mean about your wits. You observe things, you're precise.'

'Thank you.' Hwilli could barely speak. The master rarely praised any of his apprentices. He smiled as if he understood her confusion.

'Now, you've studied very hard, and you've learned remarkably fast. I'm going to put you in charge of healing Gerontos's broken leg. You can always ask me for advice, of course, but the decisions will be yours.'

'Do you truly think I'm ready?'

'Yes, I do. In a bit you can go to his chamber and take a look at him. See if he's feverish or ill in any way beyond the pain of the break. Report back to me when you've finished. Now, however, let's look at our plants. These five are all vulneraries.'

When Hwilli returned to the sickroom, she found Gerontos sitting up. His colour looked normal; his forehead felt cool; the skin on his thigh above the cast looked normal as well.

'You're doing as well as we can expect,' she said through the crystals. 'The Rhwmanes smashed the bone, I'm afraid, and there are chips.'

Gerontos blinked at her, then spoke to his brother. Rhodorix laughed and took the black crystal from him.

'The Rhwmanes aren't the white savages,' Rhodorix said. 'Our homeland's across the great ocean. The Rhwmanes conquered it, so we left with Evandar's help. We wanted to be free, you see, not their subjects.'

'I do see,' Hwilli said. 'Now.'

Rhodorix grinned at her. He had an open, engaging smile that made her feel pleasantly warm. His dark blue eyes, so different from the ice-blue common to her people, intrigued her. She liked the way he moved, too, with the muscular grace of a wolf or a stallion. *One of my own kind*, she thought. *It's a relief, to see a man of my own kind after living here so long.* 'So,' Hwilli said, 'your homeland lies to the west, then?'

'Well –' He hesitated, and his eyes narrowed in puzzlement. 'It must. Except, when we left, we sailed west, you see, toward the setting sun. But then when we arrived at the harbour up north, we were sailing east, toward the rising sun.'

'That doesn't make any sense.'

'I know. That's why I'm puzzled.' He frowned at the floor for a long moment, then dismissed the problem with a shrug and looked up. 'But here we are.'

'Indeed. I didn't know there was a harbour up north.'

'I think it was north. The way everything changes direction around here, who knows?'

They shared a laugh.

'The white savages,' he continued, 'had some villages near the harbour, anyway. What do you call them?'

'Meradan.'

'Very well. Meradan it is.'

Hwilli was tempted to linger, chatting with him, for a while more, but the master had asked her to return to the herbroom when she'd finished with her patient.

'I'll be coming back often,' Hwilli said, 'to keep an eye on your brother's progress. But if he shows the least sign of fever, call for a servant and have them come tell me immediately.'

'I will. A thousand thanks.'

When she walked to the door of the chamber, Rhodorix hurried to join her out in the corridor. She waited for him to speak, but he merely smiled, studying her face, then held out the white crystal. She took it.

'Um,' she said, 'is there something you want to ask me?'

'A great many things, but since we've just met, it would be rude of me.' He winked at her. 'May you have a pleasant evening, fair one.'

Hwilli felt her face burning from a blush. She handed back the crystal, turned on her heel, and strode away as fast as she could whilst still retaining her dignity. Yet she had to admit to herself how deeply his teasing had pleased her.

Later it occurred to her that she should tell Master Jantalaber about the actual meaning of the name Rhwmanes. To her surprise she realized that she disliked the idea of doing so, even though she knew that the master would find the information interesting and even, perhaps, important. She decided to keep it as her secret, a scrap of knowledge that the ever so learned People didn't know and wouldn't know if she never told them, something that she shared with Rhodorix alone.

In the morning Rhodorix went with Andariel to examine the herd of forty-two horses, mostly roans and greys, which they kept in a paddock behind the fortress, all of them captured in the various battles with the white savages. Some had been wounded; they trembled at the approach of the two-legged beings. Others came right up to the fence to nose the men's tunics in the hope of a bit of extra food. All of them showed good breeding with their long legs and deep chests.

Two white cows with rusty-red ears stood against the back fence. Rhodorix had never seen that particular bovine variety before. Since Rhodorix had brought the pair of crystals with him, he could talk with the captain.

'Those cows?' Rhodorix pointed to them. 'What are they doing in here?'

'Oh, they belong to the priests. They'll be the mid-winter sacrifice,' Andariel said, grinning. 'We do know the difference between a cow and these new beasts.'

That's why they're white, Rhodorix thought. *That's always best for the sacrifices.*

Not far from the cows stood the golden warhorse with the silver mane and tail that Rhodorix had seen on his first day at Garangbeltangim.

'Has anyone spoken for that horse?' He gestured at the golden gelding.

'No one's spoken for any of them,' Andariel said.

'Very well. I'll take him, then.'

'Um, should each man have a particular horse?'

'He should, truly. And he should be caring for it as well, not leaving it to the servants. It makes a bond, like, twixt horse and rider.'

Andariel looked utterly surprised at the idea.

'How many of your men know how to ride?' Rhodorix said.

'None.' Andariel smiled, a wry twist of his mouth. 'We save these beasts when we can, and we have some captured seat-things and some head-strap things, but riding on their backs – we don't know what to do or how to climb onto them.'

'I see. Do you know how to feed them? They need grain, not just grass.'

'I'm truly glad you're here. We didn't know that, either.'

As they examined the riding stock, Andariel told him more. The People, as they called themselves, lived mostly in the mountains and foothills, where the narrow valley croplands and the terraces cut into the slopes raised barely enough food for themselves. Cattle, goats, and sheep could graze on mountainsides too steep for terracing. Horses were a luxury better suited to flat ground.

Still, when the Meradan warbands had swept down on them, the People had seen the value of speed. The savages never fought on horseback, but the ability to ride fast from one scrap to another, or to make a quick retreat, had given the Meradan too great an edge in the constant raiding and skirmishing. Rhodorix and Gerontos had arrived like one of Evandar's best gifts.

With Andariel's help, Rhodorix chose forty guardsmen to learn riding and some of the menservants in the fortress to help tend the horses, then returned to his chamber to see if Gerontos had need of him. Rhodorix found his brother sitting on the edge of the bed and contemplating a wooden crutch while Hwilli stood nearby, watching him. When Rhodorix walked in, she grabbed the white crystal out of the basket.

'I wish you'd leave them here,' she snapped.

'My apologies, but I had to talk with the captain,' Rhodorix said into the black. 'Here, Gerro, I hope that leg is going to heal up fast. We've got a lot of work ahead of us. For starters, these people don't even know how to build a stall, and if they did, they wouldn't know how to rake it out.'

'I hope I'll be up and around soon.' Gerontos looked at Hwilli. Rhodorix repeated the question through the crystal.

'He's doing well,' Hwilli said, 'but I don't want him walking very far.'

'Out to the courtyard?' Gerontos said.

She shook her head. 'Too far. In a few days, maybe.'

'When can I ride again?'

'I don't know. I've never seen anyone ride a horse, so I don't know how difficult it is.' Hwilli paused, thinking. 'Well, you'll have to get well enough to walk first. We'll decide about the riding later.'

'It's probably too soon to start training with the actual horses, anyway.' Rhodorix perched on the end of the bed. 'I told some servants how to build a couple of wooden horses. We'll put them out in the court-yard so the men can learn to vault and mount.'

'It's always best to start at the beginning.' Gerontos grinned at him. 'That'll keep them busy until I can walk.'

Coming as he did from a warlike and honour-bound people, Rhodorix had seen plenty of broken limbs in his short life, but he'd never seen one as painless as his brother's leg seemed to be. The cast did bother Gerro's skin, however, especially in the warm afternoons, when he complained of the way it itched. Hwilli came in often, and several times a day she gave him a small quantity of the golden liquid. Not long after drinking it, Gerontos would drift off to sleep. Once she was satisfied that her patient was doing well, Hwilli would linger to talk.

'That yellow stuff must contain a powerful herb,' Rhodorix said one evening.

'Powerful, yes, but we make it from mead and the seeds of a red flower, not from a herb,' Hwilli said. 'I can't give it to him constantly, though. If you use too much of it, patients come to crave it. Then when you tell them they can't have it any more, they weep and rage and carry on like madmen.'

'Dangerous stuff, then.'

'A great many things here are.'

'Was that a warning?'

'Of a sort, perhaps.'

'About yourself?'

'What? Hardly!' She smiled at him, then let the smile fade. 'I meant the Meradan, the white savages as you call them. They're bound to attack us, sooner or later.'

'Now that's true-spoken, alas. With a cadvridoc like Ranadarix commanding us, we'll beat them off again.'

'We can hope so.' Her voice wavered.

'You're frightened, aren't you?' Rhodorix walked over to her.

'Of course! Any sane person would be frightened.'

'Well, true spoken. Fortunately, men like my brother and I were born insane.' He grinned at her. 'So we'll protect you. Ranadar's men are just as crazed as we are.'

'I'll hope so.'

'Are any of them mad for you?'

Hwilli blushed.

'I'll wager they are,' he went on. 'May I escort you back to your chamber?'

'You may not.' She drew herself up like a great lady. 'I'm going to join Master Jantalaber in the herbroom.'

'Then I'll escort you there, if you'll allow me.'

She wavered, looking away, glancing back at him, then shook her head. 'It wouldn't be seemly.' She thrust the white crystal toward his hands.

Reflexively he took it. With her head held high, she hurried out of the chamber. With a yawn Gerontos woke and propped himself up on one elbow.

'Huh!' Gerontos said. 'You never stop hunting, do you?'

'Why not? We'll be here the rest of our lives.' Rhodorix walked over to him. 'I thought you were asleep.'

'Awake enough to hear you chattering away.' Gerontos lay down again. 'How long will we live, once the fighting comes our way? From the things Andariel's been telling you –'

'True enough, it doesn't look good.' Rhodorix paused to pull over a chair. 'But once these men can fight from horseback, we'll have better odds. They're cursed good with bows, Gerro. Andariel set their arms masters to making javelins. He was talking about some kind of bow that they can learn to aim and loose from the saddle. That'll give the Meradan somewhat new to worry about.'

'And give us some hope. Good. Huh, I wonder if Hwilli has a sister?' Gerro smiled at him. 'Or at least, a friend who's from our kind of people, a lass who'd favour a weaponmaster's brother.'

'I'll ask her. It'll be somewhat new to talk about besides your gimpy leg.'

At first Hwilli doubted that Rhodorix was courting her, not in the midst of the beautiful women of the People. Why would he want her, so plain and awkward? The other women knew how to smile in a wicked way and say witty things, how to hold their hands just so and how to look at a man they fancied slant-wise with just the right amount of invitation. She felt so sure that she'd look ridiculous that she never tried to imitate them. Yet Rhodorix spoke only to her, he smiled only at her, he kept asking to escort her places and giving her compliments.

'Of course he's interested,' Nalla told her. 'Doesn't he follow you around?'

'Well, he does, but –'

'But what? If naught else, he's a man of your people, and he's new to our country. He's not used to us like you are.' Nalla laid a hand over her ear. 'I'll wager he thinks we're all very strange and ugly.'

Wrapped in her envy as she was, Hwilli had never considered that possibility before.

'Ask him,' Nalla went on, grinning. 'But if he says yes, he does think so, then don't tell me.'

They were walking together on their way to the herbroom, where Master Jantalaber taught groups of students every afternoon. When they arrived, they found the long narrow room already half-full and the Master laying out herbs on the marble table. In one corner Paraberiel, a pinch-faced young man with moonbeam pale hair and emerald eyes, sat on a stool, but he was reading in the book that had no name on its cover rather than looking at the herbs or the herbal that sat open on the big lectern. With a smile Jantalaber called Hwilli and Nalla over to him.

'There's no need for you two to stay,' he told them. 'I'm going to review some very basic principles for the slowest pupils. Go amuse yourselves, if you'd like.'

'Thank you!' They said it together, glanced at each other, and laughed.

Nalla hurried off on some errands of her own, while Hwilli decided to go and see what the horse-riding looked like. She went outside to a cool afternoon that threatened autumn rain and hurried across the ward to the back wall. She climbed the ladder up to the catwalks and leaned between two merlons to look out.

Behind the fortress lay a long stretch of ground that had once been open and covered with grass. The horses had eaten the grass down to dirt, and masons were building new walls to enclose the area at each side and along the back. She saw no sign of the horses, however, or of Rhodorix and the guardsmen. Her disappointment clutched her so sharply that she felt tears rise in her throat. *Oh don't be so stupid!* she told herself. *It's not like he'll ever be interested in you anyway.*

When she climbed down to the ward, one of the women servants hailed her. 'If you're looking for the riders,' she said, 'they took the horses out to the first terrace.'

'Thank you,' Hwilli said. 'But I was just looking at the clouds. Do you think it will rain?'

'Tonight, maybe. Winter's on the way.'

Hwilli argued with herself all the way to the front gate of the fortress, but in the end she left and walked down the hill to a spot just above the first terrace, a narrow strip of tall grass that ran along the face of the mountain for some hundreds of yards. At one end, some of the men were harvesting the grass with scythes, while others laid it out in the sun to dry. Seeing the arrogant men of the prince's guard working like farmers made Hwilli laugh aloud. They could barely handle the scythes, though they did keep at the task with a certain grim determination. *Good!* she thought. *Let them see what my people go through to feed them.*

At the other end of the terrace the horses were grazing in the grass, watched over by the fortress's kennelmaster and his dogs. In the middle, where the grass had already been cropped short, Rhodorix stood by a wooden structure, vaguely horse-shaped, and talked to Andariel through the black crystal. In turn, the captain repeated everything to a semi-circle of guardsmen.

Eventually Rhodorix handed the white crystal to Andariel, who held the black. Rhodorix turned, stuck two fingers in his mouth, and whistled. Out in the herd of horses a golden horse nickered in answer. Rhodorix whistled again, and the horse trotted free of the herd and came straight to him. Even at her distance Hwilli could see how the guardsmen looked at him, worshipful, almost frightened by his command of the large and – to her – ugly beast.

The golden horse stood still when Rhodorix patted its neck and whispered to it. He walked a few steps back, then ran up and leapt for the horse's back. It wasn't a graceful gesture, more of a twist and a wiggle with a kick of one leg and a wave of his arms, but Rhodorix was sitting astride the horse's back and holding the horse's halter rope in one hand before Hwilli had quite seen what he'd done. The guardsmen all cheered, and Rhodorix, grinning, bowed to them from the horse's back. He slid down again, and with a gentle slap on the horse's rump, he sent it back to its herd.

Rhodorix pointed to one of the men, who walked forward. A few more instructions, and the guardsman took a deep breath, then trotted forward and leapt for the wooden horse's back. He landed hard, stomach first athwart the wood, and slid right over and off, landing with a clumsy roll on the ground, where he lay gasping for breath. Andariel handed the crystals to Rhodorix, then hurried over to help the guardsman up. Clutching his stomach, the fellow hobbled off to join his fellows.

One at a time, the guardsmen resumed their futile attempts to mimic Rhodorix and leap onto the wooden horse. Some made it, barely, squirming and grasping at any part of the wood they could get their fingers on. A few slid off before they could get all the way on, some falling flat on their stomachs, some smack on their posteriors. Others ended up like the first guardsman and sailed right over. Hwilli could assume that many of them would end up limping into Master Jantalaber's infirmary later, seeking poultices.

The wind strengthened, chilly and sharp through her linen dress. And what if Rhodorix should notice her watching him? Hwilli turned around and hurried back up to the fortress. She returned to her chamber and spent the afternoon studying her herbal at the lectern, but her mind drifted often to the handsome man of her own kind, who had awed the arrogant men of the People with his skill.

That evening, after she'd made her usual visit to check on Gerontos's progress, Hwilli allowed Rhodorix to escort her back to her chamber, with each of them carrying one of the crystals. Once they were well out of his brother's hearing, she asked what he thought of the People. Much to her surprise, he proved Nalla right.

'They're as generous as ever any people could be,' Rhodorix said, 'and our prince strikes me as a man more noble than any I've ever met. But ye gods, they look peculiar!'

'Even the women?'

'Especially the women. Now, here, I don't mean to insult your friend Nalla, but her eyes make me uneasy, and those ears! Like a donkey's.'

'Oh, they are not! How mean!'

'Very well, then, not as bad as a donkey's.' He reached out and touched the side of her face. 'But she'll never be half as lovely as you are.'

'Come now! You're just flattering me.'

'And why would I do that?'

Before she could answer, he bent his head and kissed her, just a quick brush of his mouth across hers, but she felt as if he'd touched her with fire. He grinned, took the white crystal from her, and left without another word. She stood by her doorway and watched him disappear around the corner before she went inside.

That night she dreamt about Rhodorix. When the dawn gongs sounding on the priests' tower woke her, she lay abed for some while, smiling and remembering the dream.

After the morning meal Hwilli went to the herbroom. The day before, the apprentices had cleaned several bushels of plants and set them to dry on wooden racks. They would need turning so that they'd dry evenly. When she came in, she saw Paraberiel perching on a stool and reading from the unnamed brown book. When he looked up and saw Hwilli, he said nothing, just ostentatiously put the book into a cupboard and made sure that the door stayed shut. He caught her watching him and gave her a bland little smile. *You swine!* Hwilli thought. Master Jantalaber hurried in from the corridor.

'Ah, there you are, Hwilli, good,' Jantalaber said. 'If you'd finish working with those herbs? I'm afraid the prince has summoned me for some reason. The servant didn't know why, so I have no idea how long I'll be gone.'

'Of course, Master.'

'Thank you. Par, come with me.'

Paraberiel hesitated, turning toward the cupboard.

'You can leave the book there,' Jantalaber said. 'Hwilli can look at it if she wishes.'

Paraberiel opened his mouth as if he were about to protest, but Jantalaber was striding out of the room. Reluctantly he followed the master. Hwilli waited until they were well and truly gone, then went to the cupboard and took out the little brown book. As soon as she opened it, she realized why the master had been so casual.

Although it was written in the usual syllabary, and the language seemed the usual language of the People, she had no idea what anything meant, simply because the scattered notes – mere jottings, really, in Jantalaber's familiar script – contained a welter of unfamiliar words. Astral, convoluted, etheric, a long list of what seemed to be names, a variety of words marked with various verbal forms, another list of what seemed to be places – dweomer terms, she realized suddenly, referring to things that she'd never be judged fit to know. The master had drawn a few sketchy diagrams here and there of something he seemed to be planning on building, but she understood none of them. She shut the book with a snap and shoved it back into its cupboard.

Had the master been mocking her, when he'd told his other favoured apprentice to let her see the book? While she carefully turned each leafy plant on the wooden drying racks, that question tormented her. Jantalaber returned alone just as she'd got about half-way through her task.

'My apologies for letting you do all that,' he said. 'Par resents you, you know, because you're smarter than he is, so I knew he'd hinder rather than help you.'

Hwilli nearly dropped the rack she was carrying. Jantalaber smiled, then picked a stalk of eyebright from the tray and sniffed it.

'Yes, you can put those back,' he said. 'They're not quite ready. Did you look at the book?'

'I did. I understood none of it. Of course.'

'Of course?' He quirked a pale eyebrow.

'Isn't that why you let me look at it? Because you knew I couldn't make sense of it?'

'That wasn't it at all.'

Hwilli felt herself blush. She hurriedly turned away and carried the rack to the drying room, lined with shelves to hold the wooden racks. The scents of over fifty different herbs seemed to thicken the air, as if she'd walked into a foggy day. The master followed her.

'I've often got the impression,' Jantalaber said, 'that you're very much interested in dweomer workings.'

'I know they're forbidden to me.'

'By tradition, certainly. By common sense, not at all.'

Her hands started shaking. She slid the rack into its place on the shelves before she did drop it and disgrace herself.

'I've learned as much from you as you have from me, Hwilli,' the master continued. 'All our traditions say that your folk cannot learn dweomer, simply cannot. I suspect that those traditions arose because none of the People ever bothered to get to know your folk.'

'I —' She spun around to find him smiling at her.

'Now, I've taught my apprentices to put any guesses and surmises about healing to the test, haven't I? I'd like to put my suspicion to the test. Do you want to share Nalla's lessons?'

'I'd like naught better in the world!'

'So I thought. If you hadn't bothered to look at the brown book, I never would have offered, by the by. But I felt that you'd be curious enough, and you were.'

'Thank you, I don't know how to thank you enough —'

'You're very welcome. Now, about that book. Doubtless you noticed that it only contained notes in my hand.'

'I did.'

'They're notes toward an idea that lies near to my heart, a special place we could use for healing and naught but healing. This fortress exists to serve death. We healers exist to serve life, and we need a place free of death to study healing, somewhere that possesses healing in its very nature. You won't understand all this at first.' Suddenly he laughed, and his eyes took on an excitement she'd never seen there before. 'I don't truly understand it all myself. For now, let me just say that other masters in the healing arts agree and are planning on helping me build such a place.'

'It sounds splendid.'

'It might well be splendid, when we're done.' He let the smile fade. 'Assuming, of course, that we can finish the work now, with the Meradan raiding and killing. Ah well, who knows what the gods have in store for any of us?'

'Or what our destiny will be.' Hwilli felt abruptly cold and shivered. 'And perhaps that's just as well.'

Jantalaber laughed again, but his normally silvery voice took on a hard edge. 'Perhaps,' he said. 'For now, though, I want you to look at the first three pages of that book again. I'll wager there are words there you don't know. Memorize them, then ask Nalla or me what they mean.'

'I already have. Memorized them, I mean. I never thought I'd be allowed to ask.'

'Well, you are.' He paused, turned toward the door, and listened to a noise outside. 'Ah, yes. Nalla, come in. Hwilli's agreed.'

Laughing, Nalla rushed into the herbroom. She caught Hwilli's hands in both of hers and squeezed them. 'I know it,' she announced, 'I know you can do this!'

'Thank you.' Hwilli was thinking, *I know it, too.* 'But the others? What will they say?'

'I'm going to teach you the first steps myself, just the two of us,' Nalla said. 'Once you've caught up to the others, there'll be naught for them to say.'

Which means they won't like seeing me among them, doesn't it? Aloud, Hwilli said, 'That will be splendid, then.'

While the two apprentices finished turning the drying herbs, Hwilli learned the meaning of the words that had so puzzled her. Nalla also gave her the first principle of magical studies. All things are made of a light that has shone since the beginning of the world, but light that has convoluted, twisting around itself, bending around other rays of light, gaining substance and form with every twist and interaction, melding itself into matter in the way that a master blacksmith pattern-welds a sword from separate strips of iron.

'Meditate on that,' Nalla told her. 'The teachers say that it's the key to everything. I don't know why, because I'm not advanced enough.'

'You mean you've not worked hard enough,' Jantalaber said, grinning. 'Follow your own advice, Nalla.'

Nalla blushed, but she managed to smile.

For the rest of that day, Hwilli felt as if she were floating through her usual work and study. The door to the treasure chamber had swung open, a door that she'd been sure would always remain shut and locked. When she went to Gerontos and Rhodorix's chamber to examine her patient, her splendid mood withstood Gerontos's own foul temper. That evening he did little but complain into the black crystal. The leg ached, when could he walk on it, he hated lying still all day, the cast smelled bad and itched him, on and on until she was tempted to drug him into silence.

'If you're patient now,' she said instead, 'you'll heal properly. If you refuse to lie still for a few more days, the leg will be twisted and strange. Which do you want?'

Gerontos set the crystal down, then crossed his arms over his chest and glared at her. Rhodorix got up from his seat by the window and walked over to pick up the black pyramid.

'There's a third choice,' he said, grinning. 'Your older brother can tie you down to the bed so tightly that you can't move until the cursed leg heals.'

Gerontos said something that made Rhodorix laugh. 'Just try,' he answered. 'Not that you could right now, anyway.'

Gerontos said something else in a less angry tone of voice.

'That's better,' Rhodorix said. 'He tells me that he's sorry if he offended you. Offending me is somewhat else again, but I can't begrudge it to him.'

'Just so. Please tell him that he really will get better if he lets the leg heal in its own time.'

Rhodorix repeated what she'd told him. With a sigh Gerontos nodded his agreement. Hwilli gave him his carefully measured dose of the opium tincture, then packed up her supplies.

'I'll carry those back for you,' Rhodorix said, 'if I may.'

She hesitated, but the night had turned late enough that Master Jantalaber would have left the herbroom.

'My thanks,' she said, 'I'd like that.'

Rhodorix carried her sack of medicaments, then waited, glancing around the herbroom, watching her put things away by candlelight. Without asking he escorted her back to her chamber. Neither of them spoke on the short walk, but Hwilli could feel her heart pounding so hard that she wondered if he could hear it. At the door she hesitated, clutching the white crystal in one hand while he held up the black.

'You look particularly beautiful tonight,' he said. 'Your hair's like the winter sun, it gleams so.'

'Oh, listen to you! You should be a bard.'

'You inspire me, that's all.'

He caught her chin in his free hand and kissed her, a long lingering kiss that made her gasp for breath. She leaned back against the corridor wall, and he stepped closer to kiss her again.

'Could you favour me?' he murmured.

'Can't you see I already do?' She regretted her bluntness the instant she'd spoken.

He laughed. 'I had hopes that way, but I'd not get you in trouble with your master. What will he do if he finds out you've got a man?'

The question puzzled her. The women here in the fortress had always taken lovers when they wanted them, whether anyone else had approved or not.

'Naught,' she said. 'Why would he do anything? I'm only his apprentice, not his daughter or suchlike.'

'Well, then.' He smiled, his eyes eager, as if he were waiting for something.

'Then what?'

'Then will you invite me in?'

'Oh!' She realized that despite everything he'd said and done, she'd still been doubting herself. 'Of course.'

As they went inside, he shut the door firmly behind them. He put his crystal down on the stool by her lectern, then slipped his arms around her before she could do the same. He drew her close and kissed her with the white pyramid caught between them. When his hands slid down to her buttocks, she felt so aroused that she nearly dropped the precious crystal. He laughed, caught it in one broad hand, and turned away to put it down next to the black.

Hwilli pulled her dress over her head and let it fall to the floor. She lay down on her bed, so narrow that he barely fitted next to her, but once his arms were around her, it became all the comfort they needed.

After their love-making, she drowsed in his arms, only to wake when a pale grey light filtered through the window. He woke as well, to turn onto his side and contemplate her face. He was smiling, and with a gentle finger he traced the shape of her lips.

'You're so beautiful,' he said. 'I'm honoured that you'd favour a man like me.'

'Oh don't say daft things.' She kissed his fingertips. 'I'm the one who's honoured.'

'Indeed? You're a healer, you can read and write, and what am I? Just a fighting man who happens to know horsecraft.'

'I'd say you know women just as well. I –' Hwilli stopped, abruptly surprised. 'Wait! I'm understanding every word you say. The crystals are still over there.'

Rhodorix sat up, twisting to look at the lectern and the stool, where indeed the two crystals sat some five feet distant.

'Ye gods!' He lay back down. 'Well, that's a handy thing, then.' He started to say more, but the priestly gongs began announcing the dawn in a racket of struck bronze. Rhodorix swore and winced, then waited till the sound died away. 'Why in the name of every god do they keep making that wretched noise?'

'In the name of every god, just like you said.' Hwilli grinned at him. 'It's the priests' duty to mark the points of the passing days, and the days themselves, the cycles of the moon and the sun, the rising of some of the stars, all of the heavenly things. That's why the prince built this fortress up so high, so the priests would be closer to the stars.'

'I think me that the sun would rise without them making all that cursed clamour.'

'So do I, but the priests don't.'

'Ah. Like the cocks that crow on the dungheap, then, and the sun obeys.'

She laughed until he kissed her again, and neither of them had any need of words or laughter.

Yet once their love-making finished, sunlight was flooding in the window, and he needed to leave to rejoin his men out in the horse yard. Hwilli lay on her side and watched him pull on the funny, baggy legging-things he called brigga.

'Will you come back tonight?' she said.

'If you'll have me back,' Rhodorix said.

'Of course!'

He paused to grin at her, honestly thankful that she would want him. *Me*, she thought. *He loves me. Nalla was right!*

'Well, then, let's settle somewhat.' Rhodorix turned solemn. 'From now on, you're my woman. I don't want you looking at any other man.'

'Fear not! There's not a man in this fortress I'd want, not after you.'

He smiled again, as bright as the sunlight coming through the windows. 'Let me take the crystals with me,' he went on, 'and at the morning meal today, I'll tell the guard captain that if any other man looks at you wrong, he'll have me to answer to.'

'Truly?'

'Truly. That way if I get you with child, everyone will know the child's mine, so you'll not have to worry that I'll refuse to maintain it.'

His generosity surprised her so much that she had a hard time answering with more than a murmured 'my thanks'. He sat down on the edge of the bed to pull on his boots. She cuddled against his back and tried to think of some generosity she could offer in return.

'Rhoddo?'

'Imph?'

'Then from now on, your people will be my people, and if I have a child, I'll raise him that way.'

'Well and good, then.' He turned to look at her. 'That's a grand thing you're giving me.'

'You've done the same for me. I'll swear it on your gods, because they're my gods now.'

'Then swear it by Belinos and Evandar.'

'Evandar's not truly a god, you know.'

'Of course he is! Our priests said so. When he saved my life, I promised him I'd swear all my vows on his name.'

If it pleases him, she thought, *why does it matter?* Belinos she knew nothing of, but if Rhodorix considered him a god, then she would honour him too. 'I swear by Belinos and Evandar,' she said.

'So do I, that you're my woman now.'

They both smiled, yet deep in her heart she felt sombre, as if a cold wind had touched her. Somehow, she knew, they'd sealed some sort of bargain, one that resonated far beyond the first days of a love affair.

The guardsmen ate in Prince Ranadar's great hall, a long narrow room with tables enough for several hundred men. At one end stood a narrow dais, where the prince dined with his intimates. Frescoes covered the walls with pictures that reminded Rhodorix of those in Rhwmani villas, though these were far more magnificent. Painted roses bloomed in a vast garden that wrapped around the entire room. In the landscape behind the garden, one wall sported a view of rolling hills and forest; the other, a distant city on the far side of a river. A spiral made of bits of white glass covered half the ceiling. At night this spiral glowed with an eerie blue light, but during the day it merely glittered in the sun streaming through the windows.

Since Rhodorix sat next to Andariel at the warband's head table – an honour, he realized, to a stranger who knew so many useful things – he could talk with the captain through the crystals. When he told Andariel that he considered Hwilli his property and his alone, Andariel relayed the warning to the guardsmen, who mostly laughed and saluted him with their wine cups.

'She's always been the stand offish sort,' Andariel remarked. 'Cold as ice, we all thought. I'm impressed that you could warm her up, and so are the rest of the lads.'

As the days went by, the warning had the desired effect. From time to time, Hwilli came down to the terrace to watch the riding lessons. The other men made a great show of looking elsewhere whenever she did, and if for some reason they needed to speak to her, they made the encounter as brief as possible.

'They're afraid of you,' Andariel said. 'If you've not noticed.'

'Why would they be?' Rhodorix was honestly surprised. 'I'm naught, just an exile, in a way, a man who's lost his tribe.'

'Just for that reason. You have every reason to be desperate. You're more than a little reckless, I'd say, judging from the way I've seen you ride. No one wants to face you in an honour duel.'

'I see. Well, truly, the only trouble I'd ever cause you and the warband would be over Hwilli.'

'Good.' The captain smiled briefly and put a sliver of ice in his voice. 'That's the answer I'd hoped for. *There*, you'd be within your rights.'

But nowhere else, Rhodorix thought. 'Well and good, then,' he said aloud. 'That's fair.'

Once they'd eaten, Rhodorix and Andariel left the great hall together. They were walking across the rear courtyard when the gongs boomed from the priests' tower. A blare of horns answered them from a doorway at its base. Andariel caught Rhodorix's arm and made him stop.

'They're coming,' he said. 'We have to kneel.'

'Who?'

'The priests. Don't say a word to them unless they ask you a question.'

'Well and good, then.'

Rhodorix knelt beside the captain on the hard cobbles. When he glanced around, he saw that everyone within sight had knelt as well. Bronze horns, as harsh as the tubae of the homeland, blared from the fortress walls. Silver horns answered with a chiming melody. To the beat of small drums, carried before them by two lads, four men emerged from the tower.

Long robes of cloth of silver swirled around them with each measured step. They held their heads high and rigid, balancing the weight of their plumed and studded headdresses. Gold and sapphires gleamed at their throats and in their earlobes; a long trail of peacock feathers swayed down their backs. As they passed each person kneeling along their route, in perfect unison the priests raised one hand and lowered it again, most likely in blessing, but they never spoke a word. Behind them came eight lads marching two abreast, dressed in dark blue linen, each carrying a silver sword two-handed and upright in front of him.

They marched the entire length of the fortress, turned in a perfectly executed sweep, and marched back again. The horns blared, the drums beat steadily, until the priests and their retinue returned to their tower by the door they'd left from. After so much processional music, the silence rolled around the courtyard like sound.

'Ye gods!' Rhodorix shook his head to steady down his hearing. 'What was all that about?'

'I've got no idea,' Andariel said. 'Maybe they just wanted a bit of fresh air.' He stood up, dusting the dirt from his knees. 'They don't tell us anything, and we don't ask them anything. Those young lads with the swords? They have the right to kill anyone who insults a priest, and you never know what might insult them.'

Rhodorix got up to join him. 'Those swords don't look like they'd cut meat at table.'

'They look soft, but they're not true silver. It's some kind of mix. I don't know what it is, but the Mountain Folk up in Lin Rej make it.'

'Oh. Well and good, then, captain. I'll remember what you say about the priests. They look a fair bit different from the ones from my own tribe, not that I would have crossed them, either.' Rhodorix paused, remembering Galerinos. 'Well, except for the one who was a cousin of mine, but he was just an apprentice. Ye gods, no doubt I'll never see him again, and that's a pity.'

'It's a hard thing, exile.' Andariel paused to look up at Reaching Mountain and the huge slabs of stone towering above. 'I hope to the gods I never have to face it.' He reached out and gave Rhodorix a friendly slap on the shoulder. 'Let's go round up our lads and get to work.'

After the day's riding lessons, Rhodorix went first to the bath house, then back to the chamber he shared with Gerontos. His brother was sitting in a chair by the window and eating bread and fruit from a tray on the table.

'What's this?' Rhodorix said. 'Does Hwilli know you're out of bed?'

'She does. I'm not to walk any farther than this, but it's time, she said, to see if the leg can bear weight.' Gerontos gestured at the tray of food. 'There's more there than I can eat.'

Rhodorix sat down across from him and picked up a chunk of bread and a knife to butter it.

'I've been meaning to ask you,' Gerontos said. 'Does Hwilli have a sister or a friend who might –' He let the words trail off.

Rhodorix grinned at him. 'She doesn't, not one who's our kind of people.' He let the smile fade. 'But she's mine, Gerro. I know we've shared women before, but not this time.'

'Well and good then. I just asked.'

'Naught wrong with asking.' Rhodorix bit off a mouthful of bread and ate it while he thought. 'She has a friend named Nalla, though, who's a bit of a spark in tinder, if you ask me. She might find a different sort of man interesting, like, if you can ignore the ears.'

'I'll ask Hwilli if I can meet her, then. It'll let her know that it's not her I want to bed.'

'Very gallant of you.' He grinned again and reached for an apple. 'How is the leg, by the by?'

'Healing, she says, and fairly fast as these things go.'

'Good. You'll be riding again by winter, or so I hope.'

Eventually Gerontos managed, with the aid of a crutch and with Hwilli's help as well, to hobble out down to the terrace to teach beside his brother, though generally Rhodorix and one of the men carried him back up again. The forty men under their instruction learned to handle the captured mounts in a much shorter time than Rhodorix had been expecting, not that any of them turned into splendid riders in a fortnight's work.

The difficulties lay in the mount and dismount. Eventually the guardsmen all learned how to leap onto the wooden horse, but their nervousness communicated itself to the real horses, who usually refused to stand and hold for the practice. Until they could mount, the men would never learn anything else about riding, so Rhodorix reluctantly agreed to a set of wooden steps, such as the kitchen servants used to reach the nets of onions and apples, the smoked pork and other such preserved foods that hung from the kitchen's high ceilings. Rhodorix made his men pay for the device with jests and shaming remarks that made them struggle all the harder to learn.

On a sunny day turned cool by a crisp wind, Prince Ranadar himself and his retinue came down to watch the riding practice. Skipping along beside him was his little son, Berenaladar, or Ren, as he was usually called. Through Andariel and the crystals, Ranadar asked Rhodorix to show him what 'this riding thing is.'

Rhodorix whistled for Aur, the name he'd given his chosen horse, who trotted out of the herd at the command and joined him. His previous Meradani owner had trained Aur well; Rhodorix had spent many a morning learning what his new mount could do. When Rhodorix surreptitiously tapped the gelding on his off-fore, Aur bent the leg and seemed to bow to the prince. Ranadar smiled, and Ren clapped his hands with a laugh.

'I want one of those, Da,' the child said.

'You shall have one when you're older,' Ranadar said. 'Now hush!'

'Begging the cadvridoc's pardon,' Rhodorix said, 'but he's of an age when he should be learning to ride. The younger, the better, honoured one.'

Ranadar considered him with a twisted smile, then shrugged. 'Very well, perhaps we'll both come have some lessons with you. Show me what this all entails.'

Rhodorix saddled and bridled Aur, then leapt into the seat and caught the reins. He walked the horse down to the end of the terrace to let it warm its muscles, then trotted back. He dismounted, made Prince Ranadar a bow, then turned to the guardsmen.

'Saddle up, lads!' Rhodorix said.

The men rushed off to fetch their horses, since none had yet trained them to come when called. While they struggled with the tack under Andariel's supervision, Rhodorix lifted young Ren to Aur's saddle and told him how to sit properly. The boy's catslit eyes, lavender like his father's, widened with delight at the sensation of being up so high on horseback. He followed every instruction Rhodorix gave him, then repeated every move on his own. *If we live long enough to teach the lads*, Rhodorix thought, *the People will be as good as we are with horses.*

The presence of their rhix and cadvridoc made the guardsmen even more nervous than usual. Several of them refused to use the wooden steps, but the first man to try the leap put too much spring into his jump, overbalanced on the saddle pad, and slid off to fall in a heap. His horse snorted, danced, and very nearly kicked him. He got to his feet, his face as red as a sunset, and stared at the grass to avoid looking the prince's way until Rhodorix sent him and his mount back to their respective herds. A second man and a third tried and failed. The entire guard unit turned hang-dog, standing heads down with humiliation.

'Ye gods, that looks difficult!' Ranadar said. 'Here, let me try.'

Andariel protested in a flood of words that Rhodorix couldn't follow, not even with the crystal, but the prince laughed and insisted. Rhodorix brought Ren down from Aur's saddle.

'This is the best trained horse in the lot, honoured one,' Rhodorix said. 'He'll stand still for you.'

On his first try the prince very nearly managed the leaping mount. In fact, Rhodorix suspected that if he'd wanted to, Ranadar could have got himself onto the saddle, albeit in an ugly flurry of arms and legs and clutching hands. Instead, the prince made a great show of sliding off and falling into the grass. He laughed and picked himself up before anyone could rush forward to help him.

'Very difficult,' Ranadar announced. 'Don't feel dishonoured on my account, men.'

The guardsmen cheered him. Rhodorix felt utterly stunned. He'd never seen a man of authority, not Devetianos nor Rhwmanos, voluntarily shame himself for the sake of the men who served him.

On a wave of good feeling all round, Ranadar collected his retinue and his son and left the guardsmen to their practising. Rhodorix watched them as they walked uphill. He'd finally found a leader worth dying for, he realized, someone with ten times the honour of a Vindex or even a Brennos.

At the end of the day, when they returned to the fortress to let the men care for their mounts in the newly built stable, Rhodorix and Andariel discussed the various problems that the lesson had shown them.

'If we ride to battle, then dismount,' Andariel said, 'how are we going to get them mounted again after the fighting's over?'

'It'll be worse yet if they're unhorsed during a retreat,' Rhodorix said. 'You'll have to leave them behind. They'll never manage to remount a panicked horse.'

'We don't have enough men to leave anyone behind.'

'Well, then, I don't know what to tell you. It's all very well to provide a set of wooden steps here in the fortress, but we can't carry those with us to battle.'

Andariel sighed and considered the line of saddles perched on a railing. Crystals in hand, the two men were standing in an improvised tack room, part of a storehouse that the prince's servants had roughly converted to a stable. The saddles were much like those Rhodorix knew from the homeland, simple leather pads with a cinch that went over a heavy saddle blanket.

'Carry the steps with us?' Andariel said eventually. 'That gives me an idea. What if we hung a step of sorts from the saddle itself?'

'What?'

'I'm thinking of the rope ladders that lead up to the catwalks on the walls. What if we put straps down on each side of the saddle with loops for a man's foot to go into?'

Rhodorix grinned in sheer admiration. 'That just might work splendidly, once we got the horses used to the device. Stick your foot in the loop and swing your free leg over.'

'Just so. I'll go to the armoury and ask.'

The People knew their craft work. One of the prince's armourers delivered a saddle with the new idea attached the very next morning. Rhodorix first accustomed Aur to having straps dangle against his sides, then tried out the new way of mounting while the armourer stood watching. Although the foot-loop certainly made getting onto the horse's back easier, the simple saddle twisted to one side under the pull of his weight. Rhodorix dismounted and led the horse over Andariel and the armourer.

'We need to work on the saddle,' the armourer said through the crystals. 'Give it back to me. I think I see what's wrong.'

Back and forth the saddle went over the next eightnight between the armoury and the horse yard. Each time it returned, it was heavier and stiffer, until finally the leather ended up stretched over a wooden frame. The cinch had spawned two additional straps. One went round the horse's chest, one round its behind, and the new side loops included iron bars to keep them open and stiff. Although Aur disliked this new version of its usual tack, Rhodorix heartily approved.

With the armourer and Andariel in tow, he rode down to the first terrace, then galloped along its length once. As he walked the horse back to the waiting men of the People, he tried standing with his weight on the new, reinforced loops, then sat back down and howled with laughter. He walked the snorting, dancing horse over to Andariel, who was watching from the side of the courtyard. Still grinning, Rhodorix leaned down to retrieve the black crystal from the captain.

'A man could swing a sword from horseback like this,' Rhodorix said. 'It'll take some practice, but I think we can put the fear of our gods into the Meradan with these.' He leaned forward and patted Aur's neck. 'Whist! You'll get used to it in a bit, lad.' He straightened up again and looked at the grinning armourer. 'A splendid job! Captain, can he make us more of these things?'

Andariel spoke briefly with the armourer, who nodded his agreement. 'He says,' Andariel said, 'that he'll set his men to work on them this very afternoon.'

'I have good news for you,' Hwilli said. 'Master Jantalaber is going to take the cast off this afternoon.'

'Splendid!' Gerontos grinned at her over the white crystal, which he was holding. 'Although, alas, I'll miss seeing you every day.'

'Oh, you're not rid of me yet! Wait till you see what your leg looks like.'

'Good.' His smile turned soft.

Hwilli set the black crystal down on the table beside the bed. She felt uneasy enough to gather up her supplies and hurry out of the sickroom. *Brothers always squabble*, she thought, *but I don't want them squabbling over me.*

When she returned to the herbroom, Nalla was standing at the table, studying a row of freshly pulled plants.

'What are those?' Hwilli said.

'Comfrey,' Nalla said, 'I think, but the roots don't look right to me.'

Hwilli glanced at them. 'They've grown in very poor soil, I'd say. The rest of the plant certainly looks like comfrey.'

'Ah, you're right! I hadn't thought of that. How's your patient doing?'

'The master's going to cut the cast off this afternoon, and then I'll know. I hope he's healing well. He's been terribly bored, and it worries me.'

Nalla looked up with a grin. 'What's this, he's interested in you too?'

Hwilli felt her face burn. 'My heart belongs to Rhodorix,' she said. 'And only him.'

'It's not your heart that's the problem, but a very different portion of his anatomy.' Nalla grinned again. 'He's not bad-looking, really, despite those funny eyes.'

'I'm not going to –'

'Who said anything about you? I was thinking of providing him a little distraction.'

Nalla's grin turned so wicked that Hwilli had to laugh.

'Just be careful of his leg,' she said. 'Don't undo all my work.'

When the cast came off, the leg had shrivelled from sheer lack of use, and the skin lying underneath had turned as wrinkled as a toad's. Master Jantalaber brought all his apprentices into Gerontos's quarters to see the effects of wearing a cast for nearly two months, tested the leg, pronounced the break mended, but urged him, through the crystals, to keep his weight off it as much as possible.

'You'll be fine by the spring, lad,' the master said, 'if you're careful now. Hwilli, let's go to the herbroom. I'll give you a recipe for salve that you can make up for his skin.'

Hwilli followed the master into the herbroom as the other apprentices dispersed. Jantalaber went to the massive herbal on the lectern, thumbed through its heavy parchment pages, and opened it flat at a particular page.

'There you are, Hwilli,' he said. 'The formula I promised you. Before you start preparing it, though, tell me how your work with Nalla's going.'

'Nalla says I'm doing well,' Hwilli said, 'but I think she's just being kind. I can remember all the information she gives me, but I can't put it to use.'

'That takes time, a great deal of time. Keep at it, and the results will come. Can you see the elemental spirits yet?'

'No, I'm afraid not.'

'In good time, then, in good time.'

Hwilli could only hope that the ability would come. It galled her to think that the tiniest child among the People could see the Wildfolk, while to her and her kind, they existed only as tales and jests. And what would 'good time' be? Compared to the long lives of the People, she had very little to spare. A few days later, however, her worry proved unnecessary.

'After dinner tonight,' Jantalaber told her, 'Maraladario wants to see you.'

Maraladario, the head of the dweomermasters' guild, the most powerful mage that anyone in the Seven Princedoms had ever known – Hwilli caught her breath in an audible gasp. The master smiled at her.

'She won't eat you,' Jantalaber said. 'In fact, she wants to give you her blessing.'

Hwilli found herself unable to answer. She laid her hand on her throat and wondered if she'd gone pale. Finally, after another gasp for breath, she managed to say, 'I'm so honoured.'

The Tower of the Sages stood at the north end of the main palace, opposite the Tower of the Priests. As they entered through the door at its base, Master Jantalaber cast a silver dweomer light on the end of his staff, which he held up before him like a torch. Steep wooden stairs switchbacked up past landings, each with a chamber door marked with various sigils, none of which Hwilli could decipher.

Maraladario lived at the very top. The stairs ended at a landing of polished wood in four different browns, laid in a pattern of triangles. In the silvery light, the pattern rose up into interlocking pyramids, or so it appeared, rather than forming a flat surface. As her shadow fell across it, Hwilli noticed that the pyramids seemed to flatten under the shadow's weight.

Master Jantalaber stepped onto the landing boldly. When he didn't trip and fall, Hwilli followed him and discovered that the floor was indeed perfectly flat. The red door to Maraladario's suite bore no sigil or decoration. When Jantalaber knocked, the dweomermaster herself opened it and ushered them into a wedge-shaped room lit by golden light. Although Hwilli had seen her from a distance many times, she'd never been this close to the great sage. Maraladario was tall, even for a woman of the People, and slender with long, delicate fingers. She wore her jet-black hair bound up in a green gauzy scarf that matched her eyes, but one long tendril hung down over her cheek. Her long blue tunic shimmered as she moved.

'Come sit.' Her voice was soft, pleasantly husky. 'Would you care for wine?'

'None for me,' Jantalaber said.

'Nor me either, mistress,' Hwilli said. 'Though I thank you.'

'A prudent girl, and well-spoken.' Maraladario grinned at her.

Hwilli bobbed her head and hoped she looked humble rather than terrified, her actual feeling. The dweomermaster led them to simple chairs, with wooden backs and cushioned seats, placed near a shuttered window. A small table with a mosaic top sat nearby, the only other furniture in the room. As Hwilli sat down, she noticed movement out of the corner of her eye. When she turned her head she saw a strange little being lurking under the table. Roughly human in shape, with purplish skin and a warty little face, it stood about two feet high. When it saw her looking its way, it stuck a bright red tongue out at her and wrinkled its nose.

'My familiar,' Maraladario said, 'and a very rude little gnome, really.' She snapped her fingers, and the gnome disappeared.

I saw him! Hwilli nearly blurted but managed to keep silence. Jantalaber, however, must have noticed, because he smiled and nodded, pleased.

'So, you're Hwilli.' Maraladario sat down opposite her and considered her over folded hands. 'Do you like studying dweomer, child?'

'Very much, mistress. I've longed to study dweomer – well, not my whole life, perhaps – but as far back as I can remember.'

'Very good. Tell me, suppose you gain great power in our craft. What will you do with it?'

'To be honest, I don't know.' Hwilli felt herself blush. Her answer sounded absolutely flat and silly to her own ears.

Maraladario, however, nodded as if she were taking it under serious consideration. 'Honest of you,' she said at last. 'I suspect, though, that you'll find out what to do with it once you gain it, assuming you do. There are great dangers on your road ahead, Hwilli. Once you finish the first studies, believe you me, there are dangers for all of us, whether Children of Air or Children of Aethyr.'

'So I've been told, mistress.'

'Good. Keep the dangers always in mind.' Maraladario turned her calm emerald gaze on Jantalaber. 'She has a strong aura. I think me you've chosen well.'

'Thank you,' the master said. 'I have every hope she'll succeed.'

'Have you discussed our other plans with her?'

'I have, if you mean the place of healing, but only briefly.'

'Very well.' She looked at Hwilli once again. 'If we succeed in building this place of healing, it must be for everyone, not just the People, but your folk, and the dwarven folk of the Northlands, and yes, even the Meradan, those among them who prove worthy. Healing cannot be hoarded or begrudged, Hwilli. Your place in the work is crucial, because it means that your folk will have a share in the healing just as the People will. Do you understand that?'

'I do, mistress.' Hwilli swallowed heavily to clear her voice. 'I'm frightened I won't be worthy.'

'Work hard, and you will be worthy.' Maraladario glanced at Jantalaber. 'Thank you for bringing your new apprentice.'

Jantalaber smiled and rose with a quick gesture to Hwilli to follow. The audience had ended.

That night, when Rhodorix came to her chamber, Hwilli considered telling him about her studies and in particular, the meeting with Maraladario, but he'd been drinking with the other guardsmen and seemed muddled. Besides, she suspected that talk of sorcery might frighten him, perhaps even turn him away from her. She'd had so little joy in her brief life that she lived in terror of losing what she now had: her healing knowledge, her dweomer studies, and a man of her own, a man of her own kind who still had as much honour as a fighting man of the People.

Instead of talk she let him fall asleep on her bed. For some while, though, she stayed awake, watching him by candlelight and thanking the gods for letting him love her.

'You have to learn to ride wet and cold sooner or later,' Rhodorix told his men. 'Today's a good day for it.'

The guardsmen grumbled, but when Andariel snapped out a string of orders, they obeyed. Rhodorix had judged it time to take his new troop of mounted soldiers off the terrace and into the real terrain beyond. They rode armed. Most of the guardsmen wore a bronze breastplate and carried a long slashing sword in a baldric, though Rhodorix had his own chain hauberk and pattern-welded sword. Five of the mounted men carried the new short bows and quivers of arrows. Andariel had deemed it wise to ride ready for trouble, since trouble lay all around them.

Under a thick grey sky the men walked their horses down the mountain, following a narrow dirt track through the system of terraces, where the farm folk were planting the winter wheat despite the chilly drizzle. Like the farm folk that Rhodorix had grown up with, they were thin, bent-backed, dressed in scruffy brown clothes with their feet wrapped in rags. Overhead birds wheeled, desperate to steal the seeds that the folk flung broadcast on the ground. Children with sticks chased them away.

Back in the homeland Rhodorix had paid little or no attention to farmfolk, but here everything struck him anew.

'These farmers—' Rhodorix waved his arm in their general direction '— they're Hwilli's folk?'

'They are,' Andariel said. 'We bring this lot up here in the summer. Soon they'll go back down the mountain with the cattle. The snow up here – it's too hard on the stock. We send them to the Vale of Roses for the winter.'

Rhodorix had the distinct feeling that he was including the farm-folk with the cattle when he referred to 'the stock'. He rose in the stirrups for a last survey of the farm folk, but none of the women looked attractive enough to give to Gerontos. They rode on, heading down the mountain. Below in a narrow valley a village of wattled huts stood around a well. More fields spread out to either side. A wider road ran the length of the valley, leading to the foothills at either end.

'This isn't the Vale of Roses, is it?' Rhodorix said.

Andariel tossed his head back and laughed aloud. 'No. In the spring we'll ride back there, and you'll see how splendid it is.' His face suddenly darkened. 'Well, with luck.'

'And if the gods are willing. Are the farmers down there Hwilli's folk, too?'

'No, not at all. In the southlands around Rinbaladelan, the farmers and herders all come from the People themselves.'

'Ah. I'd wondered.' Which meant, he supposed, that he wouldn't find another woman for his brother there, either.

'It's a hard life they have,' Andariel continued. 'The priests say that they did somewhat in their last lives to deserve it, just like we earned our place as warriors.'

'Our priests always told me the same thing.' Rhodorix touched the hilt of his sword to ward off any evil that might appear at the mention of such arcane matters. 'Which way shall we go now?'

'South,' Andariel said. 'The prince told me that some bands of Meradan are raiding to the south. They must have stayed down on the flat and just bypassed us.'

'Have messengers come in? I haven't seen any.'

'The prince doesn't need messengers. He has farseers.'

'Has what?'

'Mages who can see things from afar.'

Andariel was watching him with a slight smile, as if he expected the stranger to argue. While Rhodorix had never known men with true magic, he'd heard about them back in the homeland. *What about Galerinos and that blue fire?* he told himself. *That must have been magic.* 'Well and good, then,' Rhodorix said. 'South it is!'

Although they saw no raiders that first day, after a few more days of riding patrols the mounted guardsmen had their first battle test. They had ridden a little farther than usual, once again to the south some ten miles from the fortress. When they crested a grassy hill, they saw below them some fifteen Meradan, riding along as easily and openly as if they owned the road.

'Here's a chance to try those new bows,' Rhodorix said, 'but tell the lads to try to spare the horses. We need every mount we can get.'

Andariel turned in the saddle and called back the orders. The archers looped their reins around the saddle peaks and brought their bows from their backs. Down below the Meradan had seen them. They paused their horses, then called out and waved to the guardsmen, who must have appeared from their vantage point as small figures silhouetted against the sky.

'Ye gods!' Andariel said. 'They think we're some of them!'

'Of course.' Rhodorix grinned at him. 'We're on horseback.'

Andariel shouted more orders. The archers lowered their bows but held them ready, hiding them as best they could behind their horses' heads. Rather than charge, Rhodorix led the squad downhill at a steady walk, just as if they were planning on joining up with allies. They had reached the flat before the Meradan realized their mistake.

The five archers whipped up their bows and loosed the first volley. Arrows whistled, then sank into targets as the Meradan yelled war cries – then screamed. Three of their men pitched over their horses' necks into the road. More arrows, more screams, but over the shrill rage and fear Andariel yelled for the charge. Rhodorix followed the captain as the mounted swordsmen left the archers and charged straight for the remaining Meradan.

The Meradani horses that had lost their riders bolted, galloping back south down the road. The others were milling and rearing, bucking and trying to grab their bits. Their riders could barely control them, much less fight. Rhodorix saw one savage whose black hair bristled like a boar's, tied as it was with a plethora of charms and beads. He urged Aur straight for him. Foolishly the Meradan tried to turn his horse to run. Rhodorix swung straight for his spine at the neck. His sword slashed through the man's pitiful leather hauberk with a spurt of blood.

With a last scream the rider fell just as Aur slammed into the rear of his horse. The Meradani pair went down, and Rhodorix nearly followed. Only a lifetime spent on horseback saved his balance and his life. He managed to stay on Aur's back and balance his weight at the same time so that the golden gelding kept his feet. Aur tossed his head, foaming in panic. Rhodorix threw his weight forward and kept him from rearing while he stroked the horse's neck.

'Whist, whist, lad! It's all over.'

The swordsmen had cut to pieces the few Meradan that the archers had missed. When Rhodorix turned his horse back to the battle, he had a moment of nausea at the sight – severed limbs, hacked torsos, heads rolling under hooves, and still the swordsmen cut and slashed until every single enemy had been reduced to so much butchered meat. Battle fury he knew, but he had never seen so much hatred on the field of war.

'The horses!' Andariel was calling out in what amounted to bad Gaulish, words he'd learned from Rhodorix. 'Round up the horses!'

Blood spattered and grim, the swordsmen followed orders. Andariel urged his foaming, dancing horse up to Rhodorix's mount.

'Well, that's a few less Meradan in the world,' the captain said through the crystal. 'Once we catch these horses, let's head back to the fortress.'

'What about the bodies?' Rhodorix said.

'Leave them for the ravens and foxes. They don't deserve anything better.'

With the captured horses came an equally valuable prize, a leather saddlebag with painted insignia upon it, the ship crest of the Prince of Rinbaladelan. One of the guardsmen handed it to the captain, who opened it and peered inside.

'Messages,' Andariel hissed. 'What happened to the messengers, then?'

'What do you think?' Rhodorix said. 'They must be dead.'

'I don't understand. Why didn't the farseers tell us about the messengers? We might have saved their lives.'

'Good question,' Rhodorix said. 'Maybe the savages can hide from magic. Maybe they have magic of their own.'

The colour drained from Andariel's face. Rhodorix abruptly realized that the captain – and doubtless the entire fortress – had been considering magic an important weapon on their side.

'I could be wrong,' Rhodorix said. 'Be that as it may, we'd better get these back to the prince.'

'Just so. Let's ride.'

Leading their captured horses, the guardsmen rode back to Garangbeltangim. As they entered the gates, half the servants in the fort rushed out to cheer the riders, blood-spattered and exhausted, but victors in their tiny battle. Everyone had been desperate for some kind of victory, Rhodorix realized, so desperate that the insight gave him a cold feeling in the pit of his stomach. Maybe they could find and kill a few bands of raiders, but what would happen if his pitiful handful of mounted guardsmen had to face an army?

Andariel insisted that Rhodorix accompany him when he took the captured messages to the prince. They found Ranadar in his great hall, sitting on the dais with his advisors, all of them lounging in chairs around a small inlaid wooden table and drinking from golden cups. Rhodorix wondered which ones were the mages. All three of the men with the prince looked too young, too smooth and handsome to be learned counsellors to a cadvridoc. He realized that he'd not seen one old person in the entire fortress, though Hwilli had certainly implied that her master in herbcraft had reached some great age.

Rhodorix and Andariel knelt before the prince, who leaned down to take the saddlebag from them. When he showed his advisors the crest, they all leaned forward, faces suddenly grim. Ranadar handed the messages to the nearest one, then spoke to Andariel. Rhodorix could pick out a few words and phrases of what the prince said, and he understood even more of the captain's report of the skirmish, since he of course knew what had happened. The prince listened, nodding now and then. Behind him the advisor was reading through the messages; as he finished a sheet, he handed it over to the next man at the table. All of them had turned grim as death itself.

When he finished, Andariel handed Ranadar the white crystal, apparently at the prince's request. Ranadar turned to Rhodorix.

'I'm well pleased with how you've served me,' the prince said. 'From now on, you shall have the title of horsemaster and be an honoured man among us.'

'My thanks, honoured rhix,' Rhodorix said, 'but at least half the honour goes to Andariel. He's the one who thought of the new saddles, and without them, we couldn't fight half as well.'

'Indeed!' Ranadar turned to Andariel. 'Then you're too modest by half, my friend.'

Andariel smiled, but his eyes looked suspiciously moist. Rhodorix could guess that the prince rarely referred to any man in the fortress as a friend.

'Your armourer deserves honour as well, my prince,' Andariel said.

'He shall have it, then. You must be tired and hungry. My honour goes with you.'

It was the best dismissal he'd ever heard, Rhodorix thought with a grin. They both rose, bowed, and took themselves away. At the door Rhodorix looked back to see the advisors standing up to huddle around the prince, each of them waving one of the pieces of parchment that held the messages.

Rhodorix followed his usual routine, bath house first, then back to his chamber. As he came up to the door, he heard Gerro's voice and a woman giggling in answer. Suspicion flared in his blood like fever. He flung open the door to find Gerro lying half-naked on the bed and Hwilli's friend Nalla sitting beside him. She held a pot of some sort of salve in one hand, but judging from the disarray of her hair, and from the fact that her tunic was hiked up around her waist, she'd been doing more for Gerro than treating his withered leg.

'You might have knocked,' Nalla said. She handed the salve to Gerontos and grabbed her tunic to pull it down.

'My apologies.' Rhodorix knew his face must have turned scarlet. 'I'll uh just uh go find Hwilli.'

He turned and beat a hasty retreat, slamming the door behind him. Yet despite the blush, he felt gratified that his younger brother had found a woman of his own, partly because he liked seeing Gerontos happy. *And he won't be sniffing around mine this way*, he thought.

All too soon, however, things changed.

'Hwilli, Nalla, all of you.' Master Jantalaber appeared in the door of the refectory. 'I have something important to tell you.'

At their long table the apprentices, male and female both, fell silent as he walked into the room. Jantalaber looked weary, that night, his hair uncombed, his eyes heavy-lidded and sad as he looked over his students.

'The prince has made a decision,' the master said. 'I don't agree with it, but he's the prince. Today the guardsmen brought back messages from Rinbaladelan, begging his aid. Ranadar's sending all but two of you to Rinbaladelan. Refugees are pouring into the city. Many are wounded. They need healers badly and supplies as well.'

Everyone went tense, glancing at each other.

'Hwilli, you'll stay with me,' Jantalaber said. 'I'll keep Paraberiel here, too, because he's been helping me with – well, our project. The rest of you, once you've finished your meal, go to your chambers and begin to collect your belongings. In the morning, we'll load up a wagon with supplies, and you'll set out with an escort of archers and some of the new horse soldiers.'

Hwilli caught her breath. Would the prince sent Rhodorix away? Jantalaber looked at her and smiled, just briefly. When he spoke, he used her own language, that of the Old Ones. Since he was the only person among the People who had ever bothered to learn it, they both knew that no one else would understand.

'Your friend will stay here with you,' Jantalaber said.

Hwilli let out a sigh of sheer relief.

'I decided to keep you here for two reasons beyond our project,' he continued. 'You're the best of my students, and the healers at Rinbaladelan might not treat you as you deserve.'

'My thanks, Master,' Hwilli said, and in this instance nothing poisoned her gratitude.

Jantalaber returned to speaking the language of the People.

'Par, you've advanced far enough to teach others. It will be your duty to instruct the archers in binding wounds. Hwilli will show them which herbs are vulneraries and how to prepare them. They need to be capable of healing themselves if something happens to the three of us.'

'As you wish, Master,' Paraberiel said.

'I won't lie to you all,' Jantalaber continued. 'Things are looking very grim. Apparently the Meradan have wits, after all. They've simply bypassed Ranadar's realm and are striking at the heart of the Seven Princedoms.'

Nalla's face turned white, and she caught the edge of the table so hard that the blood drained from her knuckles as well. Hwilli laid a gentle hand on her friend's arm.

'The prince is beginning to think that the best we can hope for is to fall back to Rinbaladelen eventually,' Jantalaber continued speaking, 'and help defend the city, but no one's ready for that move yet. Still, who knows? With luck and the favour of the gods, I may see you all again in Rinbaladelan one fine day.'

No one spoke. Only a few of the apprentices so much as moved in their chairs or glanced around. Hwilli felt as if a north wind had swept into the refectory and laid a coating of dirty grey frost over everything in it.

When they finished eating, Hwilli helped Nalla fold her clothing and place it into two leather sacks for the travel ahead. Her few other possessions – combs, a silver brooch, a pair of blue ribands – Nalla tucked into a small pouch that she'd carry on her belt. Neither of them spoke until they'd finished.

'Hwilli, this is horrible,' Nalla said. 'The prince believes he'll lose the war, doesn't he?'

Hwilli tried to speak, but tears clogged her voice.

'You see it, too,' Nalla continued. 'And your family – ai! they live outside the walls.'

The tears spilled and ran. Nalla threw her arms around Hwilli and held her, just for a moment, before drawing back. Hwilli tried to speak, then hurried to the door before she wept again.

'I'll pray I see you in the spring,' Nalla called after her. Hwilli ran down the corridor and took refuge in her chamber. The last of the sunlight gleamed through the window, a distant gold. She flung herself onto her bed and fought down her tears. *This is no time for weeping*, she told herself. *We all have to be strong.* Perhaps if she pleaded with Master Jantalaber, he could convince the prince to allow her mother to come into the relative safety of the fortress. Perhaps.

'Beloved?' Rhodorix opened the door and stepped into the chamber. 'Have you heard the news?'

'That the healers are leaving?' Hwilli sat up and turned on the bed to sit facing him.

'Not just the healers.' He paused to shut the door. 'The prince is sending all the farm folk with them. The Vale of Roses isn't a safe haven anymore, the captain told me. Tomorrow our warband's going to strip every bit of food they don't need for the journey south.'

'I hadn't heard that.' *How like a man of the People, even Master Jantalaber, to forget to tell me! What does he care about the slaves outside?*

Rhodorix sat down next to her and caught her hand between both of his. 'Do your bloodkin still live out there?' he said.

'Only my mother. She'll be safe, then, for a little while. Well, if she doesn't starve at the gates of Rinbaladelan, anyway.'

'The prince won't let his people starve.'

'Our prince wouldn't, true. I know naught about the prince of Rinbaladelan.'

Rhodorix started to speak, sighed instead, and drew her into his arms. His love-making gave her more comfort than any words could have done.

In a grey dawn turned cold by a drizzle of rain, the healers led out their expedition from the fortress. Hwilli walked with them down to the valley, where the farm folk waited for them in a mob of weeping humans, bleating goats, and lowing cattle. The farmers pushed wheelbarrows and handcarts laden with pitifully small bundles of household goods. Hwilli worked her way through until she found her mother, Gertha, a big-boned woman who wore her long grey hair bound back into a single braid. In one hand she held the halter ropes of two milk goats, who were complaining softly and rubbing up against their human's hips.

'Mama!' Hwilli threw an arm around her shoulders. 'I've brought you a cloak and some extra food.'

'Well, thank you.' Gertha's smile displayed the few brown cracked teeth left to her. 'I was thinking I was going to have a cold walk of it.'

Hwilli laid the cloth-wrapped bundle of bread at her mother's feet, shoved a curious goat away with one foot, then took off her cloak and placed it around her mother's shoulders. She pinned it at the neck with a bronze pin. She'd considered giving her the golden bird brooch, but she knew that someone would only steal it along the way if she did. Gertha stroked the cloak with her free hand.

'Very nice wool,' she said, 'but don't you need it?'

'No. Master Jantalaber will give me another one.' She picked up the bundle again and handed it over. 'Bread and cheese. Eat it first, before the overseers take it.'

'I will. It's kind of you to remember me. I wondered if you did, up there in the palace and all.'

'Mama, how could I ever forget you?'

Sudden tears ran down Gertha's face. Hwilli hugged her again and wept with her. The horse soldiers were riding up and down the line, yelling at everyone to get ready to move. Whips cracked, the horses tossed their heads and snorted. Hwilli gave her mother one last embrace, then turned away, half-blind with tears. She worked her way free of the mob just as the villagers began to walk away. Some turned for a last look at Reaching Mountain, the huge slabs of rock that had loomed over them every summer of their lives. Most concentrated on pushing their belongings ahead of them down the rocky path.

Hwilli stood on the first terrace and watched until the last figure, the last wisp of dust, had faded from sight. By the time she returned to the fortress, she'd managed to stop weeping.

A few nights after the refugees had started their trek to Rinbaladelan, the first snow fell, but it stayed up high on the mountains. The fortress itself received an icy rain that froze only in the deepest shadows. As soon as the sun climbed half-way to zenith, the frost melted again, but winter had arrived in a swirl of north wind as cruel as thrown knives. Hwilli worried about her mother and Nalla incessantly. Not even Rhodorix could lift her spirits.

'I feel an evil wyrd coming,' Hwilli told him one night. 'I don't know what, but I can feel it deep in my heart.'

He said nothing, merely stroked her hair, twining it lightly around his fingers, then releasing it.

'Do you feel it, too?' Hwilli said.

'I don't.' He smiled at her. 'In the spring, now, when the Meradan are on the move again, then mayhap I will. But we'll have a winter here first.'

For his sake she voiced nothing and let his kisses distract her. *The spring will come too soon*, she thought. *Far far too soon.*

With Nalla gone, Master Jantalaber took over the task of teaching Hwilli her first lessons in dweomercraft, which amounted to her learning proper words and definitions. The universe, it turned out, encompassed far more than the world Hwilli had always seen, and each of these worlds contained their own proper order of beings and creatures. At times, the lesson over, Jantalaber would talk of his dream of building a place of healing as well, particularly when Paraberiel joined them.

'I'd thought of building it of stone in the usual way,' Jantalaber said one evening. 'Down by the Lake of the Leaping Trout, I thought.'

'That's a lovely place,' Paraberiel put in. 'Very restful, if someone was ill.'

'And close enough to a forest for the wood to send our failures on to their new life.' The master smiled with a wry twist of his mouth. 'But it's so far away, all the way on the other side of the grasslands.'

'I was thinking it would be safe, therefore,' Paraberiel said.

'No place is safe any more, not with these horse beasts carrying our enemies.'

'It's too bad you couldn't build a refuge that could move,' Hwilli said, smiling. 'We could use the horses to pull big sledges or some such thing.'

The men both laughed at her jest; then Jantalaber fell silent, looking away from his two apprentices at a pair of sprites, hovering in the air. Par seemed unaware of them. Both apprentices waited, unspeaking, until the master remembered their presence.

'My apologies,' Jantalaber said. 'But Hwilli, you've given me an idea. Not sledges, no, but I wonder –' He got up from his chair. 'I need to go consult with Maral. I wonder –'

Murmuring to himself, he hurried out of the room. Hwilli felt a cold shudder of awe, that the master could just go to Maraladario without sending a message first. Even Paraberiel seemed surprised into better manners than usual.

'I'll help you finish hanging those bundles of herbs,' he said.

'My thanks,' Hwilli said. 'There's a lot of them.'

Although the work took them most of the evening, Jantalaber never returned. She could imagine that the two dweomermasters talked deep into the night about arcane matters indeed, far beyond her understanding.

From that night on, Maraladario took to coming to the herbroom in the evenings. She would sit on the high stool and idly watch the two apprentices work while she chatted with Jantalaber about their proposed place of healing. Hwilli understood very little of what they were saying, and while Paraberiel pretended he understood, he never could explain it to her when she asked. Now and then she did recognize phrases, but others, such as forced convolution of the astral light, ensouling the egregore, and sigils of evocation, slipped through her mind like fingerlings through a wide-meshed fishnet.

Gradually, however, she began to build up an understanding of the general scheme. The two dweomermasters planned to build up an illusion of a place with so much dweomer energy behind it that in ordinary times it would look and feel and behave exactly like a real place. Yet it would have some extraordinary properties, since it would be only an illusion. As a nod to the troubled times, Maral wanted to give the site the power to move itself away from threatening danger. That mysterious egregore, it turned out, meant a body of knowledge about healing that would exist in a sort of bubble out on the astral plane. Any dweomerworker with the necessary skills would be able to learn the knowledge without the intermediary of a teacher.

'Someone extraordinarily talented,' Maral remarked one evening, 'could even get to it from the Gatelands of Sleep.'

'Mistress?' Paraberiel asked. 'Does that mean in dreams?'

'Dreams of a sort, a very special sort.' Maral frowned at the far wall. 'I wish Nalla hadn't been sent away. She showed promise in that area of the work.'

'Could she perhaps come back, mistress?' Hwilli said. 'In the spring, if it's safe.'

'Perhaps so. I'll speak to the prince about it.'

'I'd like to have her join us, too,' Jantalaber said. 'Well, we'll see. Now, I think your idea of placing our site on an island is a good one. The ocean's too violent, but a lake, a good-sized lake like the Lake of the Leaping Trout, that would be ideal.' He turned and looked at Hwilli. 'Why a lake?'

Hwilli gulped and forced her scattered thoughts calm. 'The vibrations of the water veil?' she said at last. 'They'd be like sticks and stones to build with.'

'Very good!' Maral raised a surprised eyebrow. 'You have an affinity for this working, Hwilli. Excellent!'

Hwilli ducked her head and forced out a modest smile, but she felt like shouting in glee, that Maraladario had praised her.

One evening Jantalaber took his two apprentices to visit Maral in her chambers. He made a silver dweomerlight to float ahead of them as they crossed a courtyard glittering with hard frost. In the sky dark clouds hung low, and the very air itself breathed out cold. The stairway in the Tower of the Sages seemed almost warm by contrast, as did Maral's chambers when they reached them.

As the head of the dweomermasters Maral had a brazier in her reception room and the charcoal to fuel it. Spirits of the air hovered round to whisk any fumes away through a tiny vent in a nearby window.

Maral, however, had draped herself in two cloaks. As the servant ushered them in, through an open doorway they could see her pacing back and forth in an inner chamber.

'She feels the cold badly,' her servant murmured. 'Master Jantalaber, do you think she's ill?'

'No,' Jantalaber said. 'At her age we all feel the cold.'

At the sound of his voice Maral came hurrying to greet them. Once they'd all sat down, and wine had been offered and refused, the servant bowed and took his leave.

'My thanks for coming here,' Maral said to Jantalaber. 'The frost bothers me, and I didn't care to go outside.'

'Of course,' Jantalaber said. 'It's never a burden to visit you.'

She smiled briefly, then leaned back in her chair. 'I've heard from the southern mages,' she said. 'Now, you children –' she glanced at Par and Hwilli '– don't know the beginning of this tale. Some days ago your master and I decided to contact the mages of Rinbaladelan and ask them to join our project of forming a place of healing. We've been waiting for an answer.'

'It finally came?' Jantalaber broke in.

'Oh yes, but you won't like it. The head of their guild told me they simply couldn't expend any dweomer force on our project because they had their immensely important secret work on hand. He did wish us luck with it.'

'How kind of him.' Jantalaber seemed to be about to say more, then set his lips tightly together.

'Their secret work, Mistress?' Par said.

'It's a puzzle they've been working on for hundreds of years,' Maral said. 'I'm truly tempted to tell you what it is, too. I never swore any vow not to tell.'

'Oh go ahead.' Jantalaber suddenly grinned. 'It will serve them right.'

'No bruiting this about, mind.' Maral paused to return his smile. 'They're trying to discover what language was spoken in the Blessed Lands, the earthly paradise where the gods created the People.'

'What? That's daft!' Hwilli blurted without thinking. 'My apologies, Mistress!'

'That was my reaction, too, actually,' Maral said. 'No need to apologize. The guild head was not pleased with me for it, either.'

'I can well imagine,' Jantalaber said. 'With the northern princedoms crumbling around us, how can they justify –'

'They say that if they can learn the language, then they can ask the gods to intervene.' Maral suddenly laughed, an unpleasant nervous chuckle. 'They have their reasons, actually. If they could talk to the gods, they could circumvent the priests and their star-gazing and their silly sacrifices.'

Jantalaber give Hwilli and Par each a look as sharp as a dagger point. 'Never ever breathe a word of this outside this chamber,' he said. 'Do you understand? It could cost a great many people their lives.'

Both of them murmured their agreement. Hwilli could barely speak, thinking of such an impiety.

'It's not just daft.' Jantalaber turned back to Maral. 'It's extremely dangerous.'

'Dangerous?' Maral said. 'Indeed. The guild in Rinbaladelan lives for itself alone, and I think the isolation has really and truly driven them mad.'

For a moment Hwilli wondered if she might be sick and disgrace herself. She took several deep breaths and fought her fear under control. *They won't be helping us with anything, then,* she thought. *No matter how bad things get here in the north.*

Every morning, Rhodorix and Andariel walked through the stables. By that time the guards had captured a hundred and seven warhorses and trained a hundred riders. Each guardsman stood beside his horse while Rhodorix examined the horse itself to ensure that it was well cared for, and Andariel looked over the man's gear for the same purpose. Usually they found a couple of slackers who ended up doing whatever unpleasant work needed doing that day. On this particular morning, however, they cut their inspection short when an out-of-breath servant lad came to fetch them.

'Prince Ranadar is outside,' he said. 'He wants to talk with you both.'

They followed him out into the courtyard, white and glistening with the first real snowfall, and picked their way over the slippery cobblestones. Wrapped in a scarlet cloak, Prince Ranadar stood in the shelter of the doorway that led into the watchtower. When they started to kneel, he stopped them with a quick wave of one hand.

'It's too cold for that,' the prince said. 'The mages have brought me some grim news. Lin Rej has fallen to the Meradan.'

Andariel turned pale and took a sharp step back, which nearly cost him his balance on the slippery footing. Rhodorix flung out one arm to steady him, lest the captain faint and fall. So many unusual names had flooded Rhodorix's mind in his few months in Garangbeltangim that it took him a moment to remember what Lin Rej was: a city of people who were usually called 'Mountain Folk', though Hwilli tended to call them 'children of earth', whatever that may have meant.

'Your highness?' Rhodorix said. 'Isn't their city underground?'

'It was,' Ranadar said. 'But there were stairways leading up to gardens on the surface. I heard that Meradan breached the upper walls and broke in through those doors.'

'There must have been a cursed lot of them.' Andariel had steadied himself. 'Your highness, I'm surprised that anyone could get past Mountain axemen, especially in those narrow tunnels. The Meradani losses –'

'– must have been high, yes, but take no comfort in it. The mages tell me that the Meradan have reinforcements. The Children of Aethyr have risen in revolt. They've deserted the farms around the northern cities and joined up with the Hordes.'

Andariel swore under his breath. Both men glanced at Rhodorix, then quickly looked away.

'Does your highness doubt my loyalty?' Rhodorix said.

'Of course not!' Ranadar frowned at him, then smoothed the expression away. 'Though I can see why you'd ask. Have no fear on that score, Horsemaster.'

'My humble thanks, then.'

The silence hung between them like smoke, acrid and choking.

'Your highness?' Andariel broke it at last. 'Were there any survivors from Lin Rej?'

'A few.' Ranadar paused briefly, his face slack with perceived horror. 'They're on their way here. I want you and your men to ride out to meet them, just in case there are any stray Meradani patrols riding around looking for prey. The Mountain Folk are travelling on the Tanbalapalim road. They left some of their fighting men behind to winter in the fortress there. The rest and some women are heading our way.'

'We'll fetch them, your highness.' Andariel glanced at Rhodorix. 'Horsemaster, how will the horses fare in the snow?'

'Well enough unless there's a blizzard,' Rhodorix said. 'Their winter coats are good and shaggy, and we'll take blankets for them at night.'

'Yes, we may have to camp on the road,' Andariel said. 'Snow or no snow.'

'I don't think the Mountain Folk are all that far away,' Ranadar put in, 'but it's hard for the mages to scry in this weather.'

'Of course,' Andariel said. 'Understood, your highness.'

Rhodorix understood nothing of this talk of scrying, but he was willing to take sorcery on faith, since both his prince and his woman believed in it.

It took some time for the horse guards to ready themselves and their supplies for the road. Rhodorix used a bit of it to find Hwilli and tell her where and why he'd be gone.

'I heard about Lin Rej from Master Jantalaber,' Hwilli said. 'The mages can speak with each other somehow.' She went pale about the mouth. 'He said that the slaughter was dreadful.'

'No doubt. The prince looked shaken himself.' Rhodorix let out his breath in a sharp sigh. 'Well, we'll do what we can for the survivors. Tell me somewhat. Gerontos wants to ride with us. Should he?'

'No. The cold will cramp every muscle on that weak leg. He won't be able to stand up, much less fight if you need him to.'

'I'll tell him no, then.' Rhodorix laid his hands on either side of her face. 'Give me a kiss, beloved, and then I'll be on my way.'

Hwilli kissed him as eagerly, as passionately as she always did, yet as he walked away, he found himself wondering if Gerontos was truly unfit to fight, or if she merely preferred having him stay in the fortress. *Don't be a fool!* he told himself. *You've not seen one thing to make you jealous, not one!* Besides, he asked himself, *what if I die in battle one fine day?* He decided that he'd rather have Gerontos take Hwilli than any other man and put the matter out of his mind.

Hwilli hated seeing Rhodorix ride out on patrol, simply because she was terrified that he'd be killed – not an unreasonable fear, given the times. Since she had learned the basic principles of dweomer fast and easily, Master Jantalaber had begun teaching her how to scry, a skill she found elusive. The master would place a pair of objects on a table in the chamber next to hers. Since she knew what the table looked like, she could first imagine it and then try to see what lay upon it, but the image of the table in her mind stayed stubbornly empty, a memory only.

When, however, she tried using Rhodorix as the subject of her exercises in the craft, she at last had some success. Now and then she caught a glimpse of him riding on a snowy road or giving his horse a nosebag of grain. The glimpses were short and generally murky, but at least she knew that he was still alive.

'This is extremely interesting,' Jantalaber said. 'Your people scry more easily when some feeling lies behind the attempt. It's just the opposite with us.'

'Well,' Hwilli said, 'it's true for me, at least. I don't know if it would apply to everyone.'

Jantalaber laughed and nodded. 'Right you are,' he said. 'I was rushing toward a conclusion that might not exist. However, let's abandon the table exercise. From now on, try to see your horsemaster or someone else you know, Nalla, perhaps.'

'Or my mother?'

Jantalaber's cat-slit eyes went wide with surprise. 'Is she still –' he caught himself. 'Is she still with us?'

'No, she was sent to Rinbaladelan with the rest of the cattle.'

Jantalaber winced. 'I'm sorry,' he said. 'But she'll be safer there than anywhere else in the princedoms.'

'That's true. My apologies, master.' Hwilli could hear her voice begin to clog with tears. She coughed, sniffled, and managed to clear it. 'I just worry so.'

'Alas, that's appropriate enough.' He shook his head and sighed. 'But yes, by all means see if you can see your mother.'

It took Hwilli several days of trying, in short bursts of work, but at length she did catch glimpses of Gertha. Dressed in clean blue linen, she sat in a cushioned chair by a window. She was pale and thin, far too thin. No doubt the long walk south had exhausted her. She held a bowl of what seemed to be dried fruit. As Hwilli watched, she took a piece out and began to eat carefully on the side of her mouth that still had teeth. Hwilli caught a glimpse of a painted wall behind her. Shame made her wince and lose the vision; she'd misjudged the People down in the south badly, apparently, when she'd thought they would treat refugees like cattle.

Hwilli saw the truth some days later, when she scried again and found Nalla and Gertha in the same chamber she'd seen before. In the vision Nalla suddenly looked up and smiled. *She's seen me!* Hwilli thought. Nalla nodded as if she'd heard her, then mouthed the words, 'I found her and took her in.' Hwilli returned the smile in a flood of relief. The vision broke up, leaving her mind divided between bitter and sweet thoughts. On the one hand, Nalla had gone out of her way to rescue Gertha. On the other, she had needed rescuing. A glimpse of the rest of the villagers, huddled outside Rinbaladelan's walls with no shelter, convinced Hwilli of that.

Hwilli went looking for Jantalaber to tell him of her success only to be distracted. Cloaked servants rushed down the corridor toward the outer doors. Hwilli caught the eye of a young man.

'The Mountain Folk are here!' he called out and ran on past.

Hwilli ran to her chamber, got her cloak, and hurried after them. Out in the frosty courtyard the horse guards were dismounting. She picked out Rhodorix immediately thanks to his gold-coloured mount. When she called to him he saw her and waved.

'I have to stable my horse,' he called out, 'and the captain and I have to report to the prince. We've brought messages.'

'Well and good, then!' Hwilli blew him a kiss, then turned her attention to the refugees, straggling in through the gates, women and children first, and the men behind.

Some five hundred at a quick count and estimate – Hwilli felt the shock as a blow, that out of Lin Rej's many thousands, only five hundred women had survived. Perhaps half had a child with them: a babe in arms, or a toddler wrapped against the snow in every spare bit of cloth the mother could find, or older children, gaunt and squinting, snow blind and clinging to their mother's skirts. Behind them came roughly a hundred axemen, weary, bedraggled, their beards and eyebrows white with frost.

'Ye gods!' Jantalaber whispered from behind her. 'Gods help us all!'

Hwilli glanced around to see him standing to one side of the door, his eyes as wide with horror and shock as hers doubtless were. He started to speak, then merely shook his head in sorrow.

'This can't be all,' Hwilli said. 'Weren't there more soldiers at least?'

'That's true.' Jantalaber sounded weary rather than relieved. 'They're wintering at Tanbalapalim. That's where the Meradan will strike first, no doubt.'

Hwilli shivered, pulled her cloak around her but shivered the more, trembling on the edge of a faint. Jantalaber laid a steadying hand on her shoulder.

'Go inside, child,' he said. 'Get the herbroom ready. No doubt there are plenty of these people who are going to need our help.'

The master had spoken the simple truth. All the rest of that day, Hwilli, Par, and Jantalaber worked in the herbroom, doing what they could for cases of frostbite, exhaustion, fluxes of the bowels, catarrh, and a good many other complaints. They heard tales of despair as well. A good many people had died during the long winter walk down from the smoking ruins of Lin Rej to Tanbalapalim. No one, however, wanted to talk about the death of Lin Rej itself.

'You have to shut that out of your mind,' one woman told Hwilli. 'You have to shove it into a chamber, like, and lock the door over it.' Her hands shook as hard as her voice. 'Don't ask. Please, just don't ask us to remember it.'

'I won't, then,' Hwilli said. 'Take this vial of herbwater with you. One sip at night will help you sleep.'

The woman looked up at her with tear-filled eyes, whispered a thanks, and walked off, clutching the glass vial in both hands as if she feared it would leap out of them.

Yet, a few words here, a mumbled oath there, a sentence framed in tears – a few precious scraps of information did come out during that long day, some of it to the good. Another group of Mountain Folk might well have escaped the slaughter. There was reason to hope that the Meradan had never found an escape tunnel that led from one quarter of the city to a bolt hole some miles east. A few of the axemen had tried to reach that tunnel. Although Meradan had blocked the way, the soldiers had found that area of the city deserted; its inhabitants must have gone somewhere, and there were no corpses in sight.

'So we think they'd already escaped,' a woman said. 'Before the Meradan got there.'

'Not just Meradan!' an axeman with a broken wrist put in. 'The halls were crawling with a different kind of lice! The –' He stopped, glancing at Hwilli, then away. 'Ah, what does it matter now? Worms and slimes from hell, all of them.'

At the dinner hour Rhodorix came to the herbroom. He stood in the doorway and watched with bleak eyes as Hwilli cleaned a festering cut on a young child's cheek. A Meradani sword had grazed her face as she fled behind her mother. By then only a few patients still waited to be seen, and they, as Jantalaber remarked, were the ones with the least pressing injuries.

'When you've stitched that cut you may leave, Hwilli,' he said. 'Par and I can finish up here. In the morning, though, I'll need you back.'

'Of course, Master,' Hwilli said. 'My thanks.'

'I've had one of the servants bring food to my chamber,' Rhodorix said. 'The chamberlain's having the Mountain Folk camp in the refectory for now.'

Gerontos had set the bowls of food, mostly bread and some dried beef simmered in wine, out on the table in the chamber. While they ate, Rhodorix told them about the horse guards' ride north.

'We found a squad of Meradan,' he said, 'and wiped them out. We got twelve good horses out of the scrap and a couple that will do for pack animals once their wounds heal.'

'Good,' Gerontos said. 'Any losses on our side?'

'None. Ye gods, the odds were a hundred to fifteen. If we'd lost any men, Andariel and I should have been flogged!'

The brothers shared a laugh, though Rhodorix cut his short.

'And I finally managed to take a couple of prisoners,' Rhodorix continued. 'I stopped the men from cutting them into shreds just in time. They might be persuaded to part with some information.'

'Good,' Gerontos said. 'I wonder how much pain the white savages can take?'

'We'll find out, I wager. But here's a thing that creeped my flesh,' Rhodorix said. 'Some of the men we killed weren't Meradan. They were farmfolk, according to Andariel, men like us.'

'Were they fighting for the Meradan?'

'They were.'

'Then it's all the same to me.' Gerontos turned to Hwilli. 'When can I ride to war again? I'm going half-mad, sitting around here like this.'

Hwilli was so exhausted from her long day in the herbroom that she blurted the truth without thinking. 'You may never be able to,' she said, 'not standing on the ground, anyway. Your leg's mended well enough for you to ride, but I don't know what fighting from horseback is like.' She glanced at Rhodorix. 'Do you use both legs?'

'Only to stay in the saddle.' Rhodorix was staring at his brother in obvious concern.

When Hwilli looked at Gerontos, she found his face an utter mask. He could have been enraged or thinking of nothing at all as far as she could judge from his impassive gaze. He sighed once, sharply. 'That's a blow and a half.' His voice was perfectly level. 'Are you sure?'

'No,' Hwilli said. 'Neither is Master Jantalaber.'

'Then I've got some hope,' Gerontos said. 'I'd rather slit my own throat than live like a servant or suchlike.'

'I'd expect no less of you,' Rhodorix said. 'But the new bow that the archers came up with is a splendid thing. If naught else, you can learn how to use it and ride with them.'

Gerontos smiled, such a sunny smile of such evident relief, that Hwilli felt faintly uneasy. *They both enjoy killing people*, she thought – then sharply reminded herself that the Meradan deserved it.

As he usually did, Rhodorix spent the night in Hwilli's chamber. She would have gladly spent half the next day abed out of exhaustion as much as for love for him, but the bronze gongs of the priests woke her long before the winter sun had crept above the horizon. Rhodorix mumbled something unintelligible and pulled a pillow over his head to block the sound. Hwilli got up and dressed, then hurried down to the herbroom and her duties.

When Hwilli arrived, a line of patients had already formed out in the corridor. Jantalaber and two of the Mountain women were already at work examining some of the worst frostbite cases in a blaze of dweomer light.

'Have you seen Par?' Jantalaber said.

'I've not,' Hwilli said. 'I came straight from bed when I heard the gongs.'

'There's some bread on a plate in the drying room. Take some before you start work.'

Hwilli fetched a chunk of bread and stood out of the way to eat it. She had met one of the Mountain women before, a healer named Vela, who came on occasion to the fortress to trade supplies of herbs and roots with Master Jantalaber. At the moment she was sitting on the high stool, translating for Jantalaber as he worked with patients who didn't speak the language of the People.

Like all the Mountain folk, Vela was short and stocky, but this morning her face looked gaunt, her eyes deep pools of shadow in the silver light glowing from the ceiling. She'd pinned her long grey hair up to the top of her head with bone pins in random clumps, and she wore a ragged dress over a pair of the leather leggings usually worn by the men of her people. When she acknowledged Hwilli with a wave, Hwilli saw that her hand and wrist had suffered burns along the back. She remembered her patient of the day before saying 'don't ask' and refrained from mentioning it.

Hwilli had just finished her bread when Paraberiel hurried in. All that day they worked with the injured and the terrified, until Hwilli wanted to weep more from the sheer horror of what had happened than from exhaustion. More information crept out of frightened mouths, about walking through so much blood that the floors had turned slippery, or of hearing the screams of women being raped before their throats were cut, or the way the Meradan growled and slobbered with rage as they killed and killed and killed.

'They burnt through the main doors on the hillside,' one axeman told them. 'And then they got in somehow through the walled gardens.'

'The worms who tended the place let them in,' a second axeman said. 'How else do you think?'

'Worms?' Hwilli snapped. 'Perhaps you'd rather this worm let someone else tend your wounds.'

The axeman yelped, as surprised as if a statue had spoken to him. Vela slewed around on her stool and barked an order in Dwarvish. After that, the men talked only to answer the healers' questions about their injuries.

Once they'd done everything they could for every injury, Jantalaber invited the healers to come and eat in his chambers. The other dwarven woman, Othanna, begged off, because she desperately needed sleep.

Jantalaber's outer chamber, high up in the mages' tower, displayed on its walls the many treasures he'd collected over his long life, elaborately glazed pottery, silver work, tapestries, pictures painted on tawed leather. A tiny fire burned in the freestanding pottery stove, using just enough fuel to take the bitter chill from the air. Only the priests kept truly warm in winter at Garangbeltangim. Bundled in their cloaks the three healers sank gratefully into cushioned chairs while Jantalaber's manservant brought bread and wine and dried fruit to go with a dish of spiced meats, stewed beyond identifying but tasty all the same.

At first the two masters tried to talk of pleasant things, but eventually the conversation turned to the attacks. No one in Garangbeltangim could avoid them, Hwilli realized, not for more than a few moments together. Trying to chat about some other subject struck her as trying to ignore a bleeding wound.

'My apologies for that fellow with his talk of worms,' Vela said to Hwilli.

'My apologies for snarling at him,' Hwilli said. 'If they let Meradan into your city, they were worms no matter what tribe they belonged to.'

'I suppose.' Vela stared across the chamber with exhausted eyes. 'I'll never be able to forgive them, never, but I do wonder if mayhap they never realized how the Meradan would treat us. I want to believe that.'

'I think you may,' Jantalaber put in. 'No one could have anticipated what followed. I suspect that no one meant to set those fires, at least. It seems likely that the Meradan were planning on using Lin Rej as a stronghold. They had no reason to destroy it. Sometimes men go mad when a battle starts.'

Vela nodded and held out her goblet. The manservant stepped forward with a flagon of wine and refilled it. Paraberiel, who'd been growing paler as he listened, held his up for more as well.

'Everyone was so surprised that our farmfolk would join the enemy,' Vela said. 'Dolts! I have been warning the council for years and years now that we had no right to treat those people that way!' Her voice sank to a growl. 'Lackwits! Blind!'

She had a sip of wine to clear her throat. 'Still, I was shocked at how – they were so, well, savage – I didn't realize. None of us did, we just didn't realize how hot rage can burn.'

'Don't think of the horrors,' Jantalaber said in a soft, careful voice. 'Try not to dwell upon them.'

Vela nodded and drank a long swallow of wine. She sighed before she continued, 'Maybe now the council will listen to me. What's left of it.'

'And maybe the prince will listen to Maral about our farmfolk.' Jantalaber paused, and the twist of his mouth expressed something less than hope. 'I suppose.'

'Master?' Hwilli said. 'I didn't know that Maraladario cared about my people.'

'Very much, child. She cares very much.'

Hwilli's eyes filled with tears beyond her power to stop them. Jantalaber smiled sadly, then pointedly looked away while she wiped the tears on her napkin.

'The Meradan, however,' Vela said, 'have no such excuse beyond their own evil natures.'

'Indeed,' Jantalaber said, 'I wonder what started them off. It was last winter when they began raiding. They came out of nowhere, it seemed. A famine, I thought, but it seems that wasn't the case.'

'No, it wasn't,' Vela said. 'Our men have doubtless told your prince all of this already. I don't understand all of it, but I'll tell you what I know.'

'Please do.'

'First of all, you doubtless know already that Tanbalapalim's threatened.'

'I'd heard that.' Jantalaber looked Hwilli's way. 'Had you?'

'Yes,' Hwilli said. 'Rhodorix told me. The leader of the Mountain axemen had talked to him on the way here. He thinks that the Meradan have made a winter camp somewhere up in the wild mountains. Rhodorix says that the princes don't have enough men to go attack it, even if they could find it.'

'Alas, that's true.' Vela abruptly shuddered. 'I wonder, though, if they'll go back to Lin Rej. Even in ruins it's warmer than the wild hills.'

'If you could bring yourself to scry into Lin Rej –' Jantalaber said.

'Eventually.' Vela moved uneasily in her chair. 'Not yet.'

They ate in silence for some moments.

'But to go back to your question.' Vela nodded at Jantalaber. 'Some months ago the council in Lin Rej decided we should strike back instead of sitting in our tunnels like rabbits in their warren. They sent a fighting force against those Meradan who lived in – well, I suppose you'd call that mess of theirs a city. It was really a lot of villages more or less joined together around a harbour.'

'Was?' Master Jantalaber interrupted her. 'Was a city?'

'Just that,' Vela said with a grim smile. 'Messengers came back with the tale. The place had been burnt to the ground. Skeletons lay all over in pieces, pulled around by the ravens and foxes. The axemen never found any heads or skulls, though.'

Jantalaber pressed a hand over his mouth. Hwilli laid her spoon down in her bowl. She could no longer eat.

'Oh, it was horrible, all right,' Vela went on. 'A survivor told our men that a horde of strangers had come out of the sea. A god brought them, he said, in great big ships bound around with iron chains.'

'But that's ridiculous!' Jantalaber said. 'No one puts chains on their ships.'

'I suppose the disaster had driven the survivors mad.' Her voice dropped to a near-whisper. 'I can understand now how such could happen.'

'One of those ghastly Meradan feuds, I suppose,' Jantalaber considered for a moment. 'Some stronger tribe probably rode in and took revenge on them for some reason. Maybe they did come by sea, for all we know. I'll wager the trouble has spread from there, tribe turning upon tribe, and now the losers are fleeing south.'

'I agree.' Vela nodded. 'It's the only reasonable explanation.'

Vela continued talking, telling of the destruction the Lin Rej men had found all across the Meradan territory, like the swing of an enormous scythe by a reaper from the hells. Hwilli wrapped her hands together and deliberately drove a thumbnail into the opposite palm. She hovered close to fainting, but the pain brought her round. She knew who those strangers from the sea were. Rhodorix had mentioned how the Devetii bound their ships to keep them from breaking up in storms. For a moment she considered telling the truth – but what would happen to Rhoddo and his brother, if the People realized who had actually brought ruin upon them?

'Hwilli?' Jantalaber said. 'You don't need to listen to all of this, if you'd like to leave us. You look quite pale, poor child.'

'My thanks, Master,' Hwilli said. 'It's just all so horrible.'

'It is that,' Vela said. 'Get yourself a little spiced wine. It should help.'

'Thank you. I will.'

Hwilli hurried out and closed the door behind her. She stood trembling in the corridor until her legs steadied under her, then went along to the refectory. At the door she paused, looking in, then gasped for breath as the smell of so many terrified and unwashed people swept over her. Somehow she'd never realized that tragedy could stink. Sweat and excreta, dried blood, sour herbs all mingled together into a scent like that of death itself.

The Mountain Folk had moved the tables over by the walls and piled the chairs on them as well, hiding the beautiful frescoes. On the elaborately tiled floors they'd spread out their blankets and little heaps of rags and trinkets, whatever they'd managed to save as the hordes rushed down the tunnel streets of Lin Rej. Babies wailed, children wept or screamed in nightmare, women chattered at them to sleep, please sleep! as if the words were some sort of spell.

Hwilli turned away and hurried to her chamber. She wanted to shut the world and the truth out, but Rhodorix was waiting for her, lying on her bed. A candle burned in a lantern sitting on her lectern.

'What's wrong?' he said. 'You look ill.'

'Rhoddo, the Meradan. Your people slaughtered their city. Why?'

He sat up, cocking his head to one side as if he were puzzled. 'The one on the seacoast? How do you know –'

'I just heard the story. That one, yes.'

'Well, our ships came into their harbour. We sent heralds, because we wanted to buy food from them. They killed the heralds, cut them to pieces right in front of us. Our men had been shut up in the ships for a long time, and they went berserk, truly.' He grinned at her. 'The savages didn't put up much of a fight.'

Hwilli considered him, her handsome beloved, who came from a people every bit as vicious as the despised Meradan.

'How can you smile like that?'

He wiped the grin away and stared at her, his eyes narrow with confusion.

'You can't ever let any of the People know,' Hwilli went on. 'Do you understand that? You can't let them know what your bloodkin started. The wars, I mean, the raiding.'

All at once he did understand. She could see it in his eyes, a wide-eyed stare, and then a wince of shame. He twisted half away from her and swore under his breath. She waited, terrified, watching him weep. At last he looked at her with his face still wet with tears.

'It's fitting,' he said, 'that I die for your People. The sooner and more painfully the better.'

'I didn't mean that!'

Hwilli flung herself down next to him on the bed. 'Rhoddo, please,' she said, 'promise me you won't tell them. They'll kill you, and me too, probably, because I knew and didn't say. Please please don't –'

He grabbed her by her shoulders and pulled her close. She could feel herself shaking as if she were half-frozen in a winter snow.

'I won't,' he whispered. 'Hush, hush, now, I won't do anything of the sort.' He kissed her, stroked her hair, until at last she could stop trembling. 'Put it out of your mind, beloved. I'd never let them hurt you.'

In his arms Hwilli could calm herself. As long as they were together, safe and warm in her chamber, she felt safe, she realized, even though she knew how temporary the safety was. *Never stop holding me*, she thought. *If only we could hold each other forever!*

As the days went on, the snow piled up outside, and the winds from the north blew as sharp as a Meradani axe. No one could leave the shelter of the fortress. Crossing the courtyard became a battle with the gods of snow and ice. Every morning the servants of the priests had to shovel the snow from the top of the priests' tower before the gongs could ring out, oddly sour and muffled in the icy air. No one ever saw the priests themselves, who stayed snug in their heated chambers, preparing for the midwinter ceremony to come.

Thanks to the weather Maraladario stopped coming to the herbroom of an evening, though at times Jantalaber would take his two apprentices and visit her. At other times, he told them, when the air was free of snow and its etheric vibrations, he and Maral spoke mind to mind.

'We're continuing with our scheme, of course,' Jantalaber said one morning. 'We've settled on the Lake of the Leaping Trout, over on the east side of the grassland, for the site. That's just north of Elditiña, and there's a convenient bridge over the River Delonderiel.' He sighed heavily. 'The project gives us something to think about, I suppose, more pleasant than – well, everything.'

'The situation's getting pretty bad, isn't it?' Paraberiel said. 'Here in the fortress, I mean. It seems like every day there are half-a-dozen fights between the Mountain axemen and our men.'

'There are too many people here. I just hope none of these squabbles end with someone swinging their sword or axe.' Jantalaber smiled thinly. 'Or we'll have even more work to do.'

'Could you ask the prince to take away their weapons?' Par said.

'I could, and he could try, but I suspect that none of the men would hand them over. It's a horrible thing, when men that need each other so badly begin to fight among themselves. Well, when this blizzard stops, they can go out on patrol. Tire them out in the snow, and they'll be more peaceful.'

Paraberiel and Hwilli dutifully smiled at the jest, which reminded Hwilli of a problem of her own.

'Par, I meant to ask you,' she said. 'Could you take over my patient, Gerontos? His leg's nearly healed, but someone should look in on him fairly regularly. If the master agrees, of course.'

'I could, certainly,' Par said.

'What's all this?' The master turned to Hwilli.

'He looks forward too much to my visits. When Nalla was still here, it didn't matter, but now I hate to be alone with him.'

'Oh.' Jantalaber nodded in understanding. 'Very well, Par. He's your patient from now on.' He paused for a sigh. 'I'm glad he's nearly healed. We've got so many new patients among the Mountain Folk that I doubt if our herb supply will last the winter.'

The slow days piled up around them like the snow itself. More than herbs began to run short, despite the extra food taken from the farm folk. The refugees from Lin Rej had brought nothing with them, and the Mountain Folk tended to eat heartily at all times. Prince Ranadar spent much of his time answering complaints and accusations, that the People were hoarding, that the Mountain Folk were greedy, that the fortress was far too cold. Worse yet was the feeling among the prince's guard that the usual winter catarrhs and rheums were somehow the fault of the Mountain Folk. Hwilli and the other healers explained over and over again that no, the refugees had not somehow brought disease into the fortress, that those minor ills struck every year.

'They're a bit worse this year, though,' Hwilli admitted to Rhodorix, 'but then, everyone's on edge and frightened, so maybe they just seem worse.'

'I'll accept that,' Rhodorix said. 'I keep telling my men to worry about themselves and their horses and let the prince worry about the men from Lin Rej.'

'That's probably all you can do.'

'Let's hope that spring comes soon.'

Hwilli felt as if her heart stopped, just for a few moments, then started again with a wrench that left her trembling.

'Spring means the war starts up again,' she said.

'Perhaps. If it's true that the Meradan have been camping up in the mountains, there may not be a lot of them left by spring.'

'Didn't the prince tell you about the scrying?'

'No,' Rhodorix looked puzzled. 'What scrying?'

'Mistress Vela's fairly sure the horde went back into Lin Rej. She's been scrying, and she can see someone moving around in there. It's in ruins, but it would still be better than the shelter they'd find in the wild mountains.'

Rhodorix swore under his breath. 'If the prince didn't tell me and Andariel,' he said, 'it means he didn't want any of the guards to know. Not a word to anyone else about this, beloved. It could send the axemen into a blind rage, and it could sink the fighting spirits of our men. Do you understand?'

'I do, truly.'

'Good.' Rhodorix said nothing more for a long moment. 'We'll deal with them when spring comes. There's naught we can do about it now.'

That he was so obviously right wrung her heart, but she smiled and put on a brave face, just to ease his worry. Yet not two days later she received news that left her helpless against tears. Nalla contacted her during a scrying practice.

'I'm so sorry,' Nalla said, 'but you have to know. Your mother caught a fever. She died last night in her sleep.'

Hwilli tried to speak, but the only sound she could make turned into a sob.

'I know,' Nalla said. 'I'm so sorry. Hwilli, I'm leaving Rinbaladelan in the spring. I'm being sent to meet Maraladario at the Lake of the Leaping Trout. I'll tell you more then.'

Hwilli nodded to show she'd heard, then dropped her face into her hands and wept. The vision disappeared and left her to her grief.

The shortest day of the year came icy cold but clear. The gongs woke the fortress to a night darkness that hid what would have been late morning in summer. Rhodorix rolled out of bed, dressed, and then woke Hwilli.

'I'm going to fetch Gerro,' he told her. 'It's almost time for the sacrifices.'

She sat up and yawned, covering her mouth with one hand, and nodded to show she'd heard him.

'No going back to sleep!' He grinned at her. 'The gods will be angry.'

'Huh! The gods aren't going to notice someone like me.'

'Wear that new dress anyway, just in case.'

'I will, then, and my thanks to you again.'

Rhodorix had asked for cloth as part of his guardsman's pay in order to give it to Hwilli. Much to his surprise, he'd been able to get her a dress already sewn up by the prince's wife's women, a further mark of the rhix's favour toward him. 'The horses are our living wall,' the

prince had told him. 'You have my thanks.' Rhodorix treasured the
memory, letting it roll around his mind like fine music.

In the cold Gerontos had trouble walking, even with his stick.
Rhodorix let his brother lean on him as they made their slow way
outside to the courtyard in front of the palace. Women carrying torches
stood in a line at the outer walls of the buildings and ringed the inner
walls of the fortress itself. The healers stood on the steps of the palace.
Hwilli hurried forward with her fellow apprentice.

'We'll help Gerro,' she said. 'You'd best take your place. Remember,
don't say a word until the priests say it's finished.'

'Well and good, then,' Rhodorix said. 'I won't.'

Andariel had already got the rest of the guards in place, horsemen
to the right of what at first looked like a pile of firewood, infantry to
the left, archers equally divided among the two contingents. As horsemaster, Rhodorix joined the captain up in the front rank. From that
position he could see that the firewood had been carefully stacked
into a temporary altar, square in shape, some twelve feet on a side
though only about five feet high.

When he glanced up, he saw men on the holy tower beside the
gleaming brass gongs, but as yet neither the priests nor the white cows
had made an appearance in the courtyard. They were, he surmised,
waiting for the prince to arrive – soon, Rhodorix hoped. Even in their
heavy cloaks the men were shivering in place. Finally silver horns
sounded. The healers on the palace steps moved aside to let Ranadar
through. He took a torch from one of the women and stalked up to
the altar. In the flickering light he looked furious, his preternaturally
handsome face drawn tight and grim under the hood of his cloak.

With the prince in place other horns shrieked, the sour bronze cry
of the priestly instruments. Marching in lockstep, their gold and
sapphire decorations glittering, the priests were coming with their
usual bodyguards around them, the silver alloy swords gleaming like
the teeth of wolves. At the rear two of them led sacrifices, but not
the cows. Rhodorix choked back a curse just in time. The two Meradan
prisoners of war shuffled along, draped in drab cloaks, their hands
bound, their heads shaved.

Had they been back in the homeland, Rhodorix could have stepped
forward and demanded his prisoners back. They might have chosen
to live as his slaves or to face the altar and go free of him forever. As
it was, he could do nothing but watch as the priests led them to the
firewood structure. They stood heads down and hopeless as the priestly
contingent gathered around them.

With raised arms the priests began to pray, a long litany in the language of the People, but some ancient and holy form of it, just different enough that Rhodorix, who'd left the crystals back in Gerontos's chamber, could understand little of the long involved plea to a great many gods. At intervals horns blared and gongs rang out, but no one spoke or moved.

At last the head priest let out a shriek that nearly matched the horns. 'The dark, the dark!' he cried out. 'We must light the dark!'

Other priests shoved the prisoners forward. They struggled, twisted, but the priests forced them to their knees. In the glittering torchlight silver swords flashed up and swung down. The dead Meradan fell forward, their heads dangling from strips of skin and spine, as blood gushed. The bronze horns screamed over and over as the priests lifted the bodies and placed them on the altar. Ranadar stepped forward and flung his torch into the firewood.

The assembled crowd waited, gasping for breath, as the flames flickered, nearly died, then caught with an uprush of fire. The gongs clanged and clashed as the assembly let out its collective breath in a sigh of relief as the torch bearers hurried forward in long lines and began to cast their torches into the blaze.

Rhodorix looked toward the east. Although the stone walls of the fortress blocked the horizon, he could see the faint first silver of dawn. The stars were beginning to disappear at the sun's first lighting. *Well, there!* he thought. *It's back for another year.*

The priests and the prince had drawn back from the blazing altar where the prisoners burned. Ranadar turned from the altar and motioned to his men to follow him. Andariel and Rhodorix collected the guards and marched off behind their rhix in an untidy mob.

Ranadar led them all the way back to the new stables, where they clustered around him at his command.

'I want you all to know,' he said, 'that I forced the priests to kill those men before they were thrown onto the fire. They wanted to lay them alive on the altar.'

Rhodorix's stomach twisted in disgust. Andariel shook his head and shuddered. Several of the guardsmen swore.

'They told me,' Ranadar went on, 'that the times demanded sacrifices beyond the usual. The cows weren't enough, they said, since the gods were so obviously furious with us. I told them I wouldn't take part unless the men died first.' His rage vanished, and his voice suddenly wavered in self-doubt. 'They kill the cattle first, don't they? I haven't cursed us all, have I?'

'They do, my prince,' Andariel said. 'I think you've saved us all from a worse bane than any priest could lay upon you.'

'My thanks.' Ranadar paused, gathering his breath. 'And the sun is rising. Well, it's done, no matter what the outcome may be.'

Rhodorix had been hoping along with Gerontos that his brother's leg would heal straight and sound. As the winter days wore on, each a little longer than the last, his hope vanished. A month or so after the solstice rites, Gerro started walking without leaning on a stick, but he limped with a sideways roll from a frozen knee. Though neither wanted to voice it, both men knew he'd never fight on foot again at his former level of skill. Eventually, however, when the snows turned soft during somewhat warmer days, though they still froze again at night, Rhodorix brought the subject up.

'About that leg –'

'I know. I'm worried, too,' Gerontos said. 'Paraberiel suggested I go talk with his master in the craft.

'I'll go with you. You'd best take that walking stick.'

Gerontos turned on him, his face bright with rage, but he caught himself. For a moment he stared at the ground.

'True spoken,' he said at last. 'Hand it to me, will you?'

Rhodorix gave him the stick, then picked up the basket with the two crystals. While he himself could understand much of what the People said, Gerontos still knew only a few words.

They walked slowly down the long corridors leading to the herb-room, where the door stood partway open. Rhodorix could hear talk inside. When he peered around the open door, he saw Hwilli, her master, and the Mountain woman Vela. They were discussing building something they had in mind – *as if any of us can build anything*, he thought, *as if any of us will live that long!* 'Hola?' he called out. 'Hwilli, may we come in?'

'Of course.' It was Jantalaber who answered him. 'Have you brought us your brother?'

'I have. Come on, Gerro.'

Jantalaber helped Gerontos hoist himself up onto a marble-topped table, then knelt in front of him. He ran his hands along the withered leg, shook his head, tapped it here and there with a thoughtful forefinger, and finally prodded the muscles along the calf. He stood up with another shake of his head.

'This doesn't look good,' the healer said into the white crystal. 'I'm sorry, lad, but the bone was smashed, not broken cleanly. The muscles aren't adhering properly, and the long bone has healed just ever so slightly off centre.'

'I see.' Gerontos spoke into the black. 'Well, my thanks, anyway, for everything you've done for me.' He glanced Rhodorix's way. 'Will you help me get back to our chamber?'

'Of course.' Rhodorix made his voice as cheerful as he could manage. 'Looks like you're marked for an archer now.'

Gerontos shrugged. From his mask of an expression, it was impossible to tell what he might be thinking.

'Hwilli?' Jantalaber said. 'You may go back with them, if you'd like. You should tell your man your good news.'

'What's this?' Rhodorix turned to her, but her smile told him before she could speak. 'You're with child?'

'Yes, I am.' She was holding her head high, on the edge of defiance even in her happiness. 'Are you glad of it?'

'Very glad!' Rhodorix held out his hand to her.

She took it and smiled at him sideways, abruptly shy. He gave her a chaste kiss on the forehead in deference to the presence of her master. *A man needs to know that something of him will live after him*, Rhodorix thought, *but that's a bit gloomy to be telling her.*

Some days later, the last of the Mountain axemen arrived at Garangbeltangim. They'd taken advantage of the slight warming and temporary thaw to leave the northern city and head south to join up with their kinsfolk. Wrapped in his scarlet cloak, Prince Ranadar met them out in the snowy courtyard. Rhodorix and Andariel stood nearby, ready to find the men somewhere to sleep and eat in the overcrowded fortress.

'We would have stayed to the end in Tanbalapalim,' their avro, Tarl, told the prince. 'But Prince Salamondar told us it would be a waste of our lives. Go guard your women, he said. Live and remember us.'

The hardened warleader leaned on the haft of his axe and wept. As if to drown the sound of his grief, the bronze gongs on the priests' tower began to clang and clatter out the passing hour.

The winter snows melted early that year. When Hwilli looked up to the high peaks, she saw them still white and gleaming, but down near Garangbeltangim only dirty streaks and heaps of snow lay in spots with deep shade. Everywhere else brown mud lay over the land like filthy blankets.

'The winter wheat will be sprouting soon,' Hwilli told Jantalaber.

'And the farmfolk won't be returning to keep the deer and wild goats away from it.'

'Very true,' the master said. 'I'll have a word with our prince tonight.'

Ranadar listened to the word, apparently, because he ordered a contingent of those guardsmen who had no horses to patrol the wheat fields. They grumbled, but they went down to the village. Hwilli went with them that first day to tell them how to repair the huts. They needed rebuilding every spring, as did the fences that marked out the fields. Master Jantalaber was waiting for her at the gates when she returned.

'Do you think they'll be able to do the work?' he asked her.

'I doubt it, not without someone to tell them how,' Hwilli said. 'Will I have to teach them?'

'No. I've already spoken to Paraberiel. I don't want you down there, the only woman in a village full of soldiers. Par comes from a farm family, too, you know. I'm sending him down on the morrow.'

'Thank you! I can't tell you how grateful –'

'Most welcome, I'm sure. Now, the two terraces just below us are a different matter. If you could lend your knowledge there? The mounted men will be sowing hay for their horses.'

'I'll be glad to do that, yes. I'm starting to think that Rhodorix is right. The horses are the only safety we'll have as things go on.'

Jantalaber looked away, suddenly weary. 'If things go on,' he said. 'Ah well, the gods will send us what they will, and there's naught we can do about that.'

Once the last of the snow had melted, and the days were noticeably warmer though the nights still froze, Hwilli took to spending her mornings down on the terraces with Rhodorix and his men. They complained, as soldiers have always complained about undignified work, but they learned to clear ground and plough, to plant and to fend off hungry birds instead of Meradan. Those few days seemed so peaceful, so unseasonably warm and soft, that Hwilli could let herself pretend that the summer would stretch out the same, with the Meradan somehow kept far away.

But of course, news of the Meradan came early that spring as well, some days before the equinox. The sprouting hay had dusted the first terrace with pale green, and she stood at the edge of the field, talking with Rhodorix, when one of the guardsmen called out in surprise.

'Runners coming up!' He was pointing to the road. 'But only two of them.'

The royal runners, the messengers whose speed and stamina helped the mages keep the scattered princedoms together, generally travelled in groups of four. Hwilli felt her heart thud in her chest as the two men jogged, stumbling weary, across the second terrace.

'Go down and meet them!' Rhodorix designated men with a sweep of his arm. 'Carry them up here, or they'll never reach us alive.'

The men ran off to follow his orders. When they brought the messengers back, cradled on their joined arms, Hwilli realized that both runners were wounded. Old blood crusted one man's face and neck; the other had wrapped a clumsy bandage around his thigh.

'Get them to Master Jantalaber!' It was her turn to give the orders. 'I'll come with you.'

The man with the wounded leg gasped out a few words, 'Meradan. Tanbalapalim's fallen,' before he fainted.

Hwilli wanted to scream aloud, but she concentrated only on the work ahead of her, saving the runners' lives. The guardsmen carried them up to the infirmary and laid them onto plank beds. Jantalaber took over caring for the man with the head wound, whilst she cleaned, treated, and stitched the other runner's slashed leg. It was a miracle, she thought to herself, that he'd not bled to death. Once he was bandaged, she helped him drink water for his thirst and a healing infusion for his wound.

She'd barely got him comfortable, and Jantalaber was still tending the second runner, when Prince Ranadar himself strode into the chamber. Behind him clustered frightened advisors like sheep behind a ram.

'Can he speak?' Ranadar said to her.

'Some, your highness,' Hwilli said.

The runner tried to sit up. She grabbed pillows and arranged them under his head and upper back. 'Lie still,' she said. 'The prince doesn't expect you to bow to him.'

'Quite so,' Ranadar said. 'When did Tanbalapalim fall?'

A few words at a time, the exhausted runner stammered out the tale. The Meradan had appeared at the first sign of melting snow, an army of them, several thousand, perhaps, including a large contingent of the Children of Aethyr. They had surrounded the walled city but sent no heralds. When Prince Salamondar tried to parley, the Meradan slaughtered his heralds and threw their heads back over the walls.

'Why didn't his farseers warn me then?' Ranadar asked him. 'We could have marched to break the siege.'

Or try to, Hwilli thought, *with our few men.*

'They tried, your highness. They said there was too much rain and snow.'

'Of course. Somehow one always hopes –' He let his voice trail off. 'Ah well, go on!'

'They made some sort of ram, your highness, and they kept on battering, screaming, pounding . . .'

Eventually the Meradan had broken down the gates. They scaled the walls; they were reckless and fearless, apparently, because they'd gained entry to the outer city within a few days. From the walls the heart-sick defenders of the citadel had watched the Meradan loot, burn, and kill helpless civilians.

'We wanted to go down, your highness,' he whispered. 'The priests wouldn't let us. They said, guard the temple towers. They would have cursed us. They made us stay.'

'I see.' Ranadar's voice had turned into a growl of rage. 'Go on.'

The fortress held out longer, giving eight runners a chance to escape by a bolt hole dug under one of the towers. Two of them had lived to reach the edge of the Meradani camp. The others had not. The plan was for the men in the fortress to sally once the runners were well away.

'We reached the hills nearby. We looked back and saw the inner citadel burning.'

'So much for the sally,' Ranadar said. 'Very well. You and your companion rest now.'

The runner nodded and let himself sink back into the pillows.

That night, the news spread in a wave of panic through the fortress. The prince and his council shut themselves up in the royal chambers. Master Jantalaber and the mages closeted themselves in Maraladario's suite. The various court officers wandered here and there in the complex, trying to reassure the garrison that Garangbeltangim was a stronger fortification than Tanbalapalim, with its civilian population, could ever be. Hwilli doubted if anyone believed them.

'It's the numbers,' she said to Rhodorix. 'There are thousands of Meradan, aren't there?'

'A horde of them, truly,' he said. 'But what's swelling their ranks are people like us. I wonder how many others there are, off to the north, waiting to join the looting?'

'People like us. I suppose they're like us.'

'Ye gods, Hwilli, do you doubt it?'

'Not doubt it, but I don't want to think we could be so savage.'

He snorted in disgust. 'Why not? Look at how the People treated your mother! Slaves will always rise up if there's someone to lead them against their masters. The Rhwmani war taught me that, if naught else.' He smiled with a bitter twist of his mouth. 'Why do you think Ranadar sent the farm folk away?'

'To spare the food they'd eat, I suppose. Or did he think we'd rise against him?'

'Most likely both. There are more guards down in the south, from what Andariel tells me, and they have more leisure to keep the slaves under control.'

'Slaves? They never called us that, but I suppose that's just what we are to them.'

'Most of us. They make exceptions for the likes of you and me.'

'How can you go on fighting for them?'

'Because I gave Prince Ranadar my word of honour that I'd serve him. Why do you go on doing your work here?'

'Because the people I heal are sick and injured and need me.' Hwilli heard her voice begin to shake. 'They're not to blame.'

Hwilli managed to keep from weeping only through her fear of disgracing herself in front of the man she loved. He put his arms around her and drew her close to stroke her hair. *At least I have him*, she thought. *The gods have given me that much in life.* When she remembered how much she'd feared growing old, she had to suppress a mad impulse to laugh. She had wasted her fears on something that very likely would never happen.

'They'll come here next, won't they?' Hwilli said. 'The hordes, I mean.'

'Most likely,' Rhodorix said. 'I won't lie to you.'

'You have my thanks for that. And they'll take the fortress, won't they?'

'Unless the gods stop them. No one else can.'

He looked oddly calm, his eyes stripped of all feeling. She realized, that night, just how completely men like him lived to die. *I'll have to be as strong as he is*, she told herself, *when the time comes.*

In the morning, news of another sort swept through the fortress like a winter wind. The prince had decided to hold out against the Meradan as long as possible, and thus drain off men from the Meradani stampede down to the coast, in order to let Rinbaladelan reprovision and fortify. He was planning on stripping Garangbeltangim of every servant, every woman, wife or not, and every child. Even the mages and priests would leave, every single person who could not fight, but who would prove a drain on the fortress's provisions in case of siege.

They were to march east with the Mountain Folk and try to make some sort of new life for themselves in some safe place.

At first Hwilli thought little of the news. As a healer, she would stay, or so she assumed. Master Jantalaber disabused her of that delusion with the noon meal, which they ate together in the herbroom.

'You'll be coming with me and the others, of course,' he said.

'What?' Hwilli stared at him. 'No. I can't leave Rhodorix.'

'Yes, you can, and you will. This is the last meal we'll have in Garangbeltangim, Hwilli. Pack up your things as soon as you're done eating.'

'No!'

'Am I your master in your craft or not? You'll do as I say. Don't you think I'm heartsick, too? But we have our work. We have the place of healing to build.'

'I don't care –' Her voice choked on tears. 'I'm too weak to matter to the work.'

'Not so! Your life is precious, the first person of your kind to study magic and succeed.'

Cold, icy cold, despite the sun falling through the tall windows, despite the warmth of the stove in the herbroom – Hwilli could hardly breathe from the cold that had gripped her entire body.

'You'll be coming with me,' Jantalaber went on. 'Come now, Hwilli. Think about this – Nalla will be joining us when we reach the Lake of the Leaping Trout. You'll see your friend again, at least.'

Hwilli pushed back her chair and stood up. Jantalaber rose as well and held out one hand.

'Hwilli, please, think of the work! I know you love your man, but once the Meradan have been beaten off, we can return. And then, after the wars are over, won't our people – both our peoples – need the place of healing more than ever?'

She could only shake her head and stare at him.

'Go pack up your belongings,' he said. 'Say farewell to your beloved. I know it won't be easy, but –'

'No!' She screamed out the word. 'No! Once we leave, we'll never come back here. Can't you see that?'

She turned and ran, sprinting from the herbroom, running down the corridor, bursting outside into the cool spring sun with tears drenching her face. Where was Rhodorix? She would have to find Rhoddo, have to tell him that she'd never desert him, never! For what seemed like days she searched for him, running back inside to their chambers, running out again, back to the stables, up to the walls, down again to question every man she saw, 'Where is Horsemaster Rhodorix?'

At last someone told her. He'd gone down to the first terrace to bring back the men who'd been working there. She started to run to the gates, but already those who would leave were assembling in front of them. Master Jantalaber stood at the edge of the growing crowd, looking this way and that. When she came up to him, panting in exhaustion, he smiled, but it was a mournful smile, and his eyes were moist with sympathy.

'I packed your things for you,' he said.

Hwilli felt too cold, too sick from running this way and that, to do more than let a few tears fall.

'Draw back!' an officer was shouting. 'Clear the gates! Clear the gates!'

Jantalaber caught her arm and drew her gently with him as the crowd of refugees followed orders. One massive gate swung open to allow the line of mounted men to trot in. On his golden gelding Rhodorix brought up the rear, chivvying the others along toward the stables. Hwilli longed to run after him, but Maraladario herself, wrapped in a dark blue cloak shot through with silver threads, stood in her way. Her emerald green eyes narrowed.

'You'll come with us,' she said. 'Don't make me ensorcel you, Hwilli. It would go against every principle I hold, but by the gods, I'll do it if I have to.'

Hwilli could do nothing but weep. She despised herself, she felt humiliated to the core of her very soul, but still the tears ran. The People had broken her, she felt, torn out her soul and replaced it with another. Had she any true strength, she would run away and hide where no one would find her, until at last the refugees had left, and she'd be left behind, free to die with her beloved, but the tears drained her strength, or so she felt, and made it impossible to move, much less run.

Bronze gongs rang out from the priests' tower, signalling, perhaps, the end of everything. Silver horns blared in the signal that the prince himself was approaching. At the same moment Rhodorix and his men came running into the ward from the direction of the stables. They flung themselves down to kneel just as the doors of the palace opened and Ranadar, followed by his retinue, stepped out. Hwilli had no interest in the prince. Seeing Rhodorix had given her part of her soul back, or so she felt.

'Rhoddo,' she called out. 'Rhodorix!'

Before Maraladario or Jantalaber could stop her, she broke away and ran to Rhodorix. He scrambled up to face her.

'Don't let them send me away,' she said. 'I want to stay with you.'

'You can't stay here,' Rhodorix said. 'Now, listen. I've asked the prince to let my brother go with you. His twisted leg will keep him from fighting, so the prince agreed. Gerro will take care of you and the child. Do you understand?'

His words were making little sense. Hwilli grabbed his arm with both hands. 'I want to stay with you,' she repeated.

'You can't.' He pulled his arm away. 'It would mean your death.'

'I don't care.' She raised her head to let him see the tears. 'I'll die with you when it comes to that.'

She took one step toward him, but hands grabbed her by the shoulders and pulled her back. Master Jantalaber had reached her. She twisted in his hands, struggled to get free – until she heard a voice she recognized even in her grief.

'What's all this?' Ranadar, the prince himself, came striding up to them.

Rhodorix knelt, head bowed. When Jantalaber let her go, Hwilli flung herself down beside him.

'She won't leave, your highness,' Jantalaber said. 'My apprentice, that is, because of the love she bears your horsemaster.'

Hwilli looked up at the prince, who was standing with his hands on his hips, his head tilted to one side as he considered her. The afternoon sun glittered on the sapphire in his dweomer pendant and turned the chased roses as fiery-gold as the harsh light itself.

'You have to go,' Ranadar said. 'You can't fight, and so you're just another mouth to feed.'

'I can bind wounds, your highness.' Hwilli felt her voice shaking in her throat, but she forced herself to speak. 'I can tend all manner of ills –'

'We have other healers, ones who can draw a bow as well as bind wounds. You swore a vow to your master, didn't you? I pity you, but I'll order you all the same. Go! Your prince commands you. Go with your master, child!'

Hwilli stretched out her arms to Rhodorix, who refused to look at her.

'You heard him,' he said. 'Follow his orders.'

He wants me to go, she thought. *He doesn't want me here*. The thought was a spear of ice, stabbing her to the heart. Her defeat tasted like a death, a cold emptiness that chilled her mind and her soul. She got to her feet, gave Rhodorix's sullen back one last glance, and let Jantalaber lead her away.

By the gates the other refugees had drawn up in reasonable order with a squad of archers. At the rear, behind the servants and hand-carts, Gerontos sat on his chestnut warhorse.

'Hwilli!' he called out to her. 'Come here! You can ride behind me.'

Understanding broke through Hwilli's grief. Rhodorix had handed her over to his brother, just as if she were a horse he no longer wanted to ride. For a moment the courtyard seemed to move under her feet. Master Jantalaber caught her by the shoulder and steadied her.

'Go ride with him,' he said. 'The child you're carrying could suffer, if you're forced to walk the entire way.'

For the sake of Rhodorix's child Hwilli went to Gerontos. He dismounted, helped her climb up behind the saddle, then mounted again. As they rode off, she glanced back to see Rhodorix still kneeling before the prince. *Very well*, she thought. *I'll do as you say, but I'll always be faithful to you in my heart and soul.*

With a sigh that was more a gasp of surrender, she slipped her arms around Gerontos's waist to steady herself as the column began to move. He turned his head to glance her way. Despite the awkward angle, she caught a glimpse of a well-pleased smile.

Rhodorix kept silent by iron self-control as Hwilli and Gerontos rode off to catch up with the refugees, most of whom had already filed through the gates. He listened to the sound of the chains grinding through the winches as the gates closed with a rumble like thunder. Under the cover of that sound he allowed himself one long keen. Tears ran down his face; he wiped them roughly away on the back of his hand. The prince, with his hands on his hips, watched him.

'So!' Ranadar said. 'You did love that woman. Did you want her to stay?'

'I wanted her to go, your highness, but only for her sake. For mine I wish she could have stayed, but I'll hope and pray that she lives a long life and finds a little joy in it as well.'

'The thought becomes you. I doubt me if you and I will do either.'

'The only joy I can see myself finding, your highness, is dying before you do.'

'That's a boon the gods will probably grant you.' Ranadar paused, looking up at the cloud-strewn sky. 'One way or the other.'

PART II

The Northlands
Summer, 1160

The reflection in the mirror is not your actual face. No more is the world you see the world.

The Secret Book of Cadwallon the Druid

I *got my wish. I died long before the prince did.*

The silver dragon spread his wings, contemplated flight, then closed them again. A wind came up, whining through the broken towers, murmuring in the trees. A dust demon whirled across the shattered paving stones of the courtyard by the long-gone gates.

'I thought I'd die here in Garangvah,' Rori said aloud, 'but I didn't. We lived through the siege, and then I followed Ranadar when he began raiding. It was all that was left to us, raiding. We stole their horses, we killed as many of their men as we could.' He laughed with a long rumble of satisfaction, remembering the kills. 'It was my wyrd, when I died on one of those raids. Was it an arrow?' He considered one of Garangvah's broken towers, as if perhaps it had heard and might answer. 'I don't remember. It doesn't matter anymore. It's a new war now.'

With a rustle of wings the silver dragon leapt into the air and flew, heading east. He laired that night on one of the foothills, then set out again in the morning. Late in the afternoon he reached the fortress he'd seen a-building. Although he'd flown over the area a number of times, he'd never examined it carefully. In the slanted light of the aging day, he saw marks upon the ground he'd not noticed before, places where the scrubby grass grew thicker or thinner. As if they were shadows thrown by Time itself, the marks displayed a pattern of long lines enclosing areas that might have been fields and little circles the size and shape of farmers' huts. Yet nothing remained on the ground to explain them.

The fortress itself presented a further surprise. In the midst of flat scrubland it stood on a hill of sorts – very much of sorts, he realized. He flew up high and glided in a lazy loop, studying the hill and the half-finished buildings, all of wood, that stood behind a wooden palisade. Despite the clutter, he could see enough to discern a crucial truth.

Like a long sausage, the ridge rose in an oddly symmetrical shape. A circular depression marked each end, as if the earth had settled over some kind of construction underneath. In the centre, where the new buildings stood, he could only guess at the ground underneath, but it seemed oddly uneven, as if boulders or some sort of loose rock underlay the soil. At least part of the ridge, then, was no natural feature, but an ancient structure, perhaps even an enormous barrow joined to shrines at either end.

Did the Horsekin realize that they were building upon a supremely unstable foundation? Apparently not. Long barges, anchored side to shore, fringed the nearby river. Each of them held cubical blocks of grey stone. Somewhere upstream the Horsekin were quarrying. Rori could guess that they had learned a hard lesson about dwarven fire the summer before and intended to defend against it as best they could, but he doubted if any master masons were working on this citadel. The city-builders of the Gel da'Thae would have understood another lesson, that stone walls required a firm footing if they were to stand. A peculiar mound like this one would destabilize anything heavy built upon it.

They could perhaps build a stone fortress here if they drove pilings for a foundation, but after they drove the pilings, then what should they do? The more Rori considered the question, the more uncertain of the answer he became. While he could recall his days as Gwerbret Aberwyn, and the long discussions of fort craft he'd held with master craftsmen, the memories were curiously dim and hard to recall, compared with his dweomer memories of old lives and old hatreds.

The hatreds in particular burned in his mind. As he floated on the currents of the wind, he counted hem: the Horsekin, certainly. Tren. Raena. Alastyr – but, he reminded himself, Alastyr and Tren were one and the same soul. The Bear clan of Eldidd that had tried to undermine his rule as Gwerbret Aberwyn – all of them, too. Most deeply of all, he hated the dark dweomermen of Bardek, who had broken his mind and will back when he'd still been a young man and an exile. Nearly a hundred years old, some of those memories, but the hatreds still smouldered in his soul. At times they flared up, so hot and bitter that they made him uneasy, threatening every shred of mercy and justice he possessed. The years that he'd passed in dragon form were divesting him of everything that had made him a good ruler, a decent lord, a human being. *Dalla was right*, he thought. *I can't – can't what? keep living like this?*

He shuddered with a vast shiver of extended wings and tried to put the rage out of his mind. His one reliable refuge from his thoughts beckoned: flight. His wings beat the air as he gained height, until the fortress looked like a smear on the earth and naught more. The cool wind soothed his hatreds and blew them among the thin streaks of clouds.

Rori made a wide turn to the north and spotted on the distant horizon the pluming dust that meant the approach of a large number of – something. He dropped down and flew in that direction until he soared over a long column of marching spearmen, followed by a rag-tag collection of Horsekin on foot. Behind them trundled loaded wagons, drawn by horses, and oxcarts as well, piled high with lumpy, uneven cargo held down by hides and ropes. A bevy of mounted riders drove herds of horses and cattle, while behind them marched another tidy column of spearmen. Riders brought up the rear. These, some hundreds of them, rode in a straggly column, bunching up, thinning out as they travelled slowly along. Horsekin, then, not Gel da'Thae cavalry – Rori risked swooping down lower, circling the line of march, for a better look.

Although he saw chained slaves among those who walked behind the leading contingent of uniformed spearmen, the others in the line of march seemed to be travelling freely enough. Mostly women drove the wagons. Children perched on top of bulky, ill-stowed loads or sat beside the women on the wagon boxes. The rearguard horsemen wore heavy tunics of leather, painted with designs that from his height Rori couldn't read. Painted shields hung from their saddle-peaks. A migration, all right, a full migration of Horsekin tribes. Probably they were planning on settling around the new fortress to raise food and mounts for whatever plans Alshandra's rakzanir had underway.

As Rori headed south again, he realized that he wasn't far – not far as dragons reckon distance, at any rate – from the strange village and the wooden bridge that Berwynna had described to him. Any army planning on extending itself through the Northlands would want that bridge. He decided to take a look at it and headed east again. Soon he was soaring high above the Dwrvawr. He turned downriver, spotted the village and the rickety bridge that Berwynna had described, then circled lower for a better look.

Near the village a strip of sandy beach sloped down toward water reeds and what appeared to be shallow water, shaded by a cluster of willows. In deeper water a pair of enormous otters swam back and forth. Rori dropped down a hundred yards or so and circled to confirm that indeed, two otters, roughly six feet long from whiskered snout to graceful tail, were exactly what they were. As he watched, one of them swam to the beach and clambered out. It started chasing its tail like a dog. In a swirl of bluish light the otter disappeared, and a human being, dripping wet and naked, stood in its stead. The other creature paddled toward the bank, flipped onto its back, and, still in otter form, bobbed in the current.

The naked man pointed at the sky and called out – from his height Rori could just hear his voice without understanding the words. Another man stepped out of the trees, a short, stocky fellow clad in a loin wrap. He tipped his head back to look up. They'd spotted the dragon, perhaps, though Rori could assume that he looked like some sort of large bird at his distance. He banked one wing and headed back southwest. Those otters – or shapechangers – or whatever they were! The sooner Dallandra heard about them the better.

The strange white bird circled overhead, then flew off, heading southwest. Kov watched it, a silver glint against blue sky, until it passed out of sight. He ached with envy of its wings. Behind him his swimming teacher clambered out of the water. The were-otter turned, spun fast around, and in a swirl of blue light, changed back into man-form.

'Was that a crane, do you think?' Kov asked him.

'It were not,' Jemjek said. 'I know not what it may be, but the seeing of it did trouble my heart somehow.'

'Just so,' Grallag said. 'We best be going back inside.'

Since there was no arguing with his strong-armed Dwrgi guards, Kov agreed.

Kov was never allowed to go outside alone. During the day, he could walk wherever he wanted inside, though at night, Grallag slept in front of the entrance to his chamber. For days now he'd been exploring the complex around the treasure chamber and studying the walls and the ceilings in the hopes of finding a ventilation shaft, or even a chink or crack, that an enterprising dwarf could use for an escape route.

Unfortunately, the Dwrgwn were almost as clever as the Mountain Folk when it came to burrowing. They had laid a pale mud-plaster over the smooth walls, which they'd reinforced with a course or two of stone where the walls joined the hard-packed earthen floors. Stout beams supported the ceilings and kept the doorways of the various rooms trim and true. All the ventilation shafts had bronze grids embedded into the ceilings over their openings. Kov admired their skill even as he cursed it.

Although he'd never found an open shaft that might function as a way out, he had seen a surprising number of empty rooms and dusty hallways. A few pieces of derelict furniture, a dropped tunic, covered in years' worth of dust, a blackened stone beneath a vent that spoke of a cooking fire – here and there he saw signs that these rooms had once been lived in. Had there been a plague or some sort of war? He wondered, but when he asked the various individuals he knew, they all shook their heads and professed to know nothing about those signs of life.

Kov had also been asking those Dwrgwn he'd got to know, whether his guards or the other diners at the communal meals up in the village, about the heaps of treasure lying so carelessly in the big chamber.

'What I wonder,' Kov would say, 'is why gathering is so important to you all. It's not like you do anything with the treasure. You don't trade it or wear it or keep it in your private chambers.'

'We do much love to visit it,' ran the usual reply. 'When we be ill, we do go there and then feel well. When we be sad, it does make us happy.'

On the day that Kov saw the unusual white bird, he went up to the communal meal early. After he'd fetched his usual plate of boiled fish and spelt porridge, he sat down next to a young woman, Annark, whom he found attractive despite her thick half-moons of eyebrows, mostly because she seemed more intelligent than most Dwrgwn. When he asked her why she loved the treasures, she gave him the answer he needed.

'It be the mist lights,' she said. 'See you not them? The beautiful blue haze from the gold, and the lights dancing from the jewels.'

Kov was too surprised to respond.

'The blue does rise from the gold,' Annark continued, 'like mist on the river. We do waft it to ourselves, we do roll in it, and our own blue shadow, it does draw strength. See you it not, Kov Gemmaster?'

'I can't, alas, but I can feel it.' Suddenly he saw an important truth. 'All of my people can, and that's why we love gold so much. We breathe in the mist and soak it up through our hands.'

She smiled and returned to stripping the bones out of a fish with her long delicate fingers. *Our own blue shadow?* Kov thought. *I wonder what that may mean!* His heart ached to consult with Dallandra about these mysterious folk and the even more mysterious mist rising from their stolen treasures.

Kov had recruited his swimming teacher for his work in the chamber of gold, one Jemjek, a young Dwrgi man who had the muscles necessary for all the lifting and hauling ahead. An unexpected recruit had volunteered as well, a boy named Clakutt, just ten years old, with bright dark eyes and slender hands that could reach into the narrowest clay jars and bring out their contents. When together, they all spoke an odd mix of the Mountain dialect of Deverrian and the few bits of Dwrgi that Kov knew. No one had offered to teach him their language in any systematic way, leaving him to pick up what he could here and there.

On the morrow, when they returned from a swimming lesson, Kov took his helpers into the chamber of gold. As it always did, the sight of all the treasure, heaped as casually as dirty laundry but glittering in the light from their candles, turned his breathing heavy with excitement. He could feel sweat beading his back and the palms of his hands. Although he could regain control of himself with one deep breath, he wondered if some day, perhaps soon, he would stop wanting to gain control. It was the mist from the gold, he supposed, muddling his thinking. He wiped his hands dry on his brigga and turned his mind to the work ahead.

'Now, our first task for today,' Kov told his two helpers, 'is clearing one of the corners.'

'Why?' Jemjek said.

'So we've got a place to put things?' Clakutt broke in.

'Exactly. Carry everything in that corner there,' Kov said, pointing, 'into this clear space where I'm standing. Then we'll start putting all the coins in the empty corner while we move things from the next one. Jewellery pieces without gems in that one, I think. And so on around the room.'

'But we leave any coins we find in that corner?' Clakutt said.

'Just so. Good lad!'

Kov picked up a gold coin, glanced at it, and nearly swore aloud. Since the death masks were of obvious Horsekin work, he'd been expecting Horsekin coins, but the coin bore Westfolk runes on one side and a roughly stamped Westfolk face on the other. He found another coin – again, Westfolk work. He picked up a golden brooch of a horse with wind-tossed mane and realized he'd seen one like it back home in Lin Serr, displayed as a treasure from the Seven Cities. The more he examined the objects in the chamber, the more he realized that the vast majority of them had to be ancient workmanship, so delicately done of such pure metal that they made the beautiful crafts of the nomadic Westfolk look like the efforts of children.

Twice looted! he thought to himself. The Horsekin in those barrows must have been buried with the spoils of war before the plague wiped out their fellows back in the Seven Cities. Vaguely he remembered that the Horsekin stripped the flesh of their dead fellows from their bones, ate it, and then buried the bones in tidy bundles, bound with leather thongs to keep the ghosts from walking. Or so he'd been told – the story had the spiteful feel of mere legend about an enemy.

'Jemjek?' Kov said. 'Have you ever gone gathering?'

'Once,' Jemjek said.

'Did you see any bones in the mound?'

'I did. All stacked up like winter firewood, they were.'

'Were they tied in bundles?'

'They were not, not no more, but there were stains on them from thongs or ropes. Rotted clean away, if you do ask me.'

Spiteful or not, part of the tale held true. *What a lovely lot they are, the savages!* Kov thought.

'Kov?' Clakutt came trotting over. 'What be this?'

The boy handed Kov something that looked like a length of rope braided from fine strands of gold. As thick as his thumb, the 'rope' had been twisted into a semi-circle about eight inches in diameter, with a solid gold sphere for a finial at each end, leaving an opening about two inches across.

'I'm not sure,' Kov began, then paused, running through his memory. 'Wait! I heard somewhat once. I think it's called a torc. A very long time ago the men of Deverry wore things like this around their necks.'

'They did?' Clakutt's eyes narrowed in thought. 'They must have had truly skinny necks to get them on.'

Kov laughed. 'When the jeweller finished braiding this rope, it would have been a straight piece. He must have bent it very carefully around the person's neck. Then they'd never take it off.'

'But how did it get off, then, to get here?'

'Well, I suppose you could bend it one more time without breaking it.' Another detail rose in his memory. 'Or an enemy might have cut the person's head off and pulled the torc free.'

Clakutt wrinkled his nose and growled in disgust, a throaty sound so animal that it startled Kov. He'd started thinking of the Dwrgwn as just a different variety of Mountain Folk, he realized. *A mistake,* he told himself. *Don't fall into it again.*

At the end of the workday the crone, Marmeg, who'd once been Kov's captor, came to fetch Clakutt, her grandson. For the boy's sake Kov decided to be polite to her, even though he'd not forgotten the kicks and insults she'd given him during the night he'd spent tied up and helpless in her hut. When Clakutt launched into an excited recital of the day's work, she laid one bony hand on the boy's shoulder and scowled at Kov.

'You know,' Kov said, 'your grandson's unusually intelligent. I'm truly pleased he wants to help.'

At that her look softened, though not so far as a smile. Over the next few days, every time Kov saw Marmeg, he made a point of praising Clakutt and his mental abilities, which quite truthfully stood far above most of the Dwrgwn he'd met. Finally, when she came to fetch him, Marmeg brought Kov a flat basket laden with oat cakes. He'd won her over, but even as he thanked her profusely, he wondered why he'd cared to change her low opinion of him. *I may be stuck here for the rest of my life*, he thought. *No use in keeping old enemies or making new ones.*

His success came in handy the very next day. In the middle of the afternoon Kov discovered, carelessly wrapped in a twist of half-rotted linen, a pair of fire opals and a palm-sized brooch of obviously dwarven workmanship, displaying a silver hound, couchant, wound round with bands of interlace. He could place it as a style popular for trade goods some forty or fifty years past.

'This is a very different-looking thing,' Kov said.

'It be so,' Clakutt said. 'It be not gold.'

'Very good! This was made by my people, the Mountain Folk.'

Clakutt's lips formed an O, and he nodded in wonder.

When Marmeg came to fetch the boy, Kov asked her on a whim if she knew anything about this unusual piece, mostly because she was the oldest Dwrgi he'd ever seen. To his surprise, she remembered it.

'It did come from a trader from the far west,' she told him. 'Varc or Ferrik or some such name he had.'

'Verrarc,' Kov broke in. 'I met him once, when I was but a child. He came from Cerr Cawnen.'

'They all do, what traders we do see. But truly, Verrarc was his name. My man did take this bit of work and them there moonstones in trade for an old book he had, a nasty looking thing, all beaten and torn, but Verrarc, he were fair taken with it.'

'A book?' Kov said. 'Do you remember what it was?'

'Just some book.' She shrugged in profound indifference. 'None of us kenned what its marks did mean.'

'I see. Does anyone else have any old books around here?'

'They may well. There used to be a fair number of books around here, before the –' She stopped speaking and looked away, her toothless mouth working.

'Um, before the what?' Kov said.

'I forget what I did mean to say.' She gave an elaborate shrug. 'I be old. I do forget things.'

'Before the Great Scour, you mean?' Clakutt said.

Jemjek, who'd been idly listening, caught his breath with a gasp.

Marmeg turned to Clakutt and hissed, then let go with an angry flood of Dwrgic words. Clakutt crossed his slender arms over his chest and glared up at her.

'But he be one of us now,' the boy said in Mountain dialect. 'The dweomer did make him so.'

Marmeg hesitated in mid-tirade, then spoke normally, still in Dwrgic. Clakutt nodded and looked at Kov.

'She says, you might be asking Lady what we do mean by the Scour. If Lady does tell you, then all be right and proper.'

'Very well, then.' Kov gave Marmeg a conciliatory smile. 'I'll do that. I want to talk with her about another matter, as well. She told me that we'd have a scribe for the work, and I've not seen hide nor hair of one.'

'Scribe?' Clakutt quirked an eyebrow. 'What be that?'

'A person who can read and write.'

'I know not of such a thing among us.'

Then why, Kov thought to himself, *did she promise me one? Just like the wretched woman, her and her grand ideas!*

Kov hadn't seen Lady in some days. That evening, at the communal meal up in the village, he asked various people where she might be, but no one seemed to know or care. 'Down some tunnel or other,' was the usual answer to his questions. 'She does come and go as she wills.' He reminded himself that life among the Dwrgwn was – *well, fluid*, he thought. *Their minds run this way and that like water, too.* He wasn't truly surprised that few – if any – of them could read.

Yet apparently Lady heard that he wanted to see her. The very next morning she came to the treasure chamber and stood just inside the door to watch them work. That particular day she went barefoot. Her long grey hair fell to the shoulders of her simple cloth tunic, fastened with brass pins, such as all her folk normally wore.

Humble clothes or not, she was still Lady and *the* lady of this peculiar underground city. Kov, Clakutt, and Jemjek all bowed to her. She acknowledged them with a wave of her hand, but said nothing. Finally, after some little while of watching, she motioned to Kov to follow, then stepped into the tunnel just beyond the door.

'I did hear that you wished to ask me a question,' she said.

'I did, my lady.' Kov decided that it would be safer not to mention Clakutt by name. 'I don't mean to give offence in any way, mind, but I overheard one of the children mentioning this, and I'm curious. What's the Great Scour?'

'A painful but necessary thing that did happen some years ago now.' She looked down, and with one long toe began to make a little groove in the dirt floor. 'There were some among us who had to be turned out.'

'Turned out?'

'Sent away. Some among us were folk like Deverry men or the First Ones. For years my own folk had lived with them and next to them in their villages. Some of us had made households with them and even born children, impure children with both kinds of blood in their veins. Some could become Dwrgwn in the water, but most couldn't.' She frowned, hesitating. 'It was very peculiar. Most times some children in a litter could change in the water like normal folk, but not the rest. So we banished all those who couldn't change.' She looked up, her dark eyes cold under their fan-shaped grey brows. 'I lived among Deverry people. I know what evils they can work when they've a mind to. Once I became Lady here, I couldn't allow my folk to have such as they living in our tunnels.'

'So you made them leave. What if they refused to go?'

'Then we killed them. They didn't give us any choice.'

For a moment Kov could find no words. She was looking at him calmly, openly, her eyes wide, her mouth unsmiling but far from grimly set.

'I see,' he said at last. 'I'm surprised you'll let me live here.'

'Oh, you're a man of the Mountain Folk.' She smiled and patted him on the arm. 'Earth and water blend well enough.' The smile disappeared. 'It was those others we couldn't allow.'

'I see.' He repeated it for want of anything better to say. 'Um, well, my thanks for telling me.'

She smiled again, turned, and trotted off down the tunnel. Kov went back to the chamber of gold, where Clakutt was waiting for him.

'She told you,' the boy said. 'I heard her.'

'She did,' Kov said. 'What do you think of all that?'

Clakutt shrugged, looked away, his face twisted in sorrow. 'My gran, she did tell me it had to happen.' His voice wavered badly. He shrugged again and picked up a pottery jar from the floor. 'Be it that I look inside this?'

'Good idea.' Kov had no desire to force him to say his opinion of the Scour aloud. No doubt it would be dangerous to do so, if Lady heard of it. 'Lay it down on its side first and bang on the bottom. That'll scare out any spiders or suchlike.'

As they continued working, Kov found himself thinking over Lady's remark about Earth and Water blending. Apparently the Dwrgwn knew about the abstract elements and their relationships. As a boy Kov had been taught such things under the rubric of natural philosophy, an important study among the Mountain Folk. Fire and Water were the pure forms of the elements. Fire begat Air, and Water, Earth, with Earth and Air being mixed or impure forms. So did that mean that the Westfolk and the Mountain Folk were impure peoples somehow? They both lived far longer than Horsekin or, he suspected, the Dwrgwn, who were in theory at least pure peoples. Could it be that purity was more a drawback than a boon? Deverry folk, the Children of Aethyr, lived lives as short as those of the Horsekin. Was Aethyr a pure or impure element? In all his studies Kov had rarely heard Aethyr mentioned, much less its properties.

Kov wished he could consult with his old teacher, Loremaster Gwarn, an impossibility at the moment, of course. With a sigh he turned his mind back to the work at hand. When he began to tally up the coins in the hoard, he remembered that he'd never asked Lady about the promised scribe. *That's what you get for letting your mind run off after vagaries*, he told himself. *Better to stick to practical matters, just like Father always said*. He did find a bit of wood, and Jemjek had a little knife. They counted up the coins in twelves and notched the wood for each lot.

Because of the scribe, at dinner that night Kov mentioned how much he wanted to talk with Lady again. When, the next day, one of her servants summoned him, he assumed she'd got his round-about message.

'She's in the council chamber,' the young Dwrgi lass said. 'I'll take you there.'

Kov followed her through winding tunnels that led down, deep into the complex to a big chamber, where the only light came from baskets of bluish-green fungi much like those of Lin Serr. Dressed in plain pale linen, the Lady sat on a high-backed chair placed between two large light-baskets. Beside her stood a tall Dwrgi with grey hair at his temples and a bristly moustache that covered his entire upper lip. Around his waist a leather belt with a gold buckle clasped his brown tunic. Kov noticed a long knife in a sheath dangling from the belt, which he took to be a mark of some sort of position or rank. He was proved right when the Lady introduced him.

'Our spearleader,' Lady said. 'His name is Leejak.'

Kov made Leejak a bow, which the spearleader returned.

'We've had troubling news from our gatherers in the north,' Lady continued. 'The Horsekin are building a fortress.'

'Troubling indeed!' Kov said. 'How close is it?'

Lady shot Leejak a sideways glance. 'Far away, I think,' she said.

'Huh, not far enough!' Leejak said. 'Maybe ten days by tunnel. We do have tunnels that lead that way, you see. This fortress, it be south of the barrows where we do gather.'

'That's not much of a distance for men who ride horses above ground.' Kov decided that giving Leejak an honourific would sweeten their relationship. 'Does my lord agree with me?'

'So our spearleader told me,' Lady broke in. 'Now, they do build it in a place we call the Long Barrow, or on top of it, I should say.'

'It's a grave site, then?'

'I think so. We've not gone gathering there, because it lies on the wrong side of the river. Besides, a mound that large – it could well be haunted or suchlike.'

'They be putting stone walls on top of the barrow,' Leejak said. 'We did call you here because your people do ken much about building with stone. How long think you it takes them for the finishing of the fortress?'

'Without seeing it I can't possibly tell.' Kov made his voice as casual as he could, but thoughts of escape were filling his mind. 'I'd have to go there and take a look at it, but normally it takes a long time to build solid stone walls and the like, if that's what they're doing.'

'I'm told,' Lady said, 'that they have many slaves working upon it.'

'Then it could rise much faster, of course. If you and the spearleader want to prevent them from settling there, we'd need to act quickly. If I could just be taken there for a look –'

Leejak cleared his throat with an angry growl and crossed his arms over his chest. Lady glanced at the spearleader with a nervous toss of her head. 'He did suggest that,' she said, 'but I fear you'll leave us suddenly if we let –'

'There be a need on us to take some action,' Leejak interrupted her. 'It does trouble my heart, thinking of Horsekin so close.'

'It troubles mine, too,' Kov said. 'You're sure they're building in stone?'

'For now the buildings are only made of wood,' Lady said, 'or so they told me, the messengers, that is, but they say that the Horsekin are hauling in stones from the west. They come on river barges, and then big cows pull them to the fort.'

Oxen, Kov supposed. 'If they finish building stone walls around this fort,' he said aloud, 'there'll be precious little we can do about it, even if it turns out that we should do somewhat.'

She winced, then glanced at her hands, where rings glinted in the bluish light. 'As long as our people are safe in their tunnels,' she said, 'I'd rather merely post watchers up at Long Barrow.'

'Not enough.' Leejak glared at her. 'What say you, Kov?'

'I agree,' Kov said. 'Last summer I was part of an army fighting Horsekin. They're ruthless, and we'd best not take chances.'

Lady moaned under her breath and tipped her head to rest it against the back of her chair. 'I'm so afraid.' Her voice trembled on the edge of tears. 'There are so few of us. The risk – if we lost more –' She let her voice trail away.

'There be risk in doing naught,' Leejak said.

But what can we do? Kov thought. Frail Dwrgic spears would never pierce Horsekin armour. Leejak cleared his throat as if he were about to speak again, but Lady sat up straight and with a wave of one hand forestalled him.

'We'll do naught till I know more.' Her voice turned firm. 'There are so few of us. We can't risk losing anyone in some rash way.'

Leejak shrugged, rolled his eyes, but said nothing. Kov bowed to them both and left the chamber with the spearleader close behind. Out in the corridor the servant lass waited with a pair of light baskets. Leejak took one from her.

'Go sleep,' he said. 'I walk him back.'

With a bob of her head and a smile, the Dwrgi lass hurried off down the corridor. Kov and Leejak strolled after her, silent until the blue glow from her basket turned a corner and disappeared.

'When Lady be like this,' Leejak said in a soft voice, 'there be no use to argue.'

'I got that impression, my lord.'

The spearleader snorted and shrugged. 'Later mayhap we do talk more, make her think more.'

'Do you think she'll change her mind?'

'I do. She does this other times, before.' He paused, struggling for words. 'She does think good after while. There be a need on her for time to think good, I do mean. Soon you do see this or so I do hope.'

'So I do hope as well, my lord. I can assure you of that.'

They walked up a long ramp and turned into a corridor that Kov knew well. Through an open doorway a bluish glow greeted them.

'Here's the treasure chamber,' Kov said. 'I have a light basket in there, my lord. I'll just fetch it and see myself home.'

Leejak nodded and strode off. Kov went inside, picked up the basket of fungi, then lingered for a moment, letting the gold and its invisible mist soothe his troubled mind. Horsekin nearby – *Ah ye gods,* he thought. *Will we never escape these savages?* As he turned to leave, the light in his basket flickered on a heap of coins and cast the blocky shadow of some object protruding from the heap. Kov pulled it free and found a crumbling codex, missing its front cover, deeply torn along some of its folds. In the dim light he couldn't properly read it, but he could decipher the Deverrian writing enough to realize that the codex contained dweomerlore.

'I wish I could show you to Dallandra,' he said to it. 'I'll take you along on the off-chance I can escape from this ghastly place.'

With the codex tucked under his arm, he went back to his chamber, where Grallag had taken up his usual station. Kov greeted him and went inside, shutting the door behind him, to catch what sleep he could with worry for unpleasant company.

The more he mulled over what he was learning about this peculiar folk, the more Kov wished he could consult with Dallandra. She had the strange lore to understand these things better – he was certain of that. *She has dweomer, too*, he thought, *which would come in handy about now.* With the thought he realized that despite what he'd always been taught, he now believed in the existence of sorcerers.

Out on the grasslands, as Laz's mood grew blacker and blacker, and his temper worse and worse, more and more of his men deserted him. Even though Drav had started drilling his rag-tag collection of deserters with military discipline, the Westfolk camp offered enough comfort and amusement to make Drav seem tolerable, or so Krask informed Laz as he left. Finally, after some days of these slow desertions, Laz ended up with a band comprised of himself and one man.

After the last deserter had walked off in a huff, early one evening, Faharn built a small fire of twigs and dried horse dung. By its smoky light they ate dry flatbread and cheese washed down with spring water. The evening breeze brought them the drift of distant music and the occasional burst of laughter from the elven camp. Now and then Laz caught a faint scent of roasting meat. At those moments Faharn would stop fanging his leathery dinner and look wistfully across to the painted tents, glowing from the fires scattered among them.

'Why don't you just go join the others?' Laz said. 'Ye gods, just because I can't bear seeing Sidro doesn't mean you have to fester out here with me.'

'Don't be stupid!' Faharn snapped. 'I'm not going to desert you.'

'Why not? I must be the worst company in the Northlands at the moment.'

Faharn shifted his weight on the log, shrugged, and scowled at the stale flatbread in his hand. 'I was hoping,' he said at last, 'that we could take up my lessons again.'

Laz felt so sour that he was tempted to tell him the truth, that Faharn's small talent for dweomer had blossomed as much as it ever would, that in fact there was no use in his studying any more dweomer than he already knew. But Faharn was watching him so hopefully, so patiently, like a dog who knows that sooner or later his master will share the meat he's engaged in eating, that Laz threw him a morsel of reassuring lie.

'There is that,' Laz said. 'Which reminds me. I promised Salamander that I'd keep scrying for that wretched dragon book. I might as well give it another try. Now, I want you to watch me as I concentrate. To scry you have to absorb yourself in the thing you're scrying for. You can't let your eyes or your attention wander.'

Faharn nodded, his eyes bright with anticipation. Laz laid his own food aside and concentrated on the tiny flames of their campfire while he sent his mind out to the dragon book. He was expecting the usual murky dark, but this time an image built up of Wynni's saddlebags, lying upon a table, with the book open on top of them. He was so startled by success that he nearly lost the vision, but with a long exhalation of breath he steadied himself.

Men clustered around the table. All he could see were dim shadowy shapes, their blood-red auras flickering this way and that as they leaned forward to peer at the book. One of them laid a hand upon it, and with that gesture his image clarified. Laz could discern his face, strangely jowly and bloated for someone as young as this man seemed to be. His thick, glossy hair, half-hidden by the flickers of his sullen greenish-grey aura, was as pale as Evan the gerthddyn's. Laz caught a quick sight of one ear when the fellow turned his head to speak to someone. The ear, abnormally long, curled like a lily bud. *A Westfolk man?* Laz thought. The fellow turned his head the other way, and Laz saw a brand bitten into his cheek: a crude image of a Boar. *A slave! And an elven slave at that! Dalla will want to hear of this.*

Laz tried to widen the vision, but much of the view around the fellow with the book stayed murky and dark. He got an impression rather than a clear view of stone walls, roughly circular, of battered tables and rush torches, a straw-strewn floor gleaming beneath the auras of a pack of large dogs. When he returned to the book, the vision began to break up. The slave was putting it back into its wrappings, and as it slid into its leather prison, Laz lost sight of everything. He looked at Faharn, who was watching him wide-eyed.

'Horseshit and large heaps of it!' Laz said. 'I saw it, but I have no idea where it is. Here, I need to talk with Dallandra. Come with me, and they'll feed you, most likely.'

Sure enough, when Laz and Faharn came to the edge of the Westfolk encampment, the men at the nearest fire hailed them like long-lost friends. They shoved a drinking horn of mead into Laz's hand and a wooden skewer threaded with chunks of cooked lamb into Faharn's. One of their number trotted off to fetch the Wise One.

'This bodes well,' Laz said in the Gel da'Thae tongue. 'I don't see Sidro anywhere nearby.'

Faharn, his mouth full of roast lamb, nodded and went on eating. Though the Westfolk offered Laz meat as well, he turned it down. He had no desire to smear himself with grease in front of Dallandra. He did allow himself a few small sips of the mead, though he had to clutch the horn in both hands to compensate for his dearth of fingers.

The Wise One herself appeared just as Faharn was starting on his second skewer of meat. As she approached, the men around the fire fell silent; two of them knelt; the rest took a step back. To Laz's hungry eyes she looked particularly beautiful that night, her skin glowing in the flickering light of the tiny fire, her ash-blonde hair, freed of its usual braid, swirling around her shoulders in long silver waves.

'It's good to see you here, Laz,' Dallandra said. 'You're welcome to come to my fire.'

'Not where I might see Sidro,' Laz said. 'But I have news. I finally got a glimpse of that wretched book.'

Dallandra gasped with a toss of her head. 'Let's go discuss this privately.'

'Splendid idea.' He glanced at Faharn, who had acquired a pottery stoup of mead whilst Laz had been looking elsewhere. 'Don't get drunk. I'm going to consult with the Wise One.'

Laz handed the drinking horn to one of the Westfolk, then followed Dallandra out into the rustling grass. Since unlike her he couldn't see well in the dark, they didn't go far, just a hundred yards or so away to put some silence between them and the noisy camp. The soft night wind lifted her long waves of hair, shining as silver as the river of stars that flowed across the sky.

'Could you see where the book was?' Dallandra said.

'Inside what appeared to be a Lijik dun,' Laz said. 'Not much of one, either. Alas, I have no idea where it might stand, but I did see some of the men who were looking at it. Typical Lijik warriors, except for one.'

When he described the slave and his brand, Dallandra agreed with him that the fellow had to have elven blood in his veins.

'He seemed well-fed for a slave,' Laz said. 'Plump, in fact. That surprised me.'

'He may well have been castrated. The Horsekin do that to lads they capture young.'

Laz winced. 'That was outlawed in the cities years ago.'

'Well, I didn't think these men were Gel da'Thae.' Dallandra smiled briefly. 'Have you heard the tale about the temple of Bel that the Horsekin raiders destroyed?'

'Evan mentioned it, truly. Didn't they find a bit of writing there?'

'Of sorts. A single letter carved into wood next to a Boar clan mark. Prince Dar wondered if someone had left it there to tell others where he was, or where the raiders came from, or suchlike.'

'Are you wondering if this slave was the one who did? From the way he was paging through the book, I'd say he can read.'

'It's likely.' Dallandra turned her head and looked out over the grass, sighing like the sea under the night wind. 'Let me talk with Cal about this. He was there at the temple, and I wasn't.'

Cal again, always Cal. *This is ridiculous*, Laz told himself. *You have no hope of getting this woman to warm to you, none!* Sidro, on the other hand – if he could only find the right key, he was sure he could unlock her heart once again. He always had before. If he could find some way to impress her, something grand, some feat of dweomer that Pir could never match – maybe then she'd see him in the old light.

Laz returned to the fire to find Faharn stuffing himself with still more roast lamb and a half-round of thin fresh bread. Dallandra must have noticed Faharn's appetite as well. Not long after dawn on the morrow, Neb arrived at Laz's camp, his arms full of sacks of food.

'Gifts from the Wise One,' Neb said.

Faharn hurried over to take some of the sacks. Together the two apprentices went off to stow them in the tent. Laz felt an odd unease at the sight of Neb – odd because he'd liked the lad when first they'd met back in Trev Hael. Neb had been miserable and thus weak, back then, in deep mourning for his hearthkin, carried off by the pestilence that had ravaged the town. Now something about him warned of danger, but the danger lay under his surface, like an ebb tide waiting for the unwary swimmer under a pleasant-seeming sea.

Odd and twice odd, Laz thought. *Wait – what was that name Dalla mentioned? Nevyn. Neb and Nevyn.* Hearing the names sound together in his mind turned him suddenly cold with dweomer-warning. Why? He had no idea. He decided that he'd best see if he could find out.

Neb came out of the tent with Faharn right behind, carrying a basket of bread and dried apples. Laz took a chunk of bread between his thumb and forefinger and waved it in Neb's direction. 'Did Dallandra mention that I'd scried out the dragon book?' Laz said.

'She did.' Neb sat down on one side of the cold fire-pit. 'She also told me that spirits of Aethyr were guarding it.'

'That's what I saw, truly.' Laz sat down on the other side.

They considered each other, with Neb as wary as Laz. Faharn joined them, but since he knew only a few words of Deverrian, he ate steadily and said little.

'Do you have any idea where it might be?' Laz said at last.

'I don't,' Neb said. 'But Salamander thinks it must be at the Boar dun. Evan, I mean.'

'I've heard all his names now, my thanks. I am amazed by the number of names the Westfolk have, and Evan Ebañy Salamander tran-whoever-his-father-was is no different.' Laz paused, thinking. Salamander himself had acquired that same odd aura of dangerous interest. *Did I know these men in my former life?* Laz wondered.

'Things are different among the Gel da'Thae?' Neb said.

'They are. A name's something to be guarded most carefully. You only get two if you're freeborn, one if you're a slave.'

'Is that why you made up another one? You were calling yourself Tirn when first we met.'

Laz winced. He'd quite forgotten that.

'My apologies,' Laz said. 'I felt I was on dangerous ground, there among your people.'

'Ah.' Neb considered this for a few moments. 'Understandable, I suppose.' His tone of voice made it clear that he neither understood nor approved. 'But about the book, Dalla told me what you saw. You know, that would fit a rough dun built by men who are basically rene-gades, and the slave had the Boar on his cheek, too.'

'So you're guessing it's at the Boar dun, then?'

'I am, which is a pity, because if it's there, it's doomed.'

'What? Why?'

'Prince Voran's planning on razing the dun, that's why.'

'Razing it? You mean burning it? And who's this Voran person?'

'The Justiciar of the Northern Border. The Boars have been raiding into Cerrgonney, so it's his duty to gather an army and burn the place in retribution. Eventually he'll slight the dun, too, that is, he'll knock down the walls.'

'It's not likely that a mere book's going to survive all that.'

'True spoken. That's my point.' Neb paused for a wry smile. 'Dalla really needs that book, too.'

'Just so.' It occurred to Laz that retrieving the book would be a splendid way to improve Dallandra's opinion of him. 'Let me think on this. There must be some way to get it out safely.'

'Good luck.' Neb rose and smiled, a thin twitch of his mouth. 'I'd best be getting back.'

'By all means,' Laz said. 'My thanks for the information about the Boar dun.'

Seeing Neb leave made Laz sigh in genuine relief. *Danger and twice danger!* Laz thought. *And I don't have one cursed idea why I feel that way.* Unless, of course, he'd known Neb back in that previous life when he'd betrayed his own kind to run after a false goddess and serve the enemies of his true people. If that were true, no wonder he felt shamed by Neb's scorn. If. Everything, these days, seemed to depend upon some hidden truth, each bit of knowledge like one strand of a spider's web, fragile with dew, hanging from the thinnest of twigs.

All that day Laz let his mind ramble around the problem of the dragon book. He was beginning to want another reason beside Sidro to leave the Ancients' camp behind. Going after the book would provide a splendid pride-saving excuse. Like Neb, however, Faharn doubted that anyone could rescue that mysterious volume.

'I did have one idea,' Laz told him. 'Which also reminds me. You really have to work on learning the Lijik language. We're going to be stuck among these people for the rest of our lives, most likely.'

'You're right about that.' Faharn's voice wavered, but when he spoke again, it sounded as strong as always. 'So what was this idea?'

'Suppose we pretended to be sutlers. There's always a crowd of them following the armies along. Whilst there, showing our wares, we could casually ask if they had any interesting trinkets or other items they'd want to sell. I'd wager that someone would bring out that book. Prince Dar would give us the coin to buy it, no doubt.'

'And what if someone's there from Taenbalapan?' Faharn said. 'And recognizes you?'

'Under all these scars? And with my dirty cheap clothes, and maimed hands, and the like, do I look like the First Son of a powerful mach-fala? I've not been in Taenbalapan in years and years. Neither of us have. I doubt if anyone would recognize us.'

'What about Bren?'

'Who?'

'That Deverry rider Pir captured. The one prowling around our horses last summer.'

'Oh. Him. What about him?'

Faharn sighed in sharp exasperation. 'He may well still be at the Boar dun, that's what.'

'I don't understand. What's he doing there?'

'Ye gods, Laz! Haven't you ever wondered what became of him?'

'No, frankly. What did?'

'Your woman insisted we give him weapons and supplies and sent him off to the Boars to warn them about the army heading for Zakh Gral.'

'Her name is Sidro, and she's not mine any longer.' Laz heard the snarl in his own voice and noticed Faharn flinch. 'My apologies. It's still a raw wound, I'm afraid, anything to do with Sidro. But let us return to this Bren.' He forced out a smile. 'Why would he remember me?'

'Because you were going to kill him. There's nothing like cold terror to fix a face in a man's memory.'

'Oh.' Laz considered this. 'You have a very good point. Very well, if Bren's still with the Boars, then indeed, he could spoil our ruse entirely too easily.'

'I'm glad you can see that.'

'I may be reckless, but I'm not stupid. Wait! The book has guardian spirits attached to it. I wonder if I can make some sort of contact with them.'

'Now there's an idea! You told me they could move the thing.'

'Not far, probably. But there's that slave, and I think we can assume he'd be willing to entertain thoughts of escaping his masters. If the spirits could influence him –'

'Assuming we can get close enough to this wretched dun to do anything before the warlords find us there. Our heads could end up nailed to the wall.'

'You're as full of comfort as a fire on a hot night, aren't you?' Laz gave him a sour look. 'But I've got to admit that you're right about the risk.'

'Why is this cursed book so important to you, anyway?'

'A number of reasons. First off, having the silver wyrm back in human form would be a great relief. He'll probably still be an ill-tempered berserker, but he'll be a great deal smaller.'

Faharn laughed in agreement.

'And then there's the matter of Sidro,' Laz went on. 'Wouldn't she be impressed if I rescued the thing? It would make me appear far more powerful than Pir.'

Faharn's smile disappeared, buried under a look that revealed no feeling at all.

'I know you've never liked her,' Laz said.

'Why would you want her back?' Faharn blurted this out. 'She betrayed you with a man you counted as a friend.'

Laz wanted to make a jest, could think of none, and finally sighed with a melodramatic shrug. 'Once again you've made a good point,' Laz said. 'But I don't care to discuss it.'

'I didn't mean to offend you. I just wondered why you wanted the book, is all.'

'Oh, don't cringe!'

Faharn winced. Laz considered saying more, then got up instead. Faharn stayed where he was, looking up at him as if waiting for the conversation to continue. With another shrug Laz turned and strode off. Faharn never followed.

Laz walked to the edge of the beaten-down area of grass that marked where his full camp had once stood. He shoved his hands into his brigga pockets and lingered, looking west at the elven tents. The various comings and goings had left a path of flattened grass between the two camps. He could walk across it, he realized, and ask to speak with Sidro. There, surrounded by safety, in the midst of her new people, she might well agree to a talk.

But what could he say, with Gel da'Thae speakers like Exalted Mother Grallezar nearby to eavesdrop? Or do – he could hardly attempt to ensorcel her again with Dallandra and other dweomerworkers so close to hand. *Not that I would*, he reminded himself. *Of course not. I want her back of her own free will.* He was lying to himself, he realized, just as he'd so often lied to Sidro about so many things. He found himself remembering young Neb's scorn over the false name he'd used in Trev Hael.

'I don't know who I am anymore,' he said aloud. 'That's what Haen Marn did to me.'

Or perhaps he'd never really known who he was. Perhaps that was the heart of the matter. Perhaps.

Laz stood there for a long while that morning and listened to his thoughts bending this way and that, like the tall grass when a gusty wind blows, announcing a coming storm. Only much later did it occur to him to wonder how he knew that Rhodry Maelwaedd had been a berserker.

* * *

The man with the beast on his cheek had saved the book from the ugly men who stank of blood. The spirits had puzzled out that much, because at times the beast-marked man would take the book out of the leather bag. He would turn the pages, run his fingers over the letters, and weep before putting it back into the bag and hiding it under a straw mattress. Because he'd saved the book, the spirits decided to reward him. With all the loose matter in the hayloft, where he slept, they could easily create blank pages in case he wished to write upon them. They made the entire astral construct larger, too, until it would no longer fit into the bag, simply because they hated the presence of leather. The man with the beast on his cheek seemed both pleased and frightened by the changes.

His fear puzzled them. They'd done nothing extraordinary, but they reversed the changes because he was afraid. If only Evandar would come – they told each other this often – he would explain everything. Evandar or one of their lords, someone who could speak to the beast-marked man – they could only wait.

'It's time we left Twenty Streams,' Cal said. 'The sheep have torn up too much of the grass as it is.'

'So I see,' Dallandra said. 'But what about Rori?'

Cal grinned at her. 'I think he'll be able to spot which way we've gone. He flies high.'

'Of course! Silly of me.'

They had left the camp to give Dari some fresher air and to enjoy the peaceful quiet. Cal was carrying the child in a leather sling against his chest. At moments she turned her head and looked around her before resting against her father and drowsing.

'Which way does Dar want to go?' Dallandra said.

'West, I suppose. We generally do go west this time of year.'

'You sound doubtful.'

Cal shrugged. He looked doubtful as well, his eyes narrow as he stared off toward the west, where a summer haze lingered in the lowering sun.

'It's because of the Horsekin,' he said at last. 'I keep wondering if they're planning border raids out our way. They'd be more likely to attack in the west, away from our allies.'

'I can keep a watch by scrying.'

'How? You've probably never seen any of these raiders, if there are any, that is.'

'It won't matter. I'll scry for the terrain. If there's a raiding party coming our way, the grass itself will show me where they are. I won't be able to see them clearly, no, or pick out details, but I'll be able to get a general impression of riders and horses. It'll be vague, but –'

'It'll be enough,' Cal finished the sentence for her and grinned. 'Good. Do that. Oh, and thank you.'

That night, when Dallandra scried, she sent her mind out in a circle around the camp. While west may have been the likely direction for a raid, the Horsekin might well be leaving the northern tablelands by some eastern route. The forested tablelands themselves, where she'd never been, would remain closed to her scrying, a vast reddish mass of vegetable auras and dead rocks. The grasslands that abutted the maze of cliffs and ravines, however, appeared clearly to her questing mind.

Off to the east, perhaps some twenty miles distant, she saw a brilliant twist of red and gold, the mark of a campfire, and the muddled auras of a few horses and mules, standing heads-down and resting in the tall grass. At the fire she could pick out four men, that is, she saw three unmistakably human auras and one actual person seen clear and whole. She recognized him as one of Prince Voran's men who'd been wounded in the fighting of the summer before. While she couldn't remember much about him, she'd paid him enough attention to fix him in the deeper levels of her mind. He and his three companions were eating, laughing now and then as they talked among themselves.

'Messengers, they must be,' Dalla told Cal. 'And they must be looking for Dar.'

'There's nothing else out here for them to look for,' Cal said with a grin. 'No doubt they can follow our trail through the grass, but I'll have Dar turn the alar back toward the east. We can meet up with them first and head west later.'

Sure enough, as the royal alar made its slow way back in the direction of Deverry, four riders appeared on the horizon. Once they rode closer, Dallandra could pick out Voran's wyvern blazon on the shields slung from their saddle peaks. With a shout and a wave, the four spurred their horses to a trot. Calonderiel and four of his archers rode out to greet them and escort them and their messages back to Daralanteriel.

Later that afternoon, while the royal alar was making camp, Dallandra discussed the letters with Grallezar in their private language.

'Voran's in a town in western Cerrgonney,' Dallandra said. 'He's met up with Envoy Garin and his retinue, and Garin had a real prize to give him – messages from the Horsekin to the Boars. A dwarven patrol intercepted them.'

'Excellent!' Grallezar paused for a smile full of fangs. 'What did they say?'

'There he has a difficulty. No one in his retinue or Garin's can read the Horsekin tongue. Voran was wondering if you might be willing to return with the messengers and join the conference.'

'Huh! Act as his scribe, you mean. I think not.'

'I rather thought you wouldn't. He can be awfully high-handed.'

They shared a grim smile.

'What about one of your men?' Dallandra went on.

'None of my own men ken reading. Our fighting men are much like the Lijik warriors, willing to leave such things to their servants and the womenfolk.' Grallezar considered, sucking a fang. 'Drav, now. Drav was an officer, and he no doubt can puzzle out the words, whether or not you'd call it reading. But he doesn't know the Lijik tongue, so he'd not be of much use to the prince. Besides, I want him here. The others obey him, and those men of Laz's who came over – they need a man like Drav above them.'

'Laz! What about Laz?

'Now that's a splendid idea. I don't much like him, but the gods all know he's a learned man and a scholar.'

'Can we trust him?'

'I can trust him the better the farther away he is. Sidro will doubt-less be glad to see his horse's rump as he rides away, too.'

'No doubt. Do you think Voran will accept him?'

'If I write a letter to recommend him, he will. I won't even have to lie. Laz can read and write, and he's a man who understands fine words and courtly manners. Whether he chooses to use the manners is another matter entirely, but that's not our concern.'

'He's a fistful of arrows short of a full quiver, if you ask me. I hope he doesn't do anything rash in the prince's presence.'

Grallezar paused to look across the open grassland in the direction of Laz's camp. 'I met his mother once or twice. She was enough to drive any son mad, always pushing, always scheming for her mach-fala no matter whose hopes she trampled on. Her First Daughter, she was such another, too, and she wielded her position over Laz like a whip, or so our Sidro tells me.'

'That would drive any man a little mad. Well, I'll go talk with him.'

'I wonder what he'll say?'

'No, probably.' Dalla paused for a smile. 'I'll have to think up a few good arguments.'

Dallandra doubted Laz's willingness to leave on such an errand simply because he'd be riding off with men he didn't know to join up with a prince of the country he'd always considered his enemies. Much to her surprise, however, and before she brought out her first argument, Laz agreed.

'That gladdens my heart,' she said. 'You look positively eager to go.'

'Joining Voran will get me away from Sidro,' Laz glanced away, his eyes dark. 'That'll be better all round.'

'I'm afraid that's true.'

'And then there's the dragon book,' Laz went on. 'Neb tells me that Voran's going to invest the Boar dun. If I go with him, I may be able to coax those spirits of Aethyr into bringing it to me.'

'I'd not thought of that. My thanks, Laz. That's an admirable thing to do.'

'I shall endeavour to bring the book back to you and lay it at your feet.' Laz smiled at her in a way that struck her as entirely too warm.

'That won't be necessary, truly.' Dallandra felt like taking a step back, but she feared insulting a man who was, after all, offering to do her an enormous favour. 'The best thing would be to take it back to Haen Marn. Well, assuming you can even get the wretched thing.'

'Why Haen Marn?'

'It strikes me as the ideal place to perform whatever this ritual is, if I can work the dweomer at all.'

'And without, I hope, it killing you.'

'I hope that, too.' Dallandra paused for a wry smile. 'If somewhat does go wrong, then maybe you and Marnmara can set it right again, with the power of the island behind you.'

'Very well, then. No doubt the Mountain Folk will help me get there, since I'll be doing a bit of work for them.'

'They pay their debts, truly.' She patted him on the arm, a gesture such as she'd use to soothe a nervous horse. 'And may luck ride with you.'

With a little wave, Dallandra turned and hurried away. *The prince will be glad to hear this,* she thought. *And I'll be glad to have Laz gone.*

Laz turned away rather than watch Dallandra leave. Had there been anything near him to kick but grass, he would have sent it flying. *Ye gods! Here I am, riding all over the wretched Northlands to do the bidding of another woman who doesn't want me!* Sidro, on the other hand – he calmed himself with a couple of deep breaths. If he returned the dragon book to Dallandra, wouldn't Sidro find that impressive? Perhaps, assuming she'd be at Haen Marn to see his triumph, which was not, he told himself, very likely.

But a sudden thought soothed his mood. If he got the book, why should he just hand it over? He could bargain with it, use it as a lever to pry Sidro out of the elven camp. He could picture himself triumphant, knew exactly what he'd say: Send Sidro over here, and I'll give *her* the book.

In a private talk with Sidro, somewhere away from all the others, he could use every weapon he possessed in the battle to get her back. If, of course, he could get the book in the first place. And if she happened to go to Haen Marn with Dallandra for the working. With a long sigh for the injustice of everything, he returned to his tent to tell Faharn that they'd be leaving on the morrow.

'Assuming you want to leave with me, that is,' Laz said. 'You can stay with the Westfolk if you want. There's no use in both of us riding off on what most likely will turn out to be a fool's errand. Besides, it could turn dangerous. Wars often do.'

'Oh, I'll stick with you,' Faharn said. 'The Westfolk – all that noise and all those children and dogs running around – I don't know why, but they put me on edge.'

'Very well, then, but you've been warned.' Laz was only making a jest, but his words made a ripple of cold run down his back. An omen? He doubted it, since they'd be joining a large army and as mere translators would stay behind the lines during any sort of fighting. Faharn merely smiled, profoundly unalarmed.

They would travel back with the messengers, four solid Deverry men all wearing tabards embroidered with Prince Voran's wyvern. Rhidderc, their leader, a dark-haired fellow with a scar running across one cheek, looked Laz over with a cold eye.

'A scribe, are you?' he said.

'I am,' Laz said, 'and a bit more than that, considering I can read and write in three languages.'

Rhidderc made a snorting noise that might have meant anything. He jerked a thumb in Faharn's direction. 'Who's this?'

'My apprentice.'

'And just why are you two willing to help your enemies? He's a full-blood Horsekin by the look of him.'

'He's Gel da'Thae, not Horsekin. The Alshandra people are my enemies, too.' Laz held out his maimed hands. 'Look what they did to me, and all because I refused to worship their false goddess.'

Rhidderc's suspicion disappeared. He whistled under his breath. 'Must not have been a pleasant afternoon's work.'

'Most unpleasant.' Laz arranged a thin, cold smile. 'And healing them was almost worse. The herbwoman had to keep cracking open the burns so the fingers wouldn't fuse completely. She could only save a couple as it was.'

'You have my sympathy.' Rhidderc winced sharply. 'Hurts to think about, like. Well and good then, lad. My apologies for not trusting you.'

'It's most understandable. Don't let it trouble your heart. By the by, where exactly are we going? Is the prince still in Cerrgonney?'

'He was when we left, but we're to meet him elsewhere. There's an attainted dun that he's handing over to the Mountain Folk. It's north of Cengarn. Know where that is?'

'I do. Huh. The dun must be near Lin Serr, then.'

'A fair bit south of it, if you mean the Mountain Folk's town, but in that general direction. Now, get yourself ready to ride. We need to get back on the road.'

They were on the verge of leaving when Neb brought Rhidderc messages in silver tubes from Prince Daralanteriel and Exalted Mother Grallezar. A Westfolk archer followed, leading a pack horse, laden with supplies for the journey, including a set of inks and pabrus in case Laz needed to act the scribe as well as translator. Faharn took the horse from the archer and led it away. Neb waited till he'd got out of earshot before he spoke.

'The inks and such are from Salamander,' Neb said.

'Then thank him most heartily for me, will you?' Laz said.

'I will. And I owe you some thanks as well, for taking me and my brother to my uncle's. It's only been a couple of summers, but so much has happened, and I fear me I simply forgot to thank you.'

'Most welcome, I'm sure. Will you forgive me for lying to you? It's not just the name. I never was a priest of Bel, as I'm sure you've realized by now.'

'I have.' Neb paused for a brief smile. 'And truly, I do understand why you'd not want to admit to being Gel da'Thae and all that. But why a priest?'

'Sheer chance. I met an actual priest of Bel upon the road, and for a while we travelled together. Alas, he grew very ill and died just before we reached your city. So I took his tunic and appurtenances and – what's so wrong?'

Neb's face had turned dead-white. 'Ill with what?' His voice came out as a rasp.

'Oh ye gods!' Laz suddenly understood. 'With some sort of ghastly flux of the bowels, in truth, that drained him, and a fever came with it. I was sure he'd eaten spoiled food. He never ate what I did, because ordinary food wasn't pure enough for him. Whilst I feared for my life at first, I never fell ill myself, so I assumed it couldn't be an actual sickness.'

'I see.' Neb's colour began to return to normal. 'Well, I have to assume the same. He must have eaten somewhat that had turned or suchlike. Where did you bury him?'

'I didn't. I took his body to the temple of Bel just outside your town, the one on that little hill on the other side of the river. When he was dying, he begged me to do that, so he could have the proper prayers said over him.'

'No doubt. The priests hold their prayers in high esteem.'

'They buried him among those trees on the hills.'

'And then you came to town for the market fair?'

'I did. The temple sent a delegation, like, to bless things.'

'So they buried him on the hill.' Neb's voice trailed away. 'I wonder . . .'

'What?'

'Well, when it rained, the run-off from that hill flowed into the river upstream from the town. That river's where a lot of us got our water.' He paused, chewing his lower lip in thought. 'But you never felt ill yourself?'

'Only queasy at the poor fellow's symptoms. You might ask Dallandra about all this.' Laz felt a trace of dweomer-cold run down his back. 'Somewhat tells me it might be important.'

'I'll do that. My thanks.'

Neb strode off, leaving Laz profoundly uneasy. At the time, he'd been convinced that Tirn the priest's special food, kept too long in his saddlebags, had been the cause of his illness. But what if it hadn't been? Could the young priest's corpse have been the source of the corrupted humours that had ravaged Trev Hael? *May the gods forgive me!* Laz thought. *I should have buried him by the road and been done with him!* Yet he himself hadn't fallen ill. *And ye gods, I even wore his clothes!* He could comfort himself with that thought, that if anyone should have been a victim of spreading corruption, it would have been him.

'Ready to ride, scribe?' Rhidderc put a welcome end to his thoughts.

'I am. Let's get on our way.'

As they rode out, following the track the messengers had left through the high grass, Laz glanced back for one last look at the Westfolk camp. Somewhere among those tents were Sidro and Pir. He wondered if he'd ever see her again, and the wondering wrung his heart.

Branna stood at the edge of the camp and watched Elessario feeding the changelings. Although at some forty years old Elessi still had the mind of a child, she was in most respects, an ordinary child, who loved her mother, made friends, listened carefully when someone spoke to her, and made much loved pets out of the alar's dogs – unlike the changelings. As soon as they were old enough to run, speak a few words, and feed themselves, they wanted nothing more than to live apart and never be touched by anyone again.

Yet had they left the alar, they would have starved, died from accidents in the wilderness, or even been eaten by the wild animals that terrified them far more than they terrified ordinary children. The older ones, some eight souls in all, trailed along with the alar in a small crowd of their own kind, surrounded always by an absolute horde of Wildfolk. Only Elessi could speak to them, and she was the only person they would answer. 'Princess', they called her, those of them who had chosen to learn to speak.

Twice a day Elessi gathered food from everyone in the camp and took it out into the grass. The changelings would come running and gather around her to grab handfuls from the various baskets she carried. As they sat in the grass they looked like ordinary elven children, palehaired with beautiful faces if always a bit dirty, and huge cat-slit eyes, but they wore odd scraps of clothing, most of it torn and stained. Their parents had given them all decent clothing only to see them rip it, twist it, rub grass and mud or even blood upon it in oddly misshapen decorations. Branna had never seen any of them smile.

That morning Elessi had invited Branna to come with her. 'They should know you,' Elessi told her. 'If I am sick, will you feed them?'

'I will,' Branna said. 'Will they take the food from me?'

'If I say so. So they have to know you.'

While they ate, the children kept glancing Branna's way. The four girls looked frightened, three of the boys looked angry, but the fourth boy stared out into space as if she didn't exist. As they walked back to camp with the empty baskets, Elessi commented on it.

'That was bad,' she said. 'Basbar wouldn't look at you.'

'His name is Basbar?'

'He says so.' Elessi shrugged. 'It doesn't mean anything, but names don't have to mean anything, do they?'

'They don't, no. If one of the changelings gets sick, do you think they'd let Neb help them?'

'They wouldn't, not yet.' Elessi considered this with a small frown. 'They need to know Neb, too.'

'I'll ask him if he'd like to come with you next time.'

'My thanks.' Elessi grinned at her. 'I'd like that.'

Neb was more than willing to let the changelings grow accustomed to him. As he remarked to Branna, they all had hard lives ahead of them.

'What's going to happen when they grow up?' he said. 'And have children of their own?'

'I hadn't thought of that. I wonder if the children will all be changelings, too.'

'It seems likely. I'll discuss this with Dallandra.' Neb paused, thinking. 'I should have asked Laz if the Gel da'Thae ever give birth to children like this.'

'Laz is gone?'

'Off to hunt for the dragon book.'

'Did you thank him before he left?' She laid a hand on his shoulder.

'I did.' He turned his head and kissed her fingers. 'You were right. I needed to do that.'

'That gladdens my heart to hear.'

'I knew it would. Ye gods, you nagged me enough about it!'

They shared a laugh.

Branna had entered their tent to find Neb gathering up his herbal supplies. The two gnomes, the grey and the yellow, were attempting to help him, but their aid soon devolved into throwing packets of herbs at one another. Branna banished them back to the etheric, then picked up the packets and returned them to Neb's sack of medicinals.

Since she too was studying herbcraft, though not as intensely as he, Branna joined him when he went to the tent where Dallandra had set up her improvised surgery. Most of the injured men had healed enough by then to get outside to the sunlight, but Hound still lay on his blankets. When they knelt down next to him, he woke, yawning, and turned his head to look at them.

'How's the arm?' Neb said.

'It aches,' Hound said, 'and it's hot and swollen.'

Neb swore under his breath, then began to unwrap the bandages from the wound. As soon as he got them off, Branna could smell the corrupted humours.

'It's gone septic,' Neb said. 'Well, we'll have to do somewhat about that.'

'Don't cut off my arm!' Hound tried to sit up, then fell back, shivering with fear. 'Ye gods, how can I live –'

'Hush now!' Branna laid a hand on his forehead. 'That's the last resort, and there are lots of things we can do first to treat it.'

'Indeed,' Neb said. 'Branna, will you start a fire over on the hearth-stone? I'll need hot water. I –' He abruptly stopped speaking and stared at the filthy bandage in his hand. 'Ye gods!' he whispered. 'There's some live thing on this.'

Branna looked, saw nothing but pus and old blood, then opened her sight. Sure enough, the matter on the bandage had an aura, only a faint reddish glow, but a sign of life nonetheless.

She studied the wound, a deep gash in pale flesh, sticky and green with dead matter. Even if the wound had been giving off some sort of emanation, Hound's own aura glimmered bright enough to blot it out.

Neb grabbed a clean strip of linen and began to wipe the pus away from the wound. This new bandage also gleamed with the sign of something alive. As the air touched it, however, the glow faded, though it never completely vanished.

'So!' Neb said. 'I don't know what's inhabiting you, Hound, but we're going to get rid of it.'

'Fleas.' Hound attempted to smile. 'They be that what lives on hounds.'

Neb patted him on the shoulder, then turned back to her. 'Branni, the herbwoman in our town, had us boil things that the sick had used. She thought we were balancing humours, but by all the gods, I'll wager we were killing whatever an infection is.'

'Here now!' Hound tried to sit up, but Neb pushed him back down. 'You'll not be boiling my arm, will you?'

'Of course not!' Neb said. 'I'll be putting on herbs that'll kill what-ever these things are.'

If he can find the right herbs, Branna thought. The idea that some live thing too small to be visible was feeding on wounds seemed incredible to her, too grotesque to be believed. She had to remind herself that when it came to healing, Neb's lore was far greater than her own. Aloud, she said, 'I'll fetch water, and then start that fire.'

'My thanks. If you could find a skin of mead, too? And maybe fetch a couple of the men.'

'Here!' Once again their reluctant patient tried to sit up. 'What have you in mind to do to me?'

Neb shoved him back down. 'Do you want to lose that arm, or do you want me to heal it?'

Hound moaned and lay still, a gesture Branna took as capitulation to the healer's superior knowledge. The two gnomes materialized, one on each side of Hound, not that he saw either, and shook their heads in a mimicry of sad pity.

A small pile of twigs and scraps of firewood stood ready beside the hearthstones in the middle of the tent. Branna grabbed an iron kettle and hurried out with her grey gnome skipping ahead of her in the warm sunshine. She went upstream from the camp to fill it where the water would be clean. Not far from the tents she found Mic, sitting on the bank. He had a handful of pulled grass which he was throwing, one stalk at a time, into the water.

'What are you doing?' Branna said.

Mic yelped and let the remaining grass fall onto the ground. 'My apologies,' he said. 'I was just thinking how life snatches our friends away from us, just like the water takes that grass.'

'Ah. You're thinking about Kov.'

'I am, truly, and Dougie as well. Perhaps Dougie even more, because we'd ridden together back in Alban.'

'Well, they both had a harsh wyrd.' Branna knelt and tipped the kettle into the water. 'It's very sad.'

'I'll carry that back for you when it's full. It'll do Kov's soul no good to have me sitting about like a fool or laggard.'

'More to the point, it'll do you no good.'

'True enough, true enough.' Mic sighed and stood up. 'Let's see what I can do to keep myself busy and useful. That's the dwarven way, not all this sitting about.'

Branna handed him the kettle, then found mead and a pair of burly Cerr Cawnen men to hold Hound down when Neb poured the liquor on the wound. Fortunately, the patient fainted early in the procedure, allowing Neb to clean and stitch with only minimal help. The Cerr Cawnen men had left, and Hound had settled into a more normal sleep, when Dallandra entered the tent.

'Richt told me that you'd found infection in the lad's wound.' Dalla paused to sniff the air. 'Ah, mead! That should wash out the corrupted humours.'

'More than corrupted humours were at work.' Neb turned and gave her a brilliant grin. 'I think I've solved it, Dalla. I think I know what causes these infections, and I'll just wager it's true for illnesses as well. Here, let me explain what I saw.'

Master and apprentice left the tent, talking together in low voices. Branna and Mic cleaned up the filthy bandages, then put them in the kettle of water to boil. She slopped in some mead from the leather skin for good measure. As she watched, the last traces of the reddish aura glow disappeared, leaving only the dead matter of the bandages themselves.

'If living things are crawling on those,' she said, 'I want them dead.'

'Sounds like a good idea to me,' Mic said with a shudder. 'Hard to believe, though I'd wager Neb knows more about it than I.' He sighed, glancing around him. 'I'll just be seeing what my poor niece is up to, then.'

'You'll be brooding about your cousin, more like!'

Mic left without answering. With a sigh of her own, though this one expressed exasperation, Branna considered cleaning up the mess around Hound's bed, then stormed out of the tent. Nearby she saw Neb and Dallandra surrounded by her four apprentices, all of them talking fast as they questioned Neb. Branna strode up to them and nearly shouted out her words, 'I beg your pardons!'

Everyone turned to look her. Ranadario, in fact, took a step back.

'I'm not a servant,' Branna said with a toss of her head. 'Neb my dearest, if there's some nasty thing living on those dirty bandages, hadn't *you* better clean them up when you're done with them?'

Neb flinched and looked down at the ground. 'So I had,' he said. 'My apologies. You're quite right.'

Branna strode off again, but she was thinking, *That's another reason why I married him – he's not an honour-bound warrior. He can admit it when he's wrong.*

After a hot dusty afternoon in the gold chamber, Kov was more than ready for a swimming lesson. He stripped off his clothes except for his loin wrap, laid them neatly on his bed, then hurried outside to join Jemjek.

They walked a good way upstream to the bend in the river that marked the shallows. The sun lay close to the western horizon, casting ripples of gold like coins on the river. A light breeze rustled the long grass along the bank and cleared away the last of the dust and gold-greed from Kov's mind.

'It's good to get outside,' Kov said.

'It is,' Jemjek said. 'Water be good.'

At the sandy beach, caught in the river's bend, they paused to watch the water flowing and rippling. About half-a-mile downstream the timbers of the bridge cast a tangle of shadows across the river. Yet despite the peaceful afternoon, all the birds abruptly fell silent. Over the murmur and splash of the water, Kov heard a drumming sound.

'What's that noise?' Jemjek said. 'The sky's clear. Can't be thunder.'

'It's not,' Kov snapped. 'It's hooves, horses, and here the bastards come!'

Like a black wave of flies heading for dead meat, distant riders were trotting through the tall grass. They were coming from the north and riding in such good order that he knew they had to be Gel da'Thae, not Deverry men.

'Get down!' Jemjek shrieked. 'Into the water!'

The Dwrgi slid out of his tunic, grabbed it in one hand, and dived into the river. In swirls of light and bubbles he transformed. The tunic billowed like foam beside the six-foot-long otter he'd become. Kov dashed after him and slipped over the bank into the thick stand of water reeds. He could only hope to hide since his flesh couldn't transform. In the shallows he stood with his nose just above water and peered through the reeds. What he saw turned him cold.

Horsekin, all right! Regimental cavalry such as he'd seen at Zakh Graal, a troop of them, no, a regiment formed up four abreast, hundreds of them, trotting down the riverbank, heading for the village. Dust plumed as the steel-shod hooves cut down the grass and pounded it into raw dirt. Kov heard something rustling the reeds behind him, nearly screamed, turned to see Jemjek beckoning to him with one paw.

'Swim!' His mouth's new shape turned the whispered word into one long hiss.

'Wait!' Kov hissed back.

Jemjek shook his sleek wet head no and turned around to dive back into deep water. Kov had a brief thought of taking this chance to escape. With no clothes but a loin wrap, no food, not even a knife, he squelched the thought as soon as it appeared. In the gathering twilight his hiding place worked well enough. No one even looked his way as the regiment trotted onward down the river.

The last of the cavalrymen passed by just as the sun sank below the horizon. Behind them, travelling at a more dignified walk, rode a two women on white mules and a small squad of retainers, one of whom carried a banner embroidered with Alshandra's bow and arrow above a row of letters in the Horsekin alphabet. The women wore leather tunics painted with Alshandra's blazon as well. *Priestesses!* Kov thought. So, this regiment had some important job at hand. He could assume that they'd come for the bridge. The only thing he could do was watch them take it.

Kov let the priestesses and their squad get past him, then stood. He could see some riders heading across the bridge and others swarming into the village. Moving a bare yard at a time, he began to wade downriver through the shallows. Once he came within sight of an escape tunnel, he would dive and swim into it, but at the moment he wanted his feet on earth, even though it was only slippery wet sand.

Ahead of him in the twilight a sudden red glare bloomed. A huge lick of flame leapt up toward the sky. The Horsekin had fired the village. Kov's rage flared up to match the black plume of smoke that twisted upward, spreading in the evening wind. How dare they! How dare they just ride in and destroy! And what of the village folk? Had they all got underground in time?

By then he was close enough to see horsemen milling around on the downriver side of the burning village. The light from the flames picked out the priestesses' white mules as they conferred with a pair of officers. Most of the regiment had spread out, doubtless to ensure themselves that no one would offer resistance. In the dancing glare Kov could see the dark hole in the riverbank that marked an escape tunnel some hundred yards ahead of him. The river reeds, however, were thinning out. He would have to strike out for clear water and swim. He crouched down to wait till the light dimmed. The flimsy huts of the fake village would burn fast and briefly.

Just beyond the group around the priestesses, he could see a pair of dismounted men, dragging something along the ground as they approached them. Kov's stomach wrenched as he discerned the otter shape of dead Dwrgwn, two of them, one a full-grown adult, one much smaller. Not everyone had reached safety, then. A panicked child, perhaps, and its mother – just who no longer mattered to Kov. He felt a hatred that burned in his blood like poisoned mead.

One of the priestesses leaned over her mule's neck, saw the corpses, and screamed. The sound reached Kov over the crackle of dying flames.

'Mazrakir! Mazrakir!' She flung up her hands and began to chant. The second priestess joined her. One of the horsemen unseated a spear from under his right leg and used it to skewer the child's body. With a contemptuous flip he tossed it into the river. The adult corpse dismounted soldiers dragged to the bank, then shoved it into the water.

You stinking maggots! Kov thought.

As the remnants of the huts turned to ash and glowing embers, the Horsekin rode on in a rough column. Once the last of them crossed the bridge, they fanned out to make a camp on the far side. Kov left the shelter of the reeds and paddled into deep water. He swam to the tunnel mouth, took a deep breath, and dived. In the dark water he could see only a deeper darkness straight ahead of him. Choking on panic he swam straight for it, found the entrance waiting, and plunged in. His knees hit mud. When he risked raising his head, he found air. He gulped it in, realized it smelled of wet Dwrgi fur, and risked a cautious 'hola?'

'It be Kov!' Jemjek's voice answered him. 'Never did I be so glad to see a man!'

Jemjek caught Kov's reaching hand and pulled him forward to the drier mud of the tunnel floor. Beyond them Dwrgi voices chattered softly.

'They killed two of us,' Kov said. 'Who?'

'Marmeg and her little Clakutt. He did grab a spear and try to fight them, and she did run to grab him and get him to the tunnels.' Jemjek's voice caught in a sob.

'But the bodies, they were in Dwrgi form.'

'When we die, we do change in the great river of Death.' Jemjek sobbed again. 'They rode them down, and they did laugh, Kov, they did laugh when they did slay her and the lad.'

'Swine! Filthy dung-eating swine!' Kov felt his eyes fill with tears. 'They and their kind will pay for this. Some way or another, they will pay and pay and pay again. I swear it by the Mountain Gods!'

Jemjek threw his head back and howled in agreement. Behind them in the hot smoky tunnel Dwrgwn wept and moaned.

Kov wiped his eyes on his arm, then made his way through the crowd and went to his chamber to change out of his wet wrap. Someone had put a basket of blue glow-fungus on his bed. By its light he dressed, then took the basket and hurried to the gold chamber. Thanks to the fire directly above, the warren had turned hot, the air stifling, but when he walked through the heaps and jars of treasures, by the blue light of the fungus he could see that none had come to harm. *It's not hot enough to melt gold!* he told himself sharply. His irrational fear frightened him the more. He was becoming entirely too protective of these glittering piles of stolen goods.

'Kov?' The voice belonged to Leejak, standing in the doorway. 'I do come to fetch you. There be a council.'

'Well and good, then,' Kov said. 'How much danger are we in?'

'We be safe enough if we do stay deep in the tunnels. The Horsekin swine, they did burn the covers to our doors.'

It took Kov a moment to puzzle out what he meant. 'Those structures over the entrances?' Kov said. 'The things that looked like crates.'

'Those, truly. They not find us now. We all be quiet now. They not think to look under themselves.'

Underground, Kov supposed he meant. 'How long can we hold out here?'

'Not long. Not much food.' Leejak shrugged and spread his hands palms-up. 'But we need not to stay. We have deep roads.'

'Of course! The tunnels run a long way.'

'Very long way north. Also toward west. We travel, we fill in behind us, block tunnels. They do never find us. Dwrgwn dig good, very good.'

'So they do.' Kov suddenly smiled, but he knew that it wasn't a pleasant smile. 'I have an idea, Spearleader.'

'Tell me on way to council. There be need for us to go now.'

When they reached the chamber, they found it full. All of the Dwrgwn were crowding into the council chamber to consult with the Lady. They moved in silence, unspeaking, cautious. Kov entered the chamber by the door near her chair to find the room glowing with dim light from fungi baskets. Beside her chair, candles burned in small gold sconces. When he started to close the door, Lady stopped him.

'Leave that be for the air,' she said, 'or the flames will devour it all and leave us fainting.'

That night she wore a black dress, set with beads of onyx and jet, glittering in long sparks of light as if she too burned. She gestured to Kov to kneel beside her chair to her left. Leejak sat down by her right. Once they were settled, she stood. Tears ran down her face, but she wiped them away with an impatient shake of her head. For some while she spoke in the Dwrgic tongue. Kov could pick out words here and there and the occasional phrase. As far as he could tell, she was speaking of mourning their dead and of moving farther up the river or perhaps to some other river – too many unknown words baffled him. When she finished, Leejak rose and spoke as well, but only briefly.

A few at a time, the Dwrgwn got up and left the chamber, again in silence, moving carefully through the throng and out into the hall, more quietly even than the Mountain Folk could move. At last the council chamber emptied. Lady rose and blew out the candles, leaving the room awash in pale blue light. When Kov got up to join the spearleader, Lady turned to face them.

'Kov and Leejak, I beg you to forgive me. You were right, and I would not listen. Now all we can do is hide in our burrows like terrified water rats.'

'Not all,' Leejak said. 'But for now, enough.' He glanced at Kov. 'The people do collect their things. We do move everything north, then plan.'

'What about the gold?' Kov spoke so quickly that he once again realized how much he was coming to value the treasure. 'We can't just leave it.'

'We won't.' Lady's voice ached with tears, but she managed a trembling smile. 'Each of us will carry a bit of it. Many hands make light work. Kov, you go to the chamber of gold, and make sure no one has more than they can take safely.'

All that night the Dwrgwn came to the treasure chamber in twos and threes, each carrying some sort of vessel or sack. Kov stuffed each thing full of whatever gold or gems first came to hand, but he insisted on wrapping the delicate Horsekin pottery in clothing or bedding. By dawn the marvellous hoard-room stretched out empty. With a light basket in his hand, he walked around, checking each corner for dropped treasure, then went to his own chamber to pack up the few things he owned.

All that day the Dwrgwn lay silent in their tunnels. Frightened though he was, Kov slept through most of it. When he woke, Leejak came to him with the news that the Horsekin were making so much noise setting up a camp of their own that they'd never notice any coming from under their feet.

'So now we go north,' Leejak said. 'Fast we do go. There be more Dwrgwn up at joining of east-pointing river.'

'Let's hope they're still there,' Kov said. 'What if the Horsekin found them?'

'We know not that till we do get there. So we do start now.'

As Kov followed him out, he was remembering Mic and Berwynna, whom doubtless he'd never see again. Even if somehow they thought he might be alive, they could never come to look for him now, not with Horsekin camped around the bridge. And even if somehow they could, by dweomer or suchlike, he'd no longer be there to find.

Berwynna always knew when Uncle Mic was brooding about the loss of his cousin. Mic would slip into their tent and lie on his blankets, as limp as a wet rag while he stared at the ceiling. Only one person could cheer him, Salamander, who had a wealth of tricks and tales designed to lighten any heart's load, even one as heavy and grim as that belonging to a man of the Mountain Folk.

When, therefore, Berwynna looked into their tent and found Mic half-asleep in the middle of the day, she ducked out again and went to round up her other uncle. Salamander was sitting in front of his own tent and juggling three small leather balls. When he saw Berwynna, he made them disappear one at a time.

'Good morrow, fair niece.' He stood up and bowed to her. 'Come to visit your aged uncle?'

'Always does it gladden my heart to visit you.' Wynni paused to smile at him. 'But today there be a need on me to ask you for help.'

'What's this? Mic brooding again?'

'Just that.'

Salamander flicked a hand over the front of his shirt, produced one of the leather balls, then made it disappear again. 'Let's hope his troubles vanish as easily. Lead on!'

As they walked through the camp, Berwynna saw the usual children and dogs, and a few women were tending to various errands, but everything lay wrapped in a strange though welcome silence.

'Be somewhat wrong?' she said. 'All this quiet!'

'Several parties went off hunting,' Salamander said. 'Venison is a nice change from mutton, and we can't eat every sheep we own, anyway.'

In her tent Mic still lay stretched out on his blankets. When they came in, he sighed for a greeting. They sat down next to him, but he kept his gaze on the ceiling.

'Oh come now!' Salamander said. 'If you sit up you'll feel better. This wallowing in guilt isn't doing you a bit of good.'

'Wallowing, is it?' With an angry snarl Mic sat up to confront him, then laughed, a little ruefully, when he realized what he'd done. 'Well, mayhap you're right.'

'I'm always right. Now, what tale shall I tell you today?'

Mic considered, rubbing his chin. Berwynna, however, already had her request ready.

'Uncle Salamander, know you the story of the taking of Tanbalapalim?'

'I know *a* story about it. Now, whether it's the true story, I cannot know. It happened a long time ago, and the tale passed through the mouths of many a bard before I learned it.'

'You know more than I do, and that's what matters to me.' Mic leaned forward. 'Is it true that refugees from Lin Rej sought shelter there, but they were turned away?'

'In a way. The garrison in the city had run out of provisions, and they were half-starved. The Wise One among them knew that a massive Horsekin attack was on its way. The garrison could have retreated, but they decided to die there defending the city in order to delay the Horsekin and give the next fortress to the south – Garangvah – a chance to reprovision. Some of the Mountain axemen volunteered to stay and die with them, but the prince of the city – Salamondar, his name was – insisted that the rest of the refugees head east to save their women and children.' Salamander smiled with a twist of his mouth. 'Or to try to save them, anyway.'

'Salamondar?' Berwynna said. 'Be that whom you be named for? That real name of yours, I do mean, Salamonderiel.'

'It is – me and dozens of other men.'

'Ah, I see. He were a hero.'

'So he must have been,' Mic said. 'And so your Da's tale makes sense now. Salamander, they did survive. They ended up down in Deverry somewhere, or so Rori told us. He saw a dwarven colony there when he was a young man.'

'So the sacrifice wasn't in vain?' Salamander paused to wipe sudden tears from his eyes. 'How very odd, peculiar and unanticipated, to weep over it! That all happened twelve hundred years or so ago, but ye gods, it's still good to know the outcome.'

'Ai!' Mic said. 'How I wish our Otho was still alive to hear this.'

'Oh come now!' Salamander said. 'I didn't mean to make you start mourning yet another soul.'

'I'm not.' Mic grinned with a wicked gleam in his eyes. 'I'd love to rub it into the old man, how wrong he was.'

'That's better!' Salamander paused briefly to mug deep thought. 'I suppose.'

Berwynna laughed, then cut it off when Salamander raised one hand for silence. Someone outside seemed to be beating a drum, a huge drum, growing louder and louder. She could hear women outside running back and forth and calling out to one another.

'That be Da, I'll wager!' Berwynna got to her feet. 'I do hope the horses, they all be tethered and the like.'

'So do I,' Salamander said. 'Let's go see.'

Berwynna ducked out of the tent and looked up. Sure enough, the silver dragon was swooping over the camp, then turning south, away from the herds. She waited till she saw him land, then ran to greet him with Mic trotting after.

*   *   *

Dallandra had heard and seen the dragon as well. After she rounded up her medicinals, including her clay jar of leeches, she hurried out to join Rori. Berwynna had already reached him; she sat between the dragon's front legs and leaned back against his massive chest, while Mic stood nearby, watching with a fond smile. Dallandra marvelled at Wynni's courage. Many a lass would have preferred to honour her dragon father from a safe distance. Still, as a precaution, Dalla asked her to move while she treated the gash in Rori's side.

'He gets irritable when the willow water stings,' Dallandra remarked. 'And he can't seem to stop his tail from lashing.'

'It has a life of its own, truly,' Rori said.

Berwynna and Mic sat down in the grass some yards away while Dallandra readied her leeches. The edges of the wound showed only a thin stripe of morbid flesh, but she wanted to make sure the contagion spread no further. With wooden tongs she fished out the thinnest leech and set it feeding.

'And how was the scouting expedition?' Mic asked. 'What are the Horsekin up to?'

'Too many evil things,' Rori said. 'I'll give Cal and the prince a full report when they come back. For one thing, though, the bastards are building their fortress upon some sort of long barrow.'

'That can't be stable,' Dalla said. 'Good.'

'Indeed, but I saw somewhat stranger still. Wynni here told me about a bridge over the Dwrvawr, so I decided to take a look at it. I found it near that strange little village, just as you told me, Wynni. Fire and fumes! It's the most flimsy-looking bridge I ever saw, but that's not the strangest thing yet. In the water there were two huge animals with brown fur, like enormous otters.'

'Gartak,' Mic broke in. 'The folk there called the monsters gartak.'

'Mazrak's more like it.' Rori swung his head Mic's way. 'When one of them climbed onto dry land, he changed into a man.'

'What?' Dallandra nearly dropped her tongs in surprise. 'Just like that?'

'Snap of my fingers, if I had any.' The dragon paused to rumble with laughter. 'He spun in a circle, danced if you can call it that, on his short legs. Then this peculiar blue light flashed around the otter-thing, and a man stood there.'

His laughter had dislodged the leech. Dallandra used the tongs to pick it out of the grass.

'Did you see the other otter change?' She dropped the leech back into the water, then took out one of its fellows. When she held the fresh leech up to the wound, it grabbed hold with its smaller mouth and began to feed on the sour flesh with the larger.

'I didn't. It stayed in the water. Now, there was a third fellow on the river bank, but he was different-looking. I was far too high to see him clearly, but he looked like one of the Mountain Folk.'

Berwynna gasped, and Mic cried out. He clapped his hand over his mouth to stifle the noise.

'Think you it could be Kov?' Berwynna said to her uncle. 'My Dougie –' Her voice caught, but she continued on. 'My Dougie did wonder if Kov were truly dead, or if he were mayhap taken for a slave or such.'

Mic lowered his hand; he was smiling, his eyes full of sudden hope. 'Maybe it's so,' he said. 'Ah ye gods, maybe he's still alive.'

'I can find out easily enough,' Dallandra said. 'I remember him quite well, so I can scry for him.'

'I'd be truly grateful if you did,' Mic said.

Dallandra looked up at the sky, where a few streaks of high cloud offered a focus. When she thought of Kov, his image built up quickly, though at first she had trouble identifying him, since the only light, and that a peculiar blue, came from glowing baskets.

'He's in a dark tunnel with an absolute mob of other people,' Dallandra said. 'I can't tell if they're asleep or just resting, but they all seem to have big bundles and baskets and the like with them. Refugees from the Horsekin? It could be.' She banished the vision. 'He looks very much alive to me, Mic.'

Tears welled in Mic's eyes. He wiped them vigorously away on his sleeve. 'Then I've got to head back north,' Mic said. 'He's my bloodkin, distantly, perhaps, but bloodkin nonetheless, and it's my duty to ransom him.'

'It's too dangerous,' Rori broke in. 'There are bands of Horsekin raiders all over the countryside.'

'But –'

'Uncle Mic?' Berwynna laid her hand on Mic's arm. 'Remember you when I did wish to go haring off across the countryside to find Da's book? You did tell me then that the danger were too great. It be worse now, from what Da does tell us.'

Caught, Mic looked back and forth between his niece and the dragon, then nodded. 'Well and good, then,' Mic said. 'But how do we know that the danger won't come his way?'

'We don't,' Dallandra said. 'It's in the laps of the gods.' She frowned at the dragon's side, where the leeches were finishing up their work. 'As is this wretched wound, apparently. I think I'll have Neb take a look at it.'

Once she finished tending to Rori, Dallandra returned to camp. She found Neb, told him that she wanted him to examine the dragon's wound at some point, then went to her tent to nurse a hungry Dari.

Late that afternoon, in a flourish of silver horns the hunting party rode back to camp with venison to distribute. Prince Daralanteriel and Calonderiel turned their horses over to Pir to rub down and put out with the herd. Dallandra followed the pair as they hurried out to speak with Rori, who was lounging in the high grass on the opposite side of camp from the herd and the flocks. While Pir's dweomer was gradually accustoming the horses to the scent and sight of dragon, the sheep lacked the capacity to learn, and Pir knew nothing of ovine ways.

The two leaders joined Rori in the grass to hear his detailed report. A few at a time other members of the alar gathered around as well, squatting down in the golden sunlight of late afternoon. When Rori described the old cities of the far west, everyone sighed. A few of the men brushed tears from their eyes.

'So much for the splendour of the past,' was Dar's only comment. Rori's report on the new Horsekin fortress, however, brought more of a response from the prince.

'Very well,' Dar said. 'If they're putting so much work into that fortress, they won't be raiding our borders, I suspect.'

'Not this summer, maybe,' Cal said. 'Once they get their safe haven built, that's when they'll be coming south.'

Among the listeners a few whispered, a few swore in a soft breath of sound, quickly squelched when Dar began to speak again.

'Eventually we'll have to deal with them, but for now, let's continue on our way west,' the prince said. 'I want Dallandra to send messages ahead of us to Cerr Cawnen. They're our allies, and we need to consult with them. The Horsekin are closer to them than they are to us.'

Everyone turned to look at the dragon, lounging in the grass nearby. Rori nodded his massive head. 'Cerr Cawnen needs to go on alert.'

When Dar got to his feet, the other members of the alar rose too and silently followed him. Dallandra felt danger like smoke in the air, choking her. Momentarily she saw smoke, spreading out like a vast fan into the air.

'Are you ill?' Rori said.

'No, just an omen.'

'Just.' The dragon rolled his oddly human eyes.

'Well, we already know how dangerous the wretched Horsekin are. I'm surprised that I'm receiving omens about it. Usually one gets them about unknown things.' She stood up, suddenly irritable. 'I'm going back to – no, wait! Here comes Neb.'

With greetings all round Neb strode up. Sylphs clustered around him in the air, and gnomes pushed their way through the thick grass at his feet. Rori flopped over on his side to allow him to examine the gash, a stubborn pink stripe on his silvery body.

Neb ran a cautious hand over the scales just above the wound. 'Does that hurt?'

'Not truly,' Rori said, 'though I can feel it. My hide's thin about there.'

Neb made a thoughtful grunting sound, then ran his hand under the wound, back and forth several times. He muttered something too low to comprehend, then stepped back a pace. From the vague look in his eyes, Dallandra could tell that he'd opened his sight. He shook his head, then turned to speak with her. His eyes appeared normal again.

'Dalla, this is most peculiar,' Neb said. 'It almost looks like he's got a splinter under his skin, a big one, but at root just like a carpenter might get in his finger.'

Dallandra gaped at him.

'It's not somewhat natural,' Neb went on. 'I can see a dark mark in the aura, a straight flat line, though it's thicker at one end. It's like the splinter is somehow sucking the life-force into itself.'

'If somewhat's draining energy from his aura,' Dallandra said, 'it's no wonder the gash won't close. I –' She hesitated, letting elusive memories rise. 'Oh by the Black Sun! The silver dagger!'

'What?' Neb and the dragon spoke together.

'Rhodry, I mean, Rori, your silver dagger! I never found it among your clothes after the transformation. Evandar was using it as a kind of focus for the dweomer that was building you a new astral body.'

'Ye gods!' The dragon lifted his enormous head to look at her. 'I can remember that, though not very clearly. It's like trying to remember a dream, but I was holding the dagger. I threw it into the air, and then –' He growled, baffled. 'That's all I can remember. I woke, and I was a dragon.'

'Indeed you were.' Dallandra laid her hand where Neb's had been and pressed, making the dragon grunt in pain. She could feel something hard under the scaly hide. 'It's about the right size for a silver dagger. Neb, I've long thought that the daggers glow when one of the People touch them because they're absorbing force from our aura.'

'That makes sense, truly,' Neb said.

'If we held one long enough, it might well kill us, or at least, leave us gravely ill. Rhodry was only half an elf, of course, and besides, a dragon has a tremendous amount of life force. Doubtless a silver dagger would only irritate a wound rather than cause worse harm.'

'Why would Evandar have let it be incorporated?' Neb said. 'I suppose it could be a physical component for the dweomer spell.'

'It could.' Dallandra felt suddenly weary. 'It could also be a simple mistake. Evandar never much cared about consequences and details, you see. He could be very – well, the truth is – he was careless.' She sighed briefly. 'And reckless. If an action matched one of his omens, if he thought he'd foreseen a thing, I mean, he'd do that thing without worrying about the outcome.'

Neb started to speak, then bit it back. Dallandra felt like screaming at him. *I know what you're thinking. He was awful and crazed and a spirit, and it was absolutely perverted of me to go off with him! That's what everyone thinks, isn't it?* Aloud, she said, 'Well, the real question is, what are we going to do about it now?'

'Have it out, I'd say,' Neb said.

'That's my thought, too, though if it is a component – well, I suppose that doesn't matter, since we're trying to reverse the working.' She caught Rori's gaze and gave him a grim stare. 'Aren't we?'

The dragon looked away. 'Eventually,' he said. 'I suppose.'

'Try supposing this,' Dallandra went on. 'If we take the dagger out, if indeed that's what it is, we stand a grand chance of getting your wound to finally heal. Is that worth the risk to you?'

With a long sigh the dragon rolled back to a sitting position, with his hind legs off to one side and his front legs extended in front of him.

'Besides,' Neb put in, 'if we don't heal the wound first, and you do decide to be transformed back, the wound will kill you.'

Rori contemplated his front paws, then finally spoke. 'If I didn't want to return to Angmar, I'd die gladly once I was back in my old skin. My Lady Death might –'

'Oh don't start that again!' Dallandra felt like slapping him on the nose, dragon or not. 'It's so daft!'

'Very well.' Rori laughed in a long low rumble. 'If there's somewhat stuck under my hide, then I want it out, whether I'm a dragon or a man, so do your worst, chirurgeons.'

'I'm hoping we can do our best,' Neb said. 'We have one problem left to solve. I don't want to be slain by a pain-crazed dragon when I'm in the midst of slicing open that abscess. Truly, Rori, I don't know if there are enough herbs in the grasslands to ease the pain for you. I do know for certain that there's no one strong enough to hold you down.'

'Ah, but there are,' Rori said. 'Arzosah and Medea between them, Medea to sit on my tail, and Arzosah to tend to the head. I'll let you bind my mouth with rope, too, to make sure I can't bite.'

'You sound positively cheerful about this,' Dallandra said.

'I've had this cursed wound itching and smarting for over forty years now. By the black hairy arse of the Lord of Hell, cursed right I'm cheerful! It'll be worth a day or two of pain, let me assure you. Can we do it now?'

Dallandra glanced at the sky, where the sun sat just above the horizon. 'Is there enough light, Neb?'

'Just, but I'd rather wait till morning. That will give me time to brew up an herbal wash to clean the wound once we've got the dagger out.'

'And it will give me time to explain the procedure to Arzosah,' Dallandra said. 'She'll need to be careful where she puts her weight.'

That night, Dallandra lay awake in her blankets. Finally she rose and left the tent before her tossing and turning woke Cal and the baby both. The warm night air soothed her as she picked her way through the sleeping camp, as did the sight of the river of stars hanging close above. At the edge of the tents she paused and looked out across the grass, much beaten down by the day's comings and goings, to the place where Rori and Arzosah were sleeping, curled into tidy bundles. Medea lay sprawled nearby. As Dallandra watched, the young dragon flopped over onto her back, legs akimbo in the air.

In the starlight Rori's skin gleamed with silver highlights, much like his dagger from the old days, which he'd always kept polished to a high sheen. Dallandra searched her memories of the dweomer that had turned Rhodry into a dragon. She was trying to pin down the moment of Evandar's mistake, if such it was, with the silver dagger. At last the memory came clear. Rhodry had tossed the dagger away, thrown it high into the air, there in Evandar's country. She had seen it spin up high and give off a flash of light before it disappeared.

At the time she'd thought it had fallen back onto the physical plane when Evandar destroyed his etheric constructions. When she hadn't found it, she'd assumed that it had somehow dissolved. Silver, especially enchanted silver, can be profoundly unstable during dweomer workings. *But it wasn't pure silver*, she reminded herself. *The daggers are made of some sort of alloy.*

She gave up trying to solve the puzzle. If Neb's chirurgery retrieved the dagger from Rori's side, she would have her answer then and not before.

Just after dawn on the morrow, a strange group of chirurgeons assembled out in the grasslands near camp: Neb with his implements, Dallandra with her supplies, and two dragons with their great strength and weight. After Dallandra bound Rori's mouth with rope, he lay down on his side. Medea pinned her stepfather's tail under her forelegs, while Arzosah arranged herself across his shoulders. Neb stepped up to the wound. He'd found a large boning knife, of the sort a hunter would use to draw and disjoint a deer, and sharpened it to a scalpel's edge.

'Very well, Rori,' Neb said. 'Brace yourself.'

When she'd known Rhodry in human form, Dallandra had always been impressed by just how indifferent to pain he could be. Apparently the dragon shared this trait. Neb felt the splinter one more time with his left hand, then slashed the hide just under the wound. Rori never moved nor made so much as a grunt or mutter, though his wings, folded tight along his back, did tremble. Blood trickled out of the slash along with a grey thick ooze that stank worse than any excrement.

'It did form a cyst,' Neb said. 'I thought so. I'm making a second cut.'

This time Rori's tail tried to lash out. Medea threw her weight forward and held it still as Neb cut vertically up from the original slash at each end, as if he were shaping a flap out of leather for a pouch. Rori allowed himself a low moan, quickly stifled. More blood spurted out of the new wounds, and green pus followed. Neb made a gagging sound deep in his throat from the stench, but his hands were steady as he used the point of the boning knife to pry something free.

In a wad of foul matter a dagger-shaped object fell to the ground. Slime oozed into the grass.

'Got it!' Neb called out. 'Dalla –'

Dallandra stepped forward with her kettle of warm herb water and ladle. Neb picked up the disgusting object with a pair of tongs and carried it out of her way. While she washed the wound clean, and it took the entire large kettleful to get all the pus out, Rori sighed several times, perhaps in relief. Medea had to lie across his tail, however, to hold it down. Once Dallandra had cleansed the cuts, she packed them with clean linen strips, soaked in an astringent, to stop the bleeding.

Neb returned with a handful of thin gold wires. 'The prince gave me an old Deverry brooch made out of woven wires,' he said. 'He got it in trade, I think, but anyway, I unwound it. Thread isn't going to hold this cut closed. Rori, my apologies, but I'm going to have to cause you more pain. I need to make holes and lace you up like a bit of leather work.'

Rori made a sound which sounded, with his bound mouth, much like 'very well then.' He rumbled briefly, as if he'd made a jest. Medea shifted her hold on his tail to secure it, and once again Arzosah leaned over his shoulders.

'I must say,' Arzosah said, 'that it gladdens my heart to have that awful stink gone.'

'Me, too,' Neb said. 'Very well, here we go.'

Once again Rori's self-control held him rigid and still. Dallandra pulled out the linen strips, then stepped back out of Neb's way. With an awl Neb made holes in his hide, inserted the gold wires, and laced the new cuts and the old shut. With the cyst opened and the irritant gone, Dallandra could hope that the wound would heal up properly at last.

'Dragons heal quickly,' Arzosah said. 'But he'd best not fly for a few days.'

Rori muttered some inarticulate curse.

'Neb,' Dallandra said, 'you can untie his mouth now. Medea, you can let the tail go. My humble thanks for your aid! Arzosah, you were both splendid.'

She rumbled, then carefully slid off her prostrate mate. Medea let go the tail, stood up and stretched, then backed away. Neb began to uncoil the rope from around Rori's mouth.

'And my thanks to you and Neb,' Arzosah said. 'To think that nasty thing's been in there all this time! It's been a trial for all of us, living with him so on edge.'

'It must have been hardest on him,' Neb said.

'Oh, of course.' Arzosah paused to lick Rori's face, as if to comfort him. 'But you know what the old proverb says, when a dragon farts, the whole mountain stinks.'

'Indeed,' Rori mumbled. 'Ye gods, that remedy stung almost as bad as the wound! Still, the worst is over, isn't it?'

'It should be.' Dallandra patted his massive jaw. 'Neb, when you finish coiling that rope, you can wash that lump off, and we'll see what's inside it.'

'I'm going to boil it,' Neb said. 'It's crawling with live things, Dalla, just like Hound's bandages were. I can see the auras as a very faint reddish glow.'

'Fascinating!' Dallandra turned to look at the lump, held in Neb's tongs. When she opened her Sight, she could see the reddish, pulsating glow. 'It's truly remarkable, seeing it for myself. Not that I didn't believe you, mind. Ah, now the aura's fading. It's curdling, actually, like souring milk.'

'There must be a lot of tiny lives in an infection,' Neb said. 'Not a few larger ones. Gods, it stinks!' But he was grinning in the sheer pleasure of having solved the puzzle.

Once Neb had finished removing all the matter crusted upon it, both living things and dead pus, Rhodry's silver dagger did indeed appear. Although the leather binding around the hilt had long since dissolved into the grey matter in the wound, the semi-magical metal itself cleaned up to its former shine. Mic came to watch as Neb polished it with an old rag. When he handed it over to the dwarven jeweller, Mic traced out the falcon device that once had belonged to Cullyn of Cerrmor, graved on the blade.

'Otho himself made this dagger,' Mic said. 'He told me the secret of the metal, you see, when we were off in Alban. He tried to tell me how to place the two dweomers upon a piece, too, but I never could work them properly.'

'Two dweomers?' Dallandra said. 'I thought there was only one.'

'One to attune the metal to the elven aura and one to bind the dagger to its true owner.' Mic began to say more, paused for a long moment, then laughed in an oddly tense and high-pitched way. 'It stuck close to poor old Rhodry, all right, didn't it?'

Neb laughed at the black jest, and Dallandra joined in, but she was laughing in relief. *Not Evandar's fault, then*, she thought. *That's one thing no one can blame him for.* She was tempted to tell Valandario, just to defend Evandar further, but she wondered why she'd bother. *Why do I get so angry?* she thought. *I suppose because Val's right.*

One thing, however, she did tell Valandario and Grallezar as well. 'The silver dagger was a component of sorts,' she told them. 'I'm thinking that removing it could be the start of his giving up the dragon form. What do you think?'

Both of them agreed. 'If somewhat be wound,' Grallezar said, 'then the unwinding does start with but a few inches of thread.'

For the next few days, Rori stayed on the ground near the alar's camp. Arzosah brought him venison, and from time to time he would waddle down to the stream to drink. By the time the flocks and herds had grazed down the fodder around the camp, he was well enough to walk after the alar when it moved further west, a trip of a mere five miles. Dallandra relied on Arzosah's opinions about his condition; she herself had no idea when a dragon might have recovered enough to fly. Finally, on the fourth day after the surgery, Arzosah announced that he might take to the air for short distances.

'Those gold wires were a very fine trick indeed,' she told Neb and Dallandra. 'If you can leave them in, I think me he can fly again.'

'Oh, I intend to leave them in,' Neb said. 'Fear not! I want those cuts well healed before I do anything more to them. Rori, can you get up? I want to make sure the wires will hold when you extend your wings.'

'Good idea,' Rori said. 'I'd best try flapping them, too. Here, let's get a good way away from the others.'

Chirurgeon and dragon ambled off together. Neb clasped his hands behind his back and bent forward slightly as he walked to keep an eye on the wound.

'This looks very promising,' Dallandra said.

'It does indeed,' Arzosah said. 'I was truly worried, you know, that the wound would eventually poison him to death. You and Neb both have my thanks for this healing.'

'You're most welcome.' Dallandra was as surprised as she was pleased by this expression of gratitude. 'You know, while we're here, there's somewhat I've been meaning to ask you. It's about your daughters. When Rori found you and brought you to Cengarn, where were they? No one even knew that you had young hatchlings. I'm sure Jill and I would have made some provision for them if we'd known.'

'I thought of telling you,' Arzosah said, 'but I was afraid to. My experience of you two-legged groundlings had not been pleasant, you know. Medea was old enough to defend herself, but Mezza was only some twenty years old, practically an infant. Men with spears and the like could have slain her.'

'I can understand your being cautious. I gather Medea could feed them both?'

'She could and did.' Arzosah's voice rang with real pride. 'She's a splendid little darling, truly. My two gems were hiding in that cave where Rhodry found me, you see, and they saw and heard what happened with that loathsome dweomer ring. The poor wee mites!'

'That really is very sad. I don't suppose it would have occurred to Rhodry to ask if you had young ones.'

'He was a male with mannish blood. Of course he didn't. But they knew I'd come back to them as soon as I could, and Rhodry was decent enough to release me at the end of the summer.' Arzosah paused, turning her head to watch Rori and Neb walking slowly together toward open ground. 'I worried about them, of course, the entire time we were apart. The next summer I made provision for them before I returned to Cengarn.'

'Provision?'

'None of your affair.' She hissed softly. 'We dragons have our secrets, and please, don't use my name to force me to say more.'

'Very well, I won't. You're right. It's none of my affair.'

A huge drum began beating – the sound of Rori flapping his wings to allow Neb to inspect the strength of the golden wires. Since neither Dallandra nor Arzosah could have heard the other, they fell silent. Dallandra had a moment's stab of guilt. She'd not thought of Loddlaen once after she'd returned to Evandar's country, while the dragon, a female of cold-hearted wyrmkind, had fretted about leaving her young.

Rori stopped drumming and folded his wings back. Neb turned and called out, 'He's doing well! The wound's holding nicely.'

'Good,' Arzosah said. 'Almost healed at last!'

While he'd been healing, Rori had apparently been laying plans. When Dallandra had a moment alone with him, he brought up the matter of Kov.

'After I get Berwynna to safety, I'll go back for Kov. I promise you that.'

'My thanks, but what do you mean, get Wynni to safety?'

'I don't want her in Cerr Cawnen. I have a bad feeling about all of this, Dalla. I'm going to take my daughter to the Red Wolf dun and ask Tieryn Cadryc to take her under his protection.'

'No doubt he will, and truly, I think you're wise. But you can't just leave her there by herself.'

'What? She'll hardly be alone in that dun.'

'But she doesn't know anyone there, doesn't know if she can trust them or if she'll like them or what. Your poor child's in mourning, Rori, for her man. She's been dragged away from her home and every-thing she's ever known, and –'

'Stop! Yes, of course,' the dragon interrupted her with a toss of his head. 'You're right, truly. My apologies, Dalla, and my thanks as well.' He fell silent, and when he spoke again, it was in Deverrian. 'That's somewhat else I've forgotten, how a woman can feel weak and timid if she's surrounded by friends she doesn't know are friends.'

'Only women feel that way?'

His laughter rumbled briefly. 'You've caught me there,' he said. 'Men, too, at times.'

'So I thought.'

'But well and good, then. I'll take Mic with her, if he'll go, and I think he will. We don't want him sneaking off to try to rescue his cousin on his own, anyway.'

'Very true, especially since Kov isn't where Mic left him. Every time I scry for him, I see him still in some sort of tunnel with all those other people.'

'Then he's safe for the nonce. Good. I've not got the time to rescue him right now.'

Travelling underground with a pack of Dwrgwn was coming close to driving Kov insane. He was accustomed to the tightly organized and rapid marches of Mountain Folk, who could cover a cheerful thirty miles a day, even when burdened with children and household goods. Under the same conditions the Dwrgwn dawdled, dragged, whined, complained, and at moments, outright stopped to sit down and announce that they simply couldn't move one more step. At the most, Kov figured, they were making twelve miles daily, and that on a good day.

The tunnels meandered, changed direction and levels, and branched off in a welter of directions. Kov could keep track of where they'd been, but since he had no idea of where they were going, he could only listen with the others while Lady and Leejak argued furiously about the route. Eventually one or the other would win, and the ragged procession would set off again, trending generally north.

Now and then they reached an air vent where a ladder leaned against a nearby wall, the sign of an observation hole. One of the Dwrgi men would climb up, stick his head out for a look around, then climb down again to tell Leejak what he'd seen – usually mere landscape. Finally, however, after a long blur of days in the tunnels, the scout hurried down and began chattering in sheer excitement.

'He did see huts,' Leejak told Kov. 'We be here, and they be not burnt.'

Most of the Dwrgwn stayed in the tunnel to watch over their goods while Kov, Leejak, Lady, and a guard of five men climbed up and out. Waiting for them was a delegation from the new village, a half-circle of Dwrgi spearmen guarding a woman dressed in shimmering gold. When Lady hurried forward to greet her, Kov guessed that she held the same position of Lady in her tribe. The two women walked a few steps away from the crowd and began to talk in low voices.

Both sets of men crossed their arms over their chests and stared at each in cold silence. One of the men from the new village wore clothing made of leather, Kov noticed. Around his neck, a bronze knife with a long blade dangled from a chain.

When Kov looked around, he realized from the position of the sun that he faced east. Straight ahead, in a bend of a river, stood a circle of meagre-looking huts some hundred yards away.

In among them he saw two of the narrow wood booths indicating entrances to the underground domain of this new group. He turned back to the west and saw straggly fields of grain stretching out to a stand of trees. *I could be anywhere in the Northlands*, he thought. Even if he managed to escape his captors, getting home to Lin Serr was going to be an adventure at best but more likely an ordeal. At worst – what if he never found it?

The two women had finished their conversation. Lady rejoined her troop of refugees, spoke briefly to Leejak, then addressed them, speaking so fast that Kov could pick out only a few words here and there. From the way that everyone smiled and nodded, he could assume that they were being welcomed. Or at least, most of the refugees were welcome – he himself seemed to be an exception, judging from the villagers' cold stares and the fingers jabbed in his direction. The fellow in the leather clothes unhooked his knife from the chain and gave Kov an unpleasantly meaningful look.

'They no trust you,' Leejak told him. 'I go talk sense to their head woman.'

He stalked off to join the woman dressed in gold scales. Lady came over to Kov and patted him on the arm.

'Fear not,' she said. 'We won't let them sacrifice you.'

'Sacrifice?' Kov could hear an unmanly squeal in his voice and coughed to clear it.

'They want to sacrifice you to the water. You're a stranger, and not one of us, and so they're frightened, is all. With Horsekin on the move, everyone's at the edge of panic.'

'That man with the knife. I take it he's the priest?'

'Not in the sense that the Deverry people speak of priests. I think you could call him a spirit walker or somewhat like that. He knows some dweomer.' She sighed and paused to watch Leejak, who was waving his arms as he spoke. 'They do agree that we have to make some sort of strike at the Horsekin. They have good spearmen here, she told me, and now we've brought more.'

'Do they know about that fortress?'

'They do, and that's what will save you. I told them that as a man of Earth and the mountains, you understand stone and how to destroy such things.'

Kov's stomach clenched. He wished he'd paid more attention during those long meetings with the sappers and miners of Lin Serr.

'The rest of us will stay here,' Lady continued. 'Some of the men will stay to guard us, not, I suppose, that they'll be able to do much against raiders like the ones who burnt our village. We'd all best keep underground as much as possible.'

'That seems wise to me, certainly.'

Finally the woman in gold flung her hands in the air, said something abrupt, and turned back to her village. Smiling, Leejak strode over.

'She tell me no sacrifice,' he said.

'Thank all the gods for that.' Kov let out his breath in a sharp sigh of relief. His aching stomach began to ease.

'I tell them you know tunnels and such. You bring down fortress for us.'

'Ye gods, I hope I can do it now!'

'You best had. Spirit man, Gebval his name, he come with us. If you no kill the fortress, they sacrifice you and me with you.' Leejak tossed back his head and laughed. 'So dig good, Mountain Man!'

Kov's stomach clenched again, so tightly that he feared he was going to vomit. He managed to suppress the urge, then pushed out a smile that, or so he hoped, brimmed with confidence.

Kov and Leejak spent the rest of that day gathering supplies and volunteers for their long hike west to the Horsekin fortress. Although the Dwrgi men would bring their spears, their real weapons would be shovels and baskets to move the earth under the fortress. Fighting above ground would get them killed, Kov figured, and little more. Still, when he surveyed his ragged pack of Dwrgwn, he found himself wishing for a nice large contingent of Westfolk archers and Deverry swordsmen, someone to guard them while they dug, under Prince Voran, say, or Lord Gerran of the Gold Falcon.

Impossible, of course. The old Mountain proverb came to him, 'Do what you can with what you have, and if you can't do anything else, then dig your way out of danger.' It was, he reflected, the best advice he was going to get, and the only.

Lord Gerran happened to be out in the ward, talking with his foster brother, Lord Mirryn, when he heard the drumming of dragon wings, heading for the Red Wolf dun.

'Messages from Prince Dar, maybe,' Gerran said.

'A good guess.' Mirryn shaded his eyes with his hand and looked off to the west. 'I think it's Rori. It's a silver one, anyway. Here! He's carrying riders.'

Yelling for pages to follow them, they hurried out of the main gates and jogged down the hill to the meadow where the dragons usually landed on their infrequent visits. The silver wyrm circled the meadow, dropping lower each time, then ungracefully flopped into the tall grass. His two riders wasted no time in sliding down from his massive back, a man of the Mountain Folk and a pretty young woman with dark hair and cornflower-blue eyes.

'Allow me to present my daughter,' Rori said in his deep growl of a voice. 'Berwynna of Haen Marn, and her maternal uncle, Mic son of Miccala, both of Lin Serr.'

Gerran and Mirryn bowed to the visitors. Berwynna, who was wearing baggy old brigga and a man's shirt, managed to drop a decent curtsey.

'I can't tell you how glad I am to be on the ground,' was Mic's only response.

Rori laughed in his deep rumble.

'Oh come now, Uncle Mic,' Berwynna said. 'It were glorious, being up so high and seeing everything all laid out below.'

Mic rolled his eyes and moaned under his breath.

'Be that as it may,' Rori said, 'I've come to beg the tieryn to take my daughter and her escort under his protection. Mirryn, do you think –'

'Of course!' Mirryn broke in. 'I shall be honoured to escort such a lovely lady back to my father's dun.'

Mirryn led the pair away. Gerran untied the various sacks of supplies and bedrolls from the dragon's broad back. He handed them over to the pages to carry and sent them back to the dun while he lingered to have a few words with the dragon.

'I've got messages from the prince,' Rori said. 'They're in the pouch around my neck. If you'll just untie that and take it up?'

'Gladly,' Gerran said. 'Is our prince well?'

'He is, for now, but truly, Gerro, I don't like what I see up in the Northlands. The Horsekin are moving south. War might not come this year, but sooner or later, it will. We've got to get more men into the Melyn River Valley.'

'So we do, but I don't know where we'll find them.'

Gerran carried the messages back up to find the great hall full. The warband, the servants, and the noble-born alike all crowded in to see the lass who was a dragon's daughter. Gerran found his greatly-pregnant wife, the only person in the dun who could read, and handed her the pouch of letters.

'Is she truly Rori's kin?' Solla said.

'So he said, and I'll not be arguing with him.' Gerran paused to sniff the vinegar-scented air. 'She smells like one of the great wyrms, truly, but that may be from riding on her Da's back.'

Lady Galla had noticed the scent as well, apparently, because she called for servants to heat bath water and swept Berwynna off to the women's hall. Mic had to make do with the stream out in the meadow. The next time that Gerran saw Berwynna, he and Solla were sitting together at the table of honour. When Galla and the lass came downstairs, Gerran noticed that she was wearing a proper dress, a pale grey colour trimmed with bits of blue Bardek silk.

'That's Galla's very best dress.' Solla sounded on the edge of laughter. 'No doubt she wants little Berwynna to make a good impression.'

'Why?' Gerran said.

Solla rolled her eyes. 'Because of Mirryn, of course.'

'Ah, I understand now. Our lady's spotted marriage prey.'

Solla giggled, then arranged a neutral smile for Galla and Berwynna when they joined her at table. Mirryn sat next to Berwynna, begged her to share his trencher at dinner, and put on what courtly manners he had, pouring her a goblet of Bardek wine and asking her various small questions while Galla beamed at them both. Berwynna, however polite, seemed mostly weary.

Late that night, after Solla had spent the evening in the women's hall, Gerran learned the cause of Berwynna's exhausted air.

'The poor child!' Solla told him. 'Her betrothed was slain in battle not a month past.'

'I'll have a word with Mirro, then,' Gerran said. 'He needs to pull back his forces and plan for a long siege.'

'Will it trouble his heart that she's been betrothed?'

'I doubt it. An alliance with a powerful dragon, and through him to our overlord? It's worth laying aside a few scruples.' He paused to grin at her. 'Assuming Mirro has any.'

Solla abruptly winced and laid both hands on her swollen stomach. 'The baby kicked me again, and twice,' she announced. 'Gerro, I'm as sure as ever I can be that this is a lad. No lass would be so mean to her poor mother.'

'I'd tell him to stop, but I doubt me if he'll listen.'

'Oh, no doubt he wouldn't. He's your child, after all.'

They shared a laugh and a kiss.

In the morning, once Solla had written out the tieryn's answers to the prince's messages, Gerran took the pouch back down to the meadow, where the dragon lay lounging in the sun.

'Good,' Rori said. 'I need to get myself back to the prince's camp.'

'No doubt he's safer with you there.' A wink of gold on the dragon's side caught Gerran's attention. 'Here, that wound's finally healing!'

'So it is, and I thank every god for it, too. Neb's the one who cured it.'

'He's a marvel with his herbs, truly. I can parry with a shield as well as I ever could, thanks to him.'

'Good. I'd wondered about that wound. You know, there's a real wisdom to be found in wounds.'

'Indeed?'

'You sound unconvinced.' The dragon rumbled with laughter. 'I've learned that, these past years. Look at me. Do you think there's a creature alive that could kill me?'

'I don't. Maybe a squad of enemies, but then, you could just fly away from them.'

'True spoken. But you know, being invulnerable's robbed me of the joy of living. When I was a human man and a warrior, every moment of peace I had glowed and warmed me like mead, because I knew that in the end, my Lady Death would take them all away from me. Now I face years upon years of tedium.'

That sounds splendid to me, Gerran thought, but aloud he said, 'Well, your daughter told my lady that the elven mages were trying to turn you back into a man.'

'If I let them.' The dragon let out a long vinegar-scented sigh. 'Ah well, Gerro, farewell! Let's hope we meet again, but who knows where my wyrd will take me?'

'No man nor dragon either knows that. I'll hope for the best for you.'

The dragon waddled away into the clear space of the meadow. He bunched his muscles, spread his wings, and leapt into the air. Gerran watched him soar, as tiny as a white bird against the bright sky, until he disappeared.

As soon as she'd seen Lady Solla's maid, Penna, Berwynna had realized that her people belonged to the strange village folk up in the Northlands. She waited until she had a chance to be alone with Uncle Mic before she asked him if he'd seen it, too.

'Most assuredly,' he said. 'Did you notice the one-armed gatekeeper? I think his name is Taurro. He's one of them, too.'

'Twice a mystery, then! I'll see what I may learn about them.'

Fortunately, Solla and Galla both knew the tale. They told Berwynna as they sat sewing in the women's hall.

'They're a brother and sister,' Galla said, 'who used to live in a village farther west. Poor little Penna and the other village women were abducted by the wretched Horsekin, but, may the Goddess be thanked, our men rescued them last summer.'

'Now, Taurro was a rider in Gwerbret Ridvar's warband.' Solla picked up the story. 'He lost his arm in the fighting, and now he's a dependent of my husband's. He'll be our gatekeeper once we've built our own dun.'

'I did wonder if they were blood kin,' Wynni said. 'They do much resemble each other.'

'Indeed they do,' Galla said. 'Now, I've been told that the children weren't born in that village. Their mother was widowed – I'm afraid I forget how – and ended up there when she married again.'

'Her first husband was a river fisherman who drowned,' Solla put in. 'Penna mentioned that to me.'

Drowned? Wynni thought. *Caught in a weir, mayhap, or a net, when he swam as an otter?* The mystery began to intrigue her.

In the morning, Penna came into her chamber to bring her wash water and to set the chamber pot outside the door for a servant of lower rank to empty. While Berwynna washed, Penna bustled around the chamber, pulling back the heavy drape at the window, smoothing out the blankets on the bed.

'My lady Galla does say that she'll find you a coverlet by nightfall,' Penna remarked. 'She be ever so generous.'

'Most certainly she be that,' Wynni said. 'Lady Solla, she be a kindly soul, too.'

'Oh, very! I know how lucky I be, to have fetched up here.'

'You come from the Northlands, baint?'

Penna turned half-away and froze, staring at the curved stone wall of the chamber.

'Oh, here,' Wynni said. 'My apologies. Never did I mean to frighten you.'

Penna turned around, and her pinched little face had gone pale. 'How be it that you know that?' she said.

'I do come from the Northlands myself, though not from your people.'

'My people?' Penna's eyes grew wide. 'What do you know of my people? I know naught, you see. We did leave when I were so small, and my mam, she would tell me naught, no matter how much I begged to know.'

'Well, they do live in villages by the river and grow crops there. I think me they also be great fisherfolk.'

'Why?'

Wynni picked her words carefully before she spoke. 'Well, I think me they do swim in the river and catch their fish on the fin, as it were. Like you the water?'

'I do not!' Penna stamped one foot. 'My mam, she did always tell me, shun you the water. 'Twill carry you away, she did say.'

'Did she warn your brother, too?'

'She didn't.' Penna frowned, considering. 'She did let Taurro swim in the river with the other lads. I did ask her once why he might swim but not me, and she just said that I be different. When I did ask her how she looked ever so frightened. I mustn't ever ask her that again, she did say, and she did give me a good slap to help me remember her saying. So I didn't.'

Berwynna hesitated, wondering if she should tell Penna the truth. The lass cocked her head to one side.

'You know why, don't you?' Penna said. 'Do tell me, please.'

'Be you sure you want the knowing? Naught will be the same for you if I do tell you.'

Penna hesitated. As Berwynna waited, she wished that she could run to Angmar or Dallandra for advice.

'I do,' Penna said at last. 'Please, do tell me what you know.'

'Far to the north of here there be a people who do look much like you and your brother. They do have your hair, your brows, and the like. I think me you were born among them, and your mam, she did flee them for some reason with the pair of you. They be otter folk, truly, shape-changers. Know you what a shape-changer be?'

'I did hear old tales and suchlike.' Penna's voice barely rose above a whisper. 'Be they true?'

'They be so. I think me that if you were to swim in running water, a change would come over you. Why else would your mam worry so?'

Penna's face blanched. Without another word she turned and ran from the chamber. Wynni followed more slowly, cursing her own bluntness. She could only hope she'd not terrified the poor lass into avoiding her ever after. That very afternoon, however, Penna sought her out.

'I be done with my work for the nonce,' Penna said. 'Please, Lady

Berwynna, would it please you to come with me to the meadow? There
be a stream there. There be a need on me to know if you did speak
true about my kin.'

'Well and good, then,' Berwynna said. 'It be a nice warm day.'

No one noticed them when they left the dun and hurried down
the hill to the meadow. Near the stream a wide circle had been beaten
down in the grass, the place where the silver wyrm had laired during
his brief stay. At the stream bank, Penna stripped off her overdress
readily enough, then paused, her eyes wide with terror.

'Only do this if you be sure you do want to,' Wynni said. 'Truly, I
never meant to trouble your heart so deeply.'

'It be not you,' Penna said. 'I be grateful that you did tell me what
you know.' She took a deep breath, then bent down to grab the hem
of her underdress and pull it up.

Wynni helped her get the dress over her head. Wearing only a loin
wrap around her skinny hips, Penna took a step off the bank and into
the stream. She gasped aloud, then flung herself into the water with
a cry of near-sexual delight. She rolled over and over, and as she
moved, a glittering blue light sprang from her body and wrapped her
round, so bright that Wynni could barely look upon it.

The light receded, then vanished. A skinny half-grown otter, just
Penna's size, wallowed in the water with little yips of joy. Wynni could
just barely understand her words. 'Good, good.'

The stream ran too shallow for diving or even proper swimming.
After a few more splashes and rolls, the Dwrgi lass clambered out
of the water and began to shake the drops from her fur. As she
shook, she danced in a circle. In a flash of blue light the otter
disappeared.

Penna stood shivering on the bank with water dripping from her
human hair and dripping down her human back. When Wynni handed
over her underdress, the lass slipped it on, patting the cloth as if to
thank it. She looked up and gave Wynni a weak smile.

'You were right,' Penna said. 'I be half an otter, and we must come
from the Dwrgi folk, Taurro and me.'

'Indeed you must. Did that hurt, changing so?'

'It did not. It were the sweetest feeling I ever did have, a melting,
like, into the water. My thanks, Lady Berwynna, my humble thanks!
May the Goddess bless you forever for the helping of me.'

'You be most welcome, truly. Mayhap someday you'll be going north
to meet your kin, someday when the Horsekin be not prowling around.'

'Mayhap. Yet I do think my mam, she were forced to flee them.

Why else did we fetch up so far from – from home?' Penna's voice broke, and she wept, covering her face with her hands.

Berwynna threw her arms around her and held her while she sobbed. *It be a hard thing*, she thought, *to learn such dweomer truths about yourself.* For the first time in her entire life, she considered the possibility that Mara, her ever so annoying sister, might have been equally distressed to learn that she was no ordinary lass, but one with an enormous wyrd laid upon her, a burden to be carried as much as an honour to be cherished. *There be a need on me to ask her about that*, she thought, *if ever I do see her again.*

Penna's tears ended at last. She pulled away and wiped her face on her overdress before putting it on. Berwynna pulled a handful of grass and gave it to her to use to blow her nose.

'My thanks,' Penna stammered. 'For the truth, too. I just be so – well, so surprised, I think I do mean.'

'No doubt!'

Penna smiled, blew her nose, and let the ill-used grass fall to the ground. She turned and looked northward.

'We'd best get ourselves back to the dun,' Berwynna said. 'I would you not take a chill or suchlike.'

'Well and good, then.'

Yet as they walked back, Berwynna noticed how often Penna looked to the north, as if she might see her peculiar kinfolk, so far away, by force of will.

Kov, meanwhile, had seen all the Dwrgwn he ever wished to see, even though travelling with a group of dedicated spearmen proved far faster and easier than travelling with an entire village of their kind. As they marched through the narrow tunnels that led west, Kov found himself missing the treasure chamber and its gold so badly that he knew he'd escaped the glittering trap just in time. *You're like a sot*, he told himself, *moaning and shivering when there's no drink to be had.* Without the gold's invisible mist to deaden his feelings, he lived with the infuriating aware-ness that he'd been enslaved. The presence of Gebval the spirit talker became a second irritation. Every now and then he caught this supposed dweomerman staring at him with grim eyes. When Kov would catch his gaze, Gebval would ostentatiously test the sharpness of his bronze blade with a calloused thumb. *You fraud!* Kov would think. *I'll wager your supposed dweomer is just as false as that silly binding spell.* Yet he refrained from voicing the insult. Since the others believed that Gebval had magic, they doubtless would react badly to any slight to their shaman.

On the journey west, Kov might have schemed out a way to escape had he not realized that he hated the Horsekin even more than he'd come to hate the Dwrgwn. He wanted little Clakutt avenged, for starters, and then vengeance for his ancestors, slain as they fled Lin Rej, for Lin Rej itself, for the Mountain Folk slain in the recent wars, the same for the dead Westfolk, and even for the Deverry losses, the soldiers killed as allies of his people. By the time he and his band of Dwrgwn reached the fortress, Kov had worked himself into a state of icy rage.

Late on an afternoon, the tunnel they were currently following led them to a wide circular chamber, some twenty feet underground by Kov's estimate. Scraps of rotting cloth, bits of rope and leather thongs, pieces of broken pottery, and fragments of wooden boards, black with age and mould, littered half the floor, though the other half looked reasonably clean.

'This place be safe,' Leejak informed Kov. 'We do rest here.'

'Are we near the fortress, then?' Kov said.

'Not far, but not right next, they tell me.' He gestured at the Dwrgwn from the northern village. 'We reach edge of barrow land. South edge, that be.'

This chamber, Kov realized, must have served the Dwrgi grave robbers as a way station, a place to rest and free their treasures from the original wrappings. He walked over to the littered scraps and idly poked through it with one booted foot. Black hairy spiders scuttled away, but he found nothing else of interest. On the far side of the chamber stood a wooden door, roughly made of axe-split planks. When Kov shoved it open, the smell of fresh air greeted him, and a shaft of sunlight that revealed another tunnel leading north.

'That doesn't look very promising,' Kov said to Leejak. 'I want to climb up to that vent and look out.'

'Good thought.'

This vent, however, lacked a ladder, and Kov was far too short to reach it. Leejak turned and whistled, then held up two fingers. Jemjek and Grallag trotted over to join them. After a few words from the spearleader, they hoisted Kov up. He stood on Jemjek's shoulders and stuck his head – very carefully – through the mouldy wooden grating.

Through a scant cover of long grass he could see westward to a stand of trees. Between the trees, water gleamed.

'There's a river ahead,' Kov told Leejak. 'And I can just see some kind of boat – ye gods, it's a barge!'

As the barge glided downriver, it winked into and out of view through the trees. Kov caught glimpses of its cargo.

'It's carrying stone blocks,' he said. 'We must be near the fortress, all right. But that river's going to cause us a cursed lot of trouble.'

Carefully he extricated his head from the grating, then let Grallag haul him down. Gebval was standing in the open doorway, glaring again, his hand on the hilt of the bronze knife. Kov restrained his urge to make a rude gesture.

That night Leejak questioned the northern Dwrgwn, extracting every bit of knowledge they had about this stretch of country, then passing it on to Kov. As Kov had suspected, the tunnel system never crossed under the river. Even a skilled crew of Mountain men would have been hard pressed to make such a crossing water-proof and thus safe. Instead, the tunnel system turned north and ran parallel to the river until it reached the rich pickings of the barrow fields. While the Dwrgwn could have transformed and swum across, Kov could not. Even more to the point, in otter form they'd never have been able to carry their digging tools, earth-moving baskets, and other such supplies.

'We go north little ways,' Leejak said. 'Find ford, cross there.'

The northern Dwrgwn immediately objected, not that they had any other plan in mind. They voiced idea after idea, all of them unworkable or even merely silly. After a long evening of squabbling, which on several occasions nearly led to blows, everyone finally agreed with Leejak's original idea, thanks to Gebval, who finally made himself useful by delivering the opinion that Leejak was right.

Kov found himself remembering the constant arguing among his own kinsfolk. Among the Mountain Folk, the arguments arose when individuals refused to change an idea or budge an inch from a position – *the vices of Earth*, he supposed. The Dwrgwn, on the other hand, suffered from the vices of Water, endlessly flowing, always changing, unless the rare individual like Leejak could finally contain their ideas in a vessel made of hard thought.

In the morning they set off again, heading north through the tunnels. At every ventilation shaft either Leejak or Kov would climb up and look at the river, which stubbornly flowed deep and fast at the edge of the view. On the third day, however, they found a surprise: a bridge. Just at sunset Kov spotted it, a ramshackle affair of planks laid on pilings, thrown up hastily out of timber so green that the roadbed was already pulling apart. Judging from the stumps of trees he saw all along the bank, whoever had built the bridge had cut their raw materials on site. He climbed back down to report what he'd seen.

'Think it hold us?' Leejak said.

'If we're careful,' Kov said. 'The Horsekin must have built it to get horsemen across the river.'

'Ah. Maybe the ones that burn huts.'

'It could be, indeed. After we bring down the fortress, we can retreat back here, cross the bridge, and burn it behind us.'

'Good plan. If we live so long.'

'There is that.' Kov tried to smile and failed. 'Well, all we can do is hope for the best. To that end, we need to send a scout up. See if Horsekin are guarding the thing.'

Leejak snorted profoundly. 'I go myself. These –' he jerked a thumb in the direction of the other Dwrgwn '– be useless.'

Kov agreed, but he said nothing aloud.

When twilight grew thick outside, Leejak climbed up to the vent, pulled out the wooden grating, and hauled himself over the edge to the ground above. Kov stayed on the ladder and watched as the spearleader ran, half-crouching, to the riverbank. He made his way among a scatter of bushes, where he paused to take off his clothes. When Leejak slipped into the water, Kov saw a brief glimmer of blue light, then lost track of the spearleader completely in the dark ripples of water.

Twilight turned to night. The stars came out and began their slow wheeling climb toward zenith. Kov's legs began to ache on his awkward perch, but he kept watch. Without Leejak, he felt, the expedition would fail, which meant he himself would end up sacrificed to the Water gods by a gloating Gebval. *My throat slit and my blood given to the river*, he decided. *Or bound to one of those stone pillars and knifed.*

Down below him he could hear the Dwrgwn squabbling over who had received more of their diminishing rations of stale flatbread. He considered climbing out and disappearing into the night, but what would happen to him then? As much as he hated to admit it, his safety lay with Leejak and his followers.

After what seemed like half the night, though the wheel of the stars had only marked out an eighth of its journey, a damp Leejak returned. Kov climbed down to let the spearleader swing himself onto the ladder and follow.

'No guards,' Leejak said. 'I round up our men. We hurry across now. Who knows who comes later?'

'Just so,' Kov said. 'What do we do once we've crossed?'

'Hide in trees to west. Then dig.'

'Dig tunnels south, down to the fortress, you mean?'

'That too. Place to hide, place to think.' Leejak paused to look up at the opening of the shaft. 'Too strange up there. Too wide, too many stars.'

Getting all the Dwrgwn up and out, as well as hauling up all the gear, took far too much time and made too much noise for Kov's peace of mind. He kept expecting that at any moment a Horsekin barge would drift downriver and see them, or a mounted patrol would come bursting out of the woods to run them down with sabres flashing in the starlight. At last everyone had assembled in a reasonably straight line. With Kov leading, and Leejak at the rear to ensure that no one stopped or strayed from the line of march, they headed for the bridge.

When they reached it, even in the uncertain light Kov could see that it had been built on the ruins of an older structure. Stone pilings, cracked and mossy, rose a few feet out of the water. New wooden pilings had been driven next to these ancient supports only in the centre of the structure, where the bridge arched high enough for a barge to slip through. Near each shore the Horsekin had laid their rough-cut planks over the old stones.

'We go few at time,' Leejak said.

'Good idea,' Kov said. 'The gods only know how they got horses across this thing!'

'Slowly,' Leejak said, then laughed.

Despite Kov's fears, the entire expedition got across safely, though certainly not silently. The wood creaked and groaned under any greater weight than a single Dwrgi. The men kept slipping and cursing, snapping at those closest to them as if the slip were someone else's fault. Kov could only pray that the sound of water rushing along under the bridge would cover the noise, assuming that any Horsekin laired near enough to hear it. By the first grey light of dawn they all reached the stand of virgin forest that Leejak had spotted off to the west. In among the underbrush they could hide their supplies and themselves. The Dwrgwn spread out, nestling down to sleep in the bracken among the trees.

'No horses come through here,' Leejak remarked. 'Too thick.'

'You're right.' Kov felt greatly relieved. 'As long as we're quiet, no one on the river can spot us, either.'

'True. Tomorrow we dig.'

'Or maybe we can find another tunnel system. Surely some gatherers must have investigated the long barrow.'

'Maybe, maybe not. We see soon.'

Yet despite these rational reassurances, it took Kov a long time to fall asleep, even though he felt exhausted from the long day's march and the night's danger. Just as the sun broke above the horizon, he got up from his improvised bed and made his way to the forest verge. Overhead a stipple of grey clouds was sailing in from the south. *Rain!* he thought. *Ye gods, just what we don't need!*

He looked back at the bridge, some two hundred yards away across ground mostly open, though littered with tree stumps. On one of the ancient pillars he could see what appeared to be a carved design, though it stood too far for him to distinguish what it might be – dwarven runes, perhaps, cut on a bridge made by refugees from Lin Rej as they made their way east to found Lin Serr.

His curiosity would have to wait, he realized. In the light of day going back to examine the carving struck him as infinitely foolish. What if a barge came downriver? As he made his way back through the forest to warn the others about the coming rain, he told himself that he'd try to see the carving on the return journey – if he lived so long.

Down to the south and east, the warm summer storm had already broken over the grasslands. Life in the Westfolk camp moved indoors to wait out the rain. Branna had been assiduously following her teacher's advice and centreing her meditations on the problem of returning Rori to human form. Late one drizzly afternoon, when Neb was working in the healers' tent, she stumbled across a memory knot from Jill's life, the moment when that dweomermaster had seen dark wings of wyrd enfolding the man she'd once loved.

Although Jill knew she'd be unable to turn the wyrd aside, she'd sworn a vow to undo whatever it brought upon him, no matter what the risk to herself. It was enough reason, Branna supposed, for her desire to set things right for the man inside the dragon – and yet something more lay hidden at the centre of the knot. She could feel it but not identify it.

The problem reinforced another that troubled her these days. Neb had found his true wyrd when he'd resolved to use dweomer to further the healing arts. She envied the clear focus it gave him, the power it had released for his studies. She had no idea why she was studying dweomer, except that she loved it and had the gifts to master it.

'There must be some reason I'm doing this,' Branna told Grallezar.

'Something specific, I mean. I swore a vow that I'd use it to help others, but that's all kind of vague, isn't it?'

'It is – now,' Grallezar said. 'You be young yet. Wait till you reach your third nine of years, and then will you be working a ritual that tells of your true wyrd.'

'But Neb –'

'Neb be not you, and you be not Neb.' Grallezar fixed her with a narrow-eyed glare. 'And this be not some race or mock combat with lords to set a prize.'

'True spoken. My apologies. It's just so hard to wait.'

'That be because of what I did say: you be young yet.'

Branna felt a profound temptation to sulk, but she shoved it aside. *I've almost reached two nines,* she told herself. *It's not all that long till I can work the ritual. It only seems like it'll be forever.*

Dallandra had been using her tent-bound rainy days for meditation, as well, and on the same subject of dragon dweomer. She'd discovered little in these astral forays. When she discussed them with Valandario, she learned that Val had been doing the same, with the same disappointing results.

'You'd think we'd come up with something,' Val said, 'with the four of us all worrying about that wretched spell.'

'The four? Right, you're including Branna, as well we should. I suppose we can start by assuming that Evandar's dragon spell is merely a particular instance of transformation dweomer.'

'Then the problem is, how do we reverse it from the outside, as it were.' Val paused for a frown. 'It's going to take a tremendous amount of power.'

'Just that, and let's hope we don't kill the man inside the dragon if we can't earth the forces properly. Now, I've been studying Rori's etheric double ever since he reappeared last year. He seems to have two doubles, actually, one of them dragonish, the other the same shape he had before. They're somehow tied to the cycle of the moon.'

'Which one is dominant? Can you tell?'

'Fortunately, yes.' Dallandra considered for a moment. 'The mannish shape is generally stronger, but during the second quarter, the dragon double appears. It's at its peak when the moon is full.'

'So we'd best do the working when the moon's dark.'

'I'd think so, yes.'

'I really do wish that Evandar had left the wretched book in your tent or some such place instead of in Alban, wherever that may lie!

Why couldn't he ever do anything simply?' Val held up one hand to prevent a reply. 'Oh, I know, I know, it's because of what he saw in his omens. You explained all that. It just really irks me.'

'It irks me, too, to be honest.'

Valandario smiled at the admission, so brightly that Dallandra wished she'd never made it.

'You did the right thing when you convinced him to incarnate,' Val went on.

'I didn't convince him, exactly. He made the decision the only way he ever made decisions, by backing into it.'

'Like getting a balky horse into a paddock, eh? Arse first.'

Dallandra was about to make a nasty reply when Calonderiel, for probably the first time in his life, averted an argument rather than caused one. He ducked under the tent flap and came in, shaking water drops from his hair.

'Am I interrupting some working?' he said. 'I can take myself out again if so.'

'No, no.' Valandario stood up. 'I was just thinking of leaving, actually. I need to cast the omens for the day.'

You and your omens! Dallandra thought. *You're a fine one to talk about Evandar!* She managed to hold her tongue until Valandario had left. Cal flopped down on the heap of leather cushions that her fellow dweomermaster had just vacated.

'I wanted to ask you to scry out something for me, beloved,' he said. 'Assuming you don't mind and all that. I keep wondering what Voran's up to, because of the Boars, mostly. I'd like to see them brought to justice. Those priests of Bel were a loathsome lot, as arrogant as a ram in spring, but they didn't deserve what happened to them.'

'I couldn't agree more. Let's see if I can find him. This rain is a nuisance.'

Despite the water veil falling around the tent, the image of the prince built up fast. Voran was sitting at a long table inside some sort of room with wood-panelled walls. At his right hand sat Envoy Garin of the Mountain Folk, and between them on the table lay heaps of parchments, some splitting and yellowed with age, others fresh and smooth. Sunlight fell across them from a window. The rain had yet to arrive at their location, if indeed the storm was even heading their way.

'Still discussing the border, then,' Cal said when she told him what she'd seen. 'Well, eventually he'll send messages to our prince. No doubt they'll have some hard information in them.'

'And don't forget that the silver dragon's off scouting,' Dallandra said. 'He should be back soon, and he'll know more.'

'True. And, come to think of it, there's Laz, too. Can you talk with him the way you do with other Wise Ones?'

'I can't, or to be precise, he doesn't know how. That teacher of his – he wasn't only corrupt, he simply didn't know much. Or else he knew but didn't choose to teach what he knew, which is worse. But I can scry for Laz easily enough. I intend to keep track of him, too.'

'I don't trust the man.'

'No more do I, which is why I intend to keep track of him.' Dallandra had been looking for Laz at regular intervals, but she found his image difficult to clarify. Apparently he'd cast a dweomer spell over himself that hid him from scrying eyes. She could, however, find Faharn and Rhidderc easily enough, then identity Laz as the misty presence near them. *He's a cautious soul,* she thought. *Or does he even realize that he's cast up this dweomer shield?* He was hiding from himself as much as from some enemy, real or imagined, she supposed. When she considered what she knew of his earlier lives, she couldn't blame him.

'Almost there,' Rhidderc said.

'I hope our prince has reached the dun,' Laz said.

'He should have by now.'

They topped a rise and saw, ahead across a valley, the grey broch tower on its squat hill, wound with earthworks. Even at that distance, Laz recognized it. *Home.* The word burst into his consciousness and brought with it a flood of memories that washed away the present moment. Once again he felt the weight of mail upon his shoulders, the tug of a sword at his side, the stiff-backed ache of an old wound. He turned in the saddle to give orders to his warband and saw only Faharn riding behind him, leading their pack horse. The memory flood receded, but it left behind images and emotions like the detritus washed up on the beach by a storm tide.

'There they are,' Rhidderc was saying. 'Look.'

Laz looked where he pointed and saw at the foot of the dun mound the tents of a large encampment, spread out like dirty grey seafoam around a rock. At least five hundred fighting men, Laz estimated, and more horses and servants. Rhidderc and his men continued talking, but Laz had no attention to pay them. He could remember another army surrounding that dun, even larger, this one mostly made up of Horsekin and Gel da'Thae. Although they had hailed him as a friend,

Lord Tren had been shocked to meet them. Alshandra's priestesses and envoys had always been human.

As the messengers guided their horses down the hill, Laz let his mount follow its temporary herd and watched the dun grow closer and closer. The memories clustered around him, of all the times Lord Tren had ridden back to this isolated lump of ugly hillock, elaborately defended against enemies that never bothered to come. He'd spent much time with his brother, Tren had – Laz couldn't remember his name, but he felt a strong sense of gratitude for gifts given and hospitality offered, boons far beyond what a younger brother could usually expect from an elder. Someone had murdered him. Who or how, Laz couldn't remember, only his rage at hearing the news, that his brother lay dead and unavenged.

And that's the trouble with this sort of memory of a past life, Laz thought. *Vague, misty, soaked in feelings – no hard information, nothing you can ask the old people about, nothing a priest or sage can verify or deny.* But hadn't Dallandra been at the siege of Cengarn? She'd mentioned it, certainly. When he saw her again, he could ask her if she knew how Tren's brother had died.

His small party of riders had by then reached the valley floor. They followed a path beside a river and crossed a bridge, stout on its tree-trunk pilings, though the timber looked fresh-cut.

'The Mountain Folk must have built this,' Rhidderc said.

'They can work fast when they want to,' Laz said. 'There was only a ford here before.'

A slip on Laz's part – Rhidderc turned in the saddle and seemed to be about to question him, most likely to ask how he knew. Fortunately, in the encampment horns sounded, a shout went up, and a pair of riders wearing the wyvern blazon on their tabards came trotting out. With a whoop Rhidderc and his men kicked their horses to a trot to meet them. Laz and Faharn followed more slowly.

'I never thought I'd say such a thing,' Faharn said, 'but I'm glad to see the size of this Lijik army.'

'Me, too,' Laz said. 'The Northlands have become a suddenly dangerous place.'

As they rode through the camp, Laz noticed how well organized it was. On two sides lay ditches for latrines and garbage, with the dirt from their digging piled up neatly for covering the refuse when the army moved on. Tents stood in tidy semi-circles inside the ditch works. The horses were tethered out in pastures marked by rope fences, the supply wagons stowed in rows nearby. Here and there gold wyvern banners, planted among the tents, marked the fighting men clustered around them as squadrons from the King's Own.

At the base of the hill, the Mountain Folk had set up a camp just as well organized. Sentries armed with long battle-axes stood at the entrance to the winding earthworks that lined the road up to the walled dun. More sentries called out a greeting at every turn and stood at the open gates. When Laz and his party dismounted in the ward, four men of the Mountain Folk hurried over to take their horses.

'If you'd just hold our mounts for us?' Rhidderc pointed out the other three messengers to include them in the 'us'. 'We'll doubtless be going back to our camp after we give the prince his messages.'

The men nodded but said nothing. They were all looking at Faharn with suspicion in narrowed eyes.

'He's all right,' Rhidderc said, a touch jovially. 'Both of these men have good reason to hate the Horsekin. Laz, show them. They tortured him, you see.'

Laz held up his maimed hands. Two of the Mountain men winced and looked away; the others nodded their understanding.

'Don't know where you'll be quartered,' Rhidderc said to Laz. 'Up here, I'd think.'

Rhidderc's thought proved accurate. As the important translator and scholar, Laz found himself billeted in the dun itself. The prince's quartermaster gave him a chamber near the top floor, a tiny space, but it did possess an actual bed. Laz asked him to give Faharn a straw mattress to put on the floor rather than letting his apprentice sleep outside on the cobbled ward as most servants and apprentices did.

'He's Gel da'Thae, not Horsekin,' Laz told the quartermaster. 'But will the other apprentices appreciate the difference?'

'They'd make his life miserable, no doubt,' the fellow said. 'Well and good, then. He can share your chamber.'

They dumped their gear next to one of the wickerwork walls. While Faharn went off to tend their horses, Laz sat on the wide stone windowsill and looked down into the ward below. The view was shockingly, achingly familiar. Had Lord Tren come to this isolated chamber to brood or to spy on his household? Or had some servant lass caught his lordship's fancy and earned a few trinkets on that bed? Laz suspected the latter, but the memory-feeling refused to clarify itself.

That evening Laz ate in the great hall at a table headed by Prince Voran's scribe, who ignored him in an icy way that indicated the scribe saw him as a rival. This disdain allowed Laz plenty of time to look around the great hall, packed with fighting men, human and Mountain

Folk both. He was searching for Faharn, but he never saw him. He could guess that as an apprentice Faharn was being fed somewhere else with the servants. He did see a man who had to be Prince Voran, because he was sitting at the head of the honour table, a tall fellow, neither ugly nor good-looking, with a touch of grey in his brown hair and a wide mouth that gave him a froggy air when he grinned. On either side of him sat men of the Mountain Folk; the three of them stayed deep in conversation throughout the meal.

Serving lads and pages dashed back and forth, handing out food and drink while the men yelled requests and oaths. The hall stank of mouldy straw, sweat, and smoke from the rush torches burning in the wall sconces. Any kind of meditation on past lives was out of the question in the noise and heat. Laz ate quickly, then got up and slipped away while the others at his table were talking among themselves.

Back in his chamber, still overwarm from the day, Laz returned to his watch in the window. He could see over the dun walls to the grey sea of tents, illuminated here and there by tiny campfires, and beyond them to the countryside, dark under the stars. Feelings that he knew came from his life as Tren rose in his mind: a bitterness, a deep abiding resentment at someone or something, coupled with a sense that life was bleak, empty, as cold as winter frost on stone.

In his own current life, Laz had at times tasted a similar resentment, though always with some immediate cause: his sisters' privileged positions in the mach-fala, his mother's political ambitions that would have deformed him into a kind of man he hated. Still, his own feelings had been close enough to Tren's that he could use them as an entry to that other life. He set himself to meditate upon it, here in this dun where once Lord Tren had lived. At last, after the wheel of stars had made a quarter turn in the sky, Laz discovered the source, an abscess gone septic deep in Tren's soul.

Tren felt he had lost something. Some treasure was being denied him, something that mattered as much as life itself, something that should have been his, had someone not stolen it. Tren lived wrapped in a bitter certainty that he'd been cheated, denied, robbed, yet he could never find out what that something had been or who had taken it from him. Alshandra and her glorious visitations, a goddess one could see, a vast power who made herself manifest in the common world – she had seemed to supply that lack, to restore what had once been his. But in the end, she too had revealed herself to be another cheat, another lie, another robbery, when she'd died in the sky above Cengarn, torn to pieces like a fox among hounds.

But what had Tren lost?

'Sorcery,' Laz whispered. 'It had to be sorcery. I must have studied it in one of the earlier lives, then lost it or had it taken away —' He fell silent, choking on the sure knowledge that some great abuse had cost him the one thing in life he'd ever truly loved. *Dallandra said she had information about two lives,* he thought. *She never had time to tell me about the other one.*

And Marnmara had told him something about a past life, hadn't she? Something like, you did great evil —

'Ah, there you are!' Faharn kicked open the door and strode into the chamber. He carried a bucket of water in one hand and a candle-lantern in the other.

Laz could have cheerfully strangled him, but he reminded himself that Faharn had no idea of what he'd just interrupted or of the import-ance of the insight he'd just driven away. *One of these days I must tell him the great truth,* Laz thought. *Then he'll understand.*

'Wash water?' Laz managed to sound reasonably civil.

'I heated it at the cookhouse hearth, though it may or may not still be warm.'

'As long as it's not icy cold, it will do. My thanks.'

'The prince wants to see you in his council chamber,' Faharn went on. 'So I thought you might want to clean up.'

'I do, but when does —'

'In a bit, is all the page told me. He'll come fetch you. The page, that is, not the prince.'

'I assumed that.' Laz flashed him a grin. 'My thanks for the warm water.'

Laz had just finished washing and was putting on a clean shirt when the page arrived, carrying a candle lantern. Laz gathered up the wax-coated tablets and stylus that Faharn had put out for him and followed the lad into the hall.

'Beg pardon, good scribe,' the page said, 'but how can you write with those hands?'

'How?' Laz grinned at him. 'With some difficulty, that's how.'

The lad blushed and hurried on ahead of him. Laz followed the bobbing lantern light down a twist of the stone stairs and into what had once been the women's hall of the dun. Laz remembered that Tren's aged mother had once held a shabby court there for the rare visits of other noblewomen. Now it had been turned into a council chamber of sorts. A long table, lit with a lantern at either end, held a map of the Northlands, made from two whole parchments stitched together and anchored with a couple of large stones to fend off the draughts from the open window. Behind it in a half-circle of rickety chairs sat the prince, flanked by the two men of the Mountain Folk who'd accompanied him at dinner. The page bowed low. Laz reminded himself to act humble and knelt in front of the table.

'The Horsekin scribe, your highness,' the lad said.

'Not Horsekin but Gel da'Thae,' the prince said. 'Remember that. It's very important.'

'Very well, your highness, my apologies.'

Blushing again, the page backed out of the chamber and shut the door behind him.

'Do get up,' the prince said. 'That floor looks more than a little uncomfortable.'

'My thanks, your highness.' Laz rose and wiped the clinging straws from the knees of his brigga.

'Have a chair.' One of the Mountain men, who was sitting at the very end of the table, shoved a chair Laz's way with one foot. 'You come highly recommended, loremaster, in the letter Exalted Mother Grallezar sent about you. Cursed good thing you're here, too. My names' Brel son of Brellio, by the by, and I'm the avro of my lot.' He jerked a thumb in the direction of the other man of the Mountain Folk. 'This is Envoy Garin.'

Laz bowed to them both and took the chair. As he sat down, he noticed that the prince was holding a flat leather bag in his lap. He recognized it as a Gel da'Thae dispatch rider's bag. The prince passed it to Brel, who gave it to Laz. As Laz took it, he realized that dry blood crusted the flap. The dispatch rider had apparently not given it over willingly.

'I'm hoping you can read the letters inside for us,' Voran said.

'So am I, your highness,' Laz said.

The jest brought him a royal grin. Fortunately the reading turned out to be quite straightforward. When Laz unfolded the two letters inside the bag, he discovered they'd been written in a common scribal hand.

'As far as I can tell from the remnants of these wax seals, your highness,' Laz began, 'the letters come from a commander of a regiment of mounted warriors. I can't tell which one, thanks to their being shattered, but I don't suppose it would matter now, with everything so changed in the cities.'

'Probably it doesn't, indeed,' Voran said. 'Read them out.'

'*To Burc, King of the Free Boars of the North*,' Laz began, then stopped when all three of his listeners swore aloud.

'King, is it?' Voran said. 'Well, he's got his gall, but then, we could have assumed that. You may continue, Laz.'

Laz did so. '*Prataen, warleader of the Second* –' He hesitated over an unusual use of a word. '*Warleader of the Second Horde sends his greetings.*'

'Do you recognize that name?' Brel interrupted.

'I don't, sir,' Laz said. 'It looks more Horsekin than Gel da'Thae, however, as does the use of horde instead of regiment.'

'Would you stop interrupting him?' Envoy Garin glared at Brel. 'Do continue reading, good loremaster.'

'Very well. *I am sending you my last squad of men who understand fortifications* –'

'They never reached the Boar dun.' Brel glared right back at Garin. 'That's why we have the letters.'

'*Who understand fortifications,*' Laz picked up the thread again. '*Once your compound has been made ready, we will send a hundred men and wagons with supplies to maintain them. Please send me messengers once your walls are strengthened, so I may know to get these reinforcements on their way.*' Laz lowered the parchment and glanced at his listeners. 'That's the first letter, your highness, and good sirs.'

'Ye gods!' Prince Voran slammed both hands down on the table in front of him and made the candle flames dance in their lanterns. 'That's clear proof of treachery. I think we can assume that demanding the surrender of the Boar dun is well within our rights.'

'Just so, your highness,' Garin said with a nod his way.

Laz wondered if the lack of such evidence would have changed their minds about their planned attack on the Boars. He doubted it. When none of the others spoke again, Laz cleared his throat and started the second letter.

'It's from Prataen again,' Laz began. '*To our supposed King of the Boars. I have sent messengers to Her Holiness, Fellepzia, High Priestess of Alshandra in Taenbalapan, concerning your request of a temple to be built in your lands. She has responded that she'll gladly grant such a request. A temple to our most holy goddess will be a splendid way to mark our temporary southern border.*'

'Temporary?' Voran spat out the word. 'How far south are they aiming?'

'I'd assume they want a foothold in Arcodd, your highness,' Garin said. 'They sieged Cengarn once.'

'So they did.' Voran paused for a grimace. 'Bastards.' He nodded Laz's way. 'Continue.'

'*She has sent a priestess of some standing south along with a contingent of two hundred cavalrymen. They have orders to secure a bridge
somewhat to the north of you.*'

'What?' Brel broke in. 'A bridge? What bridge? What kind of madmen
would build a bridge in the wilderness?'

Laz hesitated. From Berwynna he'd learned about the strange little
village and its ramshackle bridge, but he wondered if it were wise to
admit to the knowledge. Fortunately, Garin provided something of an
answer.

'Merchants from the west pass through there,' Garin said. 'They've
mentioned a wide river, and I'm assuming they bridged it to get their
mules across.'

'Of course,' Brel said. 'My apologies. Go on, good scribe.'

Laz did so. '*Once the contingent has fortified the bridge site, the
priestess, along with a suitable escort, will proceed to your dun.*'

'I wonder how many men they deem suitable.' This time Voran
interrupted. 'Not the full two hundred, at least.' He turned to look
directly at Laz. 'Is that the last of the letter?'

'Except for some prayers and farewells, your highness,' Laz said.

'We don't need to hear those. Could you copy those letters – in
Deverrian, that is – for me? I'm going to send messengers to the High
King. I want him to realize that we need more men up here on the
border. The fear of losing northern Arcodd will doubtless inspire him
to send some.'

'Huh!' Brel snorted. 'He'd better send a small army.'

Voran ignored him and waved his hand in Laz's direction. 'You may
go,' he said. 'May I have those letters by the morrow morn? You'll find
me in the great hall.'

'Of course, your highness.' Laz rose and bowed. 'I shall deliver them
to you personally.'

With his maimed hands, carrying everything he held in his lap
turned out to be difficult. Laz paused long enough to stuff the letters
and his wax tablets into the dispatch case, and while he was doing
so, the three others went on talking as if he, a mere servant, were no
longer there, even when he got up and started for the door.

'If they're planning on taking Cengarn,' Brel was saying, 'they'll need
a bigger base camp than that fortress the dragon saw a-building.'

'Just so,' Voran said. 'A place where they can winter if naught else.
It's a long way from their cities to Arcodd. I'll wager it's Cengarn
they're after.'

'And if they take Cengarn,' Garin put in, 'what's to stop them from turning their greedy eyes to Cerrgonney? The Boars claimed all of it at one time.'

'And its iron mines.' Voran smiled in a grim, tight-lipped gesture. 'No doubt the king will realize that as well.'

A sudden thought struck Laz like an arrow. He hesitated, unsure of protocol, near the door. Fortunately, Brel noticed him and once again demonstrated his lack of concern for the niceties.

'What is it, loremaster?' Brel said. 'There's somewhat on your mind, isn't there? Out with it!'

'My thanks.' Laz bowed to him. 'About that base camp?'

'Go on.'

The prince and the envoy turned slightly in their chairs to look his way.

'Marshfort,' Laz said in Gel da'Thae, then caught himself. 'In the Deverrian speech, that is to say, Cerr Cawnen. I know Alshandra's warleaders coveted it once, some forty years ago, I believe it was. It's a fortified city with its own water supply.'

'Of course.' Garin paused to swear under his breath in a language Laz didn't know, although the tone was unmistakably foul.

'Cerr Cawnen?' Voran said. 'That's the second time that name has come up. Where –'

'I'll show you on the map, your highness.' Garin got up and stood by the table. 'It would be a grand spot to launch an attack against Prince Daralanteriel.'

'Indeed,' Brel put in, 'the bastards want grass as much as they want iron. Maybe more.'

'Cerr Cawnen is the key to taking the Westlands and the grass.' Garin slapped his hands together. 'We've been blind, your highness.'

'So we have,' Prince Voran said. 'I'll send messengers to Prince Dar on the morrow. My thanks, good scholar. I'll see to it that you're well rewarded for your aid.'

At this firm dismissal, Laz bowed and left. In the empty corridor he paused to make a small dweomer light. The silver glow bobbed along ahead of him as he returned to his chamber. There he found Faharn asleep, wrapped tightly in a blanket on his mattress near the door.

Laz considered immediately writing out the translation of the letters, but the room lacked a table, and with his maimed hands, grinding and mixing ink would be difficult. He would wake at dawn, he decided, when he usually did, and get Faharn up to help him. He laid the dispatch case down by his saddlebags, dismissed the dweomer light, then sat on the wide windowsill to consider the night view. The camp below stood mostly dark, but here and there a faint glow indicated a dying campfire. Now and then someone walked through, a twitch of motion in the gloom far below. Stars glittered on the distant river.

Lord Tren had sat here on summer nights, now and then, to take the air and brood over his cursed life. Laz pretended to be Tren once more, consciously tried to recapture his feeling that life was bleak and full of betrayals. *If only* – that was the key, Laz decided. *If only I, Tren, lord of this miserable demesne, could – do what?* He couldn't remember what it was that Tren thought he wanted. Probably Tren had never been sure of it himself. Sorcery seemed as good a guess as any, whether or not the lord had ever used the word 'dweomer' to himself.

The hair on the back of Laz's neck suddenly rose. Someone, something, had entered the room behind him. He wanted to twist around and leap to his feet in order to confront the intruder, but since he was perching on the edge of a long straight drop down to a cobbled ward, he turned and stood up slowly with great care. The spirit who had entered waited for him to face her. At first glance she appeared to be a pale, blue-haired woman, barefoot and wearing a blue dress, but when he looked more carefully Laz realized that an etheric ecto-plasm made up the dress and her body both, with the colour the only difference between them. She glowed in the dark room like a ray of moonlight falling through an arrow slit in a wall. When he gestured out the sigil of the Kings of Aethyr in the air, she smiled and nodded.

'Will you save the dragon book?' She spoke in Deverrian.

'I'll try, certainly,' Laz said in the same. 'Will you help me?'

'I shall tell those who guard it who you are. They cannot speak, but they can hear. The man with the beast on his face has the book.'

With that she vanished. Laz shuddered, suddenly cold, but pleased nonetheless. He would have help in this impossible-seeming task. This realization brought another, that the spirit called Evandar must have commanded immense power, if the fate of one of his artifacts could still trouble the Lords of Aethyr long after his death. Their concern had to be great if they'd send a messenger down the planes to a renegade dweomerman like himself. Suddenly, using the book as bait to hook Sidro looked like a less than prudent idea.

I'd best think of somewhat else, Laz told himself. *Tomorrow, though.* After a long day in the saddle, plus dealing with both royalty and astral spirits, he felt exhausted. Faharn had spread his blankets out on the narrow bed. Laz took off his boots and lay down fully-dressed on the lumpy mattress. *I'll never get to sleep on this!*

But suddenly he was awake, and the room full of sunlight. He sat up, yawning, just as Faharn came bustling in with a basket of bread and a pitcher of water for their breakfast.

With Faharn's help, Laz wrote out a translation of the two Horsekin letters on the sheets of pabrus Salamander had given him. He had enough blank space left over to add a few notes concerning Cerr Cawnen's role in Horsekin history.

'Come to think of it,' Faharn said, 'that's where the Alshandrites' supposed Holy Martyr Raena died. They probably want to build one of their cursed shrines in it.'

'You are quite right,' Laz said. 'Let me just add a note about that, too, and then I'll take these to his highness, assuming he's awake.'

'I saw him in the great hall when I fetched our breakfast.'

Sure enough, Laz found the prince sitting at the head of the honour table with Brel and Garin to either side. Laz decided that Brel would be the most approachable. When he knelt beside the dwarven warleader, Brel greeted him with a brief smile and took the proffered documents.

'My thanks,' he said. 'Your highness, the loremaster's brought back those letters.'

'Good, good!' Prince Voran favoured Laz with a nod. 'Here, good scholar, I want you to continue in my service. It's likely we'll find more letters like those. I'm offering you your maintenance for the campaign, for you and your apprentice both, of course, and a silver piece a week.'

'Very generous terms, your highness,' Laz said. 'I'll accept your commission gladly. I take it we're heading for the Boar dun?'

'We are.'

'Well and good, then.'

The prince sent a page for his quartermaster, who promptly paid over the first silver piece. Where he would spend it, Laz thought, was probably as great a mystery to the quartermaster as it was to him. After many bows and professions of gratitude, he left the prince's company and hurried back upstairs to tell Faharn the news.

'Exactly what you wanted,' Faharn said. 'Now we see if we can get that book back.'

'Just so.' Laz grinned at him. 'And wouldn't my mach-fala be proud of me? I may be only a humble translator, but I'm riding to war at last.'

Out in the Rhiddaer, the oddly circular town of Cerr Cawnen sheltered some four thousand souls. It lay in the midst of water meadows, a first line of defence against Horsekin raiders, whose mounts would have had to pick their way through the little streams and springs that turned solid-seeming ground into bog. On its outer walls, made of good stone, guards prowled the catwalks and stood at the iron-bound timber gates.

Inside the walls, a wide strip of grassy commons surrounded the town, which in turn surrounded the roughly circular Loc Vaed, the crater of an ancient volcano. Most of the buildings crammed into the pale greenish shallows: a jumble and welter of houses and shops all perched on pilings or crannogs, joined by little bridges to one another in a confusing jumble. The edge of the crannog-town bristled with rickety stairs and jetties, where leather coracles bobbed at the end of their ropes.

In the centre of the lake lay deep water, fed by underground hot springs. Drifts of mist hung over the lake on cold days and veiled the shores of the rocky central island, Citadel. On Citadel, a few large houses and a scatter of shabby dwellings clung to its steep sides, along with the town granary, the militia's armoury, shrines to the local gods and ruins of an ancient temple, tumbled in an earthquake so long ago that no one remembered exactly when.

Niffa, the dweomermaster who had once been Dallandra's apprentice, lived with her brother's family in a large house out on Citadel. Jahdo had grown up as an apprentice to a successful merchant, who had traded with Lin Serr among other places in the Northlands, though only rarely with the Gel da'Thae. After Verrarc's death, Jahdo had become rich on his own, then married Cotzi the weaver's daughter, who'd borne him a fine clutch of children. Just that spring he'd been elected Chief Speaker of the town council – an honour that had delighted him at the time. Now, however, his feelings had changed. Niffa was lingering at the breakfast table with him when he brought up the election.

'I do wish I'd turned down the post,' Jahdo said that morning. 'And kept on leading the caravans myself. Better that I'd died than our Aethel. He were so young, and I'm but an old man now. I've had my life, and –'

'Nah, brother!' Niffa said. 'Hold your tongue! Be not blaming yourself. It was his wyrd.'

'And no one can turn aside another's wyrd?' Jahdo made a sour face at her. 'That old saying does sicken me this morning.'

'It be true whether you do like it or not.'

He scowled at her, then shrugged with a lift of one skinny shoulder.

'Whether I be right or wrong,' she said, 'you be Chief Speaker now. This matter of the Horsekin –'

'– does grow more grave daily,' Jahdo finished her thought. 'I did call a council meeting this afternoon. The folk who do live in Penli, they do fear the Horsekin even more than we. They did send a man to us to petition for the right to flee inside our walls should the need arise.'

'It would be wise to grant it.'

'Of course, but the council needs must decide for themselves.' He paused for a sly smile. 'With a bit of help from me, truly.'

Niffa learned that the Council had followed her advice when Jahdo returned, bringing the Penli suppliant with him. Cleddrik, his name was, a tall skinny fellow with short black hair and a straggling moustache. He was, he informed them both, the son of a pig farmer, whose trade in salt pork had given his family a certain standing in his town.

'We be grateful that you did grant us shelter,' Cleddrik said. 'There be some fifty families in Penli, and we have not the men nor the stone to build walls of our own.'

'There be a need on us to arrange some signal,' Jahdo said. 'The Horsekin, they be most like to come down from the north and thus reach us first.'

Over the noon meal the two men continued talking while Niffa studied this stranger. Something about Cleddrik troubled her, yet he seemed sincere enough, especially when it came to his fear of the Horsekin.

'We did build a wooden palisade round our village.' Cleddrik's voice shook on the words. 'But how long might it take the Horsekin to burn that? And then, once it be done, they be amok among us and our women.'

'Dwell not upon it,' Jahdo said. 'Our stone walls, they will keep you safe enough, the gods willing.'

'But be they willing?' Cleddrik's voice abruptly turned calm. 'What about this new goddess of theirs? She has great power of her own.'

'She be not a goddess.' Niffa leaned forward into the conversation. 'And she does live no longer.'

Cleddrik turned his head to look at her with an utterly blank expression on his face, as if perhaps he'd not heard her.

'This be my sister,' Jahdo said. 'She does walk the witch road.'

Cleddrik's face lost some of its colour. He pushed out a twitch of a smile and bobbed his head in her direction.

'And I will tell you yet again,' Niffa said, 'Alshandra were but an illusion and a cheat. Fear her not.'

'If you do say so, mistress,' Cleddrik said, 'then I shall do as you say.'

Yet he was staring at the table as he spoke rather than looking her way. Niffa said nothing more, but for the rest of the meal, she studied Cleddrik, who did his best to avoid her gaze the entire time. As soon as the meal was over, he mumbled excuses and fled the house.

Niffa went up to her little chamber at the top of the rambling house. Besides her narrow bed, it held a lectern, a high stool for reading at the lectern, and a comfortable cushioned windowseat. From the window she could see all the way down Citadel, past the fine houses, past the public granary and the little annex where she'd been born and spent her childhood, past the steep paths and the retaining walls, down the strip of sandy beach and the coracles drawn up upon it, to Loc Vaed itself, where patches of pale mist floated above the greenish water.

She used the mist as a focus and reached out to Dallandra. The elven dweomermaster answered her immediately.

'Sour news,' Niffa said. 'I do think Alshandra worship has reached the Rhiddaer.'

Dallandra listened gravely while Niffa told her of Cleddrik and his odd behavior. When she finished, Dallandra agreed with her.

'This sounds ominous indeed,' Dalla said. 'I told you, didn't I, that we have a woman with us who used to be a priestess of Alshandra? She might well know more about Penli.'

'Splendid! Do ask her, and do let me know when you've done so.'

'I shall indeed. Stay on the alert would be my advice.'

'That be good advice always when the Horsekin be prowling around.'

After she broke the link with Niffa, Dallandra wandered through the alar's camp, dodging children, dogs, and Wildfolk, until she found Sidro, who was sitting in front of the tent she shared with Pir and mending one of his shirts. Dallandra sat down cross-legged in front of her.

'Tell me somewhat,' Dallandra said. 'Alshandra's Elect travelled long distances to spread the word, didn't they?'

'Very long, truly.' Sidro laid her mending into her lap. 'We did call ourselves Alshandra's messengers and speak of our duty to let all hear of her.'

'Do you know if anyone went to Cerr Cawnen?'

'Not to the town itself, though it be the place where the Holy Witness Raena did die. Lakanza did warn us away from there, saying the folk were too savage and too inclined to murder any Gel da'Thae on sight.'

'Er, that wasn't true, you know. Cerr Cawnen had an alliance with Grallezar's people.'

'Never did they tell us that! The rakzanir, they did lie and lie again.' Sidro set her lips tight in disgust.

'From everything you've told me about them, I'm not surprised. But what about the villages near Cerr Cawnen, like Penli, for instance?'

'Well, truly, that be a name I did hear. I think me one of us, Rocca most like, did go there.'

'My thanks.' Dallandra stood up, glancing around her. 'Have you seen Cal?'

'He did take Dari with him but a little while ago. He were going to the edge of camp to do somewhat, he did tell me, and thought she should have a bit of sun.'

Dallandra found them both out in the grass. Dari was on her stomach on a blanket and solemnly watching her father straighten arrow shafts by pulling them through a hole drilled in the flat part of a deer's shoulder blade.

'Cal?' Dallandra said. 'I have some nasty news. I just spoke with Niffa through the fire.'

Cal looked up and squinted at her. She realized that the late afternoon sun hung in the sky behind her and moved around to his other side while he laid his work aside. She sat down next to him in the grass, then picked Dari up and settled her in her arms.

'What's this news?' Cal said.

'Alshandra worship has reached the farms near Cerr Cawnen.'

'Oh by the Black Sun!' Calonderiel said. 'It spreads like a plague.'

'So it does. Niffa met a man from Penli, that's the village just south of the town, if you remember, who's at least heard of Alshandra. Sidro said that a priestess had visited them. Niffa suspects that he's a convert of sorts, but she's not entirely sure. He was afraid of her, but then, he might merely be afraid of what they call "witchlore". Many people are, after all.'

'It's nasty news either way. I'll tell the prince. I think we'd best hurry everyone along and get to Cerr Cawnen as soon as we can.'

'My thought exactly. One thing is clear. Whether Laz can fetch the book or not, Rori's transformation will have to wait. The danger's so thick around us that I can barely breathe.'

'A bad omen in itself. Where is Laz, by the by? And what about Voran?'

Dallandra used the sky as a focus and found them together, the prince at the head of a long convoy of riders and dwarven axemen, Laz back toward the end among the servants and wagons with Faharn beside him.

'They've left Tren's dun,' she told him. 'Beyond that, I don't know.'

'Well, let's hope they're off to attack some Horsekin,' Cal said. 'Exactly where or which ones doesn't matter all that much to me.'

When Prince Voran and Brel Avro led out their combined forces, they headed straight east from the dun. For the first day the land ran through fallow farmland and past the deserted homesteads that had once belonged to Tren's vassals. Soon they'd be farmed again, by men of the Mountain Folk, or so some of the royal servants told Laz.

'His highness settled this land upon them,' the quartermaster said, 'in return for the part they played in last summer's wars.'

On the second day the terrain began to rise, gently at first, but soon enough it turned rugged. Broken hills, gashed by steep ravines and whitewater creeks, formed a line of natural defences for the Boar territories that lay beyond. Without the Mountain Folk and their axes and picks, the army of horsemen would have had to turn back. As it was, the dwarven axemen changed their weapons of war for foresters' blades, then chopped and cleared the way through the underbrush and straggling pines. They built temporary bridges over the streams and provided rope and expertise both to keep the clumsy supply wagons moving.

'Horsekin raiders couldn't get their mounts through here either,' Faharn remarked. 'No wonder they're looking farther west.'

'Just so,' Laz said. 'And they're looking farther south, too. If they get control of the grasslands, they'll have a hundred easy roads into Lijik territory.'

In narrow valleys, where black boulders pushed through thin soil, the army passed more deserted farms. Empty houses and barns stood behind crumbling earthworks. Now and again they saw a cow or a few sheep gone wild among the hills.

'It makes my blood run cold,' Faharn said, 'seeing all this. Where are the people, do you think?'

'Dead, maybe?' Laz said. 'I've no idea.'

In such rough terrain the army made slow progress, crawling up a steep hill only to pick their way down from the crest. The supply wagons became a constant problem. Even the straked wheels of the dwarven carts broke against half-hidden rocks or tangled themselves with weeds. Whenever one of the carts lost a wheel, the army halted, slowing the march further. Faharn began to worry about food.

'The supply train's only brought so much,' he pointed out. 'What if we eat it all before the war's over?'

'Ye gods!' Laz snapped. 'Always thinking about your cursed stomach! You eat too much anyway. It dulls the higher faculties.'

Faharn blushed a dark red and fell silent. When the army stopped for its noon rest, Laz noticed that Faharn ate only a few scraps of dry flatbread and one sliver of cheese.

'Well, you could eat more than that,' Laz said. 'My apologies. I shouldn't have snapped at you like that.'

Faharn stared at him in utter surprise. *Surely I've apologized to him for my bad temper before?* Laz thought. Yet he couldn't quite remember any other time when he had.

During the journey, whenever the army stopped to rest their horses or to camp for the night, Laz made a point of scrying for the dragon book. During the day he saw only the darkness that meant the book lay swaddled in some sort of covering. At night, he got a few brief glimpses of it by the dim light of a single candle, none of which gave him the slightest clue as to its location.

'I begin to wonder if we'll ever find the wretched thing,' Laz said to Faharn. 'The impression I get is that the astral currents are pushing it away from us, not bringing it closer.'

'That's truly odd,' Faharn said. 'Or is it the work of that blue and white spirit you told me about?'

'That I doubt. She was so sincerely willing to help. Well, we'll just have to wait and see if she reappears. I don't have the slightest idea of how to summon her.'

On the fifth day out they reached an entire fortified village, some twelve round buildings surrounded by stone walls laced with timber, all of them deserted. Grass grew wild and tall upon the roofs. Unlatched doors banged in the rising wind. A flurry of chattering sparrows rose from the top of the tallest tower, circled the village once, then settled again. Otherwise not a living thing moved in the dun. Voran called a halt, then sent a squad of men down to scout out the complex.

'It's amazing,' Faharn said, 'that the Lijik Ganda never knew all this was here. It's so close to their border.'

'Plenty of people did know, Envoy Garin for one,' Laz said. 'The information never reached Dun Deverry, is all.' He rose in his stirrups for a better view of the silent fortress below them. 'Huh, one of the scouts seems to have found something.'

Inside the walls the scout was holding up a piece of cloth. When he shook it out, Laz could see the device crudely painted upon it: a Boar.

'So, some of our enemies have withdrawn,' Laz told Faharn. 'I wonder where they are, and the rest of them, too.'

Prince Voran apparently shared his wondering. The prince gave a string of orders to make the night's camp with as many men as possible sheltering inside the walls. The rest formed a defensive ring outside. While the servants and riders carried out the orders, he called a conference, including Laz, inside the broch tower. Since the departing Boars had stripped every piece of furniture, the prince and his dwarven allies all stood in the middle of the floor. Laz knelt in front of them and unrolled the map that Envoy Garin handed him. Voran squatted down to study it.

'Tell me somewhat, loremaster,' Voran said. 'Do your people know these hills at all well?'

'Only the priestesses of Alshandra do, your highness,' Laz said. 'They have some sort of secret road through them, you see, marked out by symbols of some kind, scratched on rocks and the like. Alas, they keep those signs to themselves.'

Voran muttered a few foul oaths under his breath. Warleader Brel knelt to join them at the map.

'My people don't come this far south,' Brel said. 'Neither do the merchants from Cerr Cawnen.'

'So the Boars have had it all to themselves for all these years,' Voran said. 'A nice sty to breed in.' He stood up with a stretch of his back. 'Well, this place must have been deserted some while ago. Maybe we can pick up their tracks, maybe not.'

Yet that very night help came from a completely unexpected source. As they scouted around the deserted fields surrounding the old Boar village, some of Voran's men caught a cow, left behind and turned half-wild. They slaughtered her and shared out the meat, which the servants soon had simmering at the cooking fires. Even Laz had to admit that fresh beef cooking smelled as good as any fine perfume.

The smell apparently drifted into the forest. Laz and Faharn, who found themselves attached to the prince's retinue, had been given a spot inside the walls though outside the broch. They were still eating when they heard one of the sentries beyond the gates calling out. One of the watchmen on the walls took up the cry to open up. Slowly the gates creaked open just enough to let in two armed men and a prisoner of sorts. Laz and Faharn stood and watched as the guards marched him along past their campfire.

'Bren!' Faharn said.

Laz hurriedly sat down to hide his face. He did catch a quick look at Bren, so thin he seemed starved, his hair long and matted, his clothes mere rags. The guards took him into the broch. The door had barely closed when the rumours began running through the camp, that the sentries had caught an assassin coming after the prince, or a spy for the Boars, or this thing or the other.

The truth, augmented by Faharn's memory, arrived with the morning's muster. Envoy Garin climbed up onto the walls and bellowed the tale to the men waiting below.

'The man you saw on the night past – Bren's his name – used to worship the false goddess Alshandra,' Garin announced. 'But the prince has forgiven him, and no one's to harm him. He knows where the Boars have gone to.'

The waiting army cheered. Garin held up both hands for silence, then continued.

'Bren was sent to this village with messages from a priestess. At first they treated him well, but then he learned that they weren't what he called true followers. So he escaped this spring. He's been living in the woods, but he smelled the cow cooking and came forward.'

More cheers, this time for the cow.

'Her bovine sacrifice was not in vain,' Laz said. 'I suppose that priestess was Sidro.'

'Yes, it was,' Faharn said. 'Huh, she could have got the poor man killed, sending him here. Just like her.'

'Since I was ready to kill him myself, I can hardly take issue with what she did. Be that as it may, I'm cursed glad now that I didn't kill him, so she was right, after all.'

Faharn had the decency to cringe. Laz let the gesture go without comment, because Garin was speaking again.

'The Boars had spies in Cerrgonney,' Garin said. 'They could tell that the Deverry high king would be sending an army against them. So they moved their people north to settle new land.'

General cries of 'cowards! bastards!' greeted these remarks. Garin held up his hands for silence and eventually got it.

'As for the Boars themselves,' the envoy went on, 'and this pisspoor excuse for a king of theirs, they're apparently fleeing north to join up with the Horsekin. The question is, can we catch them before they do? Prince Voran intends to try. So men, to horse! We've got to make all possible speed.'

With one last cheer the men followed orders. Laz and Faharn worked their way clear of the bustling mob to find a somewhat quieter spot on the edge of the camp.

'This is infuriating,' Laz said. 'I suppose these idiot Boars have taken that slave and the dragon book with them.'

'Seems likely,' Faharn said. 'We'd better hope we can catch up with them, then, and that we don't ride into some sort of ambuscade.'

'Ambuscade? I see that unhappy thought has occurred to you, too. Let's hope it occurred to Voran, or more likely, to Brel.'

'Just so. Here, I'd best fetch our horses. We need to be ready to ride out.'

'So we do. I sincerely hope I can stay away from Bren. I don't need him recognizing me.'

Fortunately, Bren, newly shaved, trimmed, and dressed in decent clothing, rode next to the prince at the head of the line of march, while Laz and Faharn could lurk at the rear among the servants.

On the second day, another slow crawl up hills and through twisting ravines, the prince gave orders that the fighting men should arm, ready in case of an attack on their line of march. A contingent of fifty horsemen, horse archers among them, moved back to the rear of the line to guard the supply wagons. Around noon Laz noticed that the forest was thinning out around them. A road of sorts appeared, a dirt track lined with underbrush that the Mountain Folk set about widening with their axes. When the army stopped to rest the horses, scouts on foot spread out through the trees. They returned to report that they'd not seen any sign of farms or settled land.

'It's too bad the prince wouldn't believe that I can turn myself into a raven,' Laz told Faharn. 'I could scout for him.'

'Indeed,' Faharn said. 'You don't suppose Bren was lying about this place, do you?'

'I don't. Who would want to farm in this kind of country? Don't forget that we're climbing up to a plateau.'

'That's right. A much better place to put a royal palace.' Faharn thoughtfully spat onto the ground. 'Royal. Huh!'

'I share your scepticism. Where do you think the Boars are going, anyway? Not all the way to Taenbalapan, surely!'

'I doubt it, too.'

Faharn considered, rubbing his jaw in thought. 'Most likely,' he said at last, 'they're heading to that fortress that the dragon saw a-building.

From what he told Prince Dar, it's properly sited to provide safety for a retreating force.'

'How wise of them!' Laz said. 'And may the gods curse them all for their wisdom!'

For some days Kov and the Dwrgwn had been burrowing south in the hopes of bringing a wyrd more substantial than a curse upon the Horsekin fortress. They had marched through the virgin forest rather than tunnelled under it, because they would have had to dig far too deep to avoid the impacted roots of the tall trees. Once they reached the forest verge, travelling on the surface became too dangerous. On a slight rocky rise Kov stood and looked south, a long way south over a landscape of scrub grass and stunted, twisted trees growing only beside narrow streams. If his straggling party of Dwrgwn tried to march across it, any mounted Horsekin patrol would spot them from miles away.

They took shelter underground, but the digging proceeded slowly. They found the topsoil thin over a layer of rocks – not bedrock, fortunately, but an oddly random scatter of large rocks, a few boulders, and a lot of loose gravel.

'I don't understand this terrain,' Kov said. 'I've seen somewhat like it before, up to the north of Lin Serr, but I don't know what creates it. It looks like something swept up a lot of mountain rocks, carried them along for miles, and then dropped them, but it would have happened a long long time ago.'

'Giants with brooms,' Leejak said with a shrug. 'I care not. Cursed nuisance now.'

'That's certainly true.'

Rather than try to move several tons of rock to the surface, the Dwrgwn twisted their tunnel around the biggest obstacles and used the small scatter to line the floors and brace the bottom of the walls. As much as they'd hated marching, they loved digging. They worked hard, efficiently, and relentlessly, but still, Kov considered they'd done well if they made a mile in a day. Since he had no idea how far ahead the fortress lay, he could only hope they'd reach it before the war ended.

Now and then the diggers had a tunnel collapse from above. This dangerous irritation always happened in places that someone or something had hollowed out at some time long before. Loose soil had blown in and the ceilings fallen to fill the hollows and give them the appearance of solid earth until it was too late to prevent the cave-in.

The hollows reminded Kov of Deverry root cellars. Or possibly, he supposed, they'd once been some type of dug-out dwelling. In one of these circular hollows a Grallag found a shard of reddish pottery that looked as if it had been broken out of a shallow bowl. He handed it to Leejak, who gave it to Kov to inspect.

'Someone has to have lived here,' Kov said. 'A long time ago now, though.'

'Good. No ghosts, then,' Leejak said. 'Horsekin, most like.'

'Most like, indeed.'

Unless, of course, refugees from Lin Rej had reached the area and wintered there – Kov made a mental note to ask the archivists at Lin Serr, assuming he ever saw them again. Two days later, however, when they reached another once-dug area, he found a coin, or to be precise, a corroded disk, green with silver tarnish. After he polished it up, he could see that it came from no dwarven foundry. On one side, barely legible, was a human face in silhouette; on the other, letters that reminded him of Deverry writing.

'Of course!' he told Leejak. 'The Deverrians came through here on their way from the western sea. They must have wintered in this area.'

'Interesting,' Leejak said. 'Under that Horsekin fortress, then, what lies? I wonder.'

Kov felt a sudden stab of hope. If ancient wooden structures underlay the mound, their job would be a fair bit easier. He wished that the Dwrgi scouts who'd first spotted it had given a better description – not that they would have been capable of precision, he supposed.

The Dwrgwn had fashioned a ladder out of bits of wood and tree roots. Every night Kov and Leejak would climb out of the tunnel for a cautious look around. Kov always took a stick with him to use in place of his missing staff to explore the ground around their tunnel. Some of the Dwrgwn gatherers must have burrowed into the place they called the Long Barrow in the years before the Horsekin had come south to claim it. Sure enough, on one of these expeditions he heard the slight difference in the tapping sounds that announced 'tunnel below!' to his dwarven ears. He followed it far enough to determine that it ran south. Searching further never turned up an entrance.

'They fill that in,' Leejak said. 'Hide it that way.'

'Most likely,' Kov said. 'But if this tunnel runs all the way, it'll save us a fair bit of time.'

On the morrow the Dwrgwn followed his directions. From their new tunnel, they dug a feeder shaft for some hundred yards west. When they broke through into the old tunnel, Kov saw immediately that it was solid Dwrgi work, reinforced with wood beams and a course of stone at the floor. What's more, thanks to water seepage, on the walls grew blue fungi in a lumpy carpet of phosphorescent tendrils.

The Dwrgi filled the smallest baskets with earth, then carefully transplanted nodes of fungi from the walls to the baskets. Kov took one and in the blue glimmer walked on ahead, leaving the pack of chattering Dwrgwn behind him. The silence brought him a warning. Overhead he could hear a thudding noise. He felt a trembling in the earth around him. He turned back and ran, hissing out a warning, 'Silence! hush! all of you! danger!'

Mercifully the Dwrgwn followed orders. In the resulting quiet everyone could hear the thud and rumble on the ground above. Leejak whispered to Kov, 'What be?'

'Riders. We must be near the fortress.'

Leejak murmured the news to the others in the Dwrgi tongue.

Late that night, under the light of the Starry Road and a half-moon, Kov saw the Long Barrow for the first time. In their new-found tunnel the Dwrgwn found a ventilation shaft, crumbling and filled with dried leaves and the like, but easily cleaned and repaired. With the aid of the makeshift ladder Kov climbed up and stuck his head and shoulders into the fresh air. Not more than a quarter mile ahead, possibly a bit less by his estimate, he saw orange campfires glowing among the dark silhouettes of tents. Although he couldn't spot them, he could smell horses and their manure.

Beyond the fires and the tents rose a long dark mound, some sixty feet high. At the top, jagged shapes against the starry night appeared to signify walls made of rough-cut logs. Beyond them he could just discern the uneven roofs of buildings. None of the structures appeared true to the vertical, but whether that was because of sloppy building or the mound settling, he couldn't tell. He climbed back down and told Leejak what he'd seen.

'You got good eyes for dark,' Leejak said.

'All of my people do,' Kov said. 'Now, what truly matters is what we find underneath the mound. Let's hope this tunnel runs all the way.'

'Tomorrow we send scouts. Find out. Eat, sleep now.'

In the morning the scouts came back with good news. The ancient tunnel ran another quarter of a mile, and as it ran, it rose, aiming perhaps for the middle of the mound. It ended in a crumbling wooden door, obvious Dwrgi work. They'd refrained from opening it for fear of making too much noise.

'Did you hear people moving up above you?' Kov said.

'We did,' the head scout said. 'Clomp clomp. Hollow like dead log.'

'Splendid!' Kov rubbed his hands together. 'I'll wager that means the door opens into a room of some sort. I'm going to risk taking a look. Better to do it now than wait till everyone's asleep and quiet.'

Leejak and Jemjek went with him. They hurried up the steep length of the tunnel, which rose, by his well-trained dwarven estimate, some twenty-five feet above ground level. Leejak confirmed that the original diggers must have been aiming for middle level of the barrow, where gathering parties usually found the burials and their treasures.

The door turned out to be made of planks, mossy and mouldy with age, that tore apart under Kov's bare hands like old cheese. As silently as he could he dug out a spyhole toward the bottom of one plank, then squatted down to look through. Glowing blue fungi grew in profusion in the chamber on the far side. By their light he could just make out that the walls of this room had been made of timber, whole logs, most likely, judging from the regular pattern of vertical billows under the thick crust of fungi.

He could also hear the footsteps that the scouts had described, a hollow clop clop, as if someone were walking back and forth in wooden clogs. What that person was doing escaped him – pacing the floor, cleaning something – they could have been engaged in any number of tasks.

'Anything to gather in there?' Jemjek whispered.

'I doubt it.' Kov got up. 'You can take a look, but be careful!'

Jemjek knelt down, leaned forward, and inadvertently nudged the rotted door with his elbow. With a pulpy, squishy sort of noise it pulled free of the rusted hinges and fell in a rain of mouldy splinters to reveal the further room, thick with fungus and rotting logs. Everyone froze as the footsteps above them halted. A woman's voice called out – something in a language Kov didn't know, but it sounded like a question.

The footsteps began again; the voice repeated the question. Kov waited, half-afraid to breathe, and prayed that none of the Dwrgwn would break and try to run or call out. From above a rough man's voice murmured. The woman answered, and this time she sounded afraid. Footsteps again. They slowly retreated; then silence.

Kov let out his breath in a soft sigh. 'We'd better work fast,' he whispered.

Kov got up, motioned to the others, and led them back to the waiting Dwrgwn before he risked speaking.

'We've got wood down here,' Kov told them, 'but it's damp. I don't

know how well it will burn. We're going to have to take our time and
clear out the fungus, then see how far under the fortress we can get.
But we must be silent, very very quiet.'

Leejak translated, glaring at each man in turn. Gebval stepped
forward and began talking, waving his hands, crossing them in mid-
air as if he were passing shuttles through the warp on a loom. When
he finished, Leejak gave Kov the gist of his speech.

'He say he summon water out of wood. Must dig pit for water here.
Then he summon it.'

Kov wanted to heap scorn on the idea, but working his pretend
magic would keep the spirit talker out of the way.

'Splendid!' he said. 'That will be a great help.'

Leejak raised a sceptical eyebrow but said nothing more.

Two of the Dwrgwn took shovels and began to dig an alcove into
the side of the tunnel, while the others stood ready with baskets to
take the loose earth away. Kov and Leejak walked away to talk where
they wouldn't be overheard.

'That wood,' Leejak said. 'Very old. Should be all gone.'

'Agreed,' Kov said. 'If I'm guessing aright, the Deverrians built this
place over a thousand years ago. Someone else must have been using
it since then, repaired it, even, with fresh wood.'

'Then they leave, Horsekin come?'

'Just so, but the Horsekin haven't been here long. Refugees from
the cities of the far west, would be my guess, who might have stayed
here for some hundreds of years. I don't know. If we had time, we
might find old coins and things in the ruins, but we have no time.'

'Just so. Bring it down, then get out.'

They returned to the newly-dug alcove to find the Dwrgwn digging
a cistern into its floor. Gebval stood nearby, chanting under his breath,
waving his hands back and forth. At times he shut his eyes and swayed
to some inner rhythm. On his chest the bronze knife glittered, but
the glow that fell upon it gleamed gold, too bright and too yellow to
originate with the fungi baskets. The hair on the back of Kov's neck
rose in a cold shiver. Gebval called out a sharp order. The Dwrgwn
in the cistern clambered out, whispering among themselves.

The last man out pointed to his feet – soaked through up to his
ankles. 'They've hit ground water,' Kov murmured, but he disbelieved
his own remark. Leejak shook his head in a no.

Gebval chanted on and on while the golden light grew brighter,
crept up the chain that held the knife, and covered his head like the
hood of a cloak. Kov glanced in the cistern and saw fragments of

splintered wood floating as the water rose and swirled around. Leejak suddenly swore.

'Get out of here!' he said to Kov, then turned and gave orders in Dwrgi.

Two of the Dwrgwn grabbed Gebval, who continued chanting and glowing, and dragged him along as everyone began running back down the tunnel northward. Utterly puzzled, Kov followed more slowly until he felt what Leejak had sensed – a trembling in the earth. The summoned water spilled over the cistern and began to flow down the tunnel after him as Kov ran, following the others. When they reached the level portion of the tunnel, the water slowed, but it kept on coming.

The trembling grew to a shaking. A cacophony of cracks, rumblings, thuds, and distant booms drowned out the murmur and splash of water. The Dwrgwn darted through the rough doorway from the ancient tunnel into the feeder shaft they'd constructed earlier. Gebval looked around him, then fainted, falling into the soft earth. His impromptu attendants picked him up again and ran, dragging him along. Panting and gasping for breath, Kov made it through to the new tunnel. The Dwrgwn who'd dug the cistern picked up their shovels and began forking dirt into the breach that led back into the tunnel leading to the fortress. Others pitched in, desperate to divert the swelling tide of ground water.

The noise from overhead grew louder, resolved itself into the thunder of horses' hooves and screaming from Horsekin throats. Beyond that, distantly, the cracks, booms, and rumbling went on and on. The earth around them shook as if it were trembling in fear. Kov ran back north to the closest ventilation shaft and climbed a quaking ladder. He clung to the rough wood as if he were riding a bucking horse and stuck his head out to look back.

The fortress was collapsing. Kov stared in utter disbelief as the log palings began to lean inward, slowly at first, trembling, groaning, then faster, until they fell, slamming against the roofs of the buildings inside. The buildings shook, then began to sink, tip-tilted like children's blocks. All around the mound Horsekin ran and swarmed like ants when a careless farmer ploughs up their hill. Dust rose up in huge pillars like smoke, and indeed, smoke mingled with the towering dust. Kitchen fires, most likely, had spread and caught the wooden walls.

From right below him a voice called out – Leejak. 'Get down! Run!'

Kov followed orders and splashed off the ladder into water half-way up his calves. The Dwrgwn were streaming past, rushing back north, carrying their spirit talker as well as the remaining supplies and tools. Kov and Leejak brought up the rear, splashing through the water that flowed relentlessly after them. Apparently the attempt to block the entrance into the ancient tunnel had failed. Still, as they ran, gasping and sweating, Kov realized that the flood was slowing, turning shallow, losing the race.

Under the next ventilation shaft the Dwrgwn slowed and stopped on reasonably dry ground. In the pale light that filtered down from above to meet the blue glow of the fungi baskets, they clustered around Leejak and began to all talk at once, panting between words and phrases. The spearleader held up both hands for silence while he too gasped for breath. At last the chatter stilled, and Leejak could speak.

'Very good,' he said. 'Kov, Mountain Man, what happens there?'

Kov nearly blurted out the truth, that he had no idea, but he decided that he'd best come up with some sort of explanation.

'Gebval summoned all the water out of the wood,' he began, then realized he'd stumbled on the answer. He paused often, allowing Leejak to translate. 'He also summoned water from some sort of spring or underground stream. That water was the reason the wood was so damp to begin with. The wood was so rotten that the water and the fungi were holding it together. As the fungi dried, and the water ran out, the wood couldn't bear its own weight, much less the weight of the buildings above. It fell. Meanwhile, the ground water kept rising, sweeping the dirt out from under the fortress.'

'Gebval!' two of the Dwrgwn began the chant. 'Gebval, Gebval!' Others chattered among themselves.

Leejak silenced them with a hiss and a growl. He pointed up, reminding them that the enemy still lurked above.

'They say Gebval killed fortress,' Leejak said to Kov. 'I like this not.'

'Well, he did, truly,' Kov said.

'Say it not! I tell more later.'

By then Gebval himself had roused to the acclaim. With help he stood and leaned against the burrow wall, a pale, drained little figure, as if his act of dweomer had sickened him, but malice still glittered in his dark eyes as he looked Kov's way. The northern Dwrgwn gathered around their spirit talker and turned to glare at Kov as well. Jemjek, Grallag, and Leejak stepped in front of Kov to protect him. Grallag hefted a spear. The other two growled so viciously that the northerners moved back and away.

Kov suddenly realized that if Gebval had brought down the fortress, the northern Dwrgwn would see him, the Mountain Man who'd done nothing, as fit only for sacrifice. His three protectors were outnumbered, but Leejak's authority held — at least for the moment. The other

Dwrgwn ostentatiously turned their backs and set off marching down the tunnel, heading back north toward the forest and the bridge. Leejak, Grallag, and Jemjek spoke briefly to one another, then with a gesture to Kov to follow, set off more slowly after the others.

'Tonight,' Leejak said to Kov, 'I give you spear, food, blanket. You escape. Go up shaft. I trust these not.'

'No more do I.' Kov swallowed heavily. 'But what will happen to you?'

'Naught.' Leejak shrugged the problem away. 'Cowards, these are.'

'I worry for Kov, not us,' Jemjek said. 'Horsekin all round.'

'He travel at night. He sees in dark. Horsekin do not.'

But they can sniff me out, Kov thought. Kov wondered if he were about to faint and disgrace himself. He'd be on his own, exposed, running for his life in the middle of Horsekin territory. *But free*, he reminded himself. *For all the good it's going to do me.*

His escape went smoothly. Between them Leejak, Grallag, and Jemjek smuggled supplies, a few at a time, out of the night's camp and placed them at the foot of the ladder in a ventilation shaft. Once the rest of the Dwrgwn slept, Kov crept down the tunnel and bundled the supplies in his blanket. He found a length of rope among them and used that to harness the bundle to his back. Before he climbed up, he waited, listening, peering down the dark tunnel to the faint blue glow of the camp's fungi baskets. Everyone lay still; some snored.

Kov climbed the ladder, but at the top his spear, stuck crosswise across the bundle on his back, caught in the opening. He clung to the ladder with one hand, managed to get the spear free, and threw it out ahead of him. As he clambered over the edge of the opening, clods of earth fell and landed with a plop on the tunnel floor below. He froze for a moment, but heard nothing behind him. He grabbed his spear and set off at an awkward run with the bundle thumping against his back.

Ahead he saw the dark mass of the forest, rising against the starry night. He kept running until he was gasping for breath, then drove himself to keep walking until at last, he could plunge in among the pines. In the hopes of foiling the Horsekin's keen sense of smell, he made himself a nest of pine needles. On the trunk of the tree above him, he found several globs of resin, which he smeared on his clothing. He nearly gagged on the strong scent, but he could hope that the Horsekin would smell only pine trees and not the filthy dwarf who hid under them.

Safe, he thought. *For now.*

* * *

After he'd left the Red Wolf Dun, Rori had carried Cadryc's answers to the prince's messages back to the royal alar. He lingered there for several days, lairing with Arzosah and his step-daughter, to let his wound recover from the stress of his flight east. Every morning, Neb examined the incisions, which were healing up nicely, or so the young healer said.

'No sign of infection,' Neb pronounced. 'And the gold won't become tarnished and spread corruption like the silver dagger did. I'll take the staples out later, though, once the skin's grown back together.'

'Good,' Rori said. 'It still itches, but not as badly.'

'Soon it won't itch at all. Arzosah was right. Dragons do mend fast.'

'She generally is right, when it comes to things dragonish.'

Although, he thought to himself, *human things are another matter entirely.*

Dragonish things were much on Arzosah's mind that day. When Rori rejoined her, she brought up a delicate matter. Medea had reached her hundred and twentieth year, close to the age when she would want a mate.

'I've sniffed out a few young males up north,' Arzosah told him. 'Eventually one of them will smell Medea's scent upon the wind and come flying our way. Then he'll no doubt tell the other about Mezza, as well, once she's ready. But I do worry about our son.'

'No scent of young females?' Rori said.

'None.' Arzosah heaved a sigh. 'A mother's lot is so difficult when you're a dragon. It's not like we can fly in flocks like birds or such-like.'

'Well, we have years yet before he'll be wanting a mate.'

'True, true, he's but five and thirty years old, by my reckoning. A mere child yet. But I don't want him taking an unhealthy interest in his sisters when the time comes. It's not good for the bloodlines.'

'We've raised him better than that!'

'So I hope.' She sighed again. 'I worry about the younger hatchlings in general, though, off alone like that. Don't you? One of them is yours.'

'So he is. Why not send Medea back? She doubtless finds guard work just as tedious as you do. She can care for the young ones until we return. The prince is heading for Cerr Cawnen, and our lair's not far beyond that. You can fly on home from there whilst I keep an eye on the prince.'

'Splendid! I'm looking forward to getting home. A nice cosy winter, that's what I'm longing for.'

'And so am I.'

With a yawn she snuggled closer to him. She seemed to have no idea that he was considering returning to human form. Sooner or later, he would have to tell her, if indeed he did decide to spend the winter as a man on Haen Marn instead of inside a fire mountain as a dragon. For the moment, however, he could put the decision out of his mind.

Or at least, he could try to do so. In the morning, when he was about to leave on another scouting expedition, Dallandra confronted him.

'I've been wondering,' she said. 'If you've made up your mind yet.'

'Do you mean about the transformation?' Rori said.

'What else would I mean?'

'True enough. I've not decided yet, frankly. My mind keeps going this way and that.'

'Well, it's time you steadied it.'

He considered just taking wing and flying away, but a voice in his mind whispered *coward!*

'With the dragon book still lost,' Rori said, 'I assumed that the matter couldn't be settled.'

'It may not be lost for long. Laz Moj has gone after it, and no matter what you think of him, he does have dweomer.'

'Does that mean he might find the book? Huh, I wouldn't think he could, the wretched bit of scum.'

'Rori, he's trying to make amends in this life. It's a struggle for him, but he truly wants to set his feet on the right road.'

'Well, then, more honour to him. I suppose.'

'But Laz's wyrd isn't the issue.' Dallandra put her hands on her hips and glared at him. 'Do you want to remain a dragon or not? I need an answer, Rori.'

He raised himself up on his forelegs, but Dallandra held her ground. When he snarled at her, she merely rolled her eyes in disgust.

'There's a thing I don't understand,' he said in a decent tone of voice. 'Why do I have to answer before Laz has found the cursed book?'

'Because your reluctance may well be what's keeping the thing hidden. I'm beginning to think that Evandar linked it to you, somehow or other. That may be why he put it originally on Haen Marn, because he knew you'd connected yourself to the island through Angmar.'

Rori lay down again and considered the grass directly in front of him.

'I know you've heard about currents in the astral,' Dallandra went on. 'Some waft a thing to its true owner, like the silver dagger that caused you so many years of pain. Others push a thing farther away. This book is not a real object, not as we know 'real' on the physical plane. It's drifting on the astral at the moment, waiting for you to make up your mind. It needs an answer, Rori, and by the Black Sun herself, so do I.'

With a long rumbling sigh he looked up to face her again.

'So you do,' he said, 'so you do. Ye gods, I don't know my own heart these days, and that's the honest truth. I don't know what I want. I love the freedom of the air, I'm fond of Arzosah, but there's Angmar.'

'Indeed. Perhaps you'd best go see her, and listen to what your heart tells you there at Haen Marn.'

Every muscle in his body went tense against his will. He felt himself crouch for the leap into the wind that would free him from her questions. His wings trembled, longing to spread. He fought them quiet, but his tail lashed of its own accord.

'Perhaps you're right,' he said. 'I'll think on it.'

'Please do. Sooner or later you've got to decide.'

Dallandra turned on her heel and stalked back to camp. Rori waited until she'd gone a safe distance away, then unfurled his wings and flew, heading north for another look at the Horsekin fortress.

When, on the morrow, his wings brought him gliding over the long mound, he roared with laughter at what he saw. For a long while he circled on the air currents to savour the sight. The entire top of the mound had collapsed inward like a rotted melon, revealing a jumble of stone blocks and charred wooden planks, all piled this way and that. A few of the stones showed the black marks of burning, but mud oozed among and over the rest.

From the base of the mound water oozed in rivulets that trickled off toward the river. Rori could only guess at the cause, but he assumed that the Horsekin had dug too deep and hit either ground water or some hidden spring. Near the mound stood a welter of tents and rough shelters, improvised from blankets and the like, for the Horsekin soldiers and their slaves. As he flew in lazy circles above the mess, Rori could just discern a few individuals on the edge of the camp. They were standing hands on hips and looking up at the ruins. He could imagine how forlorn and dispirited they must feel – he laughed again in a long rumble. If the Horsekin decided to rebuild at all, they'd have to build on the flat, where their enemies would have a far easier time of destroying a fortress.

Rori considered turning back immediately and bringing the news to Prince Daralanteriel and Calonderiel, but in the end, he decided to wait – just long enough to visit Haen Marn for a look at Angmar and his other daughter. He wouldn't need to land, even, merely fly overhead and spare Angmar the sight of him. He was assuming that from the air he'd be able to find Haen Marn easily, unlike the time when he'd sought it on foot. Afterwards he'd swing by the fortress on his way back to the royal alar. Perhaps by then the Horsekin would either have started to rebuild or packed up to march away, giving him more information to tell the prince.

Rori banked a wing and headed north. As he skimmed over the forest verge, he saw ahead of him a tattered bridge crossing the river. The clumsy surface of uncured timber marked it as Horsekin work, but he could tell little about it from this height. For a better look he landed, but on the solid riverbank, not the fragile structure itself.

When he saw marks like writing on the ancient stone pillars, he waddled closer to examine them. As a man and a Maelwaedd heir, Rori had known how to read, a talent extremely rare in Deverry at that time, and practically unknown among noblemen. He still remembered the mysteries of that craft well enough to recognize the marks as Deverrian letters, worn down with time, half-covered with moss. He turned his massive head this way and that as he tried to see them more clearly. *If I only had hands!* he thought. *I could brush that moss away.* Finding writing so far from Deverry proper intrigued him.

'Rori!' The voice sounded behind him. 'Ye gods! Rori! is it really you?'

Rori swung around to see a bedraggled man of the Mountain Folk running toward him from the forest. His clothes were filthy, the bundle upon his back lumpy and ill-packed, his beard long and straggly, and his face smeared with mud. It took Rori a moment to recognize the once-dapper Kov, the dwarven envoy from Lin Serr.

'It is indeed,' Rori said. 'Well met!'

'You cannot know how truly you speak!' Kov's voice trembled on the edge of tears. 'I've escaped from the wretched Dwrgwn, but now I'm at the mercy of the Horsekin, should they find me.'

'You're safe enough now. I doubt me if they'll argue with a dragon.'

Kov did weep, then. He plastered his hands over his face to hide the tears, but his shoulders trembled as he sobbed.

'Forgive me,' he mumbled. 'This last month, it's been horrible. The Third Hell, indeed!'

'No doubt! Here, Dallandra scried you out, so your cousin Mic and little Berwynna know you're safe.'

'Ah.' Kov lowered his hands. The tears had left streaks in the mud on his skin. 'Where are they? Cerr Cawnen?'

'Truly, I forget myself! You wouldn't know. After you were taken from the caravan, it was attacked by Horsekin raiders.'

'Ye gods! Maybe the Dwrgwn weren't so bad after all.'

'You might have had a bit of luck, truly. Berwynna's betrothed is dead, alas, and half the muleteers with him, but Wynni and her uncle are sheltering at the Red Wolf dun with Tieryn Cadryc.'

'Ah, I see.' Kov paused to wipe his nose on his sleeve, a gesture which only distributed the mud a bit more evenly. 'Ye gods! It saddens my heart to hear about so many deaths, but I'm cursed glad Wynni's safe, I tell you, and Mic, too. Will you take me to them?'

'Eventually.' Rori hesitated, but he knew that he had to make the trip to Angmar before his courage deserted him. 'I hope you've got a fancy to see Haen Marn, because that's where we're going first.'

'I'm sure it's the most beautiful place on earth, and all because it's not a Dwrgi hold. Never has a man been so glad to see a wyrm as I am, I'll wager.'

'No doubt.' Rori gestured with his head toward the river. 'You on the other hand need a bit of a wash, and I need your help. Can you brush the moss from those stones so I can read the letters?'

'I can. I wondered about them myself, when first I saw them.'

Kov laid aside his bundle and took off his boots, then waded into the shallows clothes and all. While he washed, Kov paused often to tell Rori about the Dwrgwn and the fortress, though the story came out in jumbled bits and pieces. Once he was reasonably clean, Kov seemed calmer, but still his hands shook as he brushed the moss off the inscribed pillar. He hunkered down and studied the letters, an act which finally soothed his troubled mind.

'Now this is fascinating,' Kov said. 'It says that this bridge was built by someone named Brennos and the council of something called vergobretes. Isn't that your King Bran?'

'It is, and the vergobretes became gwerbretion.' Rori lay down on his stomach and rested his massive head on the ground, the only way that he could get his eyes close enough to the pillar to read the words that showed how his ancestors had marched across this river over a thousand years before. 'Here, envoy, there's a thing that's bothered me for years. When I went to Lin Serr, I saw upon the doors the tale of the destruction of Lin Rej. One of the pictures clearly showed that the people of Bel were to blame for stirring up the Meradan in the first place.'

'That, alas, is indeed the case.'

'But the Westfolk didn't know that when first I joined them. Salamander had puzzled it out, but no one else. How did your people discover the truth?'

'Let me think.' Kov fell silent, but his lips moved as if he were running through memory-chains of lore. 'A long long time ago, there was a healer named Vela. She'd heard the truth from a woman of the Deverrians who was a healer, too.' He frowned, considering. 'Now, this all happened so long ago that the tale's not very complete. I think that this healer told Vela as she, the Deverrian I mean, lay dying. Her name's not been remembered, you see.'

Could it have been Hwilli? Rori thought. Her memory glimmered deep in his dragon mind, like a gold coin fallen into a stream and seen through running water. *She considered herself one of us by the end.* Kov was continuing to talk about the Great Migration of men and dwarves both.

'So this bridge,' the envoy finished up, 'has great significance as to the rightful lords of this stretch of countryside. It gives your king a claim on this stretch of country, not that the Horsekin will just give it over or suchlike.'

'Truespoken. I doubt me if the high king has the men to take it or hold it. It's not of much use to us.'

'Not now, but who knows what the future will bring?'

'You have a point. Who knows what the gods will give us? But for now, I see you've got a good length of rope. You'll have to find some way to tie yourself onto my back, because we'd best be on our way before the Horsekin or the Dwrgwn come after you.'

Once Kov had wedged himself between two of the spikes at Rori's shoulder blades, and tied himself down to boot, Rori launched himself into the air. He was expecting Kov to scream, but the dwarf merely clutched the fleshy spike in front of him a little tighter. During their long day's flight, Kov never complained once, a relief after the way Mic had moaned and screeched during the journey to the Red Wolf dun.

By sunset they reached the Dwrvawr and passed over the wattle and daub huts of the northern Dwrgi village. Kov yelled a few curses down upon them all, though doubtless no one could hear him. Rori made sure to lair that night far from the river among the rocky hills, where the Dwrgwn had no reason to go. In the morning they set off again for the east and Haen Marn. Eventually, somewhere in the afternoon, Rori's massive stomach began rumbling. He found a little valley and landed beside a stream far too shallow to harbour any Dwrgwn.

'I need to hunt,' Rori told Kov. 'Do you have food?'

'A few bits of stale bread,' Kov said. 'I might be able to catch a fish or two from this stream.'

'If I find a deer, there'll be plenty of meat for both of us. See if you can find some firewood. I doubt me if you'll want to eat it raw.'

Kov mugged sheer disgust and agreed.

With summer blooming on the hills, deer proved easy to find. Toward evening Rori spotted a herd, come out to graze on a grassy hillside. Hovering at the edge was a young stag. The herd's prime stag would lower his antlers and run a few steps toward the intruder, who would back off, only to sneak back when the elder returned to his meal. Rori waited until the young stag had retreated some distance from the herd, then plunged down and struck. One quick nip at the back of the neck, and the rival stag hung limp and dead in his claws. The herd scattered, bounding off in all directions. He ignored them and carried his prey back to Kov and their improvised camp.

Kov had managed to scrape together enough wood to cook a few gobbets of venison on a pointed green stick. While they ate, he repeated the things he'd experienced since his kidnapping all over again, but in proper order this time.

'You're telling me, then,' Rori said, 'that these otter folk have dweomer.'

'Of a sort. Very much of a sort.'

'All this cursed dweomer!' Rori paused for a long snarl that made Kov rise to a kneel, ready to run. 'My apologies!' Rori said. 'It just aches my heart, all these strange things I can't understand.'

'Mine, too.' Kov sat back down again. 'The world was so much simpler when I thought dweomer only a folk tale.'

On the morrow, Rori's heart found more to ache over when they came in sight of Haen Marn. Years before, when in human form he'd seen the island, it had appeared to him as an ordinary-looking hillock of dirt and rock rising out of a lake of ordinary-looking water. With his dragon's sight he now saw the truth.

A huge vortex of astral force shimmered before him, a twisted, convoluted mass of glimmering silver and gold threads. At moments the island appeared as he remembered it, but the image swiftly dissolved into the play of astral forces brought down and twined upon the physical plane. The entire construct glittered with strange blue lights and flashes of a pale purple unlike any natural colour he'd ever seen, whether as a man or a dragon. Every now and then he heard sounds, too, a snatch of music once, a high-pitched whistling at other times. He understood only a little, not how it had been constructed but that it had been constructed, not why it was dangerous, but that it was extremely dangerous to such as him, a less than natural form.

Rori swung wide around the vortex and saw on the lake shore a clump of shimmering grey lines forming the boulder with the silver horn. He called out to Kov to hold on tightly, then swooped down and landed near it. The dwarven envoy slid down from his back.

'There's a silver horn on that rock,' Kov said.

'It'll summon a boat that will take you to the island,' Rori said. 'I think I'll just stay here rather than fly over. Could you do me a favour?'

'But of course!'

'Tell the lady of the isle, Angmar her name is, that I'm here. She may want to come over and speak with me.'

The inhabitants, however, of the island had already seen them. Before Kov could even blow the summoning horn, the dragon boat set out from the pier to the sound of its brass gong, booming over the silent lake to frighten the water beasts away. Rori could discern Lon, still in charge of the rowers after all these years. His etheric tinged sight told him something else, too, that only one of the rowers existed as a solid, real person. The others, like the island, had been woven and crimped together out of the flickering lines of silver and gold energies. As the boat came nearer, he could discern two women standing in the bow. One he recognized as Avain, grown tall and hugely stout, her hair puffed out from her beefy face like a dragon's frill. The other was Angmar, slender and frail, her hair half-silver now, but Angmar nonetheless. The way his heart seemed to turn over in his chest told him what his decision was bound to be.

'I wish she'd not see me like this,' Rori said.

'Why not?' Kov said. 'She's known the truth for some months now, or so Mic told me. She lives in the midst of marvels, Rori. I think me she'll understand.'

'Perhaps so. But I feel shamed nonetheless.'

The boat came as close to shore as it dared. Avain jumped down into the rocky shallows and caught her mother as easily as a woman might catch a little child. As they splashed ashore, Lon called out orders. The dragon boat backed water, holding its place. Avain set her mother down on the shore, then rushed over to Rori. Her green, strangely lashless eyes were huge with excitement.

'A dragon,' she said. 'You be a dragon!'

'I am at that,' Rori said.

She clapped her hands and did a little jigging dance in front of him. He could see a bare faint shadow or mist in the sunlight, a dragon form hovering around her, but he had no idea what might have produced or caused it. Kov had arranged a polite if frozen smile as he watched Avain.

Angmar walked up slowly and laid a hand on her daughter's hip.

'Avain?' Angmar said. 'You go back now. You did promise Mama.'

'Avain go back. Avain be a good girl. Avain did see the dragon.'

Angmar turned to Kov, who bowed to her.

'Will you take the hospitality of the island?' Angmar said softly. 'I be eager to speak to my lord alone.'

'Gladly, my lady,' Kov said. 'I'd rather not intrude.'

Kov waded out and threw his bundle up to Lon, then boarded, clambering over the side. Avain took a step away from her mother, looked back, still grinning in delight, then hurried to the shore and splashed back out to the dragon boat. She climbed aboard with Lon and Kov's help. At a few crisp orders from Lon, the boat turned and glided away, leaving Rori and Angmar alone, facing each other.

With a sigh Rori settled onto his stomach, tucked his front legs into his chest, and lowered his head so they could see each other at her level. Grey mottled her pale hair, yet he could see her familiar strength when she smiled at him. Her beauty had always lain in her strength, her ability to endure and still smile.

'Well, your eyes, they be the same,' Angmar said. 'Larger, but human enough.'

'They are, truly. My love, forgive me.'

'Be this your own doing?'

'It wasn't, but I did naught to turn it aside.'

She laid one hand on his jaw and stroked it. Her touch felt cool, comfortable in such a familiar way that he remembered her stroking his human face with the same gesture. Without hands he could do nothing to caress her in return. A touch from his massive paw would likely have knocked her to the ground.

'I did return before,' he said. 'Once I'd captured the dragon I was sent to find, I returned, but the island was gone.'

'Enj did tell me so. Rori, I do blame you for naught.'

His eyes filled with tears. He shook his head to scatter them. 'My thanks,' he managed to say. 'A thousand thanks.'

'Enj did tell me that the elven folk be trying to take the dweomer off you.'

'They are, and truly, I think me they can succeed. It's not without

its dangers, but if they do, then I'll return to Haen Marn for good
this autumn, at the waning of the war.'

Her smile broke through the mist of age. At that moment he could
only think of her as young and beautiful, as lovely in her way as his
daughter was in hers.

'I'll be an old man, no doubt,' he said.

'And am I not an old woman? If we do get a few years of peace
together, then I shall be content.'

'So shall I.' He repeated the words, marvelling at them, 'So shall I.'

At the pier, the dragon boat deposited Kov and Avain, then pulled
away, ready to go fetch its mistress at her signal. Kov slung his bundle
over his shoulder and followed the young giantess – as he thought of
Avain – up the path toward the manse. She was chanting a little song
in Dwarvish, 'Avain saw the dragon, Avain saw the dragon' so happily
that he had to smile. His native language sounded so sweet that he
suddenly realized how much he'd missed it, whether speaking
Deverrian or trying to make sense of the Dwrgwn's chattering tongue.
I've been an exile, he thought, *but I'm nearly home.*

Framed by the open door, a young woman, her raven-dark hair
pinned up on her head, her slender frame draped in a blue and grey
plaid, stood on the steps of the manse. For a brief moment Kov thought
she was Berwynna, but when she walked down the path toward them,
the difference in her carriage and manner showed him his mistake.
Unlike Wynni's confident stride, her walk was graceful, her smile shy
instead of boyish. *Her twin*, he thought, *Mara.*

'There's a good girl,' Mara called out, also in Dwarvish. 'Avain, will
you come into the manse?'

'Avain go to her tower,' Avain said. 'Avain saw the dragon, Mara.'

'I know, and I'm so glad you did. Can you find your tower door?'

'Avain knows her tower, Mara.'

She skipped off, a lumbering gait that reminded Kov of a dragon
waddling on the ground, and disappeared around the corner of the
manse. Mara smiled with a brief shake of her head.

'I'll go up in a bit,' she remarked, 'to make sure she's safe and well.
I gather, good sir, that you're a friend of my father's.'

'I am that, my lady.'

Kov bowed to her, and she curtsied in return with a shy bob of her
head.

'My name is Kov,' he said. 'In Lin Serr I serve as one of their
envoys.'

'Then it gladdens my heart to meet you.' She paused, looking across the lake. 'I'd hoped to meet him as well.'

'I don't know why he stayed on the shore, but I think he feels too shamed to land here.'

'That's so sad!' Her voice carried genuine grief. 'No one here holds aught to his shame.'

'Mayhap your mother will be able to tell him so. I don't mean to intrude upon you. I'll camp across the water with the dragon, but I fear me I have to beg you for some food. Your father rescued me from captivity, you see, and I came away with naught but these clothes.'

'No need to beg,' she said. 'Come in and take the hospitality of our hall. Haen Marn welcomes everyone who finds it. A man from Lin Serr is always particularly welcome.'

'My humble thanks.'

Kov followed Mara into the manse and sat down with her at the long table. An aged servant bustled in, carrying plates. As well as bread, she brought fish, pot-roasted with wild mushrooms in the coals of the big hearth. The scent made Kov swallow hard to keep from drooling.

'My thanks,' he said to the servant woman. 'You're very kind.'

'Humph! You stink of wyrm, young man!'

Before he could answer, she took herself off again. Mara hid a soft laugh behind one hand.

'My apologies,' Kov said. 'I cut a very poor figure at the moment.'

'It's of no matter,' Mara said. 'Do eat before your meal grows cold.'

After so many days of near-starving, Kov made himself eat slowly and sparingly. He had no desire to become sick in front of this beautiful woman. She asked him polite questions, mostly centring on how he knew her father, and why her father had brought him to the isle. As he talked, she listened, resting her delicate chin on one graceful hand, with deep attention.

'Truly, Kov,' she said when he'd finished. 'You've suffered so much! War with the Horsekin last summer, then taken by the Dwrgwn this! What splendid tales you have to tell, though I'll wager that you'd just as soon have led a less interesting life.'

'My thanks, my lady,' Kov said. 'And you're quite right about my longing for a little less excitement.'

Distantly Kov heard the sound of the gong, approaching across the lake. He rose from his seat with a half-bow.

'It's doubtless time for me to leave you,' he said, 'but a thousand thanks for your hospitality.'

Mara walked with him down to the pier. When Kov shaded his

eyes with one hand, he could see the glimmering white shape of the dragon, waiting across the lake. They arrived just as the boat was pulling up. With a shout, Lon tossed a hawser over one of the bollards. The rowers feathered oars and drew the ship up snug into her berth. With Lon's help, Angmar climbed up onto the pier.

'Envoy Kov,' she said, 'you're welcome to stay here rather than fly off with the dragon. He tells me that he needs must take urgent news back to the prince of the Westfolk, and he doubts that you want to go to their camp.'

'I don't, truly, but I'd not intrude –'

'It would be no intrusion. A man from Lin Serr's always welcome on the isle. Enj is off hunting on the shore, but he should return in a day or two, so you'd not lack for company.'

'Then my thanks, my lady.' Kov bowed to her. 'I'll stay gladly.'

Angmar turned back to the boat and called up the news to Lon. He smiled, then began to strike the gong hard in a regular rhythm. The sound rippled across the lake. On the farther shore, the silver wyrm stood and seemed to bow. As Kov watched, Rori took flight. His wing beats drummed as Lon let the gong quiver into silence. The sound faded as he turned in a graceful arc and flew off to the west. Angmar watched him go in utter silence. At last, when not even Kov's dwarven eyes could find the silver point in the sky, she sighed, but only once.

'I'd best go tend Avain in her tower,' Angmar said. 'Mara, if you'll tend to our guest?'

'I will, Mam,' Mara said. 'Lonna's already fed him.'

'Good, good.' At that Angmar smiled, though briefly. 'I'll fetch Avain her dinner.'

Kov bowed again, and she walked off, heading inside the manse. He turned to Mara. 'Your servant's right. I must stink of wyrm.'

'Well, that most certainly is true!' Mara smiled wryly. 'You may heat yourself a bath at our fire. We have only the one servant – Lonna, that is – and she really can't haul water any more.'

'I can bathe in the lake. I can swim, you see.'

'Truly?' She looked at him as if he were a great marvel. 'Well, around the back of the manse there's a little bench that marks a shallow cove. You can bathe safely there. The beasts don't come right up to the shore.'

'My thanks, I'll do that. But when I'm done, I'll heat myself some water to shave, if you have a razor here I could borrow?'

'I do, one that my father left behind, all those years ago.'

Besides the razor, Mara found him a clean shirt that had once belonged to Otho. Bathed, with his neck shaved and his beard neatly trimmed, in general respectable again, Kov joined Mara at the table in the great hall.

'You cut a much better figure now,' she pronounced.

'My thanks,' Kov said. 'A lovely women like you deserves no less and a great deal more.'

Smiling, she reached out with one hand, as if she were about to take his, then hurriedly drew it back with a blush. All of Kov's weariness vanished at the gesture. *There's hope*, he thought. *Oh by Gonn himself, maybe I can gain her favour!* He felt like bursting into song.

'I'm somehow sure that Haen Marn has somewhat to do with this,' Branna said. 'In my meditations, I keep seeing a golden bird, a piece of jewellery, I mean, not a live bird. It's flat with outstretched wings, a brooch, I think it is.'

'And this does make you think of Haen Marn?' Grallezar said.

'It does, but I can't understand why.'

Grallezar considered, sucking a thoughtful fang. They were sitting in the dweomermaster's tent, early on a wet afternoon, with the rain drumming on the leather roof above them. Now and then a drop made its way through the smokehole and splashed on the cooking stones set on the floor.

'I feel like there's knowledge trying to reach me,' Branna said, 'a flood of it, like the rain outside, but all I get is the occasional drop or trickle.'

'Meditating does seem that way often. Your dreams – see you the golden bird in them?'

'Only once. In the dream I knelt by a stream and dropped the bird into it. In the Dawntime, my people gave gifts to the gods by putting things in streams and rivers. That's what my father's bard told us, anyway, when he was telling an ancient story.'

'No doubt a bard would know such things,' Grallezar said. 'But I think me there be more to it. This bird, it like to be your key to this lock. When next you sit to meditate, make you a picture in your mind of the bird. Hold it there and think the name of Haen Marn. Maybe somewhat else will rise around the image.'

'I'll do that. I'll have time alone when Neb goes to tend the wounded.'

'How be the man called Hound?'

'His wound is healing clean.' Branna smiled in deep pride. 'Neb was right about things living on wounds. Kill them, and the wound heals.'

'Splendid! Now let us hope that he does find the truth of illnesses, too, and some way to kill those tiny enemies, if truly that be the cause of illness.'

'He will. I have every faith in him. I know he will.'

That evening the rain stopped. When Branna stepped outside for a breath of fresh air, she saw stars shining through long drifts of ragged clouds. As the wind blew, the stars would disappear under the scudding grey darkness, only to re-emerge and shine as before when the clouds moved on. *That's what the knowledge is like, too,* she thought. *Bits of the old days shine through.*

As she was falling asleep that night, Branna tried to keep the golden bird in her thoughts, in hopes that she'd dream about it again. When she woke in the morning, however, she could remember nothing of her dreams except a confused image of weeping women, dressed in rags. That image was so strong that it stayed with her all morning. The more she meditated upon it, the more she felt the desire to help them. In her meditation, the golden bird seemed to speak and accuse her of somehow deserting them. It all seemed so important that Branna decided she'd best ask for help with untangling the images. She darted through the rain to Grallezar's tent, only to find Dallandra there as well. The two masters, however, told her to come in.

'We were speaking about various things,' Grallezar pointed to a leather cushion. 'But none be pressing matters.'

'My thanks.' Branna sat down on the cushion. 'I might have received a hint of my true wyrd, and it does seem to involve Haen Marn. I was meditating on the golden bird, just like you told me to. The images that rose were all of the Old Ones, the people who lived in Deverry before the Deverrians came, I mean, not the Westfolk. I saw women weeping and holding out their hands to me. So I thought, I'm meant to help them. Does that sound right?'

'It does,' Grallezar said. 'But you do have much work ahead before you do understand those weeping women fully.'

'Oh, I'm sure of that. They seemed to have somewhat to do with Haen Marn. I saw glimpses of the island, or rather, an island that my mind called Haen Marn.'

'That be an important difference, truly. 'Tis good that you do see it.'

'Well, what I see doesn't match what Laz and Wynni told us. I see the island in a big lake, not a small one, and when I looked to the shore, I saw pine forests, not oaks.' Branna frowned, considering. 'And this is silly, I know, but when I was meditating on what the island looked like, I kept thinking "trout". I'm sure a lake like the one I saw would have trout in it, but still, it seemed, well, silly.'

Grallezar considered, sucking a thoughtful fang. Outside the wind howled and shook the leather walls in a summer rainstorm.

'Tell me,' Grallezar went on. 'Saw you any new thing about the lore behind Haen Marn?'

'The one detail I remember,' Branna said, 'is that it could move. Not just to protect itself, I mean. We all knew that. But the Westfolk dweomermasters somehow or other could make it move where they wanted it to go.'

Dallandra had so far kept silent, but now she cleared her throat, just quietly. Grallezar glanced her way and nodded to give her permission to join this discussion twixt master and pupil.

'That's utterly fascinating and very important, I should think,' Dallandra said. 'Back before he became a dragon, Rhodry told me about his time on Haen Marn, and now Laz has, as well. Both of them mentioned the great hall of the manse. It has carvings on the walls, great swags of carvings, some of which seemed to them to be Elvish digraphs. Others, Laz told me, looked like the sigils of the various lords of Aethyr, and still others were sigils that he didn't recognize.'

'I do wonder, then,' Grallezar said, 'if the secrets of the isle be graved on those walls for all to see but few to read.'

Dallandra looked at Branna and raised a questioning eyebrow. Branna shuddered, suddenly cold in the warm and stuffy tent. She had, she realized, just felt an omen-touch. 'I think that's true,' she said. 'If I read the omen a-right.'

'An omen, eh? So!' Grallezar clapped her hands together. 'I think me you be linked to this isle more deeply than we did think before.'

'Indeed,' Dallandra said. 'When the time's right, you and I will go there and see if we can read the walls — well, of course, if your master allows.'

'Huh! Kind of you to ask.' But Grallezar was smiling. 'I think me it would be an acceptable thing if my apprentice did get a glimpse of grand secrets. Truly, then she might even devote herself to her beginner's studies with a bit more zeal.'

Branna felt her cheeks burn with a blush. The two older women laughed, just gently, as if they too were remembering how it felt to be young.

That evening, when they were discussing their day's work, Branna told Neb about the carved walls of Haen Marn.

'I wonder what those other sigils are,' she finished up. 'The ones Laz couldn't recognize.'

'I wonder, too,' Neb said. 'The healer who lived in Trev Hael used some odd-looking symbols for various minerals, like brimstone and quicksilver. She wrote them on labels and suchlike. She told me once that they were ancient, maybe Rhwmani or even Greggyn.'

'Do you think they might have been Elvish?'

'It could well be. I'll write them out and ask Dalla in the morning.'

By a golden dweomer light Neb found a scrap of pabrus and mixed up some ink. Branna watched as he drew the symbols. At first they looked like meaningless squiggles and naught more, but once he'd finished a row of them, she noticed that they were all composed of some dozen marks arranged in different orders.

'That one with the crescent over a straight line,' Branna said to Neb, 'is that quicksilver?'

'It is.' He looked up in surprise. 'What made you say that?'

'I don't know. But the one with the crescent under the line, is that the metal silver?'

'Right again! Dead silver, I suppose you could call it, so the crescent above the line might be the mark of some lively thing, like quicksilver.'

For hours they pored over the symbols, trying to discern which mark denoted which property. In the morning, when they took their discoveries to Dallandra, she told them that the symbols indeed belonged to an ancient Elvish way of describing various natural substances.

'What I wonder about,' Dallandra said, 'is how your herbwoman in Trev Hael learned them.'

'She told me they'd been handed down to her from her master in the craft,' Neb said. 'That's all I know.'

'In a way it doesn't matter. This is a very valuable thing you two have done, breaking these symbols down into their marks. Neb, please write the meanings up on fresh pabrus. This lore is too valuable to lose.'

'Do you think it will help when we get to Haen Marn?' Branna said.

'I do. I've been thinking about those unknown sigils on the walls. If they're composed of some of these marks, deciphering them's going to be much much easier.'

'A question,' Neb put in. 'How are you going to get everyone to Haen Marn when the time comes? I'm assuming you'll want the other masters to help you.'

'You're quite right about that, but I don't know how we'll get there.'
Dallandra smiled, a trifle ruefully. 'Dragonback, if naught else. I'm
sure Rori would carry us there – well, assuming he's made up his
mind about the transformation, but Arzosah is another matter entirely.'

When Rori left Haen Marn, he flew a wide loop north, searching for
the wagon train of migrating Horsekin. He suspected their goal to
be the fortress which Dwrgi dweomer had destroyed, but when he
flew over the remnants of that construction, he saw no sign of the
migrants. He counted up the days that had passed since he'd spotted
them and realized that they should have arrived, even allowing for
wagon breakdowns and the like.

The warriors' tent camp remained standing around the ruins. He
circled high above it to spy on the Horsekin below. Gangs of slaves were
removing the earth from the broken mound while the Keepers of
Discipline, prominent in their red tabards, kept watch. Now and then
he heard the faint sound of a whip cracking and a slave screaming in
answer. Much of the mound had turned to mud. One set of slaves filled
big baskets with the stuff whilst a second set carried it off to dump it
on the ground nearby. As far as Rori could tell, they were spreading the
earth evenly over several acres of the dusty plain, an activity that struck
him as pointless until he realized that other slaves were ploughing the
darker earth under. From the scent he could tell that the leavings of the
camp's horses and mules were also enriching the ground.

Released from its long captivity under the mound, the spring had
carved out a little stream bed in the days since he'd been gone. It
now ran gleaming into the river nearby. Rori saw not a single barge
on the river, though their previous cargoes of stone blocks still stood on
the river banks. The Horsekin might still be planning on building a
fortress at the spot, he supposed, but he'd not be able to tell that
from the air, not yet, at any rate. He'd seen enough to report to Prince
Dar. Down below the tethered horses were beginning to dance and
pull at their ropes. They had smelled him. With a flap and boom of
wing he flew up higher, circled one last time, and flew off south.

Rori found the Westfolk camp some miles west of its last location.
He circled it once, looking for Arzosah, but she was gone, off hunting,
most likely. The thought of telling her about his decision to return to
human form made him shudder and twitch in mid-air. With much
flapping of wings he righted himself and picked a spot to land down-
wind of the flocks. As he was gliding down, he saw some of the
Westfolk leaving the camp – Prince Daralanteriel, Calonderiel, Ebañy,

and Dallandra. He settled in the warm grass, furled his wings, and waited as they came jogging up to him.

'News!' Rori called out. 'Those otter folk turn out to be cursed interesting and more than a little dangerous!'

'To us or to the Horsekin?' Cal said.

'The Horsekin. And Envoy Kov has a thing or two to do with this tale, as well.'

The Westfolk sat down in the grass near his head to listen. As he talked, Dar and Cal interrupted constantly with questions and comments about the fortress and the Horsekin. Ebañy asked for details about the Dwrgwn, but Dallandra said nothing, merely listened to his recital. When Rori finished, she lingered, though the others returned to camp. She got up from the grass and stood facing him.

'Well?' Dalla said.

'I've made up my mind,' Rori began speaking in Deverrian. 'If you can turn me back to the man I was before, it will gladden my heart.'

'Well and good, then.' She smiled at him. 'I'll tell Val and Branna. We'll do a formal scrying ceremony for the book, and that should set the astral currents flowing in the right direction.'

'Will you need me to be here for it?'

'We won't. Why?'

'I'd best leave straightaway. Do you remember the Horsekin migration I saw? They should have reached the new fortress by now, if they were going there. They haven't, which makes me wonder, just where are they heading?'

Dallandra shuddered as if she'd turned suddenly cold. 'Indeed,' she said. 'I think me we'd best have an answer to that, and soon.'

'Just so.' The dragon paused to rumble with laughter. 'And we don't need dweomer to find them as long as I have eyes. The book, on the other hand –'

'Well, if we don't find it, mayhap we can devise some sort of dweomer on our own to turn you back again. It might be very dangerous.'

'To you and Val?'

'To you, my dear wyrm.' Dallandra patted him on the jaw. 'I'd hate to strip you of this form and not be able to get you back into the old one. And please!' She held up one hand for silence. 'No chatter about your Lady Death!'

'I shall hold my tongue, then.' He rumbled again. 'If you'll move a safe distance away, I'll fly off. The thought of those immigrants troubles my heart.'

* * *

Valandario had just finished casting a divination when she heard Dallandra calling her. She took a quick look at the arrangement of gems on the scrying cloth – nothing of particular interest – then went to the door of the tent to answer.

'I need to consult with you about a ritual,' Dallandra said. 'Concerning the dragon book. Laz hasn't been able to find it, and I'm wondering if the time's truly ripe.'

'Come in, then,' Valandario said. 'What's brought this on?'

'Rori's finally made up his mind. He wants to be transformed.'

'Finally, indeed!'

Dallandra ducked under the tent flap. They stood looking down at the gemstones glimmering on Valandario's divination cloth.

'Naught there about the book,' Val said. 'You mentioned a ritual?'

'I've come to realize,' Dallandra said, 'that the dragon book generates a current on the astral. That current most likely flows toward Rori. He can't retrieve it when he's flying all over the Northlands.'

'He couldn't pick it up without hands, for that matter, even if it landed on his snout.'

Dallandra laughed. 'Just so. There are spirits attached to it, and spirits are just so literal-minded. It's a very powerful artifact. All of Evandar's creations were.'

'It's a pity he didn't realize it.'

'What do you mean by that?'

'Well, do you think he considered the consequences when he unleashed these things upon the world? Or were they just toys to him?'

Anger flared in Dallandra's eyes. Valandario looked steadily back until Dallandra shrugged and turned half-away. 'Perhaps they were. Consequences – no, he didn't understand them, not at first, anyway.' Dalla sighed and turned back. 'But about the ritual, I thought we might see if the current could be redirected toward Laz.'

'Very well. I suggest we hold the ritual just before dawn. That will enlist the sun's power. As it rises, it'll shed its light upon us and the query both.'

'I like that idea. Will you take the east, then?'

'Yes. And if we put Grallezar in the south and Branna in the west, that leaves the north for you.'

'That's appropriate. I'm the one who's going to have to wrest this dweomer out of the darkness.' Dallandra paused, thinking. 'We'll let Neb stand as sentinel. He does so resent being left out of these workings.'

'I have no objection to that. I've been meaning to ask you, in fact, if he'll be part of the Haen Marn ritual.' Val smiled briefly. 'Assuming we ever find the wretched book, that is.'

'No, he won't. The dragon represents a tremendous binding of male force. I think it'll be best to have the counter-balance be as female as possible.' Dallandra paused again. 'I'll have to meet Mara – Berwynna's twin, you know – before I can tell if she should take part. From what Laz said, she's mostly untrained.'

'The sentinel again, then. Um, another question. How are we going to all get to this island? I take it you can't hold one of the roads open long enough for all of us.'

'I may not have to. It may be possible to bring Haen Marn to the Lake of the Leaping Trout. Branna had a vision while she was meditating. She thinks that might have been one of its original homes.'

'One of them?'

'That's all she knows. Speaking of being untrained and all that, she doesn't know how to extend her visions yet. We shall see, however, sooner or later. Assuming, as you say, we can find the wretched book.'

On the morrow, some while before dawn the dweomerworkers – Valandario thought of them as a warband of sorts – trooped out of the camp and walked out into an untrammelled stretch of grass. Val and Dalla trod out a ritual circle, marked it with powdered charcoal, then used their consecrated swords to level the grass within. Since they wanted to put the spirits of the working at ease, they laid the swords down to make an equal-armed cross in the circle's centre. Neb, however, kept his sword when he took up his place, not as part of the circle, but between it and the camp.

From her place with her back to the dawn, Valandario sang out the ritual evocation of Aethyr. From their stations at the other cardinal points, the other dweomerwomen sang back their responses.

'In the name of the Kings of Aethyr,' Val finished up, 'I declare this circle a place of safe visitation for their subjects.' With wide arm movements, she sketched the sigils of the Kings into the air.

'So we do pledge,' the three chanted in unison.

In the gauzy silver light of the first dawn the air within the circle became not quite visible but oddly present, as if it suddenly weighed more than the air outside the ritual marking. It seemed to quiver with unseen lives. In the centre, just above the cross of swords, a glowing point appeared and took on colour, a peculiar lavender at first, then changing to an unnaturally metallic turquoise. The point widened itself to a line. The line curled round into a circle, floating parallel to the ground. The circle expanded up and down, forming a glowing pillar of silvery light shot through with turquoise and lavender gleams and glints.

Among the glimmerings of coloured light a form appeared, vaguely human, vaguely female, her flesh dead-white, her blue dress strangely fleshy. She stepped out of the pillar and curtsied to Valandario, then turned back to point at the pillar. Inside it gleamed a long line of gold light, hovering perpendicular to the earth.

'Behold this spirit,' the white woman said, 'released from a crystal's greedy maw by she who stands in the north. He has come to aid you.'

'My thanks.' Dallandra stepped forward and addressed the light inside the pillar. 'My thanks for your aid.'

The spirit bent itself slightly as if bowing to her. Dallandra stepped back to her station.

'We have summoned you to ask about the dragon book,' Valandario said. 'We know it lies to the north. We have sent a man to find it, but it seems to flee from him.'

'The book belongs to the silver wyrm,' the white spirit said.

'True, but he cannot claim it. He has no hands. Nor can he hold a steady purpose in mind with war so close to us.'

Inside its gleaming pillar the golden line thickened and pulsed.

'Is the man with the burned hands and face your messenger?' the white woman asked.

'He is.'

The female spirit stepped back several paces until she stood up against the pillar. The golden spirit inside pulsed and shrank, twisted and pulsed the more while she stood with her head cocked to one side, as if listening. Eventually she spoke again. 'He who has the book has been bound.'

'With chains?' Valandario said.

'With custom alone. A slave, he is, and no longer a man, though he once was whole.'

'I see. Can you free him?'

'We know not, but we shall try. Shall we trust the man with the burned hands?'

Valandario hesitated, glancing Dallandra's way.

'You may,' Dalla said at last. 'To a point. If he makes any move to bind you, flee. Listen not to a word, just flee.'

'So we shall do.'

As the white spirit stepped back into the pillar, the golden line flickered once and disappeared. Slowly her form dissolved into gleams and sparks of coloured lights; then she too vanished. The pillar shrank back to a circle, the circle to a line, the line to a point – and then nothing. The air returned to mere air.

'It is over,' Valandario called out. 'May all spirits bound by this ceremony go free!' She used her foot to scatter some of the charcoal and make a wide break in the ritual circle. 'I declare this place a place on earth and naught more.'

'So do we declare,' the three responded. 'It is over.'

As they all trooped back to camp, Valandario noticed that Branna and Neb, both of them wide-eyed, their faces flushed with excitement, hurried on ahead. They were talking about the ritual in low voices, leaning toward each other as they walked. When Neb took Branna's hand and drew her a little closer, Valandario's sudden stab of envy took her by surprise. She did her best to suppress it and look elsewhere, but reaching her tent came as a relief.

Once she'd eaten, Valandario went to talk with Dallandra further. The ritual had left her tired enough for sleep, but though the sun still hung low over the eastern horizon, the camp had come alive. Children and dogs raced around, yelling and barking. Some of the adults were standing between their tents, talking and laughing. Even though Valandario's tent stood on the edge of the camp, the noise penetrated the heavy leather walls.

Dallandra's tent was just as noisy. Val found her fellow dweomer-worker nursing the baby, while Sidro sat nearby, ready to take Dari when she was done. Val sat down on a cushion and stifled a yawn. The baby pulled away from the breast just long enough to glance Val's way, then returned to her meal. *She's not Loddlaen*, Valandario reminded herself. *She's someone new now.* Dallandra yawned with a shake of her head.

'I'm tired, too,' Dalla said. 'But Dari isn't.'

'Most like she'll sleep soon enough,' Sidro said.

Valandario suddenly realized that she'd not included her apprentice in the ritual. 'I need to apologize to you,' she told Sidro. 'I should have asked you to come along this morning.'

'No need for apologies,' Sidro said, smiling. 'I do think me that my studies, they must soon take less of my day. I be pregnant again.'

'Well! Congratulations!' Valandario hoped she sounded sincere. 'That's lovely.'

'Not that I wish to leave the dweomer behind,' Sidro said. 'But until the little one be born, my mind, it will be clouded. Bearing children does take my folk that way.'

Once Dari had finished nursing, and Sidro had taken her out of the stuffy tent into the fresh air, Valandario asked Dallandra the question that was nagging at her. 'Why did you warn those spirits against Laz?'

'It's not because of Laz as he is now,' Dallandra said. 'It's because of who he was. Not in his last life, but the one before that. Alastyr treated spirits like so many slaves. I'm as sure as I can be that he's the one who bound that gold spirit into the black crystal.'

'I see. That would explain why the golden spirit reacted at the mention of the man with the burned hands.' Val considered this briefly. 'He treated his apprentices the same way, from what I've heard from Ebañy.'

'Yes, I'd agree with that. That's the way of the dark masters. They break someone down and then put them back together again on their own particular warped pattern.'

Val paused, caught by her memories of Jav, lying dead in their tent. *Was Loddlaen truly to blame?* Her own question startled her. In all the long years since the murder, she'd never considered the possibility that Alastyr might have been the true killer. He'd broken Loddlaen's will with evil magicks, then used him as a weapon. *Would I blame the knife?*

'Val?' Dallandra spoke in a hesitant whisper. 'Are you thinking about –'

'Of course I am.' Val got up from her cushion. 'But you know, I think Loddlaen was bound every bit as tightly and wrongly as that spirit.' She walked to the door of the tent. 'Don't blame yourself any longer, Dalla, not for my sake. I can forgive Loddlaen. As for Laz – well, I'll have to think this all through before I see him again.'

Valandario ducked under the tent flap and walked out into sunlight. During their conversation the sun had risen and chased the shadows away.

For some days Prince Voran's army, with Laz and Faharn trailing after with the other servants, had been struggling through the broken tablelands. When they finally crested the last ridge, they saw spread out before them the rocky plateau, the heart of the Northlands. Stumps from fresh-cut trees stubbled the gentle fall of the last hill down to the plain. Someone had been cutting timber, but the only structures Laz could see were a cluster of farm buildings, a mile or so away, encircled by a grey line that most likely signified a stone wall. The faint green blush of new grain covered the fields surrounding them.

Far off, nearly out of sight, a tuft of smoke rose, perhaps from the fireplace of yet another farmhouse. The late afternoon sun gilded the scene with a serenity that Laz instantly distrusted.

'This does not look promising,' Laz said. 'Desolate, even.'

'Just so,' Faharn said. 'I'll wager that the wretched Boars have joined up with the Horsekin by now.'

'And have taken the book with them.' Laz sighed in a flood of gloom.

The army crawled down the last hill, then spread out along a stream at its base to water their horses. Laz noticed that Prince Voran had dismounted. The cadvridoc stood off to one side with Garin and Brel Avro, while Bren knelt on the ground near the prince's feet. Brel and Voran were arguing, while Garin hovered, apparently trying to get a word in and failing.

'What's that all about, I wonder?' Faharn said.

Laz found out when Voran's manservant came running to fetch him. His worst fear – there knelt Bren, but he could find no excuse strong enough to avoid answering the prince's summons. As he followed the servant, he was calculating a few good lies. Bren glanced up, saw him, and went tense, studying his face. Although the prince never noticed, Brel Avro did, glancing back and forth between Bren and Laz both.

'Ah, there you are,' Voran said. 'Tell me, scribe, how well do you know the north country?'

'This particular stretch of it, your highness?' Laz said. 'Not at all.'

'I was afraid of that,' Brel Avro said.

Voran shot the dwarven warleader a glance that hovered on the edge of anger. 'We've been having a discussion about how far we should ride,' Voran continued. 'The avro here thinks we should turn back, and I –'

'And you are daft enough to leave your supply lines unguarded,' Brel broke in. 'And yourself miles from any allies in a country we know naught about.'

'Brel, please!' Garin snapped.

'Please, what?' Brel said. 'Hold my tongue and let a lot of good men die for naught?'

The prince and the avro glared at each other, Brel with his hands on his hips, Voran with his arms tightly crossed over his chest, as if he were subduing his sword hand by force of will.

'Er,' Laz said, 'I don't quite understand –'

'Here's the situation.' Garin stepped forward and took charge. 'Bren here tells us that the Boar planned on retreating to the north before founding a new dun. The prince wishes to go after him. The avro thinks the idea is sheer folly.'

'Ambuscades,' Brel muttered. 'Ambuscades, starvation, long sieges without reinforcements.'

'I fully intend to send messengers back,' Voran said.

'And how long will it take for help to reach us?' Brel scowled at him. 'You –'

'Your highness, honoured avro!' Garin stepped in between them, then turned to Laz. 'We were hoping you could tell us somewhat about the lay of the land.'

'I do know that this plateau stretches for a good long way,' Laz said. 'On the far side of it is Horsekin country, where doubtless this renegade clansman of yours has allies.'

'And south of that?' Brel stepped forward. 'You're a loremaster. You must know somewhat.'

'True spoken, Avro Brel,' Laz said. 'Suppose we start from my old home, Braemel, which lies in the foothills of the western mountains, far far away. The Boars may even be heading there or to Taenbalapan. Now, if you go east from either town, you reach a flat plain, which I suspect runs for hundreds of miles, crossed by rivers. The plain we see before us is doubtless an extension of it.' Laz cleared his throat. He was enjoying playing the loremaster. 'To the north is an area we call the Ghostlands, because it's filled with barrows, the graves of heroes of days gone by. Some say it's the haunt of evil spirits.'

Brel snorted in disgust.

'Some areas of the plain, those nearer the towns, are heavily forested,' Laz went on. 'There are several large rivers, including one named the Galan Targ, which marks the border of the territory the Alshandra priestesses call theirs. But I fear me I can tell you no more than that.'

'I'd think you'd know plenty about the forest.' Bren rose to his feet. 'Considering you're an outlaw and an outcast and used to live in it.'

'Here!' Voran said. 'What's all this?'

'Of course I'm an outcast.' Laz stretched out his maimed hands. 'Consider what the priestesses of Alshandra have done to me! Your highness, you know full well that I refused to bow down before their demoness.'

Bren stared at the hands, then at Laz's face, and then at the hands again. 'You weren't marked like this when last I saw you,' he said.

'What?' Laz arranged a carefully puzzled expression. 'I've never seen you before in my life.'

'Last summer, when I came to your hidey hole in the woods.'

Laz gaped at him. 'I don't have the slightest idea of what you mean by that.'

'You tried to kill me,' Bren went on. 'But the blessed priestess stopped you, and one of the men of your band gave me a horse and sword.'

'My band?'

'They were holed up in the woods with you.'

'Wait!' Laz mugged surprise again. 'Do you mean to tell me you found my brother?'

Bren's turn for surprise – he took a step back.

'I thought he'd been slain,' Laz continued. 'A nasty sort, but my brother none the less, him and his thieving ways. Are you telling me you found a man who looks much like me hiding in the forest?'

'I did,' Bren said. 'Ye gods, forgive me! This fellow was an outlaw, sure enough.'

'My heart feels torn in half.' Laz managed to squeeze out a few tears. 'Your highness, forgive my weakness!' He wiped the tears away on his sleeve and snivelled. 'It gladdens my heart that my brother still lives, but sure enough, he's a thief and an outlaw, robbing travellers on the roads, a shame and a reproach to my mach-fala, my clan, that is, in your way of speaking.'

'I see.' Voran appeared genuinely sympathetic. 'Well, mayhap I shouldn't admit this, but it's a pity we don't have him here. No doubt he knows the territory a fair bit better than any of us do.'

When Laz risked a glance at Brel, the dwarven warleader stuck his hands in his brigga pockets and arranged an utterly bland expression on his face, as if suppressing a grin. Fortunately, no one else seemed to have noticed the gesture.

'Well, one thing I do know,' Voran said. 'After the hard push we made to get this far, the men need to rest. Brel Avro, we'll discuss this further. You may go, good scribe. Doubtless you're weary and hungry.'

'I am, your highness.' Laz made him a sweeping bow. 'My thanks.'

The army spread out and made camp. While he ate his meagre rations, Laz noticed that the various captains were walking through the area and speaking to their men, appointing sentries and discussing who would stand which watch. As the sun set, the men on watch left the camp and took up posts that ringed the army round.

'That farm over there,' Faharn said. 'I wonder what the farmfolk think of all this.'

'They're doubtless terrified,' Laz said, 'and probably with good reason. Armies have been known to strip farms of every scrap of food.'

That night, after the army had camped and set its sentry ring, Brel Avro strolled over to Laz's campfire in the servants' area. Laz, who'd been sitting on the ground with Faharn, rose to greet him.

'Just a question or two, scribe,' Brel said, grinning. 'And I'll promise you that I won't be telling your answers to anyone else, unless you admit to being a Horsekin spy or suchlike.'

'Have no fear of that,' Laz said. 'They and their wretched false goddess have taken everything I cherished away from me.'

'Is that why you turned outlaw in the forest?'

Laz considered lying. The admiration visible in Brel's grin stopped him.

'It was,' Laz said instead. 'I take it you saw through my ruse about my wicked, wicked brother.'

'Of course.' The grin grew broader. 'But the prince swallowed it whole, and that's what mattered.' Brel let the grin fade. 'All I care about is you're a cursed good scribe, just as Exalted Mother Grallezar said you were.'

'She doesn't lie,' Laz said. 'It's frightening, in fact, how truthful she can be.'

'So I saw last summer. Now, I admire a man who can think on his feet, like, but be careful around the prince. He sees things a fair bit differently.'

'Apparently so. Are we really going to march out into unknown country looking for the Boars?'

'My men and I won't, no matter what his high and mightiness decides, and you're welcome to come with us when we leave.'

'My thanks. If it comes to that, my apprentice and I most assuredly will.'

'Good. We need to learn somewhat about the Horsekin tongue, and if naught else, you can teach us. As for Voran, I have hopes that Garin can talk the prince out of marching too far, for the sake of his men. It's too great a risk for too little reward. Let the cursed Boars go live with the Horsekin, say I. It'll serve 'em right.'

With a friendly wave, Brel left, disappearing into the dark between campfires. Laz sat back down and gave Faharn the gist of the warleader's remarks.

'Well, that's torn it,' Laz finished up. 'If the Boars have the book, and we're not going to pursue the Boars, how am I going to pry the thing out of the miserly grasp of Fate?'

'We don't know if the Boars still have it,' Faharn said. 'Maybe the spirits have managed to drop it by the side of the road or some such thing.'

'You know, that's quite possible. I've not scried for it today. Let me see what I can see, if anything.'

Laz considered using the campfire as a focus, but he feared that the bright flames would mask the candlelit glow that usually accompanied his glimpses of the dragon book. He fed a handful of green sticks into the fire, then stood as the smoke plumed up. In the grey billow he saw a candle gleam. He focused his mind upon the dancing glimmer and thought of the dragon book.

He saw a page by suddenly bright candlelight – the Elvish lettering, the red runes scribed at the top, and a pair of hands, long fingers, and the cuffs of rough brown sleeves as the reader turned a page. Laz tried to follow the sleeve up to the face, but the vision began to dissolve. When he returned his scrying gaze to the book, the vision clarified again.

This new page looked exactly like the last, as apparently the reader discovered. His hands turned the page back, then forward again with an irritable brush of his fingers. The hands closed the book with a snapping motion. Laz saw the dragon motif on the cover as the reader moved, standing up, walking a few steps, to judge by the motion of the book and the hands. The hands laid it down on an open saddlebag lying on a pile of sacks. Laz caught a glimpse of a wall, a rough plank wall made of fresh-cut wood, before the hands slid the book into the saddlebag, then hid the bag under the top sack.

Laz broke the vision, then sat down rather suddenly. The smoke and the scrying had combined to make him dizzy. Faharn moved closer in alarm, but Laz waved him away.

'You know,' Laz said, 'you were quite right. I don't think the Boars have the book, not if they're fleeing across the plains to reach Horsekin territory. I saw the book and the hands of the person who has it. He's inside some kind of wooden shelter, and I doubt me if the Boars are dragging a privy with them or suchlike.'

Faharn snorted with laughter.

'I suspect the astral currents have changed direction,' Laz went on. 'The candlelight seemed a fair bit brighter than usual. The vision was much clearer and more detailed, too. The flow seems to be drifting our way for a change.'

'Could that mean the book's close by?'

'No, distance has little influence over scrying. If you can see the thing at all, it doesn't matter how far –' Laz stopped, struck by an idea. 'Here! The farm buildings! They're made of wood, just like the wall of that shed or whatever it was in the vision. And I saw a pile of cloth sacks, the same kind as farmfolk use to store grain.'

'Ye gods! I wonder if the Boars left that slave behind for some reason and the book with him.'

'It would be a splendid piece of luck if they had, so splendid that I doubt it. Still, in the morning I'll scry again. Let's hope that the army doesn't turn around and retreat straightaway at dawn.'

Late that night Laz woke from a sound sleep to see that he had a different sort of visitor. The white spirit in the peculiar blue dress was standing beside the banked fire.

'Have you seen the book?' she said in Deverrian.

'I have.' Laz pushed his blanket back and sat up. 'Is it nearby?'

'It is. The beast-marked man still holds it.'

'Where he is?'

'Inside there.' She waved vaguely at the north.

'Do you mean the farm?'

'I know not what that is.' She frowned, then turned around and pointed in the general direction of the buildings. 'Inside there.' She turned back and began to fade, growing first pale, then translucent, then gone.

Laz grabbed his boots from the ground next to him, and after a brief struggle got them on. He stood up and looked around him. In the east a faint silver light lay along the horizon, though the stars overhead and to the west still shone brightly. All around him men lay asleep, wrapped in blankets or lying restlessly on top of their bedding.

Had he really seen the spirit, he wondered? Or merely dreamt the entire incident? They had never exchanged the sigils that would have confirmed a genuine manifestation. Even if she'd truly appeared to him, her comment of 'inside there' might have meant the structure he'd glimpsed in his vision, or it might have meant 'somewhere on the vast plain'. He would have to wait and see what he could learn later in the day.

It was several hours after dawn before Prince Voran, with an escort of several hundred armed men, rode over to the farm. Laz managed to talk himself into joining Envoy Garin on the excuse that the prince might need a translator. The farm buildings huddled inside an earthen wall – a round house, a barn, a scatter of sheds, all with thatched roofs. As they rode up to the stout wooden gate, three big black dogs rushed forward, barking. From inside the house a woman screamed at them to come back. Slowly, reluctantly, they obeyed.

The woman got the dogs inside, then slammed the door shut. Only the clucking of frightened chickens, back by the barn, broke the silence.

'Halloo!' Voran called out. 'We mean you no harm.'

No one answered. Garin urged his horse up beside the prince's, and they conferred about the best way to gain the farmers' trust. Laz took the opportunity to scry for the dragon book, only to see nothing but darkness, most likely the inside of the saddlebag. Still, he felt an odd tingling sensation in his maimed hands, as if he were running them over the leather cover. He could almost feel the edge of the dragon-shaped appliqué. Perhaps the spirits guarding the book were trying to send him a message, that indeed it lay nearby.

Laz rose in the stirrups and looked over the farmyard. Off to his right, back near the barn, stood a round wooden shed. He could just discern that a wooden bar held the door shut on the outside. For a brief moment a golden line of light flickered on the roof. *It's there!* He knew with an absolute certainty that the dragon book lay inside that shed. But why was the door barred from the outside? To keep the slave scribe in, perhaps?

By the gate Prince Voran and Garin had finished speaking. Voran turned his horse to face his escort.

'Men,' he called out. 'We're pulling back to some little distance. These people are never going to open up with an army at their gate. Envoy Garin and the translator here will parley.' Voran paused to point out five men at the front of the escort. 'And you five will stay as guards. Keep your hands away from your weapons unless someone threatens the parley.'

While the main force trotted off some hundred yards or so, Garin disposed his five guards a few feet away. With a wave to Laz to follow, the envoy rode back up to the closed gate.

'Halloo!' Garin called out. 'We truly do mean you no harm! I've got a good woodsman's axe here of Mountain workmanship. I'll exchange it for some information.'

Only the chickens clucked in answer, but Garin and Laz waited, listening to the silence from the house. Finally the door opened partway. A man slipped out, a tall fellow, dark-haired, dressed in shabby brown clothes. His shirt in particular was so near to rags that Laz could see skin through holes in half-a-dozen places. He walked to a spot half-way between house and gate, about twenty feet from the envoy. The way he stood struck Laz as odd, not bent-backed like every other Lijik farmer he'd seen, but straight and proudly.

'Be it I may see this here axe?' he called back.

Garin unsheathed the axe, which had been hanging from his saddle peak, and held it up. In the sunlight the good dwarven steel of its head gleamed, more precious than silver out in this isolated area.

While the fellow ambled up to the gate, Laz took the opportunity to study the shed with the barred door. From this distance he couldn't be certain, but the door seemed to be quivering, as if someone were banging or pushing on it from the inside.

'What be it you be wanting to know?' the farmer said.

'Do you serve the Boars of the North?' Garin said.

'I did once.' The fellow paused to spit on the ground. 'Bastards.'

'Do you know where their dun is?'

'The hells for all I care! They did move us out here.' He waved one arm to indicate the plateau. 'Then they did ride away, off to the north. I hear tell that they be joining them there Horsekin, but I know not if that be true or false.'

'I see.' Garin nudged his horse, who moved forward a few steps up to the gate. The envoy leaned over and handed the farmer the axe. 'Here you go, and my thanks.'

'My thanks to you.' The fellow took the axe in both hands and hefted it, then swung it one-handed as if testing the balance. 'This be a good thing.' Axe in hand, he began walking back to the house.

Laz and Garin rode off side by side to rejoin the prince, who was leading his escort forward to meet them. Laz turned in the saddle to speak to the envoy.

'Farmer my arse!' Laz said.

'Umm?' Garin said. 'What do you mean?'

'The way he stood, so proudly, and the way he swung that axe like a weapon. His hands were calloused, but his fingers weren't all twisted and deformed from grubbing in the dirt. And his legs – those torn brigga couldn't hide how bow-legged he was. He's spent most of his life on horseback, I wager.'

Garin gaped at him.

'He's not a farmer.' Laz sighed in sheer exasperation, that the envoy couldn't seem to see the obvious. 'He's either a member of the Boar's warband or ye gods, maybe even one of the Boars themselves.'

Garin let out a whoop of laughter, quickly stifled, since the prince had ridden up to them. 'Hidden in plain sight,' the envoy said.

'Just so.' Prince Voran had apparently heard enough of Laz's discourse to agree. 'You've got good eyes, scribe.'

'My thanks, your highness.' Laz made a half-bow from the saddle.

'Let's go back to camp.' Voran nodded at Garin. 'I want to discuss this with your avro. There's plenty of pine trees up on the hill. If we throw a few pitchy torches onto one of those roofs, the pigs should come running out of their sty fast enough.'

And the book will roast with them, Laz thought. He bowed again. 'Um, your highness? May I have your permission to speak?'

'You may.' Voran inclined his head in Laz's direction.

'I was thinking that it would be a great pity to burn their stored grains and the like with them. It's a long ride back to Deverry, and some of the men are growing worried about rations.'

'That's a sound point, your highness,' Garin put in. 'Food's always important to an army.'

'True enough,' Voran said. 'Well, I'll discuss this with Brel and see what he can come up with.'

Brel came up with something quite simple: let the dwarven axemen break down the gate, then have the horsemen ride straight into the farmyard. First, however, as Garin pointed out, it would be best to scout out the second farm they'd seen in the distance north of the first one.

'We'll probably want to take both of them at once,' Brel said. 'Those barns won't hide more than a couple of dozen swordsmen each, so it should be safe enough to split our forces.'

To convince their prey that they'd believed his ruse, Voran led his men to the second farm. There again Envoy Garin traded a dwarven steel axe for the information that the Boars had fled north, doubtless to join up with the Horsekin in relative safety while their disgruntled supposed supporters languished in grave danger. This second farmer looked even more like a nobleman than the first.

'Oh, it be a long way to them there Horsekin cities,' he said, 'or so I been told, all the way across this stinking rocky plain. Don't know how we're going to feed ourselves up here.'

'Then why not go back to Cerrgonney?' Garin said. 'I doubt if anyone would arrest you or suchlike. Cerrgonney lords are always short of folk to tend their lands.'

All the alleged farmer could do was stare wide-eyed at Garin. Laz suppressed a grin.

'It's their goddess, I suppose,' he said to the envoy. 'Come now, my good man, you worship Alshandra, don't you?'

The fellow swallowed heavily and glanced away.

'What be it to you?' he said at last.

'Naught,' Laz said. 'Shall we go back to camp, envoy?'

'Just so,' Garin said. 'My thanks for the information.'

Voran and Brel decided they had no reason to wait until morning for the attack. They led their forces to a spot midway between the two farms, then split them into two squads of mixed cavalry and axemen. When they marched off, Laz followed the squad targeting the first farm.

The battle, such as it was, ended quickly. The axemen broke down the gate. The prince's riders poured into the farmyard. When armed men rushed out of the farmhouse and the barn, the front rank of swordsmen cut them down with an efficiency that reminded Laz of slaughtering sheep. The man who'd posed as a farmer in the parley ran out of a back door and headed for the wall, but riders chased and caught him. They dragged him back alive, more or less, to face Prince Voran when his highness returned from the second raid.

When the swordsmen dismounted, they began to looting the farm, as methodically as they'd slain its defenders. Laz rode round to the shed. He dismounted, ran to the door, and lifted the bar free of its staples. He was about to open it when it swung wide, pushed from the inside, to reveal the portly pale-haired fellow with the brand on his face. He was clutching a leather saddlebag to his chest. He stared at Laz, tried to speak, but only stared the more.

'I'm not a lovely sight,' Laz said, 'but we're rescuing you all the same. You're a free man.'

The fellow began to weep in two thin trails of tears. His head trembled, shaking no, no, no, as if in disbelief. Laz caught him by the arm with one hand, then took his horse's reins with the other. He led them both around the looters and out of the compound to safety.

By then Prince Voran had arrived with some of his men – the rest were stripping the other farm – and other prisoners as well, two men and a woman, to join the pair captured at the first farm. Voran had Bren and a raft of servants brought from the army's camp, the servants to deal with the captured supplies and livestock, Bren to identify the prisoners. Four of the prince's riders made the prisoners kneel in front of Voran, who dismounted to look them over.

Laz and the freed slave hurried over to watch. At first the prisoners glared at the prince in cold defiance, but when Bren rode up, the men swore and the women began to weep, clinging to one another. Bren dismounted and trotted over to kneel at the prince's side.

'That fellow there on the end,' Bren said, 'he's Lord Burc himself. The other's his brother, Lord Marc.'

'And the women?' Voran said.

'Their wives, your highness. Truly they all lived little better than farmers, even in that dun where I found you.' Bren shot Lord Burc a look of sheer contempt. 'Some king you are now, eh?'

For a moment Burc seemed to be about to speak, but he shrugged and kept silent, as did his brother.

'Very well,' Voran said. 'I promise you that your women will come to no harm, Burc. I'll find them a place of refuge. But I'm taking you and your brother back to Cerrgonney to answer the charges of reiving and murder laid against you there.'

'And just who be you, then?' Burc said.

'Voran, Prince of the Gold Wyvern, Justiciar of the Northern Border by the command of the high king himself.'

Burc turned his head and spat onto the ground. The Wyvern men hauled the prisoners up and dragged them away in the direction of the army's camp. Prince Voran mounted again and led the rest of his escort after them, leaving the servants to deal with the booty from the farms.

'So much for that.' Faharn had come up behind Laz during the questioning. 'Ah, this must be the fellow with the book.'

The freed slave turned dead-pale and began to tremble.

'Here!' Laz said to him. 'You must understand the Gel da'Thae language.'

'Yes, I do.' The scribe stood a little straighter and glared at him. His voice, however, was as high as a young boy's despite the fierce edge he gave it. 'I take it I'm still a slave.'

'No, you're not. I'm an outcast from the cities, myself, a scribe and loremaster, and this is my apprentice, Faharn. My name is Laz Moj.'

'I'm truly free?' His voice squeaked on the word 'free'.

'You're truly free, and if you go back with the prince, he'll find a way to return you to your true people out in the Westlands. What's your name?'

'Pol, just Pol will do. What do you mean, true people? Horsekin raiders destroyed my village when I was a child.'

'Village?' Laz blinked at him. 'The Westfolk are wandering nomads.'

'Then, alas, they're not my people.'

'But – wait!' Laz remembered old legends about those who'd fled the Great Burning. 'Do your folk live near the sea?'

'Yes, between the mountains and the western ocean, or up in the foothills, where it's easier to hide from the raiders.'

'Then I've got somewhat of great interest to tell you, Pol, and you'll have a tale and a half for the Westfolk when you finally meet them. Come with us. If naught else, you deserve a decent meal, and I see that Faharn has snagged us a chicken.'

Faharn held the fresh-killed brown hen up by its yellow feet and grinned, all fangs.

The entire army ate well that afternoon, except for the prisoners. Faharn drew the hen, then encased her in wet clay from the stream bed, and roasted her whole in their campfire. He also collected grain from the servants and made a porridge of sorts, which they ate while waiting for the chicken to cook. Once the clay covering had baked as hard as pottery, Faharn pulled the ball out of the embers and broke off the clay. The feathers came with it, and they divided up the meat.

Between bites Pol told Laz about his people – refugees from the Great Burning who'd fled west rather than east out to the grasslands. There were, he thought, perhaps two thousand of them at most, scattered in little villages and farms, living always in fear of the Horsekin. Pol's clan had been fishermen, and their exposed village on the coast far enough south for them to feel safe – until the ships came.

'We didn't know that the Horsekin had boats,' he finished up. 'But these did, just a raiding party, but there were enough of them. They came when the men were out fishing and slew the village elders before they took the rest of us as slaves.'

'Bastards!' Faharn remarked.

'Just so,' Laz said, 'and cowards as well.'

'I thought my ancestors were the only survivors from the old days,' Pol said, 'but now you tell me there are others.'

'A great many others, actually,' Laz said. 'They live as Westfolk out in the grasslands, and then I was told that there are towns in the Southern Isles, far away across the Southern Sea, and that the People from there are slowly returning to the plains.'

Pol digested this information along with his share of the hen while Laz considered the problem of the dragon book. He'd not rescued this unfortunate man only to steal from him, though admittedly he'd stolen plenty of other property in his day. *Those days are over*, he told himself. *And that was a matter of survival*. He considered any number of plans before the obvious occurred to him. He could simply ask.

'The book with the dragon on the cover,' Laz said. 'Is that a great treasure to you?'

'Not any longer,' Pol said. 'I knew that the writing had to be in the language of my ancestors, even though I couldn't read it. It was a connection to my lost home and clan, well, of a sort, and the only one I had. I saved it when one of the servant girls back at the dun was going to use the pages to light fires.'

Laz nearly choked on his mouthful of chicken. 'I'm cursed glad you did,' he said when he'd stopped coughing. 'I'm a loremaster, as I mentioned, and I'm most curious about the book.'

'Do you want it?' Pol laid his empty bowl down. 'I'd be honoured to give it you out of sheer gratitude. If nothing else, you rescued me from that wretched hut. I was terrified that the prince's men were going to set fire to the compound, and I'd be roasted alive in it.'

'I saw the door moving as if someone were banging on it,' Laz said, 'so I thought I'd best go see. Are you sure you can part with the book?'

'Of course.' For the first time all day Pol smiled. 'I don't need it now.' His soft boy's voice quivered with joy. 'I'll be returning to my people.'

'I'll ensure that you do.' Laz rose to his feet. 'Let me just see if I can have a word with the prince.'

Laz found Voran sitting on a folding stool in front of his tent. Brel Avro sat nearby, and the dwarven warleader looked as pleased with himself as a cat with a stolen fish cake. When Laz knelt before the prince, Voran gave him permission to speak.

'Your highness,' Laz said, 'today my apprentice and I rescued a man who'd been enslaved by the Horsekin. He has Westfolk blood in his veins, and he fain would return west to his people.'

'The fat fellow?' Voran said. 'I take it that the Horsekin unmanned him.'

'I fear me they did. I was wondering if your highness might grant me a boon, that you'd take the poor man under your protection and see that he gets home.'

'Easily done. We have extra horses, thanks to the Boars. But here, won't you be returning to Cerrgonney with the army?'

'I fear not, your highness.' Laz suddenly realized that he needed a good lie to explain why he'd been leaving the prince's service in the middle of nowhere.

'I offered him a position with us.' Brel Avro saved him. 'We need to learn the Horsekin language. He and his apprentice know it.'

'So they do.' Voran swung round and scowled at the warleader. 'Which is why I gave the man a position with me.'

'Your highness, forgive me,' Laz broke in. 'But what with my maiming, and the ill-will your people bear the Horsekin, my apprentice and I live in fear when we're in your territories. My scars make me an object of scorn, and poor Faharn – your folk shun or threaten him.'

'Oh.' Voran considered this for a moment. 'Well, truly, I can under-stand that. Very well, then. I'll have my captain make provision for the rescued eunuch. We'll get him back west, one way or the other.'

'You are most generous, your highness, and my thanks.'

That night, while Pol and Faharn slept, Laz sat up by the glowing coals of the campfire and gloated over the dragon book. He'd done Dallandra the enormous favour she'd asked of him. Now he needed to see what profit he could gain from it. Yet, when he considered the silver wyrm, who hated him from lives past, and the dragon's possible rage should Laz try to withhold the book, he decided that it would be best to pass it along in the same way he'd received it – freely.

Late that night the white spirit appeared to Dallandra in her tent. In the dim glow from a dweomer light, hanging at the ceiling, her womanish form looked so substantial that both Calonderiel and Dari could see her, even though she'd created herself out of etheric substance. The baby gurgled and held out both chubby arms when the spirit bowed to Dallandra. Cal merely stared, his mouth slack in surprise.

'Greetings,' Dallandra said. 'Do you have something to tell me?'

'Yes,' the spirit said. 'The dragon book now belongs to the man with the burned hands.'

'Excellent! What about the man with the beast on his face?'

'He is safe. He'll return to you here on the grass. The prince of the Children of Aethyr has promised him aid.'

'I'm glad to hear that. Laz – the man with the burned hands – is supposed to take the book to Haen Marn.'

'So he intends. I heard him speak to the commander of the Children of Earth. He will travel with them.'

'Well and good, then. You have my heartfelt thanks for coming to tell me all of this.'

The spirit smiled and nodded in an oddly human way, then disappeared. Dallandra handed Calonderiel his daughter to hold.

'I'd best go tell the others,' Dallandra said. 'Grallezar and Ebañy will want to know.'

'What I want to know is what happened to the Boars,' Cal said. 'I assume that spirit meant Voran when she spoke of a prince.'

'Yes, I'm sure she did. I'll scry for him on the morrow, when it's light, to see if there's been a battle.'

Dallandra got up and went to the door of the tent, then paused. 'By the by, not a word about the book to Arzosah.'

'Don't worry,' Cal said with a snort. 'She doesn't deign to speak to me.'

'Doesn't she? Then consider yourself blessed.'

The dragon book and its attendant astral spirits, now safely stowed in Laz's saddlebags, were travelling westnorthwest in the company of Laz and Brel Avro's dwarven axemen, heading to the dwarven city of Lin Serr across the desolate terrain of the Northlands plateau. Even though Faharn and Laz were mounted, and the axemen on foot, the two Gel da'Thae were hard-pressed to keep up with the relentless stamina of the dwarves.

Once they left the plains behind, their route wound through the foothills rising toward Lin Serr. The situation worsened as their horses wearied fast. By mid-afternoon on the third day Laz and Faharn dismounted to spare them their weight and jogged along, leading the horses, until Laz realized that he was panting for breath. Faharn had fallen some hundred yards behind.

'Hold!' Laz called out. 'Avro Brel! Have mercy!'

At the warleader's orders, the axemen stopped, then formed a defensive circle around their carts and servants, who seemed as glad of the rest as Laz was. A sweating, blowing Faharn caught up with them just as Brel strolled back to chat with Laz.

'Huh!' Brel said, grinning. 'I didn't realize we had a pair of weaklings on our hands.'

'Kindly spare me the manly jests,' Laz said. 'Consider our poor horses, who are here through no desire of their own.'

Laz's horse tossed its head with a scatter of foam, as if to underscore the point.

'Oh very well,' Brel said. 'We'll make an early camp and let the poor beasts rest.'

The army camped that night in a valley, little more than a shallow ravine, between two hills, where ground water had collected into a slow-moving but potable stream. For the evening meal Brel and Garin invited Laz and Faharn to share their campfire. As they chewed leathery cracker bread and scraped mould from chunks of cheese, Brel discussed the journey ahead.

'Won't be long before we reach Lin Serr,' the warleader said. 'But you need to get to Haen Marn, and that can be a cursed nuisance. The island never seems to stay put, like.'

'Nuisance, indeed. I hope we can find it.'

'You'll need a bit of luck for that,' Garin put in.

'Oh, no doubt,' Laz agreed, in order to be polite. Besides, how could he tell Garin that the island was easy enough to find for someone who could fly? 'Once we reach your city, we'll head off north. There's a river we can follow for part of the way.'

Faharn had been listening, his head cocked a little to one side as he tried to puzzle out the Deverrian words. Laz turned to him and gave him the gist of their conversation in the Gel da'Thae language.

'Thank you,' Faharn answered in the same. 'I must say that I'm looking forward to seeing Haen Marn. You've told me so much about it.'

Laz started to say some pleasantry, but the words refused to come. He felt as if he were choking on lumps of ice, stuck deep in his throat. The hair on his arms and the back of his neck bristled as he shivered and gasped for air. Faharn rose to his knees and turned toward him. Brel scrambled to his feet and hurried over.

'What's this?' Garin got to his feet as well. 'A seizure?'

Laz shook his head no, gulped hard, and felt the omen pass off. A trickle of sweat ran down his back, just as if he'd not been freezing a moment before.

'Danger,' Laz said. 'Ye gods, please believe me! There's danger ahead of us.'

'What?' Garin laughed, or tried to. What came out sounded more like a dog's bark. 'Nonsense! We're nearly to Lin Serr, as the avro was saying –'

'Oh hold your tongue!' Brel snarled. 'The avro is now saying he's going to post sentries on double watch. Ye gods, Garin! Didn't you see enough dweomer last summer to recognize it when it's right in front of you?'

Garin stared at him, his mouth slack, his eyes wide. With a snort Brel hurried off, snapping orders in Dwarvish. Laz felt so drained that he might have fallen asleep right where he sat, but he shook himself and rose to a kneel.

'The Northlands were crawling with Horsekin raiding parties when last I rode through them,' Laz said to Garin. 'And one of those messages you had me read said they were sending reinforcements to the Boars. For all we know, their line of march could cross ours.'

'So it might.' Garin spoke barely above a whisper. 'My apologies.'

To spare the envoy the sight of him, Laz returned to the small tent that he and Faharn shared. In the light from the campfires around them, Faharn built a little fire of their own. Laz lit it by summoning a salamander, who obligingly caught the tinder, then settled down to bask in the flames.

'I was thinking of flying to take a look around,' Laz said, 'but I'm not sure where I can find the privacy to transform. I doubt if the guards around the camp will let me past, much less let me get back again.'

'What?' Faharn grinned at him. 'You don't want to give everyone the surprise of their lives?'

'It might be amusing, seeing the looks on their faces when a huge raven flew up from the middle of their camp, but I think that's an amusement we can forgo.'

'Why not just scry from the etheric?'

'A good point. Perhaps I will.' Yet the thought made Laz profoundly uneasy. While he couldn't say why, the thought of attempting that particular bit of dweomer filled him with dread.

Another surprise did stir the camp, however, not long after. When he was setting the sentries, Brel had climbed out of the valley holding the camp. Off to the west he'd spotted a fire-glow, some miles distant but unmistakable. As he watched, the glow had held steady, indicating not a wildfire but another camp.

'Way out here,' Laz remarked, 'that means Horsekin.'

'Most likely,' Faharn said. 'Just our luck! I don't suppose it could be an innocent hunting party or suchlike.'

'Would the gods be so kind? I doubt it.'

Curiosity conquered the dread and drove Laz to find out just who was sitting around those fires off to the west. He posted Faharn as a guard, then went into their tent and lay down on his blankets. He decided that the only way to overcome his reluctance about scrying in the etheric double was to attempt it. He reminded himself that he had only a short distance to go and that no rivers or other running water intervened.

He crossed his arms over his chest and breathed deeply and slowly. Once he felt the trance take him over, he summoned his body of light, which he'd constructed as a simple man-shape in the manner of most dweomermasters. What came to him, however, was a simulacrum of the raven, pale blue yet recognizable, and joined to his body by the silver cord. Laz banished it, broke the trance, and sat up. He was shaking, he realized, trembling like a man with palsy.

Faharn stuck his head into the tent. 'Did you call me?' he said. 'I thought I heard a yelp or something like one.'

'Did you? I wasn't aware of making one.'

'Must have been someone else, then.'

Faharn withdrew. Laz got up and joined him at the campfire.

'I'm too tired to risk scrying tonight.' The statement was true enough, Laz decided. What else would have caused him to confuse his various magical forms in such an unexpected way? 'The morrow will doubtless be soon enough.'

On the morrow, at the first light of dawn Brel Avro sent a man up the hill whilst the rest of the camp packed up their gear. The scout came back with the report that indeed, he'd spotted a plume of smoke or perhaps dust rising close to the spot where Brel had seen fire the night past. Laz sought out Brel, who was discussing the situation with Garin.

'We've got two choices,' Brel said. 'We can try to sneak around them, which won't be easy. There's about two hundred of us, and that means dust and noise. We're too close to Lin Serr to just ignore the bastards, anyway. I don't want them causing trouble for the city.'

'We're not even sure that they're Horsekin,' Garin said. 'We certainly don't know how many of them there are.'

'That's true.' Brel looked straight at Laz. 'I wonder if our loremaster here can find out.'

Laz had the quick and dishonourable impulse to say no, he couldn't. The memory of the peculiar behaviour of his body of light made his chest turn tight and cold. But – another memory kept troubling him, the sincere, grave look in Mara's eyes when she'd warned him against walking an evil path.

'I probably can,' Laz said. 'I'll need some kind of private space to work in, somewhere invisible from the camp.'

'Among the trees?' Brel turned and pointed to the hillside. 'I'll take a couple of axemen, and we'll stand guard for you.'

'Done, then,' Laz said. 'I warn you, though. Don't be surprised at what you might see or hear.'

They found a shrubby thicket of sorts about half-way up the hill, with a clearing just large enough to allow the raven access to the sky. The axemen took up places among the trees with their backs to him. Laz stripped and transformed, then considered the opening above him. He hopped back to the edge of the clearing, took a deep breath, and flew, as vertically as he could manage. With a squawk the raven just cleared the grasping branches of the trees and winged free into the morning.

Laz saw the plume of smoke immediately and headed straight west. About a mile away he found a camp full of Horsekin, a gloomy prediction come true. He circled it several times, then flew back to the valley. When he reached the clearing, he heard the guards shouting below in Dwarvish, but he could understand the alarm and surprise in their voices well enough. They had seen him. He landed in the clearing far more easily than he'd flown out of it, then transformed back into man-shape.

Brel and Garin trotted into the clearing while Laz was still dressing.

'Well?' Brel said.

'Horsekin, indeed, about a hundred of them.' Laz finished lacing up his brigga, a slow process with his maimed hands, and took his shirt from the ground. 'Some of course would be slaves and servants, but most were putting on armour and buckling on weapons, falcatas, I assume. I was too high to see things that small.'

Garin crossed his fingers in the sign of warding against witchcraft. Laz pulled his shirt over his head, then sat down beside his boots.

'I'll help you with those.' Garin knelt down in front of him.

'My thanks. They are the one thing that I have real trouble with. I just can't get a good grip on them to pull them up.'

Brel looked off into the distance and stroked his beard. 'Most of a hundred, eh?' he said eventually. 'We can take them, then. How battle-ready were they?'

'Their horses were still on tether.'

'Good. That gives us a little time to fortify the camp. What's the terrain like beyond the hill?'

'A flattish valley, a stream with thick underbrush along the banks.'

'That'll do.' Brel strode off, shouting in Dwarvish – orders to his men, Laz assumed.

Once Garin had got Laz's boots on, they walked back to the camp, where a few of the men were pulling the handcarts into a rough circle. The servants were striking the tents and tossing them into the middle of the circle along with packets of supplies and bedrolls. Laz spotted Faharn, helping haul carts. The fighting men were pulling on chain mail and readying their war axes.

'We'll stay here,' Garin said.

'Good,' Laz said. 'I used to have a little skill with a sword, not much, truly, but some. Now I can barely hold one.'

Brel left twenty-five axemen behind to guard the camp, then led the rest up the hill. Laz watched them as they reached the crest and went over, marching down out of sight one tight rank at a time. Faharn and the servants joined Laz and Garin inside the circle. The axemen left on guard disposed themselves around the perimeter.

Laz sat down in the shade of one of the carts and looked up at the sky, streaked with a few pale clouds, shimmering with heat haze. When he opened his sight and thought of the Mountain axemen, he saw them as clearly as if he flew above them from a height, marching grimly downhill to the flatter terrain near the stream. On the opposite bank the Horsekin riders had pulled up in a messy line made up of clusters and gaps rather than a true formation. Their horses tossed their heads and danced as the riders unsheathed their falcatas.

As the dwarven troop formed up into defensible squares, some half-dozen riders broke free of the Horsekin pack and trotted some distance to one side, maybe twenty yards, Laz estimated. They were holding some bulky thing.

'Archers!' Laz wrenched himself from his trance. 'They've got archers.'

Garin swore aloud and began yelling at the guards in Dwarvish. Laz felt the danger around them so strongly that he could barely breathe. He had to struggle with his mind before it calmed enough for him to return to scrying.

What he saw, half-hidden in the swirling dust from the battle, appalled him. The Horsekin raiders had indeed brought archers with them – not many, but enough to torment the dwarven line. A swift volley of arrows forced the axemen to lift their shields and swing the heavy axes one-handed in feeble strokes. The horsemen would pull back, wait for the arrows to fall, then dart forward to strike with their falcatas. The front squares broke, and the survivors pulled back. Mountain dead lay scattered on the field, while only a few horses and riders had fallen.

Laz could see Brel Avro, trotting back and forth, shouting orders, he guessed, since Laz couldn't hear sound from the battlefield. The dwarves began to fall back in orderly retreat. One of the archers grew too bold. He spurred his horse forward. A solid Mountain hand axe came flying out of the retreat and caught the fellow across his face. Laz could imagine the scream as the man toppled from the saddle and fell under the hooves of the Horsekin charge.

The lead horses reared and bucked, disrupting the Horsekin line. More hand axes flew, striking randomly. They wounded only a few Horsekin, but the half-trained cavalry began to break ranks and mill around. Laz was expecting the dwarves to use the brief respite to retreat further, but instead they suddenly threw their shields and charged straight for the enemy. Long axes swung hard. Horses reared and fell, their legs cut out from under them. Horsekin rolled from their saddles and died as the axes slashed down.

The cavalry line broke. Horses fled beyond control. Riders broke ranks and shamelessly deserted, racing back toward the west. The Mountain men swung and hacked. Blades flashed up bloody in the sunlight as the remaining Horsekin turned their mounts and ran. One remnant in utter confusion broke for the hill that separated the camp from the battle.

Laz pulled himself out of his trance and screamed, 'They're coming our way!'

A wave of lathered horses and yelling Horsekin broke over the crest of the hill and started down just as the axemen left on guard rushed forward to form a line 'twixt Horsekin and camp. At the sight of them most of the Horsekin turned their horses to either side and rode back up to the crest and over. From the screaming and warcries drifting on the summer air, Laz could guess that they'd met the dwarves and their wyrd on the way down.

One of the archers, however, decided on revenge. He pulled up his horse on the crest and began loosing arrows into the camp below. Servants screamed and dodged. The axemen trotted forward and up the hill, climbing as quick and steady as only the Mountain Folk can climb. The archer turned his horse and fled with his companions.

The danger omen left Laz as suddenly as it had appeared the night before. He turned around to speak to Faharn and saw his apprentice slumped over a dwarven cart, hands clasped around the shaft of an arrow protruding from his chest. Blood flowed from between his fingers. Laz swore with every foul oath he knew as he caught Faharn by the shoulders and gently laid him down on the ground.

Laz dropped to his knees beside Faharn and bent over his body. A quick glance showed him that pulling the arrow free would only make the wound worse. Faharn still breathed, but each breath wheezed and rattled in his chest. His mouth opened in a gasp. A thick red bubble burst on his lips. *Nothing to be done here*, Laz thought. He slipped into trance and summoned his body of light in one smooth motion of his mind. This time the man-shape appeared, as robust as ever. Laz transferred his consciousness into it and followed Faharn into what his apprentice would see as the death-world.

Faharn's etheric double, pale and stretched thin in the bright blue glow, hovered a long way above his body. The silver cord had dwindled to a mere thread, and as Laz rose up, he saw the thread snap. Faharn's utter bewilderment clung around him in a thick grey mist.

'Faharn!' Laz thought to him. 'I'm here!'

The etheric double swooped down to meet him, but Laz could hear no thought, only feel Faharn's wordless terror. His own stab of guilt made him tremble. *I should have told him, I should have told him the truth earlier.* He forced his mind steady.

'You're dead.' Laz projected as much cold calm as he could muster. 'You're dead, but it's not the end. You're going to go on and live again. I'll lead you.'

Faharn held out pale blue hands.

'You can't touch anything here,' Laz thought to him. 'You're going to a new life. Follow me!'

His years of unthinking trust brought Faharn rewards now. Whenever Laz glanced back, he saw Faharn's glowing blue form following him. Laz rose to the upper levels of the etheric, then opened a gate to the astral world beyond. As he swooped through, Faharn came after. They soared upward through the indigo tunnel, studded with stars and images, echoing with ghostly voices, past the twisting churning forms projected from both their memories, until at last they burst out into the pale lavender meadows of Death. Ahead, beyond the field of white poppies, lay the white river, where water that never flowed on earth nor reached an earthly sea slid past without a ripple or a sound.

'Cross over!' Laz said. 'Cross over to a new life!'

Yet Faharn lingered, hovering close to him. When Laz let his own form drift toward the river, Faharn came after. Close to the bank a mist was rising, reaching toward them with pale wisps like hands. Laz glanced down and saw his own silver cord stretching out thin.

'Faharn, go to the river.' He made his thought-voice as gentle as he could. 'Trust me. Life awaits you.'

With a bob of its head the etheric double obeyed. The misty hands caught the image of Faharn's hands and pulled him to the river's edge. A vast silver wave rose up and enveloped him, washing him safely to the farther bank. In the rising mist Laz could see no more.

Laz turned his consciousness to his body, left far below. With a yank the silver cord thickened and hauled him back to the gate. He plunged through. Down he swept through the indigo tunnel, down and down, until with a gasp and a wave of pain, he fell back into his flesh.

Aching and gasping for breath, Laz opened his eyes. He found himself still crouched over Faharn's body, soaked with darkening blood.

'Here, here, lad,' a familiar voice said. 'There's naught to be done for him. Come away now.'

Laz looked up to see Garin standing nearby, his eyes all sad sympathy.

'True enough,' Laz said. 'I was just saying a prayer or two for the dead. It's our custom, you see, among the Gel da'Thae.'

'Ah, well and good then.'

Laz stood up and turned away from the dead thing that had once been his friend. He would miss Faharn, he realized, another person he'd not appreciated until it was too late. *Ye gods!* he thought. *That's a nasty thread to have woven through your life!* When he glanced around him, he saw Brel nearby, barking commands as his men restored order in the disrupted camp.

'We'll bury him with our dead,' Garin said. 'Back in Lin Serr.'

'My thanks, envoy. That's an honour indeed.'

Garin bowed to him.

'It's time for the truth, envoy,' Laz continued. 'Even though remaining with your people would be another honour, I have a grave reason to leave you. The mage Dallandra charged me with the task of retrieving a book from the Boars. I've done that, and now I'm supposed to take it to Haen Marn to wait for her there.'

'Never would I stand in your way if Dallandra's behind this,' Garin said, "but if you'll come to Lin Serr, we can give you an escort to the island.'

'That's truly generous, but I'd best take my leave of you. I can get to Haen Marn faster on my own.'

'What?' Garin said. 'You'll be in danger the entire way, a lone horseman out in wild country.'

'I'll be leaving our horses with you.'

'What? But –'

Brel turned and shouted something in Dwarvish that made Garin wince. Laz could guess that it was some variant of 'he can fly, you idiot', since both the warleader and the envoy knew about his raven form.

'You know your own mind best, Laz,' Garin said in Deverrian. 'We can give you some food for the trip, at least.'

'That would be a blessing, and I thank you. I've been an outlaw for years, you know. I'm good at slipping through wild country unseen.'

'Very well.' Yet Garin hesitated.

What would he do, Laz wondered, *if I told him the truth? Or is that what Brel shouted at him?*

'If you're certain you'll fare well?' Garin said at last.

'Certain I am, good envoy! And my thanks for your aid.'

With a sack full of supplies Laz left the dwarves as they began to wrap up the bodies to take home to Lin Serr. He walked to the top of the hillock, looked around, and saw a ravine leading off to the east. He followed it, climbing over boulders, avoiding the tangled brush and thorny shrubs as best he could, until he could be sure that he was out of sight of the Mountain Folk. He took off his clothes, winced at his shirt, stained with Faharn's blood, and stowed them in the sack along with the dragon book. He tied it securely with his belt and laid it on top of one of the largest boulders.

With a cry Laz transformed into the raven. He shook his wings, picked up his sack, and flew. He circled the camp once in farewell, then headed off for Haen Marn. As he gained height, he was wondering if the silver wyrm would forgive him for whatever ancient fault it was that lay between them, now that he'd retrieved the book.

He hoped so, because he feared that even in human form, Rori would make an enemy that no man would want ranged against him.

After some days of searching Rori had found the mob of Horsekin emigrants, with their wagons, herds of cattle, horses, and slaves, a good distance away from the ruined fortress. Where the Northlands plateau began to rise into the foothills of the western mountains, they'd made a fortified camp. Although the fortifications only amounted to dirt heaped up along ditches, they troubled him, implying as they did that the emigrants were planning on spending some days behind them. He circled overhead and made a rough count of the soldiers scattered here and there in the camp – less than half as many as he'd seen before, another troubling detail.

The camp lay on the banks of another river, this one flowing south. Perhaps the leaders of this Horsekin horde were planning on following it to some goal and had sent some of their armed riders out as scouts. To test this assumption he followed its course, but he'd not travelled more than a few hours when he found another camp, this one laid out with military precision and swollen with soldiers, far more than he'd seen all summer long, as many as two thousand by his rough estimate. As he circled above, he realized that the terrain around the camp looked familiar. In the hills to the west, not far away at all, lay his and Arzosah's summer lair.

Surely the Horsekin had no idea that the dragon caves lay so close. Would they attack the great wyrms – of course not! Cerr Cawnen! The name burst into his consciousness. This river ran through canyons until it reached the flatlands again, then meandered down to the marshes around Cerr Cawnen, a town that the Horsekin had coveted before. When the war at Cengarn had left them too weak to take it, they had tried to win its citizens over to a false alliance – but failed.

Now the Horsekin had grown strong again. Little, however, had changed for the Rhiddaer since that day forty years earlier. Although the town was beautifully fortified, it could muster at the uttermost nine hundred members of an ill-trained and ill-armed militia in its defence. Rori knew that if the huge army below him could breach the walls, take even a single gate, they would slaughter every man in it and enslave the women and children. Once the town was theirs, getting them out of it again would likely be impossible with the force that Dar and Voran could muster.

By then the summer twilight was gathering in the sky. Rori banked a wing and headed south, flying until the night darkness made it too difficult for him to follow the landmarks below. He settled among rocks in the hills to rest, but with the first silver gleam of dawn he launched himself into the air again and flew onward. As he travelled, he made a rough estimate of distances. An army the size of the Horsekin threat would move slowly over this hill country. The marshy land north of Cerr Cawnen would slow them down as well. It would take them some days – perhaps even a fortnight if dragons should continually disrupt their line of march – to reach their prey.

It took Rori, however, less than a day to fly wearily into the town. Up on the central island of Citadel stood the ruins of an ancient temple, half-hidden by trees on a slope just down from the public plaza. Rori circled the plaza once and roared out Niffa's name as he did so, over and over until one of the terrified townspeople below finally understood him.

'I'll be fetching her!' the man called up to him. 'Please eat not our folk!'

'I'd never do such a thing,' Rori called back. 'I'll lair at the temple.'

The fellow ran off, and Rori landed to rest and wait.

'I be mourning Aethel as deeply as he,' Cotzi said, 'but truly, Niffa, I do try to get myself up and about, like. Your brother, he be wallowing in grief, I think me.'

'I do agree at least in part,' Niffa said. 'Well, let me go see if talk might help him.'

Cotzi smiled in thanks. She'd turned into a stout grey-haired matron, her face graved with deep lines, but still she reminded Niffa of Demet, Cotzi's brother and her own long-dead husband. The family resemblance among the weavers had always run strong. *Aethel did look like them, too,* she thought. *Ai! our poor lad!*

She found Jahdo upstairs in the long bedroom he shared with Cotzi. He was sitting at the window and looking out at Cerr Cawnen spread out below, a view tufted with clots of mist from the lake. When Niffa joined him, he looked up and managed a smile.

'What be all this?' Jahdo said. 'Did my Cotzi send you here to cheer me?'

'She did just that,' Niffa said. 'She does worry.'

'I be not mad with grief or suchlike. Truly, life on the caravan road be a dangerous thing. I nearly did die myself twice or thrice, as well you and Cotzi both do know.' He paused to lay a hand on his right knee, broken years before in a fight with bandits. 'But what does irk and gall me, sister of mine, is that one so young should die and an old man like me still live.'

'That does happen often enough that it should come as no amazement.'

'True enough, but for some daft reason, never did I think it would come to me and mine.' He stood up and smiled again. 'I'll be going down now to ease Cotzi's heart.'

'My thanks! That were best. And think on this. It may be that the gods did keep you safe for some reason we cannot know.'

Jahdo merely snorted at the idea, but Niffa knew, in the wordless way that omens often come to dweomermasters, that she'd spoken an inadvertent truth. They'd barely reached the ground floor of the house when a pounding on the front door proved the omen.

Jahdo flung open the door to reveal the blacksmith's apprentice, his face dead-pale with alarm.

'Mistress Niffa,' he gasped out. 'There be a dragon here in town. He did demand to speak with you.'

'What colour be this wyrm?' Niffa said.

'All silvery, like, with bits of blue here and there. He does lair at the old temple.'

'Rori! He be a friend, fear not.'

The apprentice looked less than reassured, but Niffa hurried past him. Her clogs clattered on the stone-laid alleyways as she trotted along. The temple stood some distance from her brother's house, round back and just down the hill. As she drew near she could smell dragon, but trees blocked the temple from her view.

'Rori!' she called out. 'Be you here?'

'I am,' he called back, his voice as deep as thunder. 'And the bearer of ill news indeed.'

Niffa turned cold all over as the omen returned to her mind. She made her way through the trees and straggly weeds to find the dragon lounging on the remains of the temple's roof. She clambered up on fallen blocks of stone until she was more or less at his level.

'I'd guess the trouble be the Horsekin,' she said. 'Bain't?'

'It is indeed. An army of them is assembling up north, and they seem to be headed this way.'

'Only seem to be?' She clutched at the tiny comfort of the words.

'Where else would they be going?'

The comfort vanished. 'True spoken,' she said. 'We be the only prize worth fighting for in this part of the land. Have we any chance of fending them off?'

'Not alone. I'm on my way to Prince Daralanteriel. He's allied with you, and he has archers.'

'Not enough. I be no fool, Rori.'

'Alas, 'tis true.' He lowered his head, and his oddly human dark blue eyes watered in sympathy. 'Still, it's far too early to give up hope. Dar can call upon his alliance with Deverry. It's obvious that if Cerr Cawnen falls, the Westlands will go next, and then the Horsekin will be at the Deverry border.'

'Will the prince of the Slavers see that be a jeopard?'

'Of course! And so will the high king once the prince informs him. Now. Is Jahdo still Chief Speaker here?'

'He is.'

'It'll be up to him to keep your people from panic, and I can't think of a better man for the job.'

'No more can I. He'll be mustering the town council as soon as I do tell him.'

'Good! Besides, if arrows won't turn the Horsekin back, there's dweomer, too, for a weapon.'

The dweomer was already warning her of disaster. For Jahdo's sake she kept that knowledge to herself.

After Rori left, flying straight south like a silver spear hurled into the blue, Niffa lingered among the fallen stones of the temple. She used the trees, swaying in the summer wind, as a focus and contacted Dallandra. She repeated the gist of Rori's message and saw her fellow dweomermaster's image turn pale.

'This be horrible news, but Rori be on his way back to you,' Niffa said. 'He'll be telling you more than I know.'

Dalla's image, floating on the surface of a shallow stream, nodded her agreement. 'Go tell Jahdo,' Dallandra said. 'I'm going straight to Prince Dar with this.'

'Well and good, then. I be remembering Cleddrik. He were the fellow from Penli, who did come to us begging for shelter behind our walls should war come upon us. I did wonder at his fear, but it did turn out that he were merely prudent.'

An exhausted Rori returned to the royal alar with the sunset and found a council of war waiting for him out in the meadow. Although Arzosah had gone off hunting earlier in the day, Dallandra and Salamander had joined Daralanteriel and the banadar. In the sky a few clouds caught the sinking light like streaks of blood across the blue, or so they seemed to Dalla's troubled mind.

When Rori finished his report, Prince Dar swore softly to himself. He turned to his banadar and raised a questioning eyebrow.

'The situation's plain enough,' Calonderiel said. 'If the Horsekin take Cerr Cawnen, then they'll have a fortified salient.' Cal turned to the dragon. 'Do you think we can defend Cerr Cawnen?'

'Not unless we move settlers up there. It's too far north, too isolated. You'd need a new gwerbretrhyn and a thousand good riders and archers to hold it.'

'And how many farms,' Salamander put in, 'would it take to feed them all?'

'Huh!' Calonderiel snorted profoundly. 'We can barely hold onto the Melyn River Valley as it is. Dar, sometimes I wish you'd never made that alliance with Jahdo's people.'

'But I did make it,' Daralanteriel said, 'and cursed if I'll break my word.'

Calonderiel sighed and shook his head in frustration.

'We've got to do something,' Dallandra joined in. 'We can't just let the Horsekin take that city and enslave everyone in it. That would be horrible.'

'The Horsekin are prone to doing horrible things,' Salamander said. 'The question is, can we stop them from perpetrating this one?'

'And the answer to that is most likely that we can't,' Calonderiel said with a shrug. 'I don't like the idea any more than you do, my darling, but we have to be hard-headed –'

'You what?' Dallandra's rush of rage made it hard for her to speak. She took a deep breath and began again. 'There are four thousand people in that town – four thousand souls who deserve better than being dragged off and sold in a Horsekin market! The ones they don't kill outright, that is, or torture to death.'

The men and the dragon merely looked at her with a certain sympathy, as if she'd been taken ill.

'I will not stand for it,' Dallandra went on. 'If I have to, I'll leave Dari with Sidro and Grallezar and go to live in Cerr Cawnen. Maybe Niffa and I can work dweomer to defend the town, since you're all dishonourable enough to turn your back on our sworn allies.'

Salamander and Calonderiel broke out talking at once. Rori silenced them with a deep rumble of laughter.

'So,' the dragon said, 'we don't want to see Dallandra in Horsekin hands, but the thousands of women and children in Cerr Cawnen don't matter? I think me she's beaten us all in this game of carnoic.'

'Well, ye gods!' Calonderiel snarled. 'I suppose having good men die with them will make matters better? Dalla, don't be a fool!'

Dallandra choked back the nasty remarks that filled her mouth. She took a deep breath. 'If you can't see reason, then I'm going to just get up and leave.'

She rose to her knees, but Calonderiel flung up one hand in a gesture that made her pause.

'Get up and leave.' Calonderiel spoke each word very carefully, as if he'd never heard them before. 'Get up and leave. Sit down, Dalla! You've just given me a splendid idea.' Dallandra sat as the idea occurred to her as well.

'So,' Cal said. 'What if we move the people out of Cerr Cawnen before the Horsekin get there?'

The other men goggled at him while the dragon laughed again.

'Well, by the silver shit of the Star Gods, think!' Cal continued. 'Dar, for months you've been saying how desperately the Melyn River Valley needs settlers.'

'So I have,' Daralanteriel said, grinning. 'Sometimes, Banadar, you put us all to shame. Do you think they'll abandon their homes?'

Everyone looked at Dallandra. 'I can't speak for them,' she said, 'but they're not stupid or mad.'

'Of course!' Dar turned to her. 'This could solve a fair many problems, like building the Falcon dun. I've seen their town, you know. The Cerr Cawnen folk know how to build fortifications. And I'll be needing a winter dun myself, soon.'

Rori slapped his tail on the ground. Everyone turned to look at him.

'It may take time to persuade them,' the dragon said. 'We'd best slow the Horsekin down to give you that time. Fortunately, my prince, you have allies in the air. Arzosah and Medea will enjoy scattering their horses as much as I will.'

'No doubt.' Daralanteriel rose, abruptly restless. 'But it's a long way to Cerr Cawnen from here. We'd best get on the road with the dawn. Banadar, we want a fast moving mounted force with extra horses.'

'Just so.' Calonderiel got up to join him. 'It would take the entire alar at least ten days to reach Cerr Cawnen.'

'A fortnight, more like, with the herds and flocks,' Salamander said. 'It's still a good hundred miles away, isn't it? We have to cross a range of hills, too.'

'That's why I want a small force. I'm not risking the alar's children, either, by taking them anywhere near the town and the Horsekin. Carra can lead everyone as well as I can. She can find a safe spot for most of the alar to wait while we –' Dar paused to glance at

Calonderiel and Dallandra '– while we travel on ahead. What do you think, Cal? A troop of twenty-five?'

'That would be a good number, and we should be able to reach the town in five days if we take extra horses. Unless, Dalla, you know a way to get us there even faster.'

'I can't open a dweomer road for more than one or two people, if that's what you mean,' Dallandra said. 'With Evandar gone, the roads get more and more unstable. They're probably not safe for anyone who's not dweomer themselves.'

'I see.' Cal considered for a moment more. 'I'd ask the dragons to carry some of us there, but frankly, I think we'd best go with a show of force.'

'I agree,' Dallandra said. 'What if the Horsekin send emissaries, like they did before?'

'They'll understand a message delivered by a troop of archers a lot better than fine words,' Cal said. 'Even with dragons hovering around.'

'Quite right,' Dallandra said. 'And they'd love to get their hairy paws on Prince Dar. He'll need guards.'

'Which brings us back to the point,' Dar broke in. 'We need to delay the main army. Can the dragons do that?'

'We can try,' Rori said.

Salamander got to his feet. Dallandra had never seen him so grim, with all his fool's pretence tossed aside. 'I need to go north with you. Valandario can receive any messages Dalla sends back. When it comes to harrying the Horsekin, I have the best weapon of all.'

Calonderiel snorted like an angry stallion and set his hands on his hips. 'And what, pray tell, might that be?'

'Alshandra herself.' Salamander crossed his arms over his chest and stared straight at the banadar. 'Or her image.'

'Oh, splendid idea!' Dallandra said.

Salamander smiled at her. Calonderiel, however, scowled and opened his mouth to speak.

'Cal, hold your tongue!' Dallandra got in first. 'Ebañy knows what he's about.'

'He does?' Cal hesitated, then turned to Salamander. 'My apologies.'

Salamander looked so shocked that everyone laughed, including the dragon.

'You can come with me, brother,' Rori said. 'Arzosah mentioned that you've ridden dragonback before.'

'It was not a pleasant experience, but I have indeed,' Salamander said. 'I suspect it will be easier with you instead of her, however.'

'It's likely,' Rori said. 'I'll ask Arzosah to travel with the prince till they reach Cerr Cawnen. Then she can come north to join us.'

'We'll be flying straight for the army, then.'

'Not quite. I want to go to our caves first and fetch Medea. It's time she learned how to harry an enemy.' Rori rumbled briefly. 'And that way you can meet your nephew.'

Calonderiel slaughtered and skinned a pair of sheep for Rori, who needed to rest rather than hunt. Rather than watch his brother eat raw mutton, Salamander went to his own tent and packed a pair of saddlebags to take north with him. Rori had told him to be ready at the first light of dawn. He'd just finished when Dallandra joined him.

'Are you riding with Cal when they leave?' Salamander said.

'No,' Dallandra said. 'I'll be travelling on one of the dweomer roads. I want to reach Niffa as soon as possible.'

'I see. What about Dari?'

'I'll be leaving her with Sidro. She's too young to wean, but Sidro's already getting milk. The Gel da'Thae seem to live for motherhood, I must say! Sidro had a child before, you see, and now she's pregnant again. That and then the amount of time she spends tending Dari has apparently got her motherly humours flowing early.' Absentmindedly, Dalla rubbed one of her own breasts through her tunic. 'It'll be a nuisance for me, but for all I know, there's a woman in Cerr Cawnen who needs a wetnurse. I've asked Niffa to look for one.'

'You'd nurse a stranger's child?'

'Why not? Someone else will be nursing mine. I can scry for Dari whenever I want, so it's not like I'll have no news of her.' Dallandra's voice turned uncertain with worry. 'Sidro can't talk mind to mind yet, but I'll contact Val every day.'

There were times, Salamander reflected, that he was grateful for having been born male.

'Very well,' he said aloud, 'but I was hoping that I could send Dar warnings, should I see something to warn him about, anyway.'

'Grallezar's offered to ride with the prince. Her city had an alliance with Cerr Cawnen, back when she was still head of their town council, and she feels she needs to do something to honour it. Drav and his Gel da'Thae riders will go with her, so the prince will have nearly fifty men to guard him.'

'Splendid! Now, when I've done performing my tricks, I'll have Rori take me back to Cerr Cawnen, so I'll see you there eventually, assuming that all goes well.'

'Let's hope it does. You'll need to husband your energy, you know. If your body of light suffers damage, I'll be too far away to help you.'

'I'm entirely too mindful of that. By the by, has anyone told Rori that Laz has the dragon book?'

'Not yet. I'll leave that up to you. Doubtless you'll have time on the journey.'

'Most likely.' Salamander paused to consider the pair of saddlebags he was taking on the journey. He'd stuffed them as full as possible, he decided. 'When are you leaving for Cerr Cawnen?'

'On the morrow.'

'Then good luck to you on the roads. I suspect you may need it.'

Salamander had touched upon one of Dallandra's fears, that the remnants of the dweomer roads might prove unstable. Evandar had created most of them, then reinforced their existence simply by passing over them. Wherever he travelled, force poured down from the higher reaches of the astral plane, allowing him to mould it into all sorts of forms, including solid-seeming dirt paths. Upon his death, most had dissolved, because no dweomermaster existed who was powerful enough to renew them. Astral force will mould itself into form easily, but keeping those forms stable over time is another matter entirely.

Yet here and there Dallandra had found some paths still open. She surmised that they had survived by virtue of a direct connection to the mother roads. Whether they existed naturally or had been formed by dweomermasters in some distant past was a question she couldn't answer. No more did she know what might happen to her if a road should dissolve when she was walking upon it. Nothing good, she assumed.

Yet she felt that she had no choice but to travel on the remnants of the roads. Although she could transform and fly, her bird form was rather nondescript, a plain grey linnet who flew slowly and lacked stamina. She needed to get to Cerr Cawnen quickly rather than flapping her slow way along over several days.

Dallandra left the royal alar early in the morning, when the astral tide of Aethyr ran at full force. If necessary, she could draw upon its power to temporarily stabilize a path, or so she hoped. She had packed a pair of saddlebags with clothes and her ritual implements the night before. She took Dari to Sidro, then walked out into the grasslands. She found a rivulet trickling toward a larger stream and followed its course. At the joining of the waters she opened her etheric sight and saw the shimmering lozenge in the air, just a few feet above the grassy bank, that signified a possible gate.

Dallandra walked straight toward the lozenge. It swelled at her approach as if in greeting. She took a deep breath, then stepped up and through into a shimmer of pale lavender mist that broke over her like a wave. As the mist cleared away, a cold bluish glare lit her way. She could see that she was standing on a flat outcrop of rock. Ahead stretched an image of another grassland with a gold-coloured footpath winding through it.

In her mind Dallandra formed images of Niffa and of Citadel. At first they were only brief flashes of memory, but one image stabilized into a clear if lifeless picture of Niffa standing near the ruined temple. As Dallandra walked toward it, the image moved away, leading her down the golden path. As it moved, it changed somewhat, adding a budding rose bush beside Niffa and behind her, a view of a kitchen garden. Dallandra walked steadily and fast, keeping her mind focused on the idea of Niffa on Citadel. The scenery around the path changed into a hillside. As Dallandra walked uphill, houses grew up like flowers, and stone walls appeared. Trees shot up to either side of her.

The image of Niffa suddenly looked straight at her and smiled. 'There you are!' she said. Her voice sounded oddly hollow, and the light falling upon her glimmered lavender.

Dallandra stepped off the path, walked through the lozenge gate, and found herself on Citadel, in the garden of the house Niffa shared with her brother. The sun hung low in the west, sinking toward its setting. As always, what she'd perceived as a few moments on the road had marked the passing of hours in the physical plane. The stench of Cerr Cawnen hit her like a blow to the face. The townsfolk dumped all their refuse into the outrunning river, but they did it where the water still ran warm from the lake. The resulting smell was one thing she wasn't going to miss about the town.

'Here I am indeed.' As her body adjusted again to the solidity of the world of form, Dallandra realized that her breasts were aching. When she rubbed them, milk oozed. 'It's good to see you. Er, did you happen to find someone who needs a wet nurse?'

'I did, and she be waiting for you inside. One of my brother's granddaughters, Hildie. Here, let me carry those saddlebags for you. You must a-weary be.'

Dallandra realized that indeed, weary she was.

In the spacious great room of Jahdo's home a scatter of finely worked chairs, each cushioned with bright fabric pillows, stood near a pair of windows with actual glass in them. Jahdo had done very well for himself over the years, Dalla realized, trading back and forth with

the Gel da'Thae as well as the Mountain Folk. A young blonde woman
sat in one chair, holding a baby who fussed and whined. She was
trying to get him to suck water from a cloth sop, but the infant would
only cry and bat at the thing with one feeble hand.

'That be Hildie,' Niffa said. 'And little Frei. He be some two months
now, and her milk, it were scant from the beginning.'

Hildie looked up with a smile so strained that Dallandra realized
that the lass was choking back tears. She decided that formal intro-
ductions could wait and strode over to sit down in the chair next to
Hildie's.

'Give him to me,' Dallandra said.

When Hildie handed the baby over, he began to wail at this rude
transfer to a stranger, but as soon as Dallandra pulled up her tunic,
releasing a waft of milk-scent, the wails changed pitch to a demand.
She settled him at her breast with a sense of mutual relief. Niffa
pulled up another chair and joined them.

'This be my friend Dallandra,' Niffa said to Hildie, 'as doubtless
you did guess by now.'

'So I did, and you have my thanks.' Hildie paused to wipe her eyes
on her sleeve. 'It be a bitter thing, to starve your own child. I do feel
so shamed.'

'Don't,' Dallandra said. 'I never had enough milk for my first-born,
but with the second I have plenty. I'll wager you will, too.'

'See?' Niffa said. 'I did tell you, but truly, I do see why you were
loath to believe me. I've not had a babe of mine own.'

'Never did I not believe you.' Hildie managed a smile. 'It just did
no good for the babe I have now.'

'Well, true spoken,' Niffa said. 'Dalla, Hildie will be sheltering here
for some days, till it be time for all of us to leave Cerr Cawnen.'

'Good, that will be convenient all round, then.'

Grateful for the cushions, Dallandra leaned back in the chair.
Feeding the baby made her drowsy, and for those few moments, as
she sat listening to Niffa and Hildie gossip about the various members
of Jahdo's large family, the Horsekin threat receded, a disturbance on
some far border, perhaps, of another country. Reality, however, shoved
itself into her consciousness when Jahdo came down to join them.

Dallandra hadn't seen Jahdo since he was a young lad. He'd grown
into a slender man, not very tall but not particularly short, and his
dark eyes and thinning grey hair had nothing particularly distinctive
about them, either. He walked with a pronounced limp, the legacy
of a bandit raid on one of his caravans.

'Good morrow, Dalla,' he said in a voice darkened with age. 'The servants, they did tell me you were here.'

'And a good morrow to you,' Dallandra said. 'It's good to see you again.'

Jahdo smiled in acknowledgement. 'I were a-wondering,' he said, 'if it be time to send a messenger down to Penli.'

Dallandra glanced at Niffa, who answered. 'I think it be so. 'Twill take the folk there some days to pack up their goods and the like. Dalla, how soon, think you, that the prince will be arriving here?'

'Five days, or so he hoped.' Dallandra paused to change the baby to her other breast. 'I doubt me if they can travel any faster, even with extra horses.'

'So be it, then,' Jahdo said. 'There be no way for me to give their horses wings. And truly, there be much to do here. Tonight I did call a special meeting of the Council of Five. We do need to decide how much to tell the town and when we should be a-telling of it. 'Twere best to have everyone know the truth before Prince Dar does arrive. The folk, they be needing time to chew things over, like.'

'Just so,' Dallandra said. 'And I want to consult with your spirit talker.'

'Artha, her name be,' Niffa put in. 'Werda did go to her ancestors many a year past. I do warn you: Artha does show forth all of Werda's holiness but few of her wits.'

On the morrow morning, Niffa and Dallandra trudged up the hill to Citadel's central plaza, a wide paved expanse at the top of the hill. To the north stood the stone buildings that housed the council and other official doings, and to the south stood a little shrine to the spirits of the lake. Four stone pillars held a roof over a cubical stone altar, laden at the moment with summer wildflowers. Artha's house lay below it at the end of some wooden steps.

Dressed in white linen trimmed with white fur, the spirit talker stood waiting for them in the doorway, but rather than let them in, Artha came out to meet them on the grassy flat in front of her door. She was carrying the staff of her office, as well, made of dark wood ringed at intervals with silver. When she held it up as if to bar their way, Dallandra went on guard. She had expected trouble from this quarter, and she got it.

'I will leave not,' Artha snapped. 'Nor may I countenance my folk deserting their gods.'

'If you stay,' Dallandra said, 'you'll all be killed or enslaved. The Horsekin will never allow the survivors to worship your gods. They believe that their Alshandra is the only god.'

A silent Artha studied Dallandra with hostile dark eyes. Her hair, a steely grey, hung in two long braids to either side of her wrinkled face. Dallandra kept her own expression carefully arranged in a pleasant, or so she hoped, neutrality.

'Artha, Holy One,' Niffa said. 'The Horsekin, they do plan to turn our town into a fortress for their impious armies. Naught we can do against them will save our folk. The gods –'

'The gods, think you they be powerless?' Artha said. 'They do protect those who give them their due. Have they not quieted the fire that lives beneath us? Have they not steadied the shaking earth?'

'Somewhat has done so. How do we know it be the gods?'

'Can you stand there and mutter blasphemies so close to the holy shrine?' Artha spat out the words.

'Have we not wrangled and snarled over all this before?' Niffa said, and she smiled.

Dallandra was expecting the spirit talker to take grave offence at that smile, but instead Artha merely heaved a sigh and rolled her eyes.

'Mayhap we have,' Artha said. 'But still, I will leave not.'

'You may choose what you choose,' Niffa said. 'What does trouble my heart is this, that other folk will heed you and stay here to meet an ugly wyrd.'

'They may choose what they will choose as well. It be no trouble of yours, witch woman.'

'Ah, but it be my charge, truly, to speak out against false counsel.'

Artha made a sound much like the hiss of a furious cat and waved her staff in Niffa's direction. The sunlight caught the silver rings and gleamed in long sparks of light. Dallandra suddenly realized that beside the rings, the staff bore runes. While Artha and Niffa continued what seemed to be a familiar argument, Dallandra studied the staff, which Artha held upright and unmoving in front of her. The runes all seemed to be Elvish. When she sidled a little closer, Artha ignored her. By craning her neck this way and that, Dallandra finally managed to read them, 'five elements, all kin, one soul.' *That's the rest of it,* she thought, *the inscription on Kov's staff!*

By then Artha had run out of invective. She and Niffa stood glaring at each other.

'Er,' Dallandra said, 'that staff. Is it permitted for me to ask whence it came?'

Artha was so startled by this sudden change of subject that she nearly dropped the staff in question.

'I know not where the first of these came from,' Artha said when she'd recovered. 'But my teacher in the spirit lore did have this one, and on her death bed she did give it to me. They be handed down over the long years, and when one does grow too frail, it be given to the holy fire, and a new one carved.'

'My thanks,' Dallandra said. 'That's most interesting.'

Artha pursed her lips and glared at her as if she were a half-wit. Niffa smothered a laugh.

'I think me we shall disagree on these things forever,' Niffa said to Artha. 'What the townsfolk will do, I ken not. I think me that what the prince of the Westfolk does say will have the true deciding of this.'

With a pleasant wave Niffa turned and began to climb the steps back up to the plaza. Dallandra said farewell to the furious spirit talker and hurried after her fellow dweomermaster. Neither said anything till they were up on the plaza and well past the shrine.

'Do you really think she'll stay here?' Dallandra said. 'The Horsekin – what they'll do to a priestess of other gods – it's too horrible to even think about it.'

'I did make a plan already. Some of my brother's muleteers, they did say they would sweep her up and tie her to a wagon if such should be the only way to, um, persuade her to leave with us.'

'Good. That sets my heart at rest. I agree with you, though, that whatever Dar says will really decide the issue for the town.'

'Then we should know soon.' Niffa glanced up at the sky, where a few white wisps of cloud were moving in from the south. 'I fear me that the rain, it be coming, though.'

'I think you're right. I hope it doesn't slow Dar and his men down too much. Well, that's in the laps of whatever gods there may be.'

As Laz winged north toward Haen Marn, the Horsekin were very much on his mind as well. Even though Laz in raven form could fly faster than he could travel on horseback, he felt as if he were crawling through the air, burdened as he was with worry. With Horsekin raiders close by, what if Haen Marn had fled back to Alban? He could return to the Westlands, he supposed, find the royal alar, and deliver the book to Dallandra there, hundreds of miles away. The very thought wearied him.

At night, when he stopped to rest, Laz found himself missing Faharn. They had met back in Taenbalapan, years before, when their dweomer studies had led them both to Hazdrubal, the Bardekian refugee. Almost from the beginning, however, Faharn had disliked Hazdrubal. He stopped his studies early on, claiming that the teacher was evil, disgusting, and probably a criminal to boot. Laz agreed with his opinion, but he stayed on, learning what he could, discarding what he hated.

· He made such fast progress that he could take Faharn on as a pupil after only a year or two with the Bardekian. When the howling mob of Alshandra worshippers began purging the city of magicians, Laz and Faharn escaped together and gradually built up their band of fellow refugees. Outlaws, perhaps, but unwilling ones – and now most of them were dead or had deserted to the Westfolk, including Pir. *I always thought he was my true friend,* Laz thought, *and Faharn just a hanger-on of sorts. How wrong I was!*

Occasionally Laz shed a few angry tears over the bitterness of Pir's betrayal. He could take comfort in thoughts of revenge, of taking Sidro back again and then mocking his former friend for losing her. Now and then he thought of scrying Sidro out, but the fear of seeing her in another man's arms always stopped him.

On his third day of flight, which happened to be the day after Dallandra arrived in Cerr Cawnen, Laz found Haen Marn, a good many miles from where he'd left it. The enormous astral vortex lay in a different lake from the one he'd last seen, this one sheltered by a horseshoe of hills that clashed with the landscape around them. Oaks and a scattering of brush grew on the lake side of the rolling hills; outside, among the rough northern mountains, stood pine forest. A river ran from the lake and flowed out of the open mouth of the horseshoe, but no river flowed into the lake from the opposite hill.

The boulder with the silver horn stood on the lake shore. Laz landed next to it and folded his aching wings. He'd been planning on flying straight to the manse, but his exhaustion made him pause. Although he felt perfectly confident that he could pick his way through the astral vortex, mistakes happened too easily when a dweomermaster had spent all his energies in the physical world. He transformed back into his human body and dressed, though he left his troublesome boots in his sack, then picked up the silver horn and blew three long notes.

Shortly thereafter he saw the dragon boat set out from the island. Its strange etheric crew of rowers brought her smartly across the lake, then backed oars and turned her in the shallows. Laz waded out, tossed his sack aboard ahead of him, and with Lon's help, clambered onto the deck.

'Well, you be back, bain't?' Lon said, smiling. 'I wager you do have a few tales to tell.'

'I do indeed,' Laz said. 'I hope Lady Angmar won't mind me imposing on her hospitality once more.'

'I doubt me that she will. You did find the island, and that be invitation enough for Haen Marn.'

Sure enough, when Laz walked into the great hall, Angmar looked up from her sewing, smiled, and waved her hand as if he'd been gone for a day or two. Mara came hurrying down the staircase and greeted him with a bit more enthusiasm but no great surprise.

'This morning Avain did see you in her basin,' Mara announced. 'Welcome back!'

'My thanks.' Laz slung his sack onto the nearest table. 'I've brought you back the dragon book, and I now know just what a treasure it is.'

'That's so splendid! Please, do tell me more. And my sister? Be she well?'

'She was last time I saw her, and your father as well.'

'Let the poor man sit, Mara.' Angmar laid her sewing into the workbasket on the floor next to her chair. 'And fetch him some ale! Envoy Kov, no doubt he'll be wanting to hear these tales as well, so do call him in.'

Mara curtsied to her mother, then hurried out the side door on her way to the kitchen.

'Mara seems to have learned courtesy,' Laz said, smiling, 'since last I saw her.'

'It be so indeed.' Angmar returned the smile. 'The hard work in the kitchen did teach her her sister's worth, as well. Come sit down, Laz. When Kov and Mara do join us, we shall trade tales.'

'Wait – do you mean Envoy Kov of Lin Serr?'

'I do.'

'Berwynna told me that he was dead.'

'He were not, but captured by the strange folk of the Northlands.' Her smile turned soft. 'My Rori did rescue him and bring him here for refuge, and I think me he be just the man our Mara does need, to be the lord here to her lady.'

'Excellent! And while I'm here, I can teach her more dweomer lore.'

'For that my heart would be grateful. There be much need upon her to learn all she can.'

In honour of his return Mara roasted a haunch of venison for the dinner that night and made a sauce of wild mushrooms to go with it. Kov baked the bread – as a young man he had in the custom of the Mountain Folk lived on a farm and learned that sort of skill. As she presided over the meal, Angmar looked happier than Laz had ever seen her. When he asked, she told him that Rori had agreed to the transformation back to his human form. 'That be, if the elven sages do have the knowledge they need to bring him back,' Angmar said.

'We have the book again,' Laz said. 'I've met these dweomermasters now, and truly, if anyone can restore him, it will be they.'

'That gladdens my heart to hear. My thanks, Laz. Truly, it be good that you did return to us.'

It occurred to Laz that it had been a long time since anyone had welcomed him to a place that felt like home. For a moment he felt close to tears, but he managed to smile and thank her in a steady voice.

After a tankard of Haen Marn's dark ale, Laz felt tired enough to excuse himself and go upstairs to his old chamber. The straw mattress and the blankets still lay where he'd left them, and the basket of extra clothes stood waiting for him as well. Outside the sun lingered above the horizon, a sign that he had flown far to the north indeed. Its warm golden light filled the tiny chamber with the peace of an approaching night.

Laz set his sack down and knelt beside it. He took out the precious dragon book and propped it up against the base of the wall. He could just discern the harsh lavender glimmer of a spirit dancing on the cover.

'Please don't leave again,' he said aloud. 'The Westfolk mages and the dragon himself will come here to fetch you.'

The spirit brightened, as if agreeing, then withdrew. Laz got up and went to the window. He leaned on the sill to look out at the lake rippling in an evening wind, and used the sunlight upon the ripples as a focus to scry for Dallandra. Although he lacked the knowledge to send her messages, he wondered what she might be doing at that moment.

What he saw surprised him. Rather than out on the grass or in a tent, she was sitting inside a room and nursing an infant that he took for Dari. He could just dimly discern that she sat in a cushioned chair, and that two other women sat nearby, though neither of them was Sidro or any other woman he'd seen among the Westfolk. Although he tried to sharpen the vision, it refused to clarify. In a fit of exhausted frustration, he broke it.

That he'd seen anything at all through the water veil around Haen Marn intrigued him. Some force must have been guiding him or lending him strength – the astral spirits of the book, perhaps. Yet the scrying left him uneasy. Something dangerous lurked close to Dallandra. That he knew; the what or why of it escaped him.

Ever since he'd met Dallandra and Ebañy, Laz had come to see just how inadequate his own dweomer training had been. Hazdrubal had left out a good many things, such as the ability to send thoughts to a fellow dweomerworker's mind. He had given Laz a good under-standing of the principles of the dweomer, but he'd slighted the practice in a good many areas, always while promising that someday, soon but never on the morrow, he would teach more. *If I hadn't been so gifted,* Laz thought, *I'd not have got very far with the work. Faharn was right about the old man. He was something of a fraud, truly.*

Be that as it may, Hazdrubal had certainly paid twice over for any sins he might have committed. Laz had a vivid memory of Alshandra's faithful holding up their blood-stained hands in the sunlight and shrieking with joy after they had clawed and hacked the Bardekian to pieces – gore under their fingernails, blood oozing down their wrists as they held up gobbets of flesh – Laz banished the image and shuddered.

But the gifts – that evening, watching the sun sinking over the hills around Haen Marn, Laz wondered about his gifts, everything Lord Tren had so longed for but lacked. Someone had given them back to him. That he could surmise, especially when he remembered Hazdrubal's scornful words about the Great Ones, who 'meddled', or so his teacher had called it, with the destiny of those who chose the dweomer road. But then, Hazdrubal had walked on the dark paths. Once again, Faharn had been right.

The dark paths. Had he himself known them? Once, in that other life Dallandra had mentioned but never revealed? Laz felt so sick that he could barely stand. He staggered back to the mattress and dropped to his knees upon it. Was that what had cost Lord Tren the only thing he'd ever truly loved?

'No,' Laz whispered in the Gel da'Thae tongue. 'By all the gods, not that!'

Yet he felt sudden eyes watching him. He looked around, saw no one, twisted this way and that, still saw not even a spirit in the chamber, yet he knew that somehow someone watched him from a great distance away, perhaps from the astral, perhaps even from the fabled Halls of Light, where the Great Ones gave their judgments. If it were true that he'd taken the path of the dark dweomer, if he'd defiled the lore he loved so much with crimes such as those, he had restitution to make, wyrd to endure. He began trembling so hard that he fell forward onto the mattress. For a long while that night he lay rolled in a blanket like a child, trying to hide from the terrors of the darkness, until at last he escaped into sleep.

'I just can't reach Laz's mind,' Dallandra remarked. 'I've been trying all evening. I can scry him out easily enough, but I can't contact his thoughts. He seems to be somewhat ill. He's shivering and rolling himself in a blanket.'

'Ken you where he be?' Niffa said.

'Inside some sort of house. I think it might be Haen Marn, because I can sense a water veil around it. I saw the dragon book propped up against a wall near his bed. I suppose that's all I really need to know, that he's safe and the book with him.'

They were sitting in the great room of Jahdo's house in front of a small fire, lit to chase away the omnipresent damp of Cerr Cawnen. Dallandra had fed Hildie's child, and his mother had taken him away to clean him and wrap him in swaddling bands for the night. As the two dweomermasters sat talking, Jahdo came in to join them. He sank into a cushioned chair with a long weary sigh.

'How does the temper of the town run?' Niffa said.

'Foul,' Jahdo said, then smiled. 'Well, half of it be foul. I understand not our folk at times. Some fear to leave more than they fear to stay, even though we all do know what evils the Horsekin will bring with them.'

'Do they think your walls will fend them off forever?' Dallandra said.

'Not forever, only to the winter, when, or so they do hope, the snows will freeze the Horsekin where they sit. It be true that winter around our town be a fierce thing. Were it not for our lake's warmth, none could live here, I think me.'

'True,' Niffa put in, 'but the Horsekin, they live in the cruel north, too. They do ken how to outlast the snows.'

'So I did say to the doubters,' Jahdo said. 'The true problem, I do believe, be a fear of what might wait for us in the southlands, so close to the Slavers' country. Some do think that we shall be slaves there again, and it does seem preferable to be enslaved by the evil we know rather than some new one.'

'Surely they don't think the Westfolk will enslave them?' Dallandra turned in her chair to look straight at Jahdo.

'None who remember Prince Dar do have such thoughts, but the young men, well, they know not what to think. They do have a hope that we might offer to join with the Horsekin to take the Summer Country back from the Slavers. I did try to impress upon them that the Horsekin, they want not an alliance this time, but a conquest.' Jahdo shrugged both shoulders. 'What will the Horsekin want with our hundreds of ill-armed warriors, when they do command their own polished thousands?'

The fire was burning low. Niffa got up and took a stick of wood from the basket by the hearth, then placed it carefully among the coals to avoid the salamanders playing among them.

'Brother?' Niffa said. 'Did the Council send messengers to Penli?'

'We did. On the morrow, most like, will we get a reply.'

The reply arrived on the following afternoon in the form of the entire village of Penli. Some twenty families showed up at the south gates driving their milk cows, sheep, and hogs, with their dogs trailing after and some cats as well, perched on the loaded wagons and hand-carts, and ferrets in cages. The town militia led them around the lake to a spot on the grassy commons where they could pitch tents, feed their livestock, and settle their crying children. Jahdo brought Cleddrik to the council chambers by the plaza, where Dallandra met them.

At the sight of her, Cleddrik took a step back. His eyes grew wide, but he stammered out a pleasant enough greeting after Jahdo's intro-duction. Dallandra disliked him on first sight. The very fact that she couldn't say why she did made her wary; the feeling had something of the omen-cold about it.

'My thanks for this shelter,' Cleddrik said to Jahdo. 'My folk be sore afraid, and I did fear they would up and run off somewhere rather than holding their ground.'

'Running off may well be what we all must do,' Jahdo said. 'The prince of the Westfolk be on his way here with an offer of land farther south. There be no hope of holding out against the Horsekin. There be thousands of them.'

Cleddrik turned dead-pale. Big drops of sweat broke out on his forehead and ran down the creases in his jowls. He pulled a rag from his brigga pocket and mopped the sweat away. It was a reasonable enough reaction, Dallandra decided, to Jahdo's news. When she opened her sight and took a look at his aura, it swirled around him in a grey-green cloud of sheer terror – again, a reasonable reaction to a marauding Horsekin army from a farmer who stood to lose the land he'd worked all his life, to say naught of that life itself. She returned to her normal vision and saw Cleddrik trying hard to put on a brave front as Jahdo explained their situation.

'Well, what must be done must be done,' Cleddrik said at last. 'My thanks, Chief Speaker, for this honest talk. By your leave, I'll be going to tell my folk what we do face. Then we must make some sacrifice to the gods of the town, some of the first apples, they might please the holy spirits.'

'True spoken,' Jahdo said. 'Tell your folk that the prince, we do expect him some three days hence.'

Cleddrik hurried away to the path down to the lake shore, where the council barge stood at its pier, ready to take him across to the mainland. Jahdo crossed his arms over his chest and watched him go with narrow eyes.

'Do you trust that man?' Dallandra said.

'I know not if I do or not,' Jahdo said. 'Niffa did tell me that the Alshandra priestesses did come to Penli.'

'As far as we know they did.'

'If Cleddrik did believe in their false goddess, it be possible that the Horsekin, they did strike some bargain with him. Messages could go back and forth, like, with the priestesses.'

'Very possible indeed.'

'But then, we all be frightened, and mayhap my mind does see things that be not there. What think you?'

'I don't know.' Dallandra managed a smile. 'He could be so utterly terrified for many reasons. The question is, is he afraid of the Horsekin or of Prince Dar?'

Jahdo laughed, one short bark that edged close to panic. When Dallandra glanced around, she saw the other members of the Council of Five hurrying across the plaza toward them.

'I'll go back to the house,' she told Jahdo. 'I see that you have a council meeting.'

'True spoken. We do meet many a time in a day now, after we do go through the town and talk to our folk. The others,' he gestured at the council, 'they do see the wisdom in leaving. So that be one battle we need not fight.'

Later that day, Dallandra contacted Salamander through the fire. He and Rori had flown a good distance since they'd left the alar. By Salamander's estimate, they were some miles to the west of Cerr Cawnen and a good bit further north.

'And the Horsekin?' she asked.

'Well, there's been no sign of them so far,' Salamander said. 'Which is all to the good. We've been following the route they must be taking, you see, just in the reverse direction.'

'Very well. Suppose the army was camping where you are now. How far is it from there to Cerr Cawnen?'

'At least three days ride for a horde such as Rori described.'

'Only three?'

'Well, they must be at least a day's ride north of where we are, so make that four days at least.'

'It's still not enough.'

'I know, oh mistress of mighty magicks, but we have yet to deploy and display our wiles, tricks, and shows of brute force and harassment. In short, we shall slow them down, never fear.'

I do fear, Dallandra thought to herself. *Profoundly so.*

To Salamander, she said, 'I just hope there are priestesses travelling with the army. I'd hate to think of you performing a dangerous feat for an audience that can't see you.'

'So would I, but I'm willing to wager high that the holy ladies have come along. These days the Horsekin never go anywhere without at least a pair or two, or so it seems.'

'Well and good, then. Do let me know how things go.' She broke the link before he could feel just how troubled she was.

Since Rori had no desire to tease his brother with sudden drops in height or near-vertical climbs, Salamander was finding the trip north on dragonback a far easier ride than the one Arzosah had given him. By the time they reached the dragons' mountain lair, the view from high in the air had come to delight him. Rivers ran sparkling in tiny silver threads through forests that billowed and swayed in the winds like one massive living thing rather than separate trees. Grassy valleys lay like jewels among the dark rocks and twisted pines of the foothills. When they reached the mountains they dodged among enormous pillars of rock and skimmed above craggy slopes. The boom and thunder of Rori's wings echoed back to them like a chant.

At last, late on an afternoon, Salamander saw the remains of a stone tower standing at the edge of a mountain meadow. Above the meadow loomed a sheer cliff, leading up and up to a streak of snow on a rocky ridge. Low on this cliff, behind the tower, he noticed a ledge of rock and the dark slash of a cave mouth.

'Hang on!' Rori called out.

Salamander tightened his grip on the rope harness around his brother's chest as the dragon swooped, flapped hard, curled his wings, and landed neatly on the ledge. Salamander slid down from his back just as Medea poked her green and gold head out of the cave and roared a welcome.

'Rori's brought Uncle Ebañy!' she called out in Elvish. 'Mezza, Devar, come meet Uncle Ebañy!'

A smaller dragon – Salamander estimated she was perhaps fifteen feet long – waddled out of the cave. Her scales shone as golden as the sunlight on a summer afternoon, darkening on her belly to the orange-red of a sunset. Behind her came a slender hatchling about the size of a plough horse, an iridescent silver like his father, though his underside was a definite dark blue to match his dragon-slit eyes. Beautiful though the three young wyrms were, the vinegar stench of dragon billowed out of the cave along with them, so strong that Salamander felt faint. He managed a decent bow to the two females, who rumbled in answer, and caught his breath at last.

Devar, his nephew, his dragon brother's son – Salamander hardly knew how to address him. His name, Salamander could guess, came from that of his and Rori's father, Devaberiel Silverhand. The young silver wyrm bobbed his head respectfully to his uncle. His dark blue eyes caught Salamander's attention. He had the vertical cat-slit eye of a dragon, but rather than round, his eyes were oval like a human or elven eye.

'Greetings.' Devar had a dark voice, but still within a human range, thanks to his youth and size. 'Did you bring my new sister, too?'

'I told him about Berwynna,' Medea put in.

'Wynni's visiting friends farther east,' Rori said. 'I hope you'll meet her someday soon.' He paused, glancing around him. 'Ebañy, that tower just below us? I thought you might want to lair in it. I know the cave's a bit dank for someone of your delicate sensibilities.' He rumbled briefly.

'Delicate as horseshit,' Salamander said, 'after everything I've been through. Be that as it may, the tower intrigues me, and it should provide all the shelter I need, this time of year.'

'Good.' Rori turned to the hatchlings. 'We have something important to discuss. Medea, it's time you learned to hunt the Meradan.'

Medea lifted her graceful green-gold head and roared with joy.

While the afternoon sunlight lingered, Salamander clambered down the cliff face to the meadow. Medea swooped down with his saddlebags and blankets in her claws, dropped them into the high grass, then swooped up again to the ledge. When Salamander looked back, he saw that the other dragons had all gone into the cave, which must have been, therefore, far larger than it looked from the outside. With a shake of her green and gold tail, Medea slithered in after them.

Salamander walked over to inspect the tower. It lacked a roof, and its wooden door and the inner ceilings had long since rotted away, but the walls still stood high, although inside green moss grew thick upon them.

In the centre of the roofless circle, where sunlight could reach, tall grass and some sort of bramble formed spiky tangles. Snakes and a variety of spiders and insects, Salamander assumed, lived under the greenery. He decided that he'd sleep outside the tower rather than in it.

He walked outside and glanced up, just idly, but carving on one of the higher ranks of stone caught his attention. He shaded his eyes with his hand and saw a line of lettering in the ancient style of the Elvish syllabary, picked out by the shadows of long light from the west. Craning his neck, he walked around the tower several times until he'd seen it all and could puzzle the meaning out.

'We, the last of they who stand on guard, carved these words. Traveller, if any travellers there be, we hold to our duty though no relief has reached us this hundred years.'

How much longer had they waited, he wondered, before making their retreat? Or had they all died in the tower, either in a Meradan attack or of simple old age, until the last of the last lay unburnt with no one to build him a funeral pyre? No one would ever know, he supposed.

'I've seen your message,' he called out. 'I stand witness that you were faithful.'

The wind sighed around the stones, and in that sound he thought, just for a moment, that he heard voices answering.

In the last of the daylight the dragons flew out to hunt, Rori first, then the young. The combined beating of their wings boomed and echoed so loudly that Salamander clasped his hands over his ears and kept them there until they were well away. He scrounged himself enough fuel for a fire from the woody shrubs growing around the meadow's edge, then considered the food he had left – half a sheep's milk cheese, some scraps of flatbread, a sack of flour, a good chunk of purified lard, and his wooden box of soda.

Not far from the tower a little spring welled up amid tall grass. Salamander took his water bottle and hunkered down beside it. As he pulled the grass aside to reach clean water, he realized that someone had lined the spring mouth with neat blocks of stone – those watchmen of the tower, he could assume. He laid the bottle down, then used both hands to clean the grass and water weeds away until the spring welled up in a basin once again. He'd just finished when he heard the thrumming of dragon wings. A flash of silver in the sunset light, Devar circled low over him and dropped two dead rabbits on the ground next to Salamander. With a flutter of blue and silver wings he landed nearby.

'The rabbits are for you, Uncle,' Devar said in Elvish. 'Da said you could roast them.'

'I can indeed,' Salamander said. 'My thanks, Nephew.'

'Da killed two horses for the rest of us. He and Medea are bringing them back.'

'Horses? I take it you found the Meradani army.'

'Yes. Da wouldn't let me attack them, but it was still great fun, watching Da and Medea scare them! The horses all bucked and ran, and some of the Meradan, they ended up on the ground.'

'Splendid! How far away was this?'

'A long way north.' Devar half-opened his wings, then closed them again in the dragonish equivalent of a shrug. 'That's why they sent me on ahead with the rabbits. I can fly lots faster than the lasses can.'

Salamander considered the size of Devar's wings and doubted it. Aloud, he said, 'The horses must be heavy even for dragons to carry.'

'Yes. They had to fly slowly once they got them. Uncle, Da says that you can fly, too. Can you be a dragon like us?'

'No, alas, but I can turn myself into a magpie.'

Devar blinked at him.

'It's a bird,' Salamander said, 'a black and white bird that chatters a lot and loves shiny things.'

'I don't think we have magpies in the mountains.'

'I doubt it, truly.'

Devar suddenly cocked his head, listening. 'Here comes my clutch.'

Salamander concentrated on listening, but a fair many moments passed before he too heard the measured drumming of wings. The twilight began to deepen just as the three dragons, burdened with their dinner, reappeared above the valley. With a high-pitched roar, Devar leapt into the air and flew up to join them as they landed, one at a time, on the outcrop by the cave mouth.

Salamander watched as Rori divided up the kill for the hatchlings. He snapped at a greedy Devar and told him to wait for his sisters to take their share, had Mezza lick her face clean after a particularly disgusting bite of horse, and praised Medea for the care she'd taken of the younger wyrms while he'd been gone. It struck Salamander as passing strange that Rori would show the concern for this family that Rhodry Maelwaedd had never shown for his human children. *He's too much at ease in dragon form*, Salamander thought. *We're pulling him back just in time.*

Salamander lit his fire with a snap of his fingers. By its light he cleaned the rabbits, then wrapped them in the fresh wet grass he'd pulled earlier and set them to roast in the coals. Overhead the twilight was deepening into night. He walked away from his fire and stood in the darkness to watch the stars appearing over the remains of the stone tower. The sight moved him nearly to tears. Why, he couldn't say, except to speculate that he had once served the Seven Cities here on the border, perhaps even among the last of the watchmen in the tower.

Dalla's right, he thought. *I must meditate more and study more and do all those things I've fled from all my life.* While normally he found such thoughts wearisome, that night they gave him a peculiar pleasure, a sense of rightness, fitting the harsh times. All night he dreamt of the western mountains. He saw confused glimpses of a splendid fortress and of a city in ruins that, even in its ravaged state, dwarfed any he'd ever seen in Deverry.

On the morrow, Salamander woke to a less than splendid reality. He was eating cold roast rabbit for his breakfast when Rori glided down to the meadow. The dragon first drank from the spring, then waddled over to join him.

'My thanks for pulling the grass and suchlike away from the basin,' Rori said. 'I tried to claw it away once, but all I managed to do was get mud in the water. Not having hands is a cursed nuisance.'

'I can well imagine.' Salamander paused to wipe his own greasy fingers on a clump of grass. 'Devar told me that you found the Meradan last night.'

'Yes, we did. They're some miles to the east of us, which doesn't matter, and about two days' march – for them, that is – to the north.' Rori considered briefly. 'Which puts them a good six days from Cerr Cawnen, assuming they recaptured all their horses in time to get a full day's march in today. How close to the army do you have to be to work whatever it is you have in mind?'

'Where I can see them but they can't see me.'

'Easily done. Are you ready to leave?'

'I am. Let me just scatter these rabbit bones for whatever wants to eat them.'

Thanks to Rori's powerful wings, they caught up with the Horsekin army just as the sun was reaching zenith. The enemy was marching through a narrow but long grassy valley, bordered on either side by forested hills. A silver riband of a river threaded itself through a stripe of trees for the entire length of the valley. Streams trickled from the hills to either side to join the river.

As he looked down from the height of dragonback, Salamander found himself thinking of the army as some sort of animal, huge, dangerous, but as awkward as a dragon on the ground as it plodded around clumps of trees and outcrops of rock. At every stream, it slowed to a crawl in order to ease its horses across the bad footing of the fords.

Rori circled high above to match its tedious pace. After a few miles the army halted, or at least, the front ranks halted, then those behind them, and so on down the entire length of the column in a sort of convulsion or ripple that at last reached the slaves and servants at the rear. *Have they seen us?* Salamander wondered, then realized that the Horsekin were merely pausing to rest their horses. Noontide heat shimmered on the hills.

Rori dropped a little lower, close enough for Salamander to see the tiny figures of riders dismounting. He noticed that they kept glancing up at the sky. As the army spread out into the grassy meadows on the western side of the river, Rori banked a wing and turned toward the western hills. On the highest hill, huge boulders and outcrops of pale brown rock emerged from the forest cover like the knuckles of an enormous fist. Rori soared up to the summit, circled once, then landed upon one of the outcrops. Salamander slid down from his back.

'How's this?' Rori said. 'You've got a clear view down to the valley floor, but you can hide among the trees as well.'

'It should do splendidly,' Salamander said. 'Are you going back to the lair?'

'No. If you're spotted, they'll come after you, and you'll need a way out.'

'I can fly, you know.'

'As fast and far as I can?'

'Well, no, and I think me I see some archers down there. An arrow that would bounce off you would skewer the magpie. Your company will be much appreciated as always.'

Salamander untied his saddlebags and bedroll from the dragon's harness. As the sun beat down on the pale rocks, sweat began to soak through his linen tunic. He took his gear and slid down between two massive boulders to the bare dirt and sliver of shade between them, but Rori stretched out in the full sun with a sigh like the sound of a wave breaking on a gravelled beach.

Thanks to the steep rise of this particular hill coupled with his elven sight, Salamander could indeed look straight down to the army below. He was searching specifically for the white garments that marked the priestesses of Alshandra and the white mules they gener-ally rode as well. Fortunately for his plans, he saw a good two dozen women in white, surrounded by slaves and servants, all in darker clothing, and among the horses, a little herd of white mules. The large number of priestesses in fact surprised him, until he remembered that their Holy Witness Raena had died in Cerr Cawnen. Most likely they were planning on founding a temple and shrine once the army had taken the city.

He could also pick out the tiny figures of the warriors by the glint and glimmer of their weapons and the mail they wore under long surcoats. It was odd, he reflected, that they'd chosen to ride in armour. Were they expecting an enemy force, out here in the wilderness? Or was it some mark of manhood among them, to expose themselves to heat and exhaustion by riding encased in metal on a summer's day?

'Rori?' he called out. 'Are you asleep?'

'I'm not.' The dragon slithered to the edge of the outcrop and hung his head over the edge to reply. 'Why?'

'The Horsekin are riding fully armed. Do you know why?'

'The slaves, of course.' Rori paused for a huge yawn. 'When you depend upon slaves, you fear your slaves. I learned that in Bardek. Here they are, some hundreds of miles from home. If all those slaves rose up to murder them, they'd have a nasty fight of it.'

'So they keep their weapons close to their hands, not on a wagon or suchlike where the slaves could steal them.'

'Exactly. Any more questions?'

'None for the nonce, my thanks.'

'Good.' Rori slid his bulk back from the edge. 'Wake me when the army saddles up again.'

Waking a sleeping dragon struck Salamander as dangerous enough for a proverb, but he could always, he decided, throw rocks from a distance.

Salamander sat down cross-legged and braced his back against the rock face behind him. He went into a light trance in order to stay fully conscious and alert while he formed the Alshandra image in his mind. He imagined her as a towering figure, her honey-blonde hair pulled back into a single braid, her face grim and glowering with disapproval. He gave her mail to wear and a bow and arrows to carry. Once she lived apart from his will, he slowed his breathing and sank down into a deeper trance.

On the etheric plane the Alshandra image took on dimension and life. She seemed to breathe; she moved this way and that in the billowing blue light. Her hands raised the bow, then lowered it. The long years of ritual worship by her cult had formed and ensouled astral images, creating a reservoir of power to quicken such creations as this. When Salamander rose up in his body of light, a silver flame that wrapped him round like a cloak and hood, the image rose with him, then drifted off on its own. After a struggle he managed to haul it back.

Below him, the army – to his etheric sight – had dissolved into a pulsing river of auras, mostly red shot with gold, while the servants moved through wrapped in darker browns and greys. He could pick out the priestesses by their silver auras, steady points of pure light glowing in the mass yet somehow set apart. All around the sunlight energized the etheric substance in sparks and ripples of silver. The astral tide of Fire was rising and merging with the tide of Aethyr.

Salamander spotted a long wave of Fire energy flowing downhill and launched his image upon it. As she floated toward her worshippers below, she raised her arms and nodded her head. A priestess saw her and shrieked, pointing at the image. In a swirl of silver auras all the holy women turned toward her and began to chant, their signal to the army that their goddess had appeared.

Salamander heard the warriors' sudden howl of greeting, 'Hai! Hai! Hai!', as a distorted wave of etheric sound, echoing and moaning through the blue light. Long streamers of red and gold swirled upward from the auras of the worshippers below. As their chant and the army's howls rose toward the image, she battened on the etheric energy that rose with it.

Now came the crux. Could he control the thing? He sent his mind out toward the image and felt as if he'd slammed into a stone wall. The priestesses, with their instinctive dweomer fed by years of worship, had surrounded their goddess with such an outpouring of emotional force that he had no chance whatsoever of reaching the image, not in any subtle way.

In a fit of ill temper Salamander sailed downhill after the false Alshandra. He invoked the Light that shines behind all gods and begged it to destroy the false image he had created. In answer the tide of Fire brightened around him. He used his flame-clad arm to draw a massive pentagram made of the sparkling light and hurled it at the image.

'Begone! In the name of the Great Ones!'

At the pentagram's touch, the Alshandra form burst in a shower of sparks as transparent as shards of broken ice. The streamers of red and gold fell back, raining down upon the auras that had originally released them. The priestesses shrieked and wailed, a horrible cry of agony to his etheric ears, while the men of the army milled around like ants when a farmer's plough opens their nest and kills their queen.

Salamander flew back to his body, still slumped against the rock face. He slid down the silver cord, hovered briefly, then let himself fall back into the flesh. He banished the body of light, then woke, panting for breath, soaked in sweat and stiff in every muscle. He staggered to his feet and, leaning against the rock for support, peered downhill at the army.

The priestesses had huddled together, a flower of white robes amidst the dark clothing of their servants. All around them confusion swirled as the warriors rushed this way and that, falcatas in hand as they looked in vain for an enemy they could fight. Horses reared, and servants ran to pull them down again.

'That gladdens my heart to see,' Rori said from above him. 'The yelling and screeching woke me, by the by. It looks like your attack struck home.'

'To some extent,' Salamander said. 'Not as much as I'd hoped.'

'Well, I can't let this opportunity go to waste.'

With a massive roar the dragon leapt from the rocks above and flew. After two booming strokes he swept his wings back and fell like a stone hurled from a sling, down and down until Salamander feared he'd dash himself to death on the ground below. At the last moment the dragon swept up again, as silver and bright as steel in the noontide sun. In his claws a Horsekin screamed and writhed – an officer, a rakzan, Salamander realized, because he wore a cloth of gold surcoat. A futile volley of arrows flew after the dragon.

Rori circled once, then deliberately dropped his prey. With one long scream the rakzan fell toward the centre of his army. Warriors and servants alike yelled in panic and ran back and forth to get clear as he plunged onto the ground. The frightened mob blocked Salamander's view of the corpse, for which he felt nothing but gratitude.

Rori flew back and landed on the rocks directly above him. 'I'm going to fly a little way away to lead them off,' he called down. 'I don't want them coming up here and finding you. I'll be nearby, though.'

Once again the dragon took flight. He glided above the milling, shouting army but kept just out of arrow range. He flew off to the north only to turn abruptly west and disappear between two hills. None of the Horsekin followed him. Apparently Rori had misjudged his enemy's courage, not that Salamander could blame them for their reluctance to chase a murderous wyrm.

Salamander sat down in the shade of the boulders and rummaged through his saddlebags until he found his leather water bottle. He could easily have drunk every drop in it, warm though it was, but he forced himself to save a third of the water for later. As he watched, the army far below regained control of itself. It took several hours, by his reckoning, but eventually the riders formed up in a marching order, the servants and slaves fell in behind, and with the priestesses leading the way, the army began to move, riding slowly and with some dignity toward the south.

Once the last of them had disappeared, and the cloud of dust they'd raised had settled, Rori returned to the outcrop. Salamander gathered up his gear and climbed back up to his brother's scaly side.

'I was hoping they'd stay here,' Salamander said. 'These rocks make a perfect watchtower.'

'There are other spots like it farther south,' Rori said. 'We'll follow them and see where they make their night's camp.'

Not far off, as it turned out. Some six miles to the south the Horsekin halted their column under steep and rocky cliffs on the west side of the valley. As they spread out to pitch tents and hobble horses, Rori and Salamander landed some hundreds of feet above them in the shelter of a scraggly growth of trees that reminded Salamander of the dark and twisted Cerrgonney pines. Some way back from the cliff edge Salamander found a stream big enough to quench both their thirsts, though Rori had to push through and trample undergrowth to reach it.

'What now?' the dragon said when he'd drunk his fill. 'Do you want to wait till morning for another strike?'

'I'm not sure.' Salamander debated briefly with his own natural caution. 'I think I'll make a feint at twilight. If that goes well, I'll make my main strike on the morrow.'

'I'll leave them be for now, then. I don't want to spoil your thrust.'

The thrust Salamander had in mind was dangerous enough without a dragon interfering with his concentration. The only way he could control the image adequately, he decided, was to turn it into a body of light and ride inside it, as it were, out on the etheric plane. The operation would drain his own life force, but if the worshippers below responded as they'd done earlier, he would have their power to absorb and replenish it. Perhaps. He'd never heard of any dweomermaster attempting this particular working. If any had, they'd not lived to record the knowledge they'd gained.

Just at sunset, when the astral tide of Water was just beginning to run in, Salamander created his image again, though this time he equipped her with a Horsekin-style falcata instead of a bow and arrow. When he slipped into the deeper trance, he banished his usual body of light. He held the Alshandra image steady in front of him, then imagined looking out of its eyes, imagined moving its arms as if they were his own arms. Suddenly he heard a rushy click like a metal sword striking a wicker shield. He was no longer imagining but looking out of the image's eyes. When he glanced back, he saw the silver cord running from Alshandra's solar plexus to that of his physical body, which lay inert well back from the cliff edge where he'd left it.

Salamander held the falcata vertically in front of the image. He sailed free of the cliff edge and began to drift downward, but he kept glancing back to ensure that the silver cord payed out smoothly, and that it glowed thick and strong behind him. Down below, the priest-esses had gathered some hundreds of yards from the main body of the army. No doubt their servants pitched the holy camp well away from the noise and pollution of the fighting men. He drifted toward them, and as he did he heard the first chant of recognition.

In a cloud of silver auras the priestesses ran free of the tents and campfires to huddle together out in the open meadowland, well away from the river and its treacherous water veil. He could just discern them lifting up their arms toward the image as they chanted a welcome. Salamander arranged a scowl, as fierce and disapproving as he could make it, on his face and thus the image's face. He turned toward the north and raised his falcata to point in that direction. The chanting changed, the voices shaking on the notes.

He kept the sabre pointing north while he made the image stamp its feet and wave its arms in an astral temper tantrum. Below him the chanting stopped. Voices cried out in fear and called out ques-tions to the goddess, questions that he had no way of answering except to point back the way the army had come.

Behind him the silver cord had stretched out dangerously thin. Salamander turned the image around and sailed back to the cliff, following the cord to his body. For a moment he hovered inside the image while the priestesses below cried out once again. He under-stood just enough of the Gel da'Thae tongue to know that they were begging Alshandra to return and speak to them. Instead, he slid down the cord to his body and transferred his consciousness back to his physical being. Before he broke the trance, he banished the Alshandra image.

Salamander sat up, exhausted and sweating despite the cool evening wind. Rori crouched nearby like a cat with all four legs tucked under him and his tail wrapped neatly around his haunches. His silver scales glimmered in the gathering twilight.

'Ye gods,' the dragon said. 'I could just make out that Alshandra-thing floating around. I take it that you created it.'

'I did, yes.' Salamander paused to grab his water bottle and drink. With a stream so close by, he allowed himself to finish off the contents before he spoke again. 'You know how children play with their dolls and little toy warriors? They hold them up and dance them around and speak for them? That's what I'm doing with this false Alshandra, though alas, I cannot make her speak. It would make my task a fair bit easier if only I could.'

'What would you have her say?'

'Go back, go back, you impious creatures! I forbid you to take Cerr Cawnen!'

The dragon rumbled with laughter. 'Too bad life is never so simple and kind.'

'Just so.' Salamander stretched his aching arms and shoulders. 'But I'll wager I've given them something to chew over among themselves. At best, mayhap the fighting men will turn superstitious and lose their morale.'

'They're superstitious already, believing what they do. As for their morale, you've made it sink, I wager.'

'Splendid! On the morrow I'll make another appearance, but I'm going to wait till they're on the move.'

At intervals throughout the day Dallandra had been scrying for Salamander, though she'd not attempted to contact him mind to mind, an operation that would siphon off some of his magical energies when he needed every pulse of them he could muster. She'd seen, therefore, both of his workings with the Alshandra image. Unfortunately, she'd received only a confused impression of the army's reactions, as she'd never seen any of the Horsekin or their priestesses in the flesh. She could only hope that the sight of their angry goddess had terrified them – those that could see her at all.

'I wonder if I should have let him try this working,' Dallandra said. 'It's immensely complicated.'

'If there be anyone who might succeed in this,' Niffa said, 'Ebañy, he be the one.'

'Let's hope so! It's a pity that he can't bring the image through to the physical, where everyone in that wretched army could see it, but he'd have to have the power of one of the Guardians for that.'

'Or one of the gods, if such there be.'

The gods were very much on Niffa and Dallandra's minds that evening. During the day, as they'd wandered around Cerr Cawnen, listening to the townsfolks' opinions on the proposed evacuation, they'd heard a number of worries about deserting Cerr Cawnen's old gods, those who lived under the lake, or up on Citadel, or in the water meadows that surrounded the town. Many citizens had a god they particularly favoured, it seemed, whether it lived in the clouds or in a particular ancient tree clinging to the rocky island.

'Your people believe in an amazing number of gods,' Dallandra said to Niffa.

'Those that do believe at all.' Niffa frowned, thinking something through. 'Most, they do know that what some call gods be truly spirits and little more. This all does trouble my heart, Dalla. Not till today did we hear people fearing to offend those spirits and godlings. I wonder if Artha be behind this, stirring up the fear with strong words.'

After the evening meal they took candle lanterns and walked across the plaza to Artha's domain. As they were making their way down the wooden steps to the shrine, they met Cleddrik coming up with a lantern of his own. He raised it high, peered at Dallandra, and flinched so sharply that he nearly missed the step below him and tumbled down. Just in time he caught himself, recovered his balance, and mumbled a 'good eve to you.'

Vandar's spawn. The Alshandrite name for the Westfolk rose in Dallandra's mind. *Is that what he thinks I am?*

'And a good eve to you,' Niffa said. 'Come you to lay an offering to the gods?'

'I so did, truly,' Cleddrik said. 'Ye gods, I be so tired tonight, missing that step as I did! Do forgive me, but I must return to my villagers.'

Dallandra and Niffa stood to one side and let him climb up past them. They continued down to find Artha standing outside her cottage door. She crossed her arms over her chest and glowered at them.

'What be so wrong?' Niffa said.

'I did spend much time today,' Artha said, 'thinking upon what you did tell me concerning the Horsekin. I do think me that if we did take the holy altar with us, in a wagon or suchlike, the gods might well travel south along with their folk.'

Niffa grinned at her. 'I do wager we can find a wagon, indeed. The farmers from Penli, they did bring their plough horses, and they can pull a fair heavy load.'

'If their masters do let them. That fellow from Penli, Clod Rik or whatever his name may be, I like him not. He were here just now, nattering about the gods, begging me to tell the folk to stay behind safe walls.' Artha suddenly smiled. 'I do think me that it were his nags and whines that did change my mind to your way of thinking.'

The three of them shared a laugh. Dallandra wondered suddenly if Cleddrik were lurking above on the plaza to eavesdrop, and if so, if he could hear them. She turned and glanced back but saw no one on the wooden steps or at the plaza edge.

'Well and good, then,' Niffa said. 'Let us talk more upon the morrow morn. The blacksmith, he does have two wagons, and no doubt will gladly offer one to you and the gods.'

Neither Dallandra nor Niffa spoke until they'd gained the plaza and walked half-way across it, well out of the spirit talker's earshot. Dallandra kept watch for Cleddrik or, more likely, the glimmer of his lantern as he hurried off, but she saw neither. At the public well they paused in their pool of lantern light and looked around them – no one in sight on the wide cobbled expanse.

'I like this not,' Niffa said. 'This Cleddrik – I ken not his heart or mind.'

'No more can I,' Dallandra said. 'He's so terrified that his fear's like a coat of mail. I can't penetrate it. He could be a traitor of some sort, or he could just be a panicked creature who hardly knows what he's doing or saying, like a rabbit in its hole when the weasel crawls in.'

'I do agree. Alas, though, I do fear me the answer will come in some hateful way.'

'True spoken. We'll have to keep an eye on him.'

On the morrow morning the Horsekin army lingered in camp. Since Salamander had seen it with his physical eyes, he could scry it out by using the running water of the stream as a focus and thus spare himself the strain of scrying in the body of light. Once he had a clear image of the camp, he sharpened the image and magnified it until it seemed that he hovered some ten feet above.

There he had a stroke of luck. He had seen in the flesh one of the Horsekin priestesses in Zakh Gral, both before and after that fortress had been destroyed. By following her he could see as clearly and in as much detail as if he stood among the holy women.

Unfortunately, what he couldn't do was hear. Everything unfolded in silence, just when he desperately wanted to hear their talk. Some of the priestesses looked as grim as death; others openly wept; all of them milled around their special area of the camp and talked with

each other in little groups that formed and broke up like autumn
leaves swirling on the surface of a stream. He could guess that they
were discussing the two ill-omened appearances of their goddess,
but what they might have said about them remained beyond him.

Salamander was on the verge of breaking the vision when a
messenger came running from the main army's camp. He knelt to a
woman who wore an elaborate head-dress – likely the chief priestess,
Salamander decided – and spoke briefly. She nodded, then turned
and beckoned to the other women. Together in an orderly crowd they
followed the messenger out to the empty stretch of grassy ground
between the camps.

Four Horsekin men, with cloth-of-gold surcoats over their mail, stood
waiting for them. They talked at some length, until the head priestess
shook her head no. One of the rakzanir began waving his arms as he
spoke. From the way that the head priestess stepped back, Salamander
could assume that the rakzan was bellowing. A second officer grabbed
his arm and calmed him. The chief priestess turned and stalked away
with her women following her. The rakzanir returned to the army, talking
among themselves. The rakzan who'd lost his temper earlier kept
pounding his fist into the palm of the opposite hand.

With a shake of his head Salamander broke the vision, then got
up and walked over to his brother, who was lounging on the ground
in a patch of sunlight among the trees.

'We've certainly stirred them up,' Salamander said. 'The priestesses
and the rakzanir are arguing among themselves.'

'Good.' Rori yawned with a show of fangs. 'Are you planning on
making things worse?'

'I am indeed, but I need to get ahead of them on the road.'

'Easily done. Get your gear together.'

When Rori and Salamander took to the air, Salamander looked
down to see the army lining up for its day's march in a somewhat
different order from before. First came the fighting men, then directly
behind them the cluster of priestesses on their white mules. Servants,
carts, and slaves formed an untidy mob at the rear as usual. Rori kept
circling as the army moved forward, one rank at a time, until the
entire cumbersome parade was at last marching down the valley. When
Rori flew off to the south, Salamander looked back and noticed that
the ranks of servants had fallen some yards behind the main line of
march, as if perhaps they followed even more reluctantly than before.

While the western rank of hills remained steep, the eastern range
was beginning to lower and flatten out, ultimately to merge with the

downs bordering the Northlands plateau. The army was drawing closer
to Cerr Cawnen. Soon they'd reach easy terrain and could march faster.
If Salamander was going to disrupt them, he would need to do so that
very day. When he spotted another rocky outcrop to the west, he yelled
at Rori to land. The silver wyrm banked a wing, soared over the outcrop,
then landed on the hillside just behind the boulders.

'My thanks, brother of mine,' Salamander said. 'This looks like a
splendid spot for my final thrust. If I can hurl confusion, commotion,
and stupefaction into their ranks, then I shall buy another day of
safety for Cerr Cawnen.'

'You do all that,' Rori said, rumbling softly, 'and I'll stand ready to
pick off a horse. I'm hungry.'

'Then if the gods allow, we shall gain at the same time both a
victory and a meal.'

A cloud of dust approached from the north, the signal that the
army was arriving. Salamander retrieved his leather bottle of water
from his saddlebags, then lay down in the shade of the rocks and
went into trance. He summoned the Alshandra image with the falcata,
transferred his consciousness to it, then rose into the etheric. As he
hovered above the twisted, throbbing mass of red and gold auras, he
saw the priestesses clearly, their silver auras tinged with the blue of
doubt and worry as they rode upon their white mules.

On the tide of Aethyr, Salamander drifted down toward the women
below. They saw the image and halted, turning their mules out of
line, then raised their chant. The main body of the army also came
to a halt, but in a disorganized mob that spread across the entire area
between the hills to the west and the river bordering them on the
east. The front ranks travelled nearly a quarter of a mile onward before
they realized what was happening behind them and turned back.

Salamander swung his falcata with a flourish and pointed north.
He scowled, danced back and forth, then floated over the priestesses
and let himself drift northward, still holding his sabre high. The priestesses turned their mules and followed, while the swarm of servants
and slaves tried to get out of their way. Some trailed after the priestesses, others merely ran to one side or another.

Salamander glanced back. His silver cord had stretched out as far
as he dared take it. He sailed up higher and began to drift back toward
his body just as a troop of horsemen broke away from the army and
came charging down the valley, waving their falcatas and screaming
at the priestesses to stop. The magnetic effluent from so much iron,
both in their weapons and their armour, pulled at Salamander's silver

cord and made it twist. As it unfurled, it became dangerously thin, then swung back and forth as they rode under the image and past.

Close to snapping – Salamander rose up fast and barely in time. He soared back to the outcrop of rock and his body, lying in the shade. As he hovered over it, he saw Rori launching himself into the air, but he had no time to watch his brother from the etheric. The silver cord had weakened until it appeared as a trail of mist, no longer a cord. Salamander slid down and slammed into his body so fast that he shrieked aloud with pain.

Freed from his control, the Alshandra image drifted away toward the valley and the worshippers whose devotion would feed it. Salamander could do nothing to stop it. Sitting up took the last of his strength. He leaned against the rough rocks behind him and panted for breath while he listened to the distant screams and shrieks from the valley below. The water bottle lay to hand. He drank as much as he could get down, but the taste seemed wrong, somewhat sweet and meaty. When he wiped his hand across his mouth, his fingers came away bloody. His abrupt return to his body had burst a vein in his nose.

Salamander staggered to his feet. By clinging to a boulder he could stand and look down. The entire army was milling about in confusion. Horses reared and kicked. A few riders lay on the ground. Alshandra's image had disappeared, but the priestesses and the supply train had both withdrawn some hundreds of yards back the way they'd come. The priestesses, still mounted on their white mules, had drawn themselves up like a wall between the servants and the main body, as if to protect them.

Wingbeats drummed in the sky. With a dead horse hanging from his massive claws, Rori swept down and landed on solid ground, a good distance from the edge of the outcrop. He laid the horse down, then waddled back to Salamander.

'What happened to your face?' he said.

'Carelessness,' Salamander said. 'It's just a nosebleed.'

'You have two black eyes as well.'

'Oh? Well, those came up fast! Doubtless I'll have bruises all over me by the morrow. I need to soak in cold water. That stream will –'

'No, you need to get onto my back. A few of the cursed Meradan have found their courage, and they're climbing up the hill below. I'm going to roll this horse down on top of them, and then we're flying off.'

Salamander stuffed his water bottle down the front of his shirt, then clambered onto his brother's back. Hanging on to the rough rope harness made his hands ache and in spots, bleed. Rori flew up into the air, then swooped down to pick up the dead horse. As he circled up with the prey in his claws, Salamander caught glimpses of some twenty determined Horsekin warriors, falcatas drawn and ready, struggling on foot through the tall grass of the hillside. From a good height Rori dropped the horse onto the steepest angle of the hill. It bounced, burst open with a shower of blood and spray of guts, then slid straight into the squad.

Curses rose up as those it hit fell, one on top of another. In a tangle of arms and legs they rolled back down the grassy slope, furious, disgraced, but probably mostly unharmed. Their companions scrambled back down after them. Rori flew off fast, heading west while Salamander held on as tightly as he could. His muscles, shocked by the impact of his etheric double, were beginning to stiffen. The aches turned into pain.

By the time they reached the meadow below the dragons' lair, late that afternoon, Salamander ached so badly that he tumbled rather than slid from his brother's back. He lay panting in the grass, then managed to sit up when Devar glided down to join them. When Salamander looked up, he could see Medea and Mezza peering down from the ledge above.

'Is Uncle Ebañy hurt?' Devar said to Rori in Elvish.

'No,' Salamander broke in. 'Or rather, yes, I am hurt, but not in any imminent danger of dying or suchlike. What I need to do is get my gear from your father's back so he can go off and hunt for supper.'

Devar allowed Salamander to lean upon him for support. With his help Salamander managed to untie his bedroll and saddlebags from Rori's rope harness. Moving eased his muscles enough for him to refill his water bottle from the spring and spread out his blankets in the shade of the tower.

'I'm going to go hunt now,' Rori said. 'I'll fetch some venison, and you can have a share.'

'My thanks,' Salamander said. 'You needn't fear my leaving without you.'

Rori rumbled, then leapt into the air and flew with a drumming of wings. As soon as Salamander lay down on his blankets, he fell asleep. In dreams his highly trained mind could ignore his aching body and sail back to the Horsekin army. Although the dream was so vivid and detailed that Salamander could take control of it, he doubted its accuracy out of simple caution.

He saw an army disintegrating into an armed mob. All along the river stood clots of dismounted men, their horses still saddled and bridled, their tents and gear lying on the ground. The rakzanir in their gold surcoats and the Keepers of Discipline in their red worked their way through, shouting orders, cracking whips, drawing weapons. He watched one rakzan kill a man who shouted back at him. One angry swing of the rakzan's falcata tore the fellow's head half-off his body.

Salamander abruptly woke, revolted by what he'd just seen, and sat up with some difficulty. For a few moments he found it hard to remember where he was, but the sharp vinegar smell of dragon brought his consciousness back to the meadow. Devar was crouching nearby, watching him.

'Are you truly well, Uncle Ebañy?'

'Well enough, my thanks. A bit hungry. Are you?'

'Very, but Da will bring us back something good.' Devar spoke with perfect confidence. 'He always does.'

Salamander felt a stab of guilt that he and his fellow dweomer-masters were going to take Devar's father away from him forever. He had the vague thought that he might bring the young dragon back to the grasslands when that happened, if of course Dallandra could lift the dweomer upon Rori. He put family matters firmly out of his mind. Such worries needed to wait until the people of Cerr Cawnen had made their escape.

'I have to scry,' Salamander said. 'Do you know what that is?'

'I do. Mama does it sometimes. I'll be quiet, I promise.'

'Well and good, then.' So! Salamander thought. *That wretched Arzosah knows a fair bit more dweomer than she's ever admitted.*

Overhead a few wisps of clouds were sailing in from the east. Although the sun had set behind the western hills, casting the meadow and the tower into shadow, the sky above still shone brightly with blue. Salamander lay down on his back and fixed his gaze upon the clouds as he invoked the powers of Air. The vision of the army – a vision he could trust, this time – built up fast.

He saw immediately that his earlier dream had shown him truth. The army had spread out into a wide but thin scatter of men and horses. The rakzanir and the Keepers still stalked among them, but now the Keepers carried long spears to threaten those who disobeyed with the worst punishment of all. Salamander saw, in fact, one man already stripped naked and impaled, still alive and screaming, down by the river. Although Salamander couldn't hear him, he could read the victim's agony from his contorted face. A few more examples such as that, and no doubt the rakzanir would regain control of their men.

The priestesses were another matter. They had withdrawn a good half-mile away from the main army and taken many of the servants and supply carts with them. As he watched, Salamander saw a troop of some hundred fighting men ride up. His heart pounded – what were they going to do to the women? Nothing, as it turned out, but join them. Their leader knelt before the head priestess, who laid her hands on his head in blessing. A few at a time, other men slipped away from the army and took refuge among the white dresses and white mules of Alshandra's Elect.

Although he wanted to see more, Salamander's exhaustion cost him the vision. He returned to normal sight to find the clouds above dyed pink by the sunset. Devar still crouched nearby, but just as Salamander sat up again, they both heard the drumming of wings, a slow booming in the air as the burdened Rori flew back with two deer, one in his front paws, the other dangling from his mouth.

'Dinner!' Devar leapt up and with a rustle unfolded his wings.

'You go eat,' Salamander said. 'I need to find firewood so I can cook my share.'

'Medea got you some. It's in the tower.'

Devar bunched his muscles, stretched his wings, and leapt into the air. He landed on the ledge above a moment before his father dropped the two deer upon it. Medea and Mezza came waddling out of the cave, chattering in Dragonish, to join the meal. Rori landed among them and began apportioning the venison.

Salamander got to his feet – slowly – and staggered to the empty doorway of the tower. Inside, leaning against the wall, stood an entire dead pine tree, crisp with orange needles. Fortunately – since Salamander had only a small hatchet in his gear – a number of branches had fallen off, and a reasonable amount of splinters and dead bark lay around as well. Salamander got the impression that Medea had simply dropped the tree into the roofless tower from a great height.

Still, it made good fuel. Salamander had a decent fire going by the time Rori glided down to the meadow. His brother laid a mangled-looking haunch of venison, still wrapped in its original owner's hide, down in the grass.

'It's a bit gnawed around the edges,' Rori said. 'I can't handle a knife, of course, to disjoint anything cleanly. My apologies.'

'No need. I've had naught but soda bread to eat for days, and this will be splendid stewed, gnawed or not.'

Salamander skinned the haunch, then cut down to the tender meat by the bone. He set chunks to simmering in his cooking pot, then

tried roasting a slice threaded on a green stick. The result was edible
if tough. After he ate, he could think of nothing but sleep. He forced
himself to stay awake until the rest of the meat had cooked, then put
out his fire and lay down.

In the morning the rising sun woke Salamander. He had to struggle
to sit up; his sore muscles had turned so stiff in the night that he
could barely get to his knees. When he looked down at his arms and
hands, he realized they'd turned a mottled red and purple. The bruises
had come out in the night, transferred slowly from his etheric double,
unlike the normal, immediate bruises caused by physical blows. That
his face had suffered damage so quickly showed him just how much
danger he'd been in. He shuddered retroactively and reminded himself
that he'd survived.

Eventually he got to his feet. When he looked up at the cave, he
saw no sign of the dragons. He took an experimental step toward the
spring and found that he ached in every joint, but the more he moved,
the more he was capable of moving. By the time he'd made soda bread
and eaten it with cold stewed venison, he felt restored enough to scry.

In the upwelling spring by the powers of Water, Salamander
summoned images of the Horsekin army, or, as it turned out, of the
two armies. The priestesses had gathered several hundred fighting
men around them, as well as a good many servants and slaves. As
Salamander watched, this gathering of the devout mounted up. With
the chief priestess on her white mule at their head, they started off
– north. They were leaving the main body and marching off the way
they'd come, heading home.

Grinning like a fiend, Salamander turned his attention to the main
body, which was also preparing to move out. Most of the fighting
force remained under the control of the rakzanir, though they were
leaving some twenty men behind them, dead on the long spears, the
price of restoring order. In a reasonable show of discipline, the army
began to ride southward, still intent on reaching Cerr Cawnen, or so
Salamander could assume.

Salamander broke the vision, then used the spring as a focus to contact
Dallandra. Her image floated upon the water and smiled at him.

'I'm glad to hear from you,' she said. 'I've been worried, and – wait!'
The smile disappeared. 'Ye gods, what happened to your face?'

'I was forced to rejoin my physical body a bit hastily,' Salamander
said. 'But I reached it, and it's still here intact, more or less.'

Dallandra's image rolled her eyes, but she listened intently as he
described his work with the Alshandra image.

'So I've managed to throw some confusion into their ranks,' Salamander finished up. 'The army must be well and truly demoralized to have their priestesses hare off without them.'

'I should think so.' Dallandra smiled again. 'Good. You've certainly managed to slow them down.'

'Have you scried for Dar and his escort recently?'

'I have. They're nearly here, but of course, we'll need time to get the refugees well clear of the city. Most of the folk have been packing up their goods, but there are always people who refuse to believe bad news and because of that put off doing anything about it.'

'The name of that kind of person might be "Horsekin slave" if they're not careful.'

'That, alas, is true spoken. What are you going to do now?'

'Stay here in the tower in Dragon Meadow, or so I've been calling it in my thoughts. Rori and Medea will cause the Meradan a bit more trouble while I rest. Rori will bring me back to Cerr Cawnen once Arzosah returns to the lair.'

'I'm glad you're going to rest. What you did can't have been easy.'

'No, it wasn't, much as I hate to admit it. And now, oh mistress of mighty magicks, it behoves me to break this link. The astral tides are changing, and it's hard to see your face.'

'Indeed. Contact me again later, if you can.'

Salamander refilled his water bottle, then went back to his gear, lying scattered on the ground by the dead fire. He knelt to tidy it up, then paused, looking up at the tower looming above him. How hard would it be, he wondered, to repair the roof and put in an upper floor and some steps to reach it? An idea, or perhaps it was only an image, the glimmer of an idea, was rising in his mind, a few shy thoughts at a time, like the streaks of sunlight breaking over the eastern hills.

Once Rori returned to his human form – or died in the attempt – the Northlands would need this watchtower again to guard against prowling Meradan. Perhaps he could man it, in the company of his dragon nephew and his sisters. Devar would need someone to help him come to terms with his mixed heritage of elven blood. *I could live among dragons*, Salamander thought. At last he could give himself over to the dweomer in the complete and committed way he'd always shunned before. The idea gave Salamander a sense of satisfaction, an intense sweetness of feeling, such as he'd not known since his marriage to Marka, all those years ago in Bardek.

All morning he thought over his idea. Toward noon Rori flew down to join him. When Salamander told him what he was planning, his brother's oddly human eyes filled with tears. With a growl the silver wyrm shook his head and scattered them.

'This eases my heart,' Rori said in Deverrian. 'The one thing that's been troubling me about returning to human form is leaving Devar. He's but a lad as a dragon's life goes. He needs a father – or an uncle.'

'An uncle he shall have, then, assuming Dallandra approves my little scheme. Shall I ask her?'

'If it pleases you, ask away.'

When he let his mind reach out to Dallandra, she returned the contact so quickly that he knew she'd been waiting for him to reach her.

'How are you?' she said. 'You were so bruised and exhausted looking that I've been worried, but I didn't want to risk waking you if you were asleep.'

'I'm awake,' he said. 'Also full of insight. Oh Princess of Powers Perilous, I have seen the rest of my life work's stretch out in front of me like a road.'

'What?' Dallandra's intense surprise translated itself to his mind as a wave of laughter. 'Tell me!'

The tower, the dragons, his plans – Salamander sent their images and words to her in a jumble of excitement and delight. She listened calmly, and he could feel her caution as she thought over what he'd told her, thought it over for a very long time, or so it seemed to him, fearing as he did her disapproval.

'Can you really live alone like that?' Dallandra said at last. 'You of all people?'

'Me of all people, indeed. I am sick to my heart of playing the fool, Dalla, of travelling through Deverry with my tricks and tales. And yet, I'll never feel truly at home in the Westlands, either, nor will I ever be the bard my father wants me to be.'

'Very well, then.'

Salamander waited for her to voice nagging doubts and irritated sneers, but none came.

'You truly mean it, don't you?' Salamander said. 'You approve?'

'You know your own heart best.' Her image smiled at him. 'But Valandario was your teacher. You owe it to her to sit down and talk this over.'

'Well and good, then. We can discuss this once we all return to the alar.'

'Assuming, of course, we all do.' Her face darkened. 'Well, Dar's nearly here. The future's in the laps of the gods.'

*　　*　　*

The prince and his escort rode into Cerr Cawnen late on a damp afternoon. In the sky grey clouds were scudding away, as if perhaps withdrawing from the royal presence. As the rain slacked off, the occasional shaft of sunlight broke through to dance upon the surface of the steaming lake. From their places on the catwalks, the town watch greeted the prince with a shout and a blare of signal horns. Dallandra, who had been waiting with Jahdo on the lake shore, hurried down to the south gates of the city. When she looked back at Citadel, she could just make out Arzosah, as black as a raven, circling the lake once, then landing somewhere on the island out of sight – the ruins of the ancient temple, Dallandra assumed.

Daralanteriel led his men inside to the grassy commons, a ring between the town walls and the welter of buildings and crannogs at the lake shore. When a crowd of townsfolk came running to cheer the men who'd ridden to their aid, a weary, dust-stained Dar acknowledged them with an upraised hand and a grim sort of smile, a gesture that made him look more princely than Dallandra had ever seen him. He was growing into his position in life out of raw necessity, she supposed, more than some instinct of breeding.

'Citizens!' Jahdo called out. 'Stand back! On the morrow morn we'll be gathering up on Citadel, and then will you hear what his highness shall tell us.'

Calonderiel pushed his way through the retreating crowd and reached Dallandra's side. He too looked weary to the bone. He threw one filthy arm around her shoulders and squeezed, then let her go.

'What's the mood in the town?' he said in Elvish.

'Not panicked,' Dalla said, 'which is the best thing I can say. Most people are resigned to leaving. A lot depends on what Dar says on the morrow.'

'It's going to be a splendid speech. He's been working on it ever since we left the alar. Devaberiel helped him.'

'Dev's here?' Dallandra stood on tip-toe and craned her neck, but she could catch no sight of the bard. 'At his age –'

'Yes, the long days in the saddle were too hard on him.' Cal finished her thought. 'Two days out he turned back, but by then, Dar had the ideas he needs.'

'Wait! Dev rode back by himself?'

'Of course not! I sent a man back with him. Besides, the alar was following us along, so the two of them probably only spent one night out alone.'

One of the archers strode up to Calonderiel to ask him a question

about pitching their camp. Dallandra looked up at the torn grey clouds
and used them as focus. When she thought of Devaberiel, she saw
him sitting in front of a tent and talking with Carra. She broke the
vision with a small sigh of relief.

Although Jahdo invited the prince to stay in his house up on Citadel,
Daralanteriel insisted on camping on the commons with his men.
Grallezar, however, did accept Jahdo's hospitality.

'I be too old for all this sleeping on hard ground,' Grallezar said.
'Still, I do feel that my place be here. I do wish the townsfolk to see
that they may trust Gel da'Thae, though not Horsekin.'

After the evening meal, Jahdo left the house to meet with his fellow
council members. Dallandra nursed Hildie's baby, then left the house
to go speak with Arzosah. She found the black dragon lying on the
roof of the ruined temple, facing west and contemplating the red and
purple streaks of sunset clouds. As Dallandra picked her way through
the fallen stones, Arzosah wiggled around to face her.

'I wanted to thank you,' Dallandra said, 'for guarding the prince.'

'You're most welcome,' Arzosah said. 'Do you want me to stay here
for another day or two?'

'No, there's no need. No doubt your hatchlings want to see you.'

'So I'd hope, though I must say, hatchlings can be wretchedly
ungrateful at times! Be that as it may, I'll be off with the dawn on
the morrow.'

Later that night the Council of Five sent messengers through the
town to announce a meeting – a council fire, as custom called it –
some hours after dawn. As soon as the sun rose, workers carried the
planks and beams of the Chief Speaker's platform out of the council
house and began to assemble it, a solid wood structure wide and long
enough for twelve people to stand upon it. Jahdo and Dallandra stood
to one side of the plaza and watched the work go forward.

'Dar needs to speak, of course,' Dallandra said. 'And Grallezar wants
to say a few words as well. Cal and I should probably stand with Dar.'

'That be true, to show that the prince, he does have a retinue,'
Jahdo said. 'Grallezar may wish to have one of her guards as well,
that fellow Drav, mayhap. I shall be there, and Cleddrik, for he be
the only chief speaker Penli has, though he be not much of one.'

'You may want to add a couple of the men of the town militia.'

'That I shall do.'

Jahdo was about to say more when a louder drumming sounded
over the hammering of the workmen. Arzosah flew up from the temple
and circled the plaza once. She roared out a farewell, then headed

off north. They watched until she dwindled to the size of a crow and disappeared into a trail of mist.

'Ai!' Jahdo said. 'It does make my heart beat faster, to see a dragon fly, still till yet after all these long years.'

Once the workmen had finished the platform, the town drummer climbed onto it and set up his enormous leather drum. When Jahdo gave the signal, the drummer began to beat upon it with two sticks in a slow but steady rhythm. A few at a time, at first, the townsfolk who lived on Citadel began to climb the path and gather on the plaza. When Dallandra looked down to the lake, she saw a bobbing flotilla of coracles making their way across from the crannog town.

It took some while to assemble the citizens on the plaza and the officials on the platform. Dar stood off to one side, his eyes fixed on the horizon, his lips moving as he mouthed parts of his speech to come. Jahdo and Grallezar conferred briefly, while Calonderiel and Drav talked with the two militia men who'd been chosen to stand with them as a show of joint force. Cleddrik kept off by himself, his face grey with fear. Occasionally he took a rag out of his brigga pocket and mopped sweat from his face.

Artha arrived and Niffa with her, squabbling over some fine point of theology, to stand behind the platform with the rest of the Council of Five. As she watched the two women together, Dallandra realized that they had known each other since childhood. Their arguments, doubtless continued over the years, offered them as much comfort as reassurances would have given to someone else.

At last the pounding drum fell silent. Jahdo stepped forward and raised both hands in the air. The crowd quieted down, quickly in front, slowly at the rear.

'Citizens!' Jahdo called out. 'We all do know why we did gather here. The times be grave and fearsome. Let us delay no longer in facing what we must do.'

The citizens clapped their approval. The older people in the crowd called out Dar's name with some enthusiasm, though some of the younger women looked as grey and fearful as Cleddrik. Grallezar, however, spoke first, with Drav standing behind her on guard.

'Ye good folk of Cerr Cawnen!' Grallezar began. 'I come here in shame to offer my apologies to you all. My own city of Braemel once did count you as allies, and faithful allies you were. Alas, as you well know, the foul swine who serve the demoness Alshandra did wrest that city from me and mine and send us into exile.'

The crowd murmured in acknowledgment. Dallandra kept a sharp watch on Cleddrik and saw him wince over Grallezar's sneer at Alshandra.

'All I can offer you now is my advice,' Grallezar continued, 'to take or spurn as you will. Behold Prince Daralanteriel of the Westlands, another faithful ally of yours. I would ask you all to listen most carefully to what he does say.'

Grallezar and Drav moved back to allow Daralanteriel to come forward on the platform. He bowed to the crowd, then launched straight into his speech.

'Exalted Mother Grallezar called me a prince, but truly, the lands I was born to rule lie in ruins far to the west. You may have heard of them as the Seven Cities of the far mountains and the Vale of Roses. The Horsekin destroyed them, burning, looting, raping our women, killing anything that lived within our walls. The bards have passed the tale down, and truly, I think your scops, as you call them, know it as well.'

Among the crowd, the older people murmured their agreement.

'I am not your prince,' Dar went on. 'I cannot command you or enslave you. You are a free people. All I can do is offer to help you stay free. I have archers, I have swordsmen, I have riders who have fought the Horsekin before and won. You have brave soldiers who can fight beside mine. Yet neither you nor I have enough men to save this city. All we can do is save your lives, your children, your livestock, and whatever you can carry away.' He paused, looking out at the assembly, staring directly at one person, then another, and by catching their individual gaze, he caught the entire crowd. 'I can give you land, but you shall rule that land. Not me, not mine, not the lords who have sworn to me – but you in your free assemblies. In return I ask only for food to feed my army and yours, food and supplies for the men and women who will keep us all free.'

The crowd had fallen silent, so quiet that Dallandra could hear the wind in the trees behind the plaza. Dar cleared his throat, then continued.

'If you agree, we will swear a solemn bargain, you and I, under the eyes of the gods of both our peoples. I will swear that forever you will be free. You will swear that you will help me keep your lands free. We shall build together a new Rhiddaer – a land that's free indeed, a land free of the tyranny of kings and priests alike.' He paused, then held out both hands in supplication. 'Will you join me?'

The assembly roared like a breaking wave, cheering, screaming out 'we will' over and over. The noise echoed around the plaza, booming like the sea against rocks at high tide. Dallandra glanced around and saw Cleddrik glowering, glaring – and slowly, carefully, drawing a dagger from its sheath.

'Dar! Ware!' Dallandra screamed, but in the noise he never heard her.

She turned and flung up both arms to summon Wildfolk, but Drav had seen the threat. With a howl of warning he lunged at Cleddrik, who twisted away and made a feeble strike in Dar's direction. The Gel da'Thae grabbed Cleddrik's left arm and swung him away from the prince. Cal leapt forward, but Cleddrik slashed up with the dagger in his right hand. Drav made no noise, merely stared at Cleddrik with a look of mild annoyance as blood gushed from his throat. His knees gave way, and he fell, crumpling over like an empty sack stood on end.

From behind Cal threw one arm around Cleddrik's neck and hauled him back while he choked and writhed. Dar grabbed his wrist and twisted so hard that Cleddrik howled and dropped the dagger. Dallandra rushed forward and flung herself down in a kneel beside Drav, but all she could do for his physical body was to close its eyes. As she bent over him, she felt the touch of Grallezar's mind on hers. She looked up to see Grallezar kneeling at the back of the platform, bent over in trance. Dalla knew that her fellow dweomermaster would lead him to whatever after-death place of peace the Gel da'Thae might have.

The entire scuffle ended so fast that only those in the first few rows of the assembled townsfolk even saw the murder. They began to shout the alarm. As the news of this treachery spread, the crowd began to move, to pull back, to shout in response, a slow churn toward panic. Dallandra got up, wondering if she should try to calm the crowd, but Jahdo limped forward and held up the staff of his office.

'Citizens!' he called out. 'Citizens, hold and stand! The traitor's been caught.'

The two militia men stepped forward and took Cleddrik from Calonderiel. They twisted his arms behind him, then shoved him to the edge of the platform on display while Jahdo went on speaking in a calm, steady voice that worked on the crowd like dweomer. The citizens held still, stopped shouting, began to reassure each other, and finally fell silent to listen.

'Tomorrow we shall do one last piece of business here in our beloved town,' Jahdo called out. 'The traitor shall have a fair trial according to our laws. In the meantime, may his men guard our prince well.'

'Cursed right!' Calonderiel muttered. 'I blame myself for Drav's death. I should have been –'

'Hush!' Dallandra said. 'He took us all by surprise.'

'We did doubt his good faith,' Jahdo put in, 'but none did think he had the courage for such a strike.'

Calonderiel shrugged, started to speak, then knelt down by the Gel da'Thae's corpse. 'Let's give him a decent funeral at least,' he said.

'Just so.' Dar stepped forward. 'I owe him my life. I only wish I could have saved his.'

Between them Calonderiel and Daralanteriel picked up the corpse and carried it off the platform. Dallandra glanced at the pool of blood, turning thick in the sunlight, and nearly vomited. Jahdo caught her arm to steady her.

'Come away,' he said. 'There be naught more to say here. The prince did win them over.'

The crowd was beginning to disperse. Those at the back of the plaza were turning and filing down the path, heading for the lake shore, while those waiting milled around, finding friends, talking amongst themselves, picking up frightened children, but always moving steadily off the plaza like slow water running over an outcrop of rock.

Dallandra allowed Jahdo to help her down from the platform, but they lingered, waiting for the crowd to thin. Some of the militia men filled buckets at the well and sluiced down the platform. Dallandra turned her back rather than watch Drav's blood run along the cobbles.

'Well,' she said, 'now we know for certain that Cleddrik was a traitor. I just wish I'd seen it sooner.'

'I do wish the same for myself,' Jahdo said. 'Niffa did have her doubts, and now I do wish I'd listened more carefully. But there be naught we can do now. I be remembering my time in Cengarn, and what the folk there might say, "It were Drav's wyrd, and no man can turn his wyrd aside." Somewhat like that, at least.'

'That's true enough. But I still wish I'd sniffed out Cleddrik earlier.'

That afternoon, the Council of Five walked through the town to speak to the citizens. They came to the conclusion that they had no need to call for a formal Deciding, as the Cerr Cawnen people called their method of voting. Almost everyone in town wanted to leave now that Dar was offering them a destination. Those few who didn't would be coerced by their kin. Still, it would take several days for the town to pack up and leave in a orderly fashion, as Jahdo pointed out that night at the evening meal.

'We don't have two days,' Niffa's voice shook. 'I did scry out Rori this morning. He be harrying the army, but they be close, mayhap four days' ride at the most. If they do find us gone, but we do linger close by, then they will be riding after us.'

'Slaves are a valuable commodity to the Horsekin,' Calonderiel said. 'We'll have to fight some kind of delaying action.'

'We don't have the men to spare,' Dar said, 'so we have to make all possible speed. Jahdo, please, tell your people to take only what they can grab and carry away fast. If they're dead or enslaved, their possessions won't do them any good, will they now?'

'True spoken, your highness,' Jahdo said. 'Food first, clothing and blankets next, and then whatever trinkets do pack fast and easily. I think me we all ken what evil comes toward us, and none will linger to feel its whips.'

'Good. Once we're all heading south, then I'll give you horses for messengers. They can ride to the farms with the ill news and collect those people, too.'

Late that night, Dallandra and Calonderiel were talking over the evacuation plans in their chamber when she heard Jahdo calling for her. She opened the door to find the Chief Speaker pacing in the corridor. Two town guards stood nearby.

'Ill news,' Jahdo said. 'Cleddrik did hang himself.'

'Ye gods!' Dallandra said. 'How?'

'He did manage to tear his clothes to strips and braid himself a noose.' Jahdo shuddered profoundly. 'The cell he were in, the ceiling, it be not high enough for him to drop, like, so he did fasten the noose to the iron bars in the little window and lean forward, trying to kneel, like, till he did choke.'

'I can't see how anyone could – by the Black Sun!'

'He would have gone into a faint, methinks, early on, and then kept strangling till he died.'

'Mayhap, but still! He must have been incredibly determined to die.'

'He were sore afraid to face his Horsekin masters, I do wager.'

'Now that's true spoken. Most likely he took the easier way to his death, ghastly though it sounds.'

'A quicker one, at the least.'

'The militia men, they be hanging his corpse again, from the north gate this time.' Jahdo allowed himself a thin smile. 'Just to let the invading Horsekin know, like, when they get here, that their traitor, he did fail them.'

Salamander and Rori had left the young hatchlings in Medea's care and followed the Horsekin army. On that first day after the defection of the priestesses, it managed only a few miles. Fights among the men kept breaking out. The carts kept losing wheels – with the help of the remaining servants, Rori suspected, since the wheels had lasted much better before. The rakzanir would call a halt, then ride up and down the ranks with the Keepers of Discipline, whose whips cracked among the trouble-makers. Once they'd restored some sort of order, the army would lurch forward again.

The army made camp early that afternoon. As soon as it had stopped, and before the servants could tether and hobble the horses, Rori left Salamander out of sight on the crest of a forested hill and plunged down. He killed one horse and panicked the rest as he carried the bleeding carcass away. Although most of the soldiers took out after their fleeing mounts, the Keepers of Discipline had to beat some of the men into joining the chase. Rori stayed on guard in case a squad came after him, but apparently no one had the courage, this time around.

The two brothers made their own camp in a clearing among the trees, a good distance from the army. Salamander was eating cold venison, and Rori was busying himself with the dead horse, when they heard the drumming of dragon wings coming up from the south.

'That will be Arzosah,' Rori said. 'The prince must be safely in Cerr Cawnen.'

'I'd assume so, yes,' Salamander said. 'You know, you really need to tell –'

'I do know!' Rori snarled and clambered to his feet. 'I – my apologies. I'm not looking forward to this, not in the least.'

Rori waddled to the edge of the clearing. He made a quick run across, then took to the air, circling up clear of the forest around him, while Arzosah's wingbeats drummed closer and closer.

He gained height, saw her off to the south, and roared. She roared in answer and changed course to fly straight for him. When they met in mid-air, they swerved and circled around each other twice in greeting. With a dip of one wing he led her back to the south a little distance to a grassy hillside he'd spotted. They landed some yards apart, then walked toward each other until they could sit, crouching nose to nose.

'Where's that chattering elf?' Arzosah said in Dragonish. 'I hope you've lost him.'

'No, he's in a camp in the forest,' Rori answered in the same. 'I wanted to have a private talk with you.'

She laid her ears back and narrowed her eyes. 'What's wrong?' she said. 'Something is.'

'It's about that book of dragon dweomer. Laz Moj has found it.'

She hissed and stretched out one front paw, claws splayed. Rori took a deep breath and decided that he'd best blurt the truth and be done with it.

'Dallandra thinks she can return me to my human form,' Rori said. 'It would be best if she did. I can't live like this.'

Arzosah raised her head and roared so loudly that the earth trembled under them. 'I should have known,' she said in a normal voice. 'That meddling bitch! I suppose she wants you for herself again.'

'Don't talk like a fool! Of course she doesn't. It's just not my wyrd to live life as a dragon.'

Arzosah hissed, raised herself up, then flopped back into the grass with another long roar.

'I'm sorry,' he said. 'It aches my heart to hurt you like this, but I never should have let Evandar –'

'Oh hold your tongue, you wretched stinking male!'

It was, he supposed, the worst insult she could think of at the moment. He took refuge in silence.

'I'm going to have a talk with her,' Arzosah said. 'I doubt very much if she and her minions have the power to turn you back. It's no certain thing, Rori.'

'She did warn me that the spell or whatever it is might be beyond her unwinding.'

'Then she's wiser than I thought.' Arzosah growled deep in her throat. 'But there's no use in my vexing myself until we see if she can succeed without me.'

'Without you?'

'Do you think you would have survived Evandar's meddling without me there to lend you strength?'

Rori opened his mouth, then shut it again. He could feel his tail lashing through the grass of its own accord.

'Hah!' Arzosah said. 'You did think so, didn't you? You were dying, Rori. I refused to lose you, and that nasty clot of ectoplasm finally did something useful when he built the matrix for your new life. But something had to fill it, something beyond the astral light, that is.'

He wondered if she spoke the truth. He had never known her to lie outright, but her definition of falsehood tended to be far narrower than his. He managed to calm himself at last. His tail quieted and lay still. One thing he'd not miss about dragonhood, he decided, was that wretched appendage and its independent mind.

'Now then,' Arzosah said. 'Dallandra told me that you were going to take Ebañy back to Cerr Cawnen.'

'I am, yes.'

'No, you're not. I will, and yes, I promise you that I'll do naught to harm him. He's your blood kin, and that means much to me even if it means naught to you.' Her tail raised and slapped down hard, scattering torn grass. 'I should have known the wretched elves would find some way to break my heart.'

'I'm sorry.' It was the only thing he could think of to say at first. He forced himself to find something better. 'I'll always hold you dear, you know. It's nothing you've done.'

She was staring at him so reproachfully that he could barely look her way. He found himself remembering the night that Jill had left him, so many years ago now, and how bitterly he'd wept as soon as she could no longer hear him. He doubted if Arzosah could weep, but in her own way she was suffering. Finally he could stand her sad gaze no longer.

'I've got a dead horse back at camp,' he said. 'Are you hungry?'

'I was until you told me about this.' She hissed, and her tail thrashed of its own accord. 'But I suppose I could get a haunch or two down.'

'Then follow me back.' He turned and began his run downhill before she could say more.

He launched himself into the air, then glanced back to see her following. He hardly knew what he was feeling at that moment: regret that he'd caused Arzosah pain, certainly, and a sneaking hope that Dallandra would be unable to reverse the spell, but at the same time, a more urgent hope that she'd succeed. *I can't go on like this*, he told himself. *Better to die from the dweomer than risk staying a dragon much longer.* For the first time he realized how close he'd come to losing, just as Dallandra had warned him, his human soul.

During their last day in Cerr Cawnen, the citizens finished gathering what goods and supplies they could carry. Some few had wagons, more had handcarts, and even more could scrounge up a wheelbarrow. The town blacksmith fired up his forge and began binding wooden wheels with iron strakes. The council barge took Prince Dar and his escort on a tour of the crannogs and wharfs that ringed the lake. The archers helped the townsfolk wherever they could, and Dar stopped often to offer encouragement and repeat his promises.

As she wandered through the town, Dallandra was impressed by how willing the citizens were to help each other. No one would be left behind, not an elderly woman, not a man with a twisted leg or a sickly orphan child. When she returned to Citadel, she saw the council members dividing the stored food in the town granary and distributing it evenly among the citizens. Up at Jahdo's house, the servants were bustling around, putting food and moveable goods into mule packs.

'There be room for other goods as well,' Niffa told her. 'The eldest townsfolk may put in them what they cannot carry themselves.'

By sunset, the citizens had finished their preparations. The town militia stood guard over the loaded wagons and handcarts lined up at the southern gates. The Council of Five met for one last evening meal in Jahdo's house, where the heavy wood furniture, stripped of its cushions, stood randomly around echoing rooms without drapes and tapestries. The house felt cold, as if it knew that it was about to be abandoned. To feed everyone the servants had set out a long trestle table in the great room. Although Prince Dar ate with the Council at the head table, he insisted on taking a seat at the side, leaving the position at the head for Jahdo himself.

Dallandra ate little and left the table early. She walked outside into the golden sunset light, climbed up to the plaza, and stood looking down at the town across the lake. Silence lay everywhere, as heavy as the mist rising from the steaming water. The last meals in all the houses would be sad, she supposed, with mothers choking back tears and fathers muttering to themselves in anger while nervous children fussed and whimpered.

The sound of dragon wings broke through the silence. Dallandra looked up, expecting to see Rori, but Arzosah was gliding down from the sky. She dipped her wings in greeting and headed for the ruined temple to land. Dallandra hurried down the slope and reached it just as Salamander climbed down from the dragon's back. Bruises mottled his face and hands, but he waved to her cheerfully enough.

'Let me just get my gear down,' he called out. 'Ye gods, is it me, or does this place stink to high heaven?'

'It's the lake and the garbage,' Dallandra said. 'If you can stand to eat in this perfumed setting, you're just in time for dinner.'

'I cannot tell you how welcome that is, after days of scrounging in the wilderness. I shall grow used to the smell, as I suppose most people do.'

Dallandra turned to the black dragon. 'Arzosah, you have my thanks for —'

The dragon looked her way, curled her lip, and hissed. *What?* Dallandra thought, then realized that Rori must have told her the truth.

Arzosah confirmed that insight later. Dallandra took Salamander to Jahdo's house, saw him seated and fed, then returned to the temple, where Arzosah had stretched out in the early evening sun. At her approach the great wyrm roused herself and sat up with a great show of extending her wings and snarling.

'We'll be leaving on the morrow,' Dallandra said. 'Do you want to go back north to your hatchlings?'

'Perhaps.' Arzosah opened her mouth to expose her fangs, as long as sword-blades. 'I have a bone to pick with you, elf!'

'Oh ye gods! You spoiled and petulant wyrm!' Dallandra set her hands on her hips. 'This is a fine time for you to turn nasty!'

Arzosah paused, startled by this answering display of ill temper. 'Um, well,' the wyrm said eventually, 'Rori told me about the dragon book and his decision.'

'And?'

'I suppose you were going to sneak around and turn him back before I had a chance to say one word against it.'

'Naught of the sort.' Dallandra decided that the time had come for plain truth. 'Now, listen to me before you storm and rage.'

Arzosah hesitated, wings half-extended, mouth open, then suddenly shut her massive jaws and folded her wings. She lay down with her forepaws tucked under her chest like an enormous cat at a hearth.

'My thanks,' Dallandra said. 'First off, just because we finally have the book doesn't mean I can work the dweomer in it. I've not even seen the thing yet. Laz has it on Haen Marn.'

'Oh.' Arzosah's voice sounded calmer. 'I didn't know that.'

'Which is why I'm telling you. Second, and here's the crux, I'll need your help. You were feeding Evandar some of your life force, weren't you, when he transformed Rhodry into Rori?'

'How clever you are! I'd wondered if you noticed that.'

'I did. So no doubt I'll need you to re-absorb that power while I'm working the dweomer.'

'Do you really think I'd help you take away my mate? You must be daft.'

'I was assuming you'd feel that way, frankly. You have the winning stone in this game of carnoic, and so there's no need for you to whine, is there?'

Arzosah rumbled, then pulled one of her paws free and curled it to contemplate her claws. Dallandra waited, hands on her hips, and tried to think of some argument that might change the dragon's mind.

'Humph!' Arzosah laid the paw down again. 'Why doesn't anyone ever consider my feelings on these matters?'

'Because you always do it for them,' Dallandra said. 'You're so busy considering your own feelings that no one else can get a word in edgewise.'

'The gall!'

'You've got a fair bit of that, too.'

Arzosah opened her mouth, then shut it with a clack of fangs.

'You're only angry,' Dallandra went on, 'because I'm right.'

'You don't need to be smug about it.'

It was, Dallandra decided, as much of an admission as a dragon could possibly make.

'I suppose,' Arzosah continued, 'that if I refuse, you'll only force me to do it, anyway. If I could think up some new curses for Evandar, I would, giving away my true name the way he did. That slimy little clot of ectoplasm!'

'No, I won't. I'd never force anyone to work dweomer.'

'You must be jesting, just to add to my misery.'

'I'm not doing anything of the sort. Forcing you to use dweomer against your will – that's a kind of slavery I could never ever countenance.'

Arzosah's head jerked up, and she slithered around to look Dallandra in the face.

'Slavery.' Arzosah spoke so softly that the word was almost a hiss. 'You bring memories to mind, dweomermaster.' Her tail slapped the ground hard. 'Do you truly mean this, that if I refuse, that will be the end of the matter, and Rori will stay mine?'

'That's exactly what I mean. The decision is yours and Rori's.'

The great wyrm went very still, crouching, her eyes fixed on some far distant thought or time.

'You're free to go,' Dallandra said. 'But please, think well on this.'

'Now that I can promise you. I shall think long and hard.'

She turned and waddled some yards away, where she could spread her enormous wings without causing Dallandra harm. With a shudder of muscles she leapt into the air and flew, flapping hard as she gained height with her greenish-black wings drumming the clear sky. Dallandra watched as she headed north, dwindled to a speck of shadow, and then was gone.

Rori had followed the Horsekin south all that day, but the army made slow progress. Some hours after noon, when they stopped yet again for no discernible reason, his impatience got the better of him. He suspected that Arzosah would be returning as soon as she possibly could after speaking with Dallandra. His life hung on that conversation like the sword that hung from a single thread in the ancient Greggyn fable, whether he lived five hundred years as a dragon or only a few as a man on Haen Marn. Waiting to hear became intolerable. He took out his dread on the army below. He swooped down, scattered their horses, killed one, grabbed one of the Keepers of Discipline and let him fall to his death, then made his escape from the cloud of angry arrows and javelins that followed him without doing him harm.

In a considerably better mood Rori headed south, but he'd not gone more than a few miles when he saw Arzosah, flying north in the last of the long summer daylight to join him. They circled round each other in greeting, then flew back toward the army together. That night they made a lair on a long ledge of rock tucked into the side of a hill. Below, at a good distance, they could see the campfires of the Horsekin army spread out along a stream.

'I spoke with Dallandra in Cerr Cawnen,' Arzosah said. 'But I suppose you realized that I would.'

Rori winced and braced himself for a tirade. None came.

'She says Laz Moj has that book,' Arzosah went on. 'She doesn't know if she can work the dweomer in it or not because she's yet to read it.' She paused to consider him with narrow eyes. 'But Dallandra also told me that she can't reverse the transformation unless I help her.'

'That settles that, then,' Rori said. 'I'll be staying in dragon form.'

'And I suppose you'll fly off and sulk for a hundred years, leaving me all alone.'

'No. Why would I do that?'

'To punish me, of course.'

'For what? Wanting my company?'

Arzosah sighed and crossed her front paws. For some while she stared off into the gathering night.

'Do you remember Evandar's silver ring?' Arzosah said abruptly.

'Of course. It's the beginning of everything between us.'

'I like the evasive way you say that. You're beginning to speak like a dragon, Rori. Are you sure you want to turn into a despicable two-legged earth-bound creature again?'

'Does it matter?'

'Think back! You threw me that ring, and I ate it, and I was free of its spell over me. You set me free when I might have been your slave. Why wouldn't I do the same for you?'

Hope sprang up in his heart. Slowly Rori swung his head her way. She uncrossed her paws and held one up, curling it to contemplate her claws.

'You'll help Dalla?' he said.

'If you want me to. Say so, and I will.'

'I don't want to lose you and your company forever.'

'Why would you? You were Rhodry Dragonfriend before, and you'll be Rhodry Dragonfriend again.'

He felt his eyes, those traitorous human eyes, fill with tears. 'When Evandar was going to work the change upon me, there in Cerr Cawnen, Dallandra warned me that I'd be throwing my human soul away. That's what I wanted, then. I remembered too many evil things, and I wanted to forget them all.'

'Your soul seems a rather high price to pay to purge some evil memories.'

'Oh, I never paid it. Dalla was wrong. I've never been able to rid myself of that human soul, and now it's calling me back.'

'Back to your true form?'

'Back to my true home.'

Arzosah lifted her wings as if she were about to spread them, then let them fall to her sides in a rustle like the wind in a thousand oaks. 'So be it,' she said. 'We'll fly to Haen Marn together.'

'My thanks.' His voice broke, and he laid his head upon the hard rock. He heard her scales scrape on the ledge as she moved close to lick his face, comforting him as she'd done so often before.

'But do one last thing for me while you have wings,' she said. 'Bid farewell to our son.'

Rori hesitated, thinking back to his other, mostly human sons. He'd never said farewell to them because he could never have told them why he was leaving without disinheriting them. This son, at least, could hear the truth.

'When the time comes, I will,' he said aloud. 'In the morning let's fly to our lair. I'd like him to help guard the evacuation, anyway. Part of his heritage comes from the Westfolk, and part from Aberwyn, as well. He needs to become a friend to both.'

'So he does, and that's the one doubt I have about your leaving us. How will he know whom he may trust and whom he should despise?'

'Ebañy will be here. He wants to repair the old watch tower, he tells me, to live in. He'll teach Devar while he studies more dweomer.'

'Oh fires and fumes! You mean I'll be afflicted with that chattering elf for years to come?'

'Would you rather he stayed away? Or you could find a new lair away from the tower.'

Arzosah growled and turned her head away. He waited while she thought the matter through.

'For Devar's sake I can put up with your brother,' Arzosah said eventually. 'Medea's fond of his antics, and I suppose Mezza will be, too, once she sees his silly tricks and the like.'

'As long as you won't see him as some kind of affliction.'

'I won't, no.' All at once she rumbled with laughter. 'Let me think about this new wretched annoyance! Somehow or other, it must be Evandar's fault.'

Dallandra woke long before daylight. She fed Hildie's son Frie, dressed, and wandered outside to look down at the town below. The lake mists were beginning to clear in a soft rising wind, and she could see in the windows of every house the gleam of candles and cooking fires. The town had woken early as well. She turned to the east and saw in the dark grey sky a sliver of pink dawn just breaking. When she turned her mind to Dari, she saw her daughter just waking in her hanging cradle. Nearby Sidro sat up and rolled free of her blankets without waking Pir to tend the baby. Dallandra smiled at them all, then broke the vision. Soon she'd see them all again in the flesh.

As the sky brightened she returned to Jahdo's house and found it awake. The servants were setting out the last of the food while the family and guests stood around the table to eat rather than sit. Few people spoke, no one smiled. The farewell to their beloved city had begun. Dallandra took a chunk of bread, then beckoned to Niffa and Salamander, who followed her out to the morning light.

They walked round the back of the house. Below them they could see the ruins of the old temple, and beyond that, down the steep hill, tangled brush and shrubs. The slope led down to the lake, where black rocks raised jagged heads out of the water. As the morning sun gathered strength, the mists began to clear away, revealing the turquoise water.

'This be a beautiful sight,' Niffa said. 'It does break my heart to think I'll not see it again.'

'I know you love it,' Salamander said, 'despite the fiery earth-blood under your feet, but truly, it's a dangerous spot.'

'It did be our home for so long.' Niffa paused to wipe a few tears from her eyes. 'Still, better to leave than stay. I be well pleased that our citizens did make the better choice.'

'I am, too,' Dallandra said. 'I was terrified that they'd choose to stay.'

'So was I.' Salamander looked off to the north. 'The Horsekin aren't coming with a real army. It's a mob, a horde, a howling crowd that's only barely under control of its officers. If they conquered the town with the people in it, the slaughter and rape would be horrifying, worse even than what your usual army would perpetrate. They're Children of Fire, after all. Their rage escapes the control of their will and flares up like burning grass.'

Niffa shuddered profoundly. 'I do pray that we might get far enough away before they do reach our gates and find us gone.'

From their perch, they could see the council barge crossing the lake toward the north commons. Niffa pointed it out.

'The load it carries, that be the mule packs. My brother, he does keep his mules over there. His men will load them up and take them round to the south gate. I think me it be time for us to ready ourselves to ride.'

With the morning Rori and Arzosah took wing. They made one disrupting pass over the Horsekin army, then headed north to their lair above the ruined tower. On their way they saw a flock of wild sheep, grazing on a grassy hillside, descendants of animals that had once grown wool for Tanbalapalim or Bravelmelim. The dragons wheeled round in the sky, stooped, and killed a sheep each to take to the lair. When they landed on the ledge, the three young dragons slithered out of the cave mouth, all talking at once in Dragonish to greet Arzosah. She made a maternal clucking noise and licked each of their faces in greeting.

'I'll be sending you south to guard the Prince of the Westlands and his friends,' Arzosah told them. 'So eat up while I tell you why and how.'

'Devar,' Rhodry said, 'I want you to listen especially carefully. You and your sisters have a very important job to do, guarding the Prince of the Westlands. I want you to fly up now and join them. Someday, when you're grown and the Prince of Dragonkind, Prince Dar will be your ally, someone you can count on to help you. So you need to help him now.'

'I will, Da. I promise.'

'Good lad! Now you can have your breakfast.'

While her young ate mutton, Arzosah repeated her instructions several times, just to make sure, as she put it, that they'd heard her.

'Hatchlings, you obey Medea,' Arzosah finished up. 'She's the eldest, and she knows how to be cautious. Now lick your faces clean, everyone. It's time for us to fly.'

Once they saw Mezzalina, Medea, and Devar well on their way, Rori and Arzosah flew east. For Cerr Cawnen's sake, they spent one last day harrying the Horsekin army. First Rori would swoop down upon them from one side; then, as he flew up, Arzosah would attack from the other. They would both retreat, allow the army to gather itself again, then repeat the attacks. Finally, when the sun had reached zenith, the army came to a narrowing of the valley where the western hills rose in steep, stony cliffs. It huddled against the cliffs and made camp, barricading the horses between cliffs and a line of wagons. Rori and Arzosah flew off, well pleased at the delay, but by then, the army was a scant twelve miles from the town.

That night the two dragons laired in the empty town, up on Citadel's highest peak. Rori could remember Cerr Cawnen as a lively, noisy place – children laughing and playing, market vendors crying, the men of the militia joking together, their weapons and armour clanging and jingling as they went about their rounds on the town walls. Now silence lay over everything as thick as the mist rising from the lake.

'It gripes my soul,' Rori said, 'to think of those white savages taking over the town.'

'Mine, too,' Arzosah said. 'You know, we can't stop them from taking it, but we don't have to let them keep it.'

'What? We could summon every dragon in the Northlands, and we still wouldn't have the strength to drive these hairy rats out of their hole.'

'Quite true. But I can turn the place into an oven and bake them. Don't you remember what I told Dallandra, all those years ago when you'd been stabbed?'

'The fire mountain!'

'Exactly that! Cerr Cawnen's lake is fed by springs deep, deep under the land. What heats the springs? An ancient fire mountain, worn down by its own erupting, but still alive, deep inside the earth. It's a sullen creature, that fire mountain, hateful and ready to snarl and spit hot earth-blood from its crumbling mouth.' Arzosah raised her head and stared at the starry horizon. Her eyes gleamed in the faint light. 'I'll teach you the insults and curses that will wake it again, and together we'll call forth its fire.'

Rori found himself remembering the day he'd met her, when she'd looked much the same, grand and dweomer-proud. He realized that consorting with him had diminished her, made her petty and demanding.

'You need to be free of me,' he said, 'as much as I need to be free of this body.'

She turned toward him with a clack of fangs, as if she were about to argue, but she hesitated, then sighed.

'True spoken,' she said. 'I hate to admit it, but true spoken.'

They looked out at the town in silence while the moon rose, a few nights past its full, but still bright in the sky. The silver light lay over the silent houses and gleamed on a chimney there, a glass window here. At its final mooring the council barge bobbed by a rickety wooden pier over on the northern shore.

'If we burn the town,' Rori said eventually, 'I don't want the fire spreading. Can you keep it within the walls?'

'I can't, but the water meadows will. The ground all round here was a swamp years and years ago. The Rhiddaer folk drained it a few stretches at a time. But once the fire comes, and the walls tumble down, then the water will burst free.'

With the first light of dawn they woke. Arzosah announced that she had preparations to make and sent Rori off to scout the Horsekin column. He found it breaking camp where they'd left it, some ten miles away. Even though he glided far above it, he could see the thousand glints of dawn on metal that meant the warriors were arming. Apparently they'd sent out no scouts of their own to discover that the townsfolk had fled.

Despite the desertions over the Alshandra sighting, the army still presented a formidable enemy. Horse warriors, of course, a thousand of those left, he estimated, along with about five hundred spearmen, and archers, more archers than he'd ever seen with one of their armies, maybe a hundred in all. They must have stripped their cities of their best soldiers for this attack. Scurrying around, packing supplies, saddling horses, and the like were menservants – slaves, he supposed, and he pitied them, but only briefly.

Before they could notice him, Rori soared up high. The wind that day was blowing steadily from the south. He tacked into it as if he were sailing a little boat in Aberwyn's harbour, all those years before when he'd been a boy. *Never a hatchling*, he thought. *Maybe that's why I can't be happy like this.* With his decision made, he felt oddly calm, at peace despite the war brewing beneath him.

When he returned to Cerr Cawnen, Arzosah flew up to greet him. She led him off to the west and a hillside several miles from the town, where they could settle and wait.

'Will they invest the town today?' Arzosah said.

'Toward sunset,' Rori said.

'Good. Then they won't be marching out again right away. We'll work the spell in the dark of night, when the tide of Earth is flowing. Now listen carefully.'

Since Dallandra had spent her entire life travelling with the Westfolk flocks and herds, the disorder of the townsfolk's retreat surprised and appalled her. It took a couple of hours for all the refugees to march out of the town gates. Next came the water meadows, where they had to pick their way through on narrow trails. The mob split up into a myriad of lines and columns. By the time everyone had got through to the firm ground of the grasslands to the south, the sun hung close to noon. The entire column seemed to think as one. Without asking their leaders, they stopped to rest and feed their live-stock and children.

Dallandra used the interval to scry for Rori. She saw him just leaving the embattled Horsekin army under the western cliffs, but she had no idea of exactly where that spot was in relation to the town.

'By the Black Sun herself,' Dallandra said, 'we've got to get these people moving faster.'

'I agree,' Calonderiel said. 'Let me go talk with Jahdo.'

Jahdo agreed as well, but the logistics of the move defeated them all. It simply took time to get a mob of civilians ready to move on, more time to get them actually moving, and still more time to deal with wagons, children, dogs, horses, oxen, and the like during the march. Dallandra felt as if they were crawling south on hands and knees. At least the weather would hold clear and dry, or so the Wildfolk assured her. They'd spotted no rainstorms anywhere near.

A further delay arrived with the young dragons, who appeared in mid-afternoon, flying high over the refugee column. With Medea leading them, they landed a good half-mile ahead and to the east of the vulnerable livestock. Still, everyone stopped walking and paused to watch them, so graceful in the air. Cal, Dar, and Jahdo managed to get the line moving again while Dallandra turned her horse – one of those Pir had accustomed to dragon scent – out of line and trotted over to join them. She dismounted, dropped the reins to make the roan gelding stand, and walked over to Medea.

'Here we are,' Medea said. 'Mama said we're to help guard the prince.'

'And I'm very grateful that you will,' Dallandra said. 'Do you know where the Horsekin are?'

'Not very far from the town, last I saw them.'

Dallandra swore under her breath.

'Mama and Rori are planning something,' Medea went on. 'I don't know what, but I know what it means when Mama gets that look in her eye. She told us she'd do something to the Horsekin, and then she and Rori would come south, too.'

'Splendid! That lifts my spirits considerably.' Dallandra paused, glancing at Mezza and the young silver wyrm. 'Is that your half-brother?'

'It is.' Medea turned her head. 'Devar, come meet the dweomer-master.'

Devar was still young and slender enough to move with some grace on the ground. He trotted over, ducked his head in greeting, then looked at his sister as if asking what to say. *Rhodry's son!* That reality still had the ability to shock Dallandra, but she smiled and fell back on platitudes.

'My thanks to you, too, Devar,' Dallandra said. 'Your uncle's riding with us, by the by.'

'Good! I do like him.' Devar hesitated briefly. 'Mama said that you have dweomer.'

'Yes, I do.'

'Will you show us some?'

'Hush!' Medea snapped. 'Mama said you weren't supposed to bother Dallandra.'

Devar hung his head, so abashed that Dallandra pitied him, dragon or not. She patted his broad jaw. 'I will,' she said, 'but I don't have the time to do it now. We have to keep these refugees moving, or the Horsekin will catch and kill them.'

'They won't, not with me on guard!' Devar raised his head high and lashed his tail.

He was acting so like his father at that moment that Dallandra found herself speechless. Medea turned to him and hissed.

'Oh listen to you!' Medea said. 'Very fierce, I'm sure, for a hatch-ling!'

'Well, there's the three of us,' Devar said. 'That's triple fierce!'

'Just so,' Dallandra said. 'And now I suggest you all get ready to fly. I see the column's moving again.'

By some hours before the late sunset, the disorganized throng of townsfolk had managed to travel fifteen miles from their town walls. Dallandra realized that while they dithered and complained and spread out randomly, they also had a grim persistence that ignored exhaustion and drove onward. The column began to remind her of the slow

tides in the estuary of the Delonderiel that crept in a few inches at
a time, barely noticeable, until the sea water filled the channel and
threatened to drown anyone caught in it.

Still, once the Horsekin held the town, they could send out fast-
moving patrols to search for the refugees. Once they spotted the
townsfolk, they would be able to strike fast, too, without worrying
about their supply train, safe behind good stone walls. When Dallandra
scried for Cerr Cawnen, she saw the town clearly. Just to the north,
she spotted the tangled mass of the army's auras. As she watched,
the red and gold clouds of etheric energy, shot through with the black
lightning of sheer hatred, poured in through the north gates.
Detachments broke off and swirled east and west to secure the other
breaches in the walls.

Oh dear gods, Dallandra thought. *Our only hope now is whatever
Arzosah has in mind.*

Rori had followed the army for the last mile or so as it approached
Cerr Cawnen. He too saw the Horsekin ride up to the north gates
and find them open. The rakzanir at the head of the line of march
drew their horses up to one side and conferred for a few brief moments.
Squads trotted through and paused their horses to look around, then
trotted out again. Brass horns blared as shouts spread up and down
the line. Although he couldn't understand them, he could assume that
the men were being warned to ride ready for a trap.

Detachments of several hundred cavalry each broke off from the
main army and trotted round the walls to secure the east and west
gates. Another hundred horsemen rode straight through the north gates
to the commons, where they paused, guarding archers who climbed up
the catwalks on the inner wall and secured the high ground. Only then
did the rest of the army ride in, breaking into two columns, one spreading
east, the other west, along the grassy area below the walls.

Citadel presented a nice military problem. The rakzanir rode down
to the lake shore and drew up on horseback. Rori could see them
shading their eyes with their hands as they peered through the lake
mists at the rocky island across the water. The council barge, tied to
a nearby pier, sat invitingly close at hand, but Rori doubted that the
rakzanir would risk using it, not so close to nightfall. If the townsfolk
had planned some sort of ambuscade or armed surprise, they would
have laid it on Citadel, and doubtless the rakzanir could figure that
out for themselves. Sure enough, they turned their horses and rode
back to the army.

Brass horns blared once more. The army began to ride, half east, half west, around the lake, spreading out as they rode. Some men dismounted and peered into the houses built onshore. Some, bolder than the rest, found their way through the maze of steps and piers to the crannog houses and gardens. As the sunset turned the lake mist pink and gold, the Horsekin slowly took over the entire town. Rori circled high above and watched them tethering out their horses in the various sectors of the grassy commons near the gates. Squads climbed the catwalks and manned the walls while down below them, slaves pulled the gates shut under the eyes and whips of the Keepers of Discipline.

The rats had helped build their own trap. With a rumble of laughter Rori flew back to Arzosah through the gathering twilight.

Still bruised and sore as he was, Salamander had spent a painful day riding south among the Westfolk archers. Sleeping on the ground proved worse. In the middle of the night, just as the tide of Water was flowing out and that of Earth flowing in, he woke, squirmed, turned over several times, swore, squirmed some more, and finally got up. Besides his stiff muscles, he felt a sense of dread, a coldness in his mind and very soul. The Horsekin were near, too near – he could feel it. He put on his boots and picked his way through the sleeping camp. Out among the sentries Prince Dar greeted him in a voice just above a whisper.

'What are you doing here, Dar?' Salamander said. 'You should be sleeping.'

'I can take a turn on watch with all the rest,' Dar said. 'What about you?'

'I'm too bruised to sleep. Why not let me take your position, and you go get some rest? You'll need your wits about you tomorrow, dealing with this lot.'

Dar chuckled and agreed. Salamander watched him as he made his way back to the archers' camp. Dawn would be soon enough to apprise the prince and the banadar of the omens he was feeling, the dread and the sense of death hovering close on widespread wings. When he turned his mind to Cerr Cawnen, he saw in vision that the Horsekin army had invested the town. His stomach knotted so badly he nearly vomited. Too close, indeed. He thought of alarming the camp right there and then, but the two dragons, the silver and the black, were flying toward the lake. He waited, watching them in vision.

Rori and Arzosah flew high above Cerr Cawnen in an odd path, back and forth in long loops, one flying deosil, the other widdershins, while the waning moon shone upon their scales and made them glitter in the night. Back and forth as if they were weaving – they were doing just that, Salamander suddenly realized, weaving a dweomer spell over the sleeping army. All at once the pattern changed. Rori spiralled down toward Citadel while Arzosah flew a spiral up toward the stars. It seemed that he might land on the island, but he smoothed his flight and began to spiral up, whilst she changed her course and spiralled down.

Three times they danced out the dweomer, then met in the sky and began to wheel in tandem. Salamander focused his vision upon them. Their mouths moved as if they spoke, but he could of course hear nothing. Around and around – the earth shook under him, breaking the vision. Salamander dropped to his knees as the camp behind him exploded with shouts and screams of fear. The earth trembled and rolled yet again. He twisted round and saw everyone in camp getting to their feet only to fall to their knees as the earth quaked a third time. Horses whinnied and pulled at their tethers. Children shrieked, and the young dragons took flight, wheeling high about the panic.

Salamander forced his mind steady and brought all his trained will to bear upon his second sight. The vision returned. It seemed that he hovered above Cerr Cawnen with his brother and Arzosah as below the town shook and rolled. The water in the lake broke into waves as large as a stormy sea, rushing onto the crannogs, then pulling back to expose the lake bottom. Steam rose in great gouts from the lake and between the houses. Once again the earth trembled under him, but Salamander managed to lock his scrying onto the town.

Cerr Cawnen's walls were shaking and twisting as the earth beneath them quaked and bucked like the terrified horses tethered on the commons. The wooden gates shattered and tore away from the stone. The horses reared, kicked, and broke free, racing in panicked herds out of the town at every gate. Behind them men went running back and forth. Some rushed out of the broken gates behind the horses just as the walls began cracking into huge hunks of mortared stone. They fell, crushing anyone beneath them. Out in the lake the water rose into huge waves that bubbled and steamed. They came roaring toward land and slammed onto the crannogs. Houses ripped apart and fell. Salamander saw men slide, open-mouthed and screaming, into scalding water and tore his gaze away.

Citadel shook the worst of all. The sides of the island were giving way, crumbling like a child's sand castle at high tide. Rocks, houses, huge lumps of soil – they all slid into the lake below. Above the island,

Arzosah and Rori still flew their long loops, weaving their dweomer. The peak of the island cracked open and split in avalanches of rock and dirt. Ugly yellow steam rose in tendrils through the cracks. Through the shimmering curtains of this deadly mist Salamander saw the gleam of fire.

With a roar that reached the camp, some fifteen miles away, the ancient caldera sprang to life. Liquid fire, the boiling blood of the earth, rose high into the air in long streamers, then plunged down. A deadly rain of glowing rocks fell with it, pounding down on the Horsekin camp and the Horsekin soldiers. Salamander saw men catch fire as they rushed back and forth, their mouths open in an agony that he couldn't hear. As much as he hated them for Meradan, Salamander could no longer bear to watch. He scried for the two dragons, saw them flying safely south, and broke the vision.

Salamander staggered to his feet just as Dallandra came running.

'Did you see?' she called out in Elvish.

'Yes, and it's horrible.'

'Very, but hurry! We're moving the camp out. I have no idea of how far or fast the molten rock will run.'

In the grey light of first dawn the refugees rushed to gather goods, livestock, and children. Salamander mounted the horse that an archer brought him, then scried again. He could see nothing of the town under a huge blanket of steam. The water meadows were boiling around Cerr Cawnen's grave. From the centre of this cloud ash rose in a tower like an enormous fist thrust into the sky.

When Salamander expanded the vision, he saw terrified horses, dusted with ash and cinders, still running south, and a few men as well, staggering through air that seemed as thick as porridge. He broke the vision to find Calonderiel and his archers forming up around him.

'Some of the horses escaped,' Salamander called out.

'We'll worry about that later, you drooling idiot!' the banadar called back. 'Ride!'

At a fast walk the warband set off with the prince at its head and the banadar at the rear, herding the refugees along as quickly as they could possibly move. Every now and then the earth trembled, but more and more gently, as if the shocks were dying away in slow waves. At intervals Salamander scried; he could assume that Dallandra and Grallezar were doing the same. Steam mostly obscured the smoking crater that once had been a town and an army, but occasionally Salamander could see enough of the fringes of the disaster to realize that the lava had stopped spreading some five or six miles from the eruption. He reminded himself that he'd witnessed no natural event, but one caused and thus to some extent controlled by dweomer.

Yet the tower of ash, grey flecked with black, continued to rise into the sky, like the smoke from a funeral pyre for the Horsekin army. All that morning he could see it, rising on the horizon, until a south wind sprang up and began to push it to the north, spreading it out into a vast fan, letting it fall like deadly snow upon the farmland and the grass.

Dallandra was riding near the middle of the column of refugees when she saw Rori and Arzosah arrive. The two elder dragons joined their young, then sorted the clutch into a formation like that of flying geese, with Rori at the head. They glided as much as flew, swinging first to one side, then the other as they kept pace with the slower refugees below.

Dallandra had seen so many horrible deaths during the eruption that she hated the thought of scrying out the destruction again. Grallezar, however, had more steel in her soul. At times she tossed her reins to Dallandra and let her lead her black gelding along while she herself scried. She came out of one vision trance with a grimly satisfied smile upon her face.

'It be safe to let the folk stop and rest,' Grallezar said. 'The earth's blood flows not our way.'

'Well and good then.' Dallandra tossed Grallezar's reins back to her. 'I'll go tell the prince.'

Dallandra turned her horse out of line and rode at the trot up to the head, where Prince Dar rode beside Calonderiel. She guided her horse in between theirs.

'We can stop now,' she said. 'The molten rock's not spreading our way.'

'Good,' Dar said. 'Everyone's weary, especially the horses.' He glanced up at the dragons wheeling in the sky. 'I want to send one of the wyrms off with messages. We need to let Gerran and Cadryc know what's happened.'

'Just so,' Calonderiel said. 'And I suppose we should send a letter to that spoiled child in Cengarn.'

'It would be politic.' Dallandra glanced Cal's way with a smile. 'If Rori takes the messages to Cadryc, Cadryc will probably agree to pass the news on to Ridvar. For now, though, everyone needs to rest, even the dragons.'

'Especially the dragons, I'd say,' Dar put in. 'They worked that dweomer, and it must have been draining. Maybe that young green one can take the messages on.'

At the prince's orders, the grateful refugees spread out along a stream and made a rough camp in the tall grass. The dragons landed a good way off to the south. Dallandra and Salamander left their horses with the Westfolk archers and made their way over the rough footing to join them. The two elder dragons were rolling on their backs in the grass, wiping away ash and cinders. At the sight of the two Westfolk, they rolled back onto their stomachs and arranged themselves in more dignified poses, front paws outstretched.

'I suppose you're wondering how I worked that dweomer,' Arzosah said. 'It's a dragon secret, and I shan't tell you.'

'Even if I knew,' Dallandra said, 'I couldn't make it work, even if I wanted to. I've never seen such a astounding act of magic in my life. I never dreamt that anyone could do such a thing, frankly.'

Arzosah rumbled and ducked her head in a modesty that Dallandra suspected of being false.

'You've saved the townsfolk,' Dallandra said. 'I doubt me if we have to worry about being chased now.'

'I doubt it, too,' Rori said. 'Dalla, I'd be willing to wager high that the dead troops were the flower of the Horsekin army. They had the best warriors, the best equipment, and a fortune in horseflesh. It'll take them a long time to recover from this.'

'And the priestesses of Alshandra will have plenty to say about it, too,' Salamander broke in. 'I can hear them now, nattering about how the army refused to listen to their goddess's warning and thus paid for their stubbornness, arrogance, and so on and so forth. The rakzanir are going to have a cursed lot less authority from now on, well, the ones that survived.'

Dallandra knew that she should feel joyful over this defeat of an enemy that would have slaughtered her and her entire people, had they been given the chance, but the memories of scalded men and burning horses rose up in her mind and turned the victory ugly and sour. Yet a victory it was. As she walked back to camp she saw the children and the townsfolk, huddled together around their wagons — refugees, exhausted, impoverished, but alive.

That afternoon the townsfolk laid campfires and lit them with no fear of attracting their enemics' attention. The women cooked soda bread and tried to quiet their frightened children while the men talked together in soft voices. Every now and then the earth shook, but each tremor felt weaker than the last. Still, Jahdo insisted that the town watch – he still thought of it as the town watch – post sentinels, just in case. No matter how many times the dweomerfolk told him what had happened, even his own sister, he found it hard to believe that the threat had died with the enemy army.

Late in the day he walked out to the northern edge of the camp and stood looking back in the direction of the place that had once been his home. An enormous smear on the horizon, the plume of ash still rose, and the south wind still blew it back toward the north. How long, he wondered, would the caldera vent? He could ask Arzosah, he supposed, and eventually he would. For the moment he only wanted to stand and look at the end of everything he'd loved.

Niffa walked out to join him. When he turned his head to look at her, she slipped her arm through his.

'Be you mourning?' she said.

'Of course. Be not you?'

'I do, truly. As you do say: of course.'

Jahdo forced out a twisted smile. 'Ai! Our homeland it be gone now past all reclaiming. The cursed Horsekin, they be welcome to it now.'

Niffa nodded and patted his arm. While he knew that she mourned Cerr Cawnen in her own way, he doubted if the loss meant as much to her as it did to him. He'd realized years before that her true home lay with the dweomer. Where her body might dwell mattered very little.

'On the morrow,' Jahdo continued, 'we'd best try to make speed. When we do reach this promised farmland, there be much work to be done ere winter falls, building shelter and planting the seed grain. Our time of mourning best be short.'

'True spoken. Think of it this way, brother. We be finally going home. The wretched Slavers stole our land so many years ago, but now they do need us so badly that they be forced to give some of it back.'

Jahdo laughed, one startled bark. 'Truly, I never thought of it in such a way. But you be right enough. Let me go back now and summon the rest of the council. We shall tell everyone we be going home to the Summer Country. And this time we be a free people!'

As the news spread through ragged camp of the refugees, laughter and cheers spread with it. Later, Jahdo knew, there would be more tears and regrets for what they'd lost, but from this moment onward, they once again owned a future.

*   *   *

With Carra and her children riding in the lead, the royal alar had been travelling toward Cerr Cawnen – slowly, of course, the way alarli always travelled. They were still over fifty miles away when the earth's blood boiled and rained down on the distant town. Even so, they felt the earthquake as a hard trembling of the earth. The flocks of sheep immediately panicked. Ewes and wethers bleated, shoved one another, and finally ran off in all directions. The alar had to stop to allow the dogs to round them up again with the help of some of the men while the rest of the riders, under Pir's direction, kept the horse herd under control.

By the time order had been restored, the sun was sinking low in the west, and the alar decided to camp where it was. Valandario had scried for Dallandra and the prince, seen them safe, and then contacted Dalla mind to mind. When the news spread through the alar that the Meradani army lay entombed in the boiling remains of Loc Vaed, such a loud cheer went up that the sheep nearly bolted again. The Westfolk broke out skins of mead and passed them around. Those who could play unpacked their harps and flutes. The music began as soon as the tents were raised, and the singing followed.

Branna, however, found it impossible to share in the celebration. As she told Neb, slaves and other innocent souls had died in the eruption along with the army.

'That's true,' Neb said. 'But I still thank the gods for Arzosah's dweomer. If the Horsekin had followed the retreating townsfolk, the army would have slaughtered the prince, his guards, the townsmen – everyone they couldn't enslave and sell.'

'And then they would have come for the rest of us. I know that. It just must have been such a horrible way to die.'

'Well, that I can't argue with.' Neb shuddered and tossed his head as if he'd throw off the truth of it. 'Truly horrible.'

Others also stayed away from the general merriment – Sidro, Pir, and the rest of the Horsekin left with the alar. Branna and Neb joined them at Valandario's tent, which as usual stood some way away from the noisy camp, for the evening meal. Young Vek had had a seizure, in fact, when he'd heard about the grim wyrd that had fallen upon the army.

'I did give him his usual medicaments,' Sidro told Branna. 'He be inside Val's tent, sleeping.'

'Well and good, then,' Branna said. 'I – oh by the gods! Sisi, do you remember that vision he had, back at the end of winter?'

Sidro caught her breath in a little gasp. 'The tower of smoke,' she said, 'and snow did fall upon the crops! The snow, it be ash, I think me.'

'Indeed.' Valandario joined them. 'When I spoke to Dallandra, she told me how the smoke rose up in a pillar, and she thought of Vek.'

When they fell silent, the nearby music and laughter spilled over them. In a blaze of golden light as thick as honey, or it seemed, the sun hovered just above its setting. When Branna shaded her eyes with her hand and looked off to the west, she could see a jagged edge etched along the skyline instead of the straight-as-a-bowstring horizon more usual to the grasslands. Neb joined her and followed her gaze.

'We've come a long way west, haven't we?' Branna said.

'We have,' he said. 'Those must be the western mountains you hear so much about, or at least their foothills. The remains of Zakh Gral are over there somewhere.'

'I was thinking more of the Seven Cities than Zakh Gral.'

'Those, too, and what do the songs call that? The Vale of Roses, that's it.'

'All gone now. They must have been lovely.'

'Truly.' Neb looked briefly solemn, then grinned at her. 'Ah well, are you hungry? It smells to me like someone's roasting a sheep somewhere.'

'They are. One of the poor stupid things broke its leg in the general panic.'

'No use in letting it suffer.' Neb took a deep breath. 'Lots of pot herbs, and some wild garlic, too.'

After everyone had eaten, Valandario took Branna aside. They walked out into the silent grass and turned toward the east, where the last crescent of the moon hovered in the starry sky. Crickets sang in the grass, and a soft breeze blew away the sweat and heat of the day.

'Dalla asked me to relay a message to you,' Val said. 'You know that she wants you to come to Haen Marn with her.'

'I do. Will we go on dragonback?'

'She'd rather use one of the hidden roads. In the morning she'll arrive back here, and then the two of you will leave once she's rested.'

Branna yelped aloud in sheer excitement, and Val laughed at her.

'My apologies,' Branna said. 'I've seen so many dweomers in the past year, but I've only watched, except for that one ritual about reversing the astral currents. Even then, I just filled the station in the circle. All I did was speak when everyone else did. But this – getting to travel on the astral roads – it's truly an adventure, isn't it?'

'Very much of one.' Val turned solemn. 'It could be dangerous. You'll need to do everything Dalla tells you and do it exactly right. Do you understand that?'

'I do, and I will.' Branna did her best to calm herself. 'It just sounds so fascinating, though.'

'It does, at that.' Val sighed and glanced away. 'I remember being so young and enthusiastic, myself.'

'But you're still young, I mean, for one of the Westfolk.'

Val kept silent for so long that Branna began to fear she'd offended her. All at once, though, Val laughed with a rueful shake of her head.

'I am,' Val said. 'You know, it's good to be reminded of that every now and again. But now, as for Dalla, she needs to read that book Evandar left before she can decide who will work with her in the ritual, though I'm assuming that I will.'

'Well and good, then. I have hopes I'll get to take part.'

'That's up to her. Now, the rest of us will join up soon with the prince and the Cerr Cawnen people. They'll be heading east, eventually, to the Melyn River Valley. Dalla particularly wants Neb to accompany them, because the prince is minded to settle some of them on the site of Neb's old village.'

'No doubt my uncle will be pleased. He's talked for years about needing settlers for the valley.'

'The prince is sending him messages about just that. And those will go by dragon.'

'Well and good, then. I'd best go give Neb the news.'

With the help of some of the other men, Neb had just finished setting up their tent. Branna followed him inside to help spread the floor cloth and arrange their blankets upon it. She was expecting him to be unhappy that she would be making the trip to Haen Marn without him, but to her surprise he agreed it would be best.

'I've done much thinking over the days past,' Neb said. 'I think your wyrd lies more with the dweomer than mine does.'

'What?' Branna said. 'Of course you're marked for it.'

'True spoken, but that's not what I meant. We know I'm meant to be a healer. You'll need to know some healing lore. There's a difference. To me the dweomer's a tool. To you, it will be your life. Do you see?'

'I do, truly.' She felt a cold chill run down her spine. 'But I want us to be together.'

'So do I. Never doubt it! But there may be times we're forced to be apart. I think that may be why I had to go play the fool in Cengarn.

So I'd know I could go away and yet come back again. Now it's your turn to go off, but you won't be playing the fool.' He paused to grin at her. 'Some of us learn more slowly than others.'

She laughed and threw her arms around him. He kissed her, and for the rest of that night, they talked of very little indeed.

With the dawn Branna went out with Elessi to feed the changelings. As they left the camp, the pounding of wings split the silence. She looked up and saw Medea, flying east on the prince's business, like a sleek green arrow in the rising light.

It had taken Berwynna some days to realize that Mirryn considered himself to be in love with her. Since they hardly knew each other, she doubted if he actually did love her, but he followed her around the dun, took her riding, ate with her at meals, smiled whenever he saw her, and in general made a nuisance of himself. She took to staying in the women's hall as a refuge, where Lady Solla, who was finding the stairs leading to the great hall more and more difficult thanks to her advanced pregnancy, tended to join her.

Usually the tieryn's widowed daughter, Adranna, sat with them, although sadly enough she rarely spoke. Generally Adranna sat in a chair by the window and sewed upon an elaborate embroidered coverlet for her daughter's dower chest. At times tears filled her eyes; she would brush them away and bend to her needlework as if her life depended on filling up the wolves drawn into the pattern with scarlet thread. *Will I end up like her?* Wynni would think. *Mourning Dougie all my life?*

Now and then Solla tried to draw Adranna into the conversation, but generally the lady answered briefly, then withdrew into herself again. Berwynna and Solla had taken to sitting at the other side of the chamber where their talk wouldn't disturb her.

'About Mirryn now,' Wynni asked Solla one afternoon. 'Know you if he does realize that I were betrothed to another man?'

'He does,' Solla said. 'But it doesn't matter to him, and for that I honour him. Gerro asked him outright, you see, and told him that you needed time to mourn.'

'That be true-spoken! Not a night does go by when I do fail to dream about Dougie. My thanks to your lord, truly.'

'He's a good man, Gerro.' Solla hesitated briefly. 'But so is Mirryn, in his way. You'll not always be mourning your Douglas.'

'That be true as well. I do know it be so. Yet it be like a knife in my heart to be thinking I might forget him.'

'Nah nah nah, never that!' Solla smiled at her. 'That's not what I meant. You'll never forget him, but you'll find room in your heart for a second love. You're too sensible a lass not to.'

Berwynna managed to smile. 'My thanks, and I think me you have the right of it.'

That night at the evening meal Berwynna found herself looking at Mirryn in a new way. When his father died, he'd be lord of the Red Wolf dun, right there on the border near the Westfolk, part of a wider world than Haen Marn could ever offer. If she stayed on the island, whom would she meet to marry someday, she wondered, if Solla were right and her heart healed? One of the Mountain Folk and live underground all her life? The thought made her shudder.

'Is somewhat wrong?' Mirryn said.

'Naught, my apologies,' Wynni said. 'Just thinking of a painful thing.'

'I realize, my lady, that there's been much pain in your young life.' Mirryn sounded as if he were reciting a bit of bard lore that he'd got off by heart. 'I only hope that someday all such trouble will be behind you.'

She glanced at Gerran, who sat across the table from them. He'd probably told Mirryn what to say, judging from his approving smile. When a servant girl put baskets of bread upon the table, Mirryn took one. He drew his table dagger and cut a chunk off the loaf before passing it across. He tore it in two and offered half to Berwynna, who took it from him, had a bite, then laid the rest on the wooden trencher they were sharing.

'What be the thing you truly hope for, Mirryn?' Wynni said. 'I do wonder if somewhat lies behind those fancy words.'

Mirryn blushed scarlet. Wynni rested her chin on her hand and smiled at him until the blush receded.

'Well, I'm hoping you'll favour me, of course,' he said. 'Surely that's obvious.'

'It be so, which is why I did want to drag that fox out of his hole.'

'Now that you have, does the colour of his fur please you?'

'In some small way. I think me that with much time the day will come when such things do please me greatly once again.'

'When that day comes, I hope with all my heart that it's a wolf that pleases you, not a fox.'

'A red wolf, it be a fine sight, truly, yet none of us know what wyrd the gods have in store for us.'

'That's so, and wisely said.'

Berwynna suddenly realized that Lady Galla was leaning so sharply their way, desperate to hear in the noisy great hall, that she looked as if she might be feeling faint. In his seat at the foot of the table, Uncle Mic was struggling not to laugh. Mirryn had noticed his mother's angle as well.

'I hear that Lord Pedrys is planning on holding a tourney,' he said, a trifle loudly. 'I think mayhap I'll ride to it. Gerro, are you up for a little sport?'

'Depends,' Gerran said. 'On how my lady fares. I don't want to be away from the dun when she's delivered of the child.'

Conversation, and Lady Galla's posture, returned to normal.

Berwynna had barely finished her dinner when she heard drumbeats thrumming through the sky. With a murmured apology to Mirryn, she got up and left the table to run to a window and look out. By then the rest of the great hall had heard the sound as well. Everyone stopped talking to listen as it came closer.

'Is that your father, Wynni?' Galla called out.

'It be not so, but my step-sister.' Wynni saw a flash of green and gold circling the dun. 'I think me I'd best go meet her.'

Uncle Mic joined her as she left the great hall. In the warm summer twilight they hurried down the path to the meadow by the dun, where Medea was drinking from the stream. She lifted her head in a scatter of drops and rumbled in greeting. Strapped to the tallest spikes on her neck was a leather pouch.

'Messages for the tieryn!' Medea sang out. 'And one for you, Wynni, though that one's not in the pouch. I'm here to take you and Mic back to Haen Marn.'

'Oh ye gods!' Mic muttered. 'Another wretched, sick-making ride through the air!'

'It be too far to walk, Uncle Mic,' Wynni said. 'My thanks, stepsister! My heart does long to see my mother again.'

'I assumed it would, truly,' Medea said. 'Mic, will you untie this itchy pouch and get it off me?'

'I will, and I'll take it up to the tieryn as well.'

Carrying the messages, Mic hurried off, but Berwynna lingered to ask her step-sister for news of Rori. 'He's in splendid form,' Medea began, 'so, now that the war's over –'

'The war be over? Wait, go not so fast in your telling! I knew that not.'

'My apologies. Here I was thinking you'd have dweomer, so you'd know.'

'Our sister Mara has all of that on my side of the family. I have none, and truly, I be glad of it.'

Berwynna sat down in the grass. She stayed in the meadow for some time, listening to Medea's report of the destruction of the Horsekin army, while the twilight slowly faded into night. Above them in the clear sky the stars came out and seemed to hang close to earth as if they too rejoiced in the death of so many enemies.

Eventually Berwynna heard someone calling her name. Medea stopped talking and swung her head toward the sound. A gleam from a lantern, held in someone's hand, bobbed down the path toward them.

'Uncle Mic?' Berwynna called out.

'It's not,' Mirryn answered her. 'It's Mirro. I thought you might be glad of the light and an escort back to the dun.'

He had used the familiar form of the second person, 'ti', she realized, perhaps as a token of friendship, perhaps in hope of something more. She hesitated, then decided that it would be ungracious to deny him that hope.

'It does gladden my heart,' she said. 'My thanks i ti.' 'To you', again in the familiar form.

As he walked up to join her, he was smiling so softly that Berwynna made a decision.

'We'll be leaving you on the morrow,' she said, 'Uncle Mic and me. My heart does ache to see my mother again.'

Mirryn's smiled disappeared. 'Ah well,' he said. 'I can understand that.'

'But if my step-sister be willing to be so kind,' Berwynna continued, 'mayhap she'll come to the island to fetch me here again in the spring.'

'Of course I will,' Medea said.

'Then I'll look forward to the spring doubly this winter.' Mirryn made as much of a bow as he could without swinging the lantern so hard that the candle went out. 'My thanks to you, fair ladies both.'

'Most welcome, I'm sure,' Medea said. 'Wynni, Dallandra asked me to tell you that Laz Moj has returned to the island with the missing book.'

Berwynna let out a whoop of pure joy that made Mirryn jump back a step. She laughed as she apologized to him.

'You ken not how that news gladdens my heart,' Berwynna said to Mirryn. 'I'll be telling you the tale should you wish.' She turned to Medea again. 'Will Dalla be going to the isle to fetch it?'

'She will, and knowing her, I wager she'll get there before we do.'

Laz had taken to doing what kitchen work he could with his maimed hands. He'd worked out a way to hold a broom reasonably well, and

every morning he swept out the kitchen hut while Lonna went outside
to toss scraps to the island's cats. Since the Gel da'Thae relied on
ferrets to control the rodents who inevitably attack stored food, Laz
had never seen housecats before coming to Haen Marn. In fact, he'd
assumed that they were some species of Wildfolk until he'd seen
Lonna and Mara feeding and stroking them.

After she tended the cats, Lonna would come back into the kitchen,
look at the swept floor, and grunt a brief thanks. The moment was
Laz's chance to fish for information.

'Lonna,' he said that morning, 'I heard the name Lin Rej once. Was
it a dwarven stronghold?'

'It was,' Lonna said. 'And a grand one, or so I heard as a child. It
stretched for miles and miles underground, but there were gardens,
too, up above. That's how your folk got in, through the garden stairways, when they were a-burning it and slaughtering my folk.'

'My apologies! I —'

'You weren't there.' Lonna fixed him with a gaze as sharp as a knife
point. 'My thanks for the sweeping.'

Laz bowed to her for want of anything to say and left the kitchen
hut. He found himself wondering if he had been 'there', one of the
Horsekin who'd destroyed the dwarven city. If so, it had happened
too many lives ago for him to worry about, he decided, especially
since he had a more recent set of transgressions to brood over.

Every afternoon Laz spent several hours teaching Mara dweomer
lore. The need to organize the material efficiently showed him that
his own training had a good many gaps, things that Hazdrubal had
never told or shown him. The Bardekian, of course, had expected to
be paid for his lore. Most likely he'd held things back in order to get
a better price for them later, not that he'd lived to see that 'later'.
More and more Laz was coming to agree with Faharn, that Hazdrubal
was — not a sham, certainly — but suspect.

Had Hazdrubal studied the legendary dark dweomer? Something
had made him flee his home in the islands. Now and then Hazdrubal
had made sharp comments about meddling government officials or
cowardly masters of magic who refused to see and take the strange
powers available to those who dared to use them. While Faharn had
bristled at such talk, Laz had found it oddly familiar, even though he
couldn't place where he'd first heard it.

That life before Lord Tren, he would think, *the one that Dalla and
Ebañy never talked about. What did I do then? What was I?* As the
drowsy summer days rolled by on Haen Marn, Laz began to feel that

he knew the answers to those questions. His mind merely recoiled every time he tried to voice them.

Yet in the event, it was neither Ebañy nor Dallandra who forced him to the answer. One hot afternoon Laz stood under an apple tree, holding out the basket while Kov, up on a ladder, picked the ripest fruits and tossed them down. Flies buzzed, birds sang, a breeze from the lake stirred the air, and Laz was fighting off the urge to sleep where he stood when he saw a lozenge of astral force appear nearby.

His first thought, in fact, was that he slept and dreamt, but Kov had seen the quivering silver shape as well.

'What in the name of Gonn's hammer is that?' Kov said.

'I'm not sure,' Laz said, 'but I'd get down from that rickety ladder if I were you. Something's made a gate from somewhere, and I've got no idea what's going to come out of it.'

Kov swore aloud and climbed down. Laz set the basket of apples on the ground and watched as the shape began to drift toward them. A bare foot across at first, as it travelled it grew until it was some six feet high and four across. Its colour turned from solid silver to a strange bluish-green, spitting and snapping with silver sparks. It stopped some three feet from the two men and hovered briefly, then split open like a pair of double doors.

Dallandra and Branna stepped out of it, both of them laden with packs like pedlars. Dalla turned and snapped her fingers. The lozenge disappeared.

'Good morrow,' she said. 'We've come to take a look at the island.'

Kov started to speak, rolled his eyes, and sat down suddenly upon the ground.

'Put your head between your knees,' Dallandra said. 'And my apologies for startling you.' She knelt beside Kov, whose face had gone white. 'Breathe deeply.'

Branna shrugged off her pack, laid it down, then turned to look at Laz. Although he'd seen her from a distance during his time near the Westfolk camp, he'd never been close enough to speak with her. She stared at him with a gaze that seemed to be looking through his eyes and plunging into his mind and memory as if she would pierce his very soul. For a brief moment he saw a lass with dark hair and a twisted harelip; then the image dissolved back into Branna's face and a scorn that sliced into his pride.

She turned her back on him and walked over to help Kov stand.

'He'll be all right in a bit,' Dallandra said cheerfully. 'We'd best go introduce ourselves to Angmar, and I've got somewhat to give her as well.'

'I'll come with you,' Kov said. 'I think I need a sip or two of ale.'

Dallandra smiled at Laz as if she expected him to accompany them, but he let them all troop up to the manse without him. He walked along the lake shore to the little bench under the willow tree and sat down with a sigh. Out on the lake the wind rippled the water, and the sunlight glinted upon it like gold coins, but all he could see was the memory image of Branna's face, ice-cold with scorn.

She had looked at him like that once before, but when? Not in the Westfolk camp, certainly. He had not a trace of a memory of knowing her when he'd lived as Lord Tren. That life before – suddenly he saw in vision the different face, the dark-haired lass with a harelip, sneering at him, then laughing with a sound as raucous as the cry of a raven while he wept. Others stood around and stared at him, all men, these shadowy figures of memory.

Loddlaen. The name rose up and attached itself to one of the men. A friend who'd turned on him, a friend upon whom he'd revenged himself once he'd gathered the power to break Loddlaen's will. The power came from –

'No.' Laz began to tremble. 'No, no, I couldn't have done that.' But he had done it, whatever it was. His memory balked like a terrified horse and refused to go any further.

Laz sat and watched the sun on the water for hours, that afternoon, until at last Mara came looking for him to tell him that the evening meal was on the table.

'I'll eat in the kitchen, my thanks,' Laz said.

'What?' She laughed at him. 'Why?'

He could never tell her. 'Oh well,' he said. 'I thought mayhap you had too many guests already.'

'Be not so foolish! There always be room for my teacher at table.'

Yet Laz made sure to take the place at the foot of the table, because Branna was sitting at Angmar's right hand up near the head, just across from Dallandra at Angmar's left. Enj and Kov sat next on either side, a welcome barrier between him and the women. Yet now and then throughout the meal, he noticed Branna glancing his way with a look that might have melted glass, had there been any on the table. When at the end of dinner Branna went upstairs with Dallandra, he let out his breath in a long sigh of relief.

'Branna?' Dallandra said. 'Why do you hate Laz?'

'I don't hate him.'

'Oh indeed? I saw the way you looked at him. Ye gods, I thought he'd shrivel like a moth in a candle flame.'

'Very well.' Branna gave her a sheepish smile. 'I don't know why I hate him, and that's the truth.'

'Much better! I suggest you meditate upon it.'

They were sitting in the chamber Angmar had prepared for them, a long narrow room with a window that opened out to the east and a view across the lake to the low hills. The last of the sunset light picked out the oak trees scattered along the far shore.

'This is such an odd house,' Branna said. 'I can't see how this chamber fits into what we see from the outside.'

'Remember that it doesn't truly exist, which explains a great deal.'

Branna agreed with a laugh.

Dallandra glanced around and saw the basin she'd brought up earlier. 'My breasts ache again,' she said. 'I'd better express some of this milk. I wish I could have brought Dari, but it would have been too dangerous, travelling on the roads.' She paused, struck by a surprising thought. 'I miss her.'

When she was finished, Dallandra returned to the great hall, where Laz was waiting at the honour table. In the sconces at either side of the two hearths, an array of candles burned, or at least, the illusions of candles seemed to be burning. Dallandra noticed that none of them dripped wax nor did they get shorter as time went by.

Laz looked up warily, nodded her way, then craned his neck to glance at the staircase.

'Branna's staying in our chamber,' Dallandra said.

'Ah. You noticed the way she looked at me.'

'I did.' Dallandra sat down next to him. 'So. There's the book at last.'

'Indeed.' Laz slid it over to her. 'I'm cursed glad to hand it over to you. I kept worrying that it would take off on its own one fine night.'

They shared a pleasant laugh.

'I owe you a great many thanks,' Dallandra said. 'It must not have been easy, fetching this.' She glanced around. 'Where's Faharn, by the by?'

'I'm afraid he's dead. As you say, it wasn't easy.'

Dallandra felt herself gaping at him like a half-wit. 'It saddens my heart to hear that,' was all she could find to say.

'We were travelling with the Mountain axemen contingent,' Laz continued. 'We were set upon by Horsekin raiders.'

'I see. Truly, my heart aches for your loss.'

'So, oddly enough, does mine.'

'Oddly –'

'Oh, never mind!' Laz snarled, then took a deep breath. 'Forgive me. It's a sore spot.'

'I can understand that. My apologies.'

Yet she wondered if she did understand it or much of anything that Laz might be thinking or feeling. His knife-sharp face betrayed no feeling whatsoever when he looked at her. She'd been planning on simply taking the book upstairs to examine it in private, but Faharn's death made her feel that she owed Laz a debt. At the very least, she decided, she should satisfy his curiosity about the dweomers Evandar had woven.

As soon as she laid her hand on the cover, she felt the tingle and snap of astral spirits. She opened her sight and perceived the pair as geometric shapes, one a blazing white, the other a peculiar turquoise colour that reminded her of Evandar's eyes. Laz leaned onto the table on folded arms to watch.

'My thanks for your aid,' she said to the spirits. 'I come in the name of Evandar.'

The wards glowed brightly, then shrank and disappeared. Under her fingers the cover felt like ordinary leather. When she opened it, she saw a page of elven script, just as Laz had described. The next page, and the next – the same digraphs in the same order on every page – she stared at the writing and wondered why she was so surprised.

'Uh, is somewhat wrong?' Laz said.

'This is utter nonsense,' Dallandra said.

'What?' Laz straightened up and slammed his maimed hands palm down on the table.

'Except for the occasional word, like drahkonnen, it means nothing at all.'

Laz swore under his breath in a mix of several languages.

'I agree,' Dalla said. 'How like Evandar! He never could do anything simply. I wonder what sort of lock he's put on this? An elaborate one, most like.'

'Oh.' Laz leaned back in his chair. 'You mean there's some sort of meaning under all of that.'

'So I hope, anyway.' *Ye gods*, Dalla thought, *if poor Faharn died for no reason!* 'I'll have to work with this. I just hope it doesn't take me days and days.' She stood and picked up the book. 'I'll let Branna have a look at it, too. She seems to have a good mind for symbols. The key might well be hidden in this welter of runes, for all I know.'

'Very well. If you could tell me eventually what it says, I'd be quite grateful.'

'Of course. Tonight I'm truly weary from travelling the roads and all, or I'd try to open the lock right now.'

She hurried to the staircase before he could ask any questions. At the top of the stairs she glanced back to see Laz still sitting at the table, staring at the place where the book had once lain.

Branna could make no more out of the writing in the dragon book than Dallandra had. Dalla sprawled in a cushioned chair and watched as Branna examined each page by dweomerlight. Finally she looked up and shut the book with a snap.

'I can't make any sense out of this,' Branna said. 'Maybe Val can. My Elvish still isn't very good.'

'That's true,' Dallandra said. 'I keep hoping there's some sort of cipher hidden among the runes, but of course, it would be in Elvish. If there is one! Maybe Val's right about Evandar and his wretched riddles.'

'Well, he really did make things difficult, I must say.' Branna frowned at the book in her hands. 'Omens tucked here and there, and dragon rings. And that scroll, the one in the strange language.'

'It was very strange, indeed. The ritual we worked with it did have some effect on the island, I think. I'll have to keep that in mind.'

'And then there's the crystal, the black one, I mean, with the visions in it. And –'

'Wait!' Dallandra leaned forward. 'The black crystal held a vision of the book and Haen Marn. Salamander saw it there. He must have mentioned it to you.'

'He did, one day when he was helping me with one of the lore lessons.'

'Good. We've all been assuming that the point of the vision was to tell us that the book was on Haen Marn. But what if the crystal itself is part of the vision's meaning?'

Branna blinked at her, then suddenly grinned. 'What if the crystal holds the key to the book, you mean?'

'Just that!'

'I hope we don't need both of them. Salamander told me that Laz lost the white one.'

Dallandra's excitement disappeared as fast as it had arrived. 'Oh by the Black Sun!' she said. 'Let's hope we don't, indeed! I also hope that Val hasn't smashed the black one. She wanted to at one time.'

'Can you contact her from here?'

'Let's hope so! If I have to go across to the mainland, it'll mean waiting till morning, which will drive me daft.'

Dallandra got up and walked over to the window. Outside the stars glimmered high above in the moonless night. She leaned a little way out of the window and used the Snowy Road as her focus, then let her mind reach out to Valandario. Although Haen Marn's astral forces turned the vision fuzzy and small, eventually she saw Val sitting in her tent and studying her array of scrying gems.

'Dalla?' Valandario looked up suddenly. 'I can barely see you.'

'Yes, it's because I'm on Haen Marn.' Dallandra thought to her in Elvish. 'Do you still have that wretched black crystal?'

'The spirit stone, you mean? Yes, I do. I was going to smash it, but somehow I just couldn't. I kept thinking that it still had secrets inside it.'

'It does, and thank every god that you still have it! When you come here, bring it, will you? It might be the key to one of Evandar's wretched riddles.'

'Very well, I won't let anything happen to it. Wretched riddles, are they? I'm glad you can see –'

Dallandra broke the link. She was in no mood for one of Val's little lectures, even though she had to admit that on this occasion at least, Val was right.

'She still has it,' Dallandra told Branna. 'And I'm exhausted.'

'You need to sleep.' Branna stifled a yawn. 'And so do I. You take that big bed. I'm the apprentice, so I'll take the trundle.'

When Laz woke, just after dawn on the next morning, he dressed and left his chamber, then hesitated at the head of the stairs to look down into the great hall. He saw no sign of Branna, but Dallandra was standing at the wall near the main hearth and studying the carvings. He trotted down the stairs and strolled over to join her.

'These are fascinating.' Dallandra traced a group of marks with one fingertip. 'They must be the sigils of Aethyr that you told me about.'

'There's another group next to the other hearth,' Laz said. 'When we stand here we face north, most of the time, at least, though you never know with this island.'

'Does it move often?'

'It twitches.' Laz paused for a grin. 'Never very far, but it does stir in its sleep like a dreaming dog. Anyway, if we were looking at that other group of identical sigils, we'd face south. I think the two groups define an axis.'

'You're doubtless right. Branna and I have a theory about these carvings, that somehow or other they contain the information we need to control the construct. I think we may be able to convince the island to move itself to the Westlands.'

'Truly?' Laz whistled under his breath in amazement. 'That's very impressive.'

'My thanks, but it's only a guess.'

'When the island came here from Alban, these groups of sigils glowed lavender.' Laz frowned, searching his memory. 'And another group, these here –' he laid his fingertip on a set of asymmetric loops and spirals '– glowed turquoise, but with curiously unpleasant orange-red flecks in them.'

'Ye gods! I've never seen marks like that before.'

'That's a pity. I was hoping you had and could explain them.'

Dallandra shook her head and glared at three little circles, each sprouting four pairs of thin wavy lines, as if they'd personally insulted her.

'I have no idea if we can make the dweomer work,' she said at last. 'But be that as it may, I told Rori to wait till I send word before he and Arzosah fly all this way to Haen Marn.'

'Ah.' *Good*, Laz thought, *that gives me time to figure out how I can avoid him.* 'I take it that the other dweomermasters in your alar won't be coming here until you know.'

'Just so. Why?'

'I was wondering if Sidro would come with them.'

'She won't.' Dallandra hesitated for an ominous moment.

'I suppose she doesn't want to see me.'

Dallandra said nothing.

'Here!' Laz felt a stab of worry. 'She's not ill, is she?'

'Not truly. Ah well, you might as well know. She's with child.'

'Pir's child?' The words seem to stick in his mouth like phlegm. He had to force them out.

'It is.' She hesitated again, then patted him on the arm. 'I'm sorry.'

Laz turned on his heel and strode out of the great hall. *She'll never come back to me now*, he was thinking, *never!* The word tolled in his mind like a bell. He made his way through the underbrush down to the lake shore, where the little bench stood under the willow tree, only to see Kov and Mara sitting there, holding hands and smiling at each other. With a snarl Laz trotted back to the manse.

He banged through the door into the great hall. Dallandra had left. Cats scattered at his approach. He ran to the stairway and rushed up with the word 'never' still ringing in his mind. Sisi was gone, she'd left him once and for all, she was carrying another man's child. He hurried into his chamber and slammed the door behind him, then leaned against it while he panted for breath.

'I can't stay here,' he whispered. 'They'll have to read the wretched book without me. Cursed if I'll help them!' He paused on a wave of self-pity. 'Not that they even asked me to.'

Faharn was dead, Sidro gone forever, Dallandra profoundly un-interested – what was left to him? The charity of some Deverry lord? Life among the Westfolk? A line of cold sweat ran down his back. He was maimed, lost, alone – nothing left to him but pleading for shelter somewhere from someone who might or might not grant it. Angmar and Mara would have taken him in, but once the dragon had turned back into Rhodry and claimed his place as lord of the island, what then?

He might kill me for one wrong word. I'd best get myself gone.

Laz found his sack, packed up his belongings, then stripped off his clothes and crammed them in, too. By then he hovered on the edge of weeping. As he laid the sack on the window sill, it occurred to him that he'd felt happy here in Haen Marn. A few tears came. He wiped them off on his arm and swallowed heavily. It took all his will for him to steady his mind enough to transform into the raven. In bird form he hopped onto the sack, sank his claws in deep, and flew, dropping out of the window and heading for the distant shore.

Ahead loomed the astral vortex that surrounded and interpenetrated Haen Marn. Laz did think – briefly – of returning to his chamber and man form, then asking to be ferried across, but his old reckless-ness caught him up. *Maybe it's better if I just die!* He made one turn over the peaceful manse below to say farewell to the apple trees and the tower, then banked a wing and turned straight for the loch and its astral matrix.

With a cackle of raven-laughter, he plunged straight into the swirling, snapping lines of light. Blue and silver, gold and brilliant white – they wrapped him round and snared him like a fowler's net.

Branna happened to be out walking on the island when she saw Laz in raven form come swooping out of the upper window of the manse. For a moment, when he made his turn around the island, she lost sight of him. He reappeared from behind the tower and headed straight for the open water of the loch. When she realized what he was going to do, she screamed at the top of her lungs.

'Laz, don't! Dalla, Dalla! Laz, stop!'

Branna took off running, following the raven as he flew toward the water. She'd found him disgusting at first sight, but at the moment she saw only a troubled soul rushing to some unknown disaster.

'Stop!' she yelled as loud as she could. 'Laz!'

Too late. The raven slammed into an invisible wall high in the air. For a moment he hung there, his wings splayed, his head thrown back. With a flutter he fell, spiralling down like a bird arrow-pierced, to land sprawled on the sandy shore.

Branna rushed over and flung herself to kneel beside him. He still lived, because he'd fallen across his sack of clothing, which had broken some of the fall. The raven was gasping for breath and rolling its yellow eyes, its beak open and helpless.

'Hold still,' Branna said. 'Help's coming.'

She heard voices behind her, Dallandra and Mara both, and the sound of running footsteps. The raven gasped out a word.

'I can't understand,' Branna said. 'Just lie still.'

On impulse she reached out and stroked the ruffled feathers on his head, smoothing them back into place. Laz shut his eyes, and slowly his breathing quieted. Mara dropped to her knees beside Laz and gently lifted a wing. With her help he folded it close to his body.

'What happened?' Dalla knelt down beside Branna.

'He tried to fly through the vortex,' Branna said. 'I don't know why.'

The raven spoke, and this time she understood him: crazed.

'You were that!' Dallandra said. 'Is somewhat broken? Your wings? Arms, I mean?'

The raven turned his head and seemed to be thinking.

'Be the strength to change back be with you, Laz?' Mara said. 'We then could see if somewhat be wrong after you did change back.'

The raven nodded. With Branna's help he got to his feet, then shook his wings with a great shudder and flapping to balance himself on one leg.

'That ankle's bad, isn't it?' Dallandra got to her feet, then pointed to the dangling leg. 'Or more than just the ankle.'

The raven nodded again.

'We'll turn away,' Dalla went on, 'to let you concentrate.'

Branna followed her lead and looked out over the water. From behind them she heard a shriek, a long cackle and croak of pure despair. Branna spun around and saw that Laz had fallen again – still in raven form, sprawled like a black cloak over the pale sand.

'Can't! Can't change.'

Dallandra's eyes suddenly went unfocused; Branna could assume that she was studying him with the Sight.

'Just rest now,' Dallandra said. 'Later you'll have more energy, and you can try again. You're exhausted, Laz. Here, Mara – will you go back to the manse and fetch the boatmen? We'll need them to carry him back.'

With a nod Mara turned and ran. Dallandra knelt down next to the raven and began to stroke his injured leg with gentle fingers, assessing the damage. As she watched, Branna realized that something far worse than a broken bone was wrong with Laz, just from the limp way he sprawled. He tried to lift his head, then let his eyes roll back and slumped again. Dallandra, however, went on speaking in a quiet soothing voice to her patient, a sure sign that she too saw some more serious injury.

Enj, Kov, Lon, and the one real boatman carried the raven up to his chamber, where Mara waited with splints and other supplies for Laz's broken leg. Branna squatted down in a corner out of the way and watched as Dallandra set and bound the leg with Mara's help. Now and then Laz made a croaking sound and tossed his head from side to side, but he kept himself remarkably still.

'That should do it,' Dallandra said. 'Mara, I'll leave soothing the patient to you. He's been in a lot of pain, and he's absolutely got to rest.'

'Well and good, then,' Mara said. 'I'll be trying to calm him.'

Dallandra gestured to Branna to follow and led her out to the corridor. They walked to the head of the stairs and paused there to speak in whispers.

'Shouldn't you have waited to set that break until he's back in man form?' Branna said.

'He may never return to it,' Dallandra said. 'What's happened is truly horrible. Getting caught in the astral vortex – it stripped away his etheric double, the human part of him, that is. It should have killed him. Fortunately, his body of light is strong enough to replace the double and keep him alive. Unfortunately, it exists in the shape of a raven. As far as I can tell, he'll be trapped in that form until he dies.'

Unthinkingly Branna laid her hand over her mouth, fearing she'd vomit.

'He always did fly too much,' Dalla continued. 'Over the years, his body of light must have taken over some of the functions of the etheric double, or perhaps warped it, somehow. I don't understand exactly what happened.'

'But the end result be obvious enough.' Mara spoke from behind them. 'He does ken the truth, Dalla, and he does agree with you.'

They turned to include her in a circle.

'He does talk of killing himself,' Mara went on. 'But I doubt me if he will. The talk, his voice – they convinced me not of true despair.'

'You can understand him, then?' Branna said.

'Mostly. He be my teacher, and there be a bond between us.' She tried, briefly, to smile. 'I did tell him that it were his wyrd to live, for much remains for me to learn.'

'Excellent!' Dallandra said. 'That's exactly what he'll need, some reason or purpose for his life, since he'll be the raven until he dies.'

'But how much longer will that be?' Mara said. 'Birds, they do live but a short time.'

'I have no idea, but I'd wager he'll live out a long span of years if he stays here. The island will give him strength. That's its purpose, isn't it? To act as a talisman of healing.'

'I kenned that not. Truly, there be so much dweomer yet to learn.'

'Well, Laz can teach you some of it, and I can help as well. For now, though, your task is to help Laz heal.'

'Well and good, then. He be welcome as long as he wishes to stay.'

'And our task, Dalla?' Branna said.

'Is to understand the carvings on the walls. Now that I've seen them I've no doubt that they'll teach us everything we need to know about the island, if we can only read them.'

'Well and good, then. Will it take long?'

Branna was all wide eyes and enthusiasm. Dallandra suppressed a laugh. 'I have no idea,' she said. 'I hope not.'

'I was just thinking of poor Rori, waiting for our aid.'

'The best time for unwinding the dweomer will be at the dark of the moon, but Rori's been a dragon for nearly fifty years. I don't suppose waiting another month will strike him as unreasonable, if we should have to.'

'Well, true spoken.' Yet Branna looked saddened by the thought of such a wait.

When Dallandra considered the moon that night, she saw that it had reached its third quarter.

They spent several days studying the vast and elaborate carvings to fix them in their minds. Dallandra drilled Branna mercilessly until they both knew the position of every cluster of design, every sigil that they knew, every digraph, and every unknown mark. Dallandra had been hoping that the digraphs would identify the various portions of the designs, but they seemed to be mere abbreviations, perhaps well known to the founders of Haen Marn, a mystery to her.

In between their sessions of study, Dallandra would look in on Laz. His delicate leg, turned hollow as bird bones are, would heal very slowly, she realized.

'You'll have to be patient,' she told him one day.

He answered with a croak that might have meant anything. Only Mara could truly understand him, though she had hopes that in time, as he worked on speaking more clearly, others would be able to as well.

'He does say that he wishes not for you to see him in this pass,' Mara told her.

Laz croaked out a fairly clear 'that's true'.

'Very well,' Dallandra said. 'Mara can do everything for you that can be done.'

When Dallandra left his chamber, Mara followed her out. They stood at the head of the stairs to talk.

'Think you that you may ken the secrets of the isle?' Mara said.

'Eventually, perhaps,' Dalla said. 'It's a very tangled puzzle.'

'No doubt. I do think me, though, that the isle will go nowhere till all its people come home. You should call my father to us.'

'I know you're eager to meet him, but I doubt me if the time is right for that.'

Mara smiled, but her eyes flashed anger. With a toss of her head she strode away, followed by half-a-dozen cats. *You may be the lady of this place one fine day,* Dallandra thought, *but that doesn't mean you can give me orders.*

Berwynna discovered that she enjoyed flying on dragonback, even though Uncle Mic's constant shrieks, moans, groans, and heavy sighs did detract from much of the pleasure during the first two days' travelling. By the time they found Haen Marn, though, he had lapsed into a welcome if abject silence. Although Medea had worried about her ability to find the island, with Wynni along, a true daughter of Haen Marn, they flew straight to the river that led to Lin Serr. From there, following it upstream to the island itself proved simple.

Through wisps of mist Berwynna saw the lake and in its centre the island. The sight of the familiar manse and Avain's tower moved her to tears. Only then did she realize how badly she'd missed her mother and Avain and Lonna and even, she had to admit, her sister. *I'll see my brother Enj again, too,* she thought. *It be good to be home!*

'Down we go!' Medea called out.

With a swoop of wings the green dragon sailed through the mists, made a wide turn over the lake, and landed with a graceful flapping on the shore by the boathouse. Berwynna and Mic slid from her back just as Avain came running with a howl of joy.

'Wynni bring a dragon!' Avain was chanting the words in Dwarvish as she lumbered along. 'Wynni bring a dragon!'

Behind her came Angmar, walking with some dignity, but smiling like the sun itself, breaking through clouds. Berwynna rushed to her mother's arms and, holding her, wept again in sheer joy.

A smiling Dallandra turned from the window. 'Let's just stay inside,' she said. 'I don't want to intrude on the family. They all look so happy to have Wynni back, even Mara.'

'Well and good, then,' Branna said. 'It gladdens my heart that Medea could fly through the vortex – safely, I mean.'

'She's a true dragon, that is, "dragon" is her natural body form. It's not like the situation with Rori or Laz.'

'Of course! I should have thought of that. Mara's not the only one with much to learn.'

'All of us have much to learn.' With a sigh Dallandra walked over to join Branna. 'Especially about Haen Marn.'

They had spent the morning studying a particular section of the carvings on the east wall. In the centre of an oval, delineated by an arrangement of small sigils of Aethyr, stood a depiction of a tree, half of which had stylized leaves on its branches but the other half, stylized flames. Across the room behind them, on the west wall, stood another, similar design but with its oval defined by repeated sigils of Air. The trees had to refer to the tree that stood by the gate between the worlds, Dallandra realized, but the realization had not got her much farther.

'So far,' Dallandra said, 'we've got four places on the walls that seem to refer to travelling, the patches of sigils of Aethyr and Air that Laz pointed out to me, and then these two trees. And then –' She paused to walk along the wall until she reached another set of symbols that at first glance looked like a design element and naught more. 'And then there's these. They're the key to the egregore, I'd wager. Mara mentioned how the healing lore began to come into her mind the night after she'd been studying this bit of the wall.'

'If you say so.' Branna frowned at the designs. 'Oh, wait, I think I do see. Birds plucking things from a garden? Is that it?'

'In a very stylized way. Now, over here –'

Laughing, calling out to one another, the inhabitants of Haen Marn came trooping in, Berwynna arm in arm with her mother, and behind them Mara, Avain, and Enj, with Mic and Kov bringing up the rear. From the east door Lonna hurried in and Lon after her to greet Berwynna. Even Medea joined in by the simple expedient of sticking her green and gold head through the window closest to the long table. So much for study and meditation, Dallandra decided.

'We'd best pick this up again later,' Dallandra told Branna.

'True spoken,' Branna said. 'Though I can't say I begrudge them their joy.'

Yet at dinner that night, in the midst of laughter and the noisy telling of tales, Dallandra found herself glancing over at the huge swags of carving that swooped across the walls of the great hall. Somewhere among them lay the secrets she needed.

In the middle of the night Branna woke from a dream too strange and unfocused to be one of her true dreams, yet she felt that she'd been given a kernel of important lore. She got up and made a small dweomer light, shielding it with her body to keep from waking Dallandra, only to realize that the master had already got up and gone before her. Branna allowed the light to swell, then dressed and went downstairs. Dallandra was standing in the great hall beside the door in the west wall.

'Did I wake you?' Dalla said. 'My apologies, if so.'

'You didn't,' Branna said. 'I had a dream. I was looking at a part of the wall and a voice said, this bit was made to be yours. Or something like that. You know how dreams are with words. So I woke and felt I had to come look for the piece that's mine before the memory faded.'

'Very good! Which bit is it?'

'The pair of Aethyr sigils in the midst of some animals that might be horses. It's on the east wall by the other door.'

'Very good! I've been looking at this pair of Air sigils here. Look, they're surrounded by what look like ships. It must have somewhat to do with motion and travel.' Dallandra touched one of the ships with her forefinger. 'I have the feeling that maybe this piece is mine, somehow, now that you mention it.'

Branna ran across the room to the back door. When she tossed her dweomer light on to the wall, she saw the sigils and the animals, clearly horses now that she was awake.

'Here they are!' she called out to Dalla.

'Good!' Dalla called back. 'I see the two groups are on an east-west axis, and both of them are near the burning trees.'

'So they are!'

Branna reached out and ran her fingertips along the sigils, then glanced back just in time to see Dallandra laying a casual hand on the sigils by the other door. The entire manse lurched and trembled. Branna yelped and nearly fell, but her hand seemed to have become stuck to the wall – or into the wall. She stared open-mouthed as her hand sank into the astral illusion up to her wrist. When she heard Dallandra call out, she glanced over her shoulder to see Dalla similarly pinned.

'The tree, Branna! Put your other hand on the tree!'

By stretching Branna could just reach the carving of the tree. Half of it began to flicker with red and orange light as if it burned, whilst the other half glowed green with fresh leaves. Once again her hand sank into the wall.

'We're moving,' Dallandra called out. 'Pray to every god we don't end up in Alban!'

Branna tried to speak and failed. A cool lavender mist was seeping through the great hall. The sigils of Aethyr were glowing brightly. Beside them two Elvish digraphs gleamed a turquoise flecked with a poisonous-looking green. She could just see out of the nearby window to the space between manse and kitchen hut. Even though the purple mist drifted around her, Medea lay curled up, asleep and apparently unaware that the entire island was flying like a dragon itself.

At the far end of the hall Dallandra began to chant but not in Elvish. Branna could only pick out the occasional phrase, not that she understood any of them.

'Hanmara, Hanmara, ol duh um duh non ci ol zir doh no co. Ol pir tay day ol pir tay, Hanmara.'

Dallandra chanted these phrases over and over, with other words in between that Branna's mind simply could not parse. A spirit voice, very high and clear, began to sing the words in descant harmony with Dallandra's chant. After some little time, it faded away, and Dallandra fell silent as well.

Branna had no idea of how long they travelled. Trapped as she was by the astral forces of the illusory wall, she was forced to stand still, unable even to lean against the carvings to rest for fear of starting off some other dweomer process. The construct shook so hard at moments that she nearly fell. Her outstretched arms first pained her, then became numb. Her legs began to ache in their stead, and she felt shivering cold from the lavender mist that swirled around her.

At moments the mist grew so thick that she could no longer see Dallandra. She became so terrified in those moments that it took all her will to keep from screaming. Eventually the mist would thin. Once she could see Dallandra again the fear would leave her.

After some long while, Branna became aware of noises, the muffled sounds of people calling out, the croak of a raven voice, the sounds of footsteps running back and forth, all of them coming from above her. She could guess that the other inhabitants of the manse had woken up and realized what was occurring around them. When she glanced out of the window, she saw that Medea too was awake. She'd sat up, and Avain huddled between the dragon's front legs.

Bit by bit, the normal noises became louder. Branna could pick out individual voices, including Laz's raven cackles. The lavender mist began to thin out. Sunlight streamed in through the window as suddenly as the lighting of a giant candle, when but a little while ago the night had wrapped everything in darkness. The mist vanished, one soft curl at time.

The wall became only a wall. Branna's left hand rested on a carving of horses and her right, on a stylized carving of a tree. All of the spirit lights had gone out. She pulled her hands away fast, lest they sink in again, and rubbed them together to regain some feeling in her cold fingers. Her shoulders ached as if she'd been carrying a heavy load for miles.

'Branna!' Dallandra came hurrying toward her. 'Are you unharmed?'

'I am,' Branna said. 'Are you?'

'Just very tired. Here come the others.'

Enj came pounding down the stairway, followed by Berwynna and Mara, all of them talking at once. Behind them a white-faced Kov led a silent Angmar, who leaned heavily on his arm. Branna was relieved to see that the raven had stayed in his chamber; despite his broken leg, he could still fly, had he wanted to come down.

'What happened? Where are we?' Everyone began speaking at once and kept it up until Dallandra shouted at them to be quiet. They stood in a shocked semi-circle around her and waited.

'Haen Marn moved,' Dallandra said calmly. 'As to where, I don't know yet. I suggest we go outside and look.'

Dallandra let the others go outside ahead of her. She was dreading the news that the inadvertent dweomer she and Branna had stumbled upon had sent them all back to the mysterious land of Alban, though she could take comfort in knowing that she had an idea of how to get them back again if so. When she went out, she saw the others hurrying to the pier that jutted out into Haen Marn's lake, which offered an unobstructed view of the surrounding landscape.

As Dallandra walked toward the water, Branna fell in beside her. Together they studied the view. The island still sat in a lake, but one easily three times the size of its original location. Dallandra could see across the water to a grove of pine trees, planted in straight rows like a garden. Along the shore stood little wooden structures and stone fire pits.

Branna began to laugh.

'What?' Dallandra said.

Branna merely shook her head. Apparently she couldn't stop laughing. She raised her arms, leapt into the air, and jigged a few dance steps, laughing all the while. Dallandra grabbed her right arm in both hands but stopped short of shaking her.

'What is it?' Dalla snapped. 'Is somewhat wrong?'

'I know where we are.' Branna got her voice under control at last. 'Trout! I know now, why the trout. We've done it, we've done it! We've brought the island home.'

Branna pulled her arm free of Dallandra's grasp and dropped to her knees. She covered her face with both hands and wept. Dallandra stood close and patted her shoulder to comfort her but said nothing. It was far too soon to ask Branna why she wept, or how she could know such things, not that it mattered, in a way, because Branna was incontrovertibly right about one thing. They were gazing upon the elven death ground by the lake that Deverry men term the Cint Peddroloc, but the Westfolk call the Lake of the Leaping Trout.

Dallandra glanced up and saw, high in the eastern sky, the pale sliver of the last of the old moon. Another night, and the moon would disappear into her dark.

Branna had stopped weeping. She pulled a handful of grass and blew her nose, then got up, wiping her face on her sleeve.

'My apologies.' Branna's voice sounded thick with recent tears, but she was smiling. 'I just had the strangest feeling, that at last I'd paid back some sort of debt.'

The icy cold of recognition ran down Dallandra's spine. 'Then most likely you have, and you should discuss that with Grallezar when she gets here. At the moment, we need to go explain things to the others.'

✳   ✳   ✳

The day after Dallandra and Branna had left them, the royal alar and the Cerr Cawnen folk had met up at last. Under Prince Dar's leadership, they continued their slow march eastward toward the Melyn River Valley. Every morning Valandario scried the surrounding terrain for Horsekin raiders. Once she did see a small squad, but they were heading north. At odd moments during the day, she followed them in vision until they disappeared into the broken tablelands.

'It looks to me,' she told Dar that evening, 'that they were cut off from some larger body, and they're desperate to get back to safety.'

'Good,' Dar said. 'We've got no time to worry about them now. Do you think this good weather will hold?'

'Yes, for a few more days at least. Which reminds me. Where is the alar going to winter this year?'

'Down on the coast as usual. I've been consulting with Chief Speaker Jahdo. The townsfolk are going to need the rest of the year to mark out their farmland, plant their grain, build shelters and the like. They won't have the leisure to worry about us and our bargain till the spring. The same holds for Gerran. He'll get his dun once our people have got themselves settled and reasonably secure. They'll need to take care of themselves before they can take Gerran's money for building it. If there's nothing to eat, the coin won't do them one cursed bit of good.'

Our people. Dar's choice of words struck Valandario as somehow momentous, as if they echoed down a long tunnel of years.

'Why?' Dar continued. 'Do you want to winter with us or in Mandra?'

Val was about to answer when she felt Dallandra's mind tugging at hers. She muttered a quick excuse to the prince, then trotted off to seek a scrying focus. The sun was hanging low in the cloudless sky, but not far from camp a small stream ran over rocks. She concentrated on its swirling water and sent her mind out to Dallandra. The image built up fast of her fellow dweomermaster grinning in sheer delight.

'Where are you?' Val said.

'On the shore of the Lake of the Leaping Trout,' Dallandra said.

'What by all the gods are you doing there?'

'Studying the walls of Haen Marn, for one thing.'

All at once Valandario understood. 'You've done it,' she said. 'You've moved the island!'

'Well, not precisely. Branna did as much as I, and frankly, we were very very lucky. Either that, or we had help from the inner planes.'

'Did you hear knocks?'

'No, which is why I'm invoking sheer blind luck as an explanation. Although, you know, I think it simply may have been time for the island to come home.' Dallandra's image, floating on the surface of the stream, frowned briefly in thought. 'Branna's been receiving omens and odd flashes of memory. I've come to believe that she was involved – deeply involved – with the creation of the island. If she'd been farther along in her training, working the dweomer might have been a good deal less harrowing, but neither of us died, so I suppose you can call us successful.'

'Yes, certainly I can! I'm overwhelmed, in fact. It's utterly amazing, what you've done.'

'Amazing, perhaps. Exhausting, certainly. On the morrow, can you get the elder dragons to bring you and Grallezar here? I'm hoping that Arzosah hasn't changed her wretched wyrmish mind about helping us unravel the dweomer.'

'They're both off hunting at the moment, but I'm sure that Rori will talk sense into her if she has.'

When the two great wyrms returned to camp, each laden with a dead deer, they both proved willing to do what Dallandra had asked, though neither seemed joyful at the prospect. Arzosah kept her ears laid back and hissed even after she agreed.

'I do understand,' Val said to Arzosah, 'how heavy your heart must be. I lost my mate many years ago now, and I miss him still.'

'My thanks,' Arzosah said. 'Yours is the first sympathy I've got out of any of you wretched dweomer people. I'm glad to see that at least one of you understands my heartsickness.'

Both Valandario and the dragon turned their heads to look at Rori, who was assiduously studying the ground in front of him. When he stayed silent, Arzosah turned away with a snort and waddled off to return to her dinner. Valandario waited, but in a moment Rori did the same without another word.

That evening Valandario and Grallezar packed up what few things they'd need for the journey. Valandario emptied out a quiver of arrows and put the black crystal, wrapped in several layers of cloth, into it in their stead. She could sling the quiver across her chest, she decided, and keep the crystal right close to her during the journey.

While the prospect of flying troubled her not at all, Valandario did worry about leaving the alar with only Ebañy and Neb as dweomerworkers – Niffa had more than enough work to do among the townsfolk – and only the two youngest dragons for protection from the air as well. In the morning, however, Medea returned, full of chatter about the astonishing island and its dweomers. Her presence reassured Valandario immensely, but she took Ebañy aside for a private talk.

'If you run into the slightest trouble,' she told him, 'contact me immediately.'

'I shall, oh learned lady of little-known lore,' Salamander said. 'But truly, after all these years of dweomer work, I do think I'm capable of scrying for enemies.'

'Well, very true, and I don't mean to be insulting. It's just that –'

'I know.' Salamander grinned at her. 'It's just that in the past, I've been less than studious, indeed rather more flippant, frivolous, and downright stupid.'

'Well and good, then. Self-knowledge is always the beginning of wisdom.'

Salamander opened his mouth to reply, then shut it again. Valandario had the exquisite pleasure of seeing him speechless.

At some distance from the camp Grallezar and Arzosah were waiting for her. As she walked out to join them, Valandario looked around her but saw no sign of Rori.

'He had one thing to do before we leave,' Arzosah said. 'We've already explained everything to the girls, but he's gone to speak with our son.'

After the hatchlings had eaten, Rori told Devar to follow him to the stream beyond the camp. As they took turns drinking, watching his young son stretch his wings to the sunlight wrung Rori's heart. He would miss Devar more than he'd ever missed any of his human sons, more even than Cullyn Maelwaedd, his favourite out of the lot.

'I have some evil news to tell you,' Rori said.

Devar slewed around to face his father, his eyes wide with fear.

'I have to leave you,' Rori went on. 'It aches my heart, lad, to tell you this, but now that the prince and his people are safe, I have to leave the clutch forever.'

'No!' Devar wailed out the word. 'No, Da, don't go!'

'I have to. I'm sorry. It's my wyrd. What have I told you about wyrd?'

'That no dragon can turn his aside, but –'

'There's no but or if or mayhap about this, lad. From now on, you're going to be the male in this clutch. You'll have to be brave, very brave in fact, but you won't have to face it all alone. Soon your uncle will come to live in the tower below our lair, and he'll teach you what you need to know.'

'I like Uncle Ebañy, but he's not you.'

'I know, and I'm sorry, but wyrd is wyrd, and it can't be denied. Can you be brave?'

'I'll try.' Devar hung his head. 'I'll try very hard.'

'That's all you or anyone can do. You're growing daily, and soon you'll be able to protect your sisters while your mother's off somewhere, rather than them protecting you.'

Devar nodded, looked away, and spoke in a choked wet voice. 'Can't you even come back to visit?'

'No. I'm sorry. If I could I would, but I won't be able to. Here's the worst news of all. I probably won't live very long, not as dragons measure our lives, a few years perhaps.'

'You're ill?'

'Very ill.' It wasn't precisely a lie, Rori decided, and might make the parting a little easier for Devar. 'You know the dragonish way. When our time comes, we go off alone to await our end.'

'I do know that.' His voice began to tremble. 'I don't want you to die.'

'No one wants to die, but when their time comes, what can they do against it?'

'Naught.' Devar sounded one small step away from weeping. 'I know that, too.'

'Still, one day we may well meet again. I'll be in a different body then, a human one. I'll hope and pray that we do meet. But while you'll recognize me, I'll not be able to recognize you, not at first, anyway. Don't feel slighted. It's merely the way things are. Do you understand? If I have a new body, I'll not be able to recognize you.'

'I'll remember.' Devar looked up, and his eyes, that strangely elven mix of dragon and human, glistened with tears. 'If I tell you, will you remember?'

'I don't know. You may have to be patient and explain things.'

'Da, I wish you didn't have to die.'

'But I do. Your mother will explain more when you're older. Now, I need you to be brave, but your sisters need you even more. You need to be strong for their sake.'

'I will then.' His young clear voice strengthened. 'I promise.'

Rori knew that if he stayed a moment longer, he would weep and shame them both. He turned and walked a safe distance away, then leapt, wings beating hard, and soared the brief distance to the gathering place in the grass where the others waited for him. Once Grallezar and Valandario had secured themselves, Val on Rori, and Grallezar on Arzosah, the two wyrms took flight, wheeled once over the sprawling camp, and headed south and east for the Lake of the Leaping Trout.

*   *   *

'Mara?' Dallandra said. 'I need to speak with you.'

Mara, who'd been studying one of the egregore keys on the north wall, turned to her with a smile and curtsied.

'I'm wondering if you want the island to stay here or return to where it was, eventually, I mean,' Dallandra continued. 'There are certainly more people living here on the Deverry border than live up north of Lin Serr.'

'That be very true,' Mara said. 'I did spend some time in thought over that myself. The Mountain Folk be hardy, and their women do possess much healing lore of their own. Mama does remember not one soul from Lin Serr ever coming to the island for help, and she did live here for seventy-some years before the taking of us all to Alban.'

'That says to me that the island should stay here, then, if you agree.'

'I do, indeed.'

'Splendid! How does Laz fare this morning?'

'As well as can be expected.' Mara frowned, biting her lower lip in thought. 'I do wish he would allow you to see him, but he be still so heartsick and so – well – humiliated. He does curse himself for a fool and croak on and on about a woman. Her name be Sidro, but I do understand few of his words. I think me he does then speak in the language of his childhood.'

'Most likely he does. Perhaps when his leg stops paining him so much he'll grow calmer, and then we can talk with him.'

'I shall hope so with all my heart.'

'Now, I've got some good news to give you. Your father is on his way here. He and your step-mother should arrive soon, in fact. He can't fly through the vortex to reach the island, so you and your mother will need to go over by boat to greet him.'

Mara smiled, and at that moment she looked more like a child filled with joy by the prospect of some splendid gift than the accomplished healer she was. 'Let me be off to tell Mam,' she said. 'We must make ourselves and the manse ready.'

The sun stood just past zenith when the two dragons settled upon the farther shore. The dragon boat immediately set out from the island with Mara and Angmar, who'd been waiting on the pier. Berwynna stayed behind and joined Dallandra and Branna in the great hall.

'I did have Da to myself for some weeks,' Wynni told them. 'It be Mara's turn to greet our father.'

'That's generous of you,' Dallandra said. 'Wynni, have you thought at all about the rest of your life?'

'I have, and I think me I may marry Mirryn of the Red Wolf.'

'He'd be a splendid choice,' Branna put in. 'He's my cousin, and I know him fairly well, you see. He'll make a better lord than many another man I've known.'

'Well and good, then, if ever my heart heals from the losing of my Dougie.' Berwynna got up from her place at table. 'Wish you some ale or suchlike? I could fetch it.'

'None for me,' Dallandra said.

'Nor me, either,' Branna said. 'We've got a lot of work ahead of us.'

'Very well. I'll be taking myself to the kitchen hut to help Lonna and Kov with the meal.' Wynni glanced at Branna. 'I do think my sister, she'll be marrying far sooner than I. She be fair taken with Kov, and the island demands she give it heirs.'

With a nod all round, Berwynna hurried out. Branna moved around the table to sit next to Dallandra, who had brought the dragon book down with her. Dallandra opened it randomly at one of its infuriatingly identical pages.

'I've tried all the simple ciphers I know,' Dallandra told Branna. 'Reading the first rune of each line, and then the last, and every third word and the like. None of them make sense except by chance. Down here –' she pointed to the bottom third of the page '– if you take every third word starting at the last word, you can put together "after the rabbit tree". I doubt me if that has much to do with anything.'

Branna laughed and nodded her agreement. The sound of a bronze gong drifted in through a window, growing louder as the boat made the journey back across the lake. Dallandra left the book with Branna and walked outside in time to see Valandario and Grallezar disembarking at the pier. With a shout of greeting she trotted down to meet them.

'I've got the crystal!' Valandario patted the quiver slung across her chest.

'Splendid, and my thanks,' Dalla said.

'My heart aches to see the dweomer book at last,' Grallezar said. 'Though truly, my mind does need a few quiet moments to recover from riding upon dragonback.'

'Well, the lady of the manse has planned a feast for tonight,' Dalla said, 'so I suggest we find some quiet spot outside and study it there.'

Dallandra went to the nearest window and called to Branna to bring the book. They walked around the manse in the opposite direction from the pier. Branna joined them at the back door, and they trooped down to the lake shore. As they walked along, looking for a place to sit, Dallandra heard a sound she couldn't quite place at first. A bird, perhaps?

'Someone weeps,' Grallezar said. 'The sound does come from that willow tree.'

On the little bench under the willow they found Avain, sitting slumped over and sobbing into her cupped hands. When Branna rushed over to her, Avain looked up but continued weeping.

'Here, here,' Branna said, 'what's so wrong? You sound as if your heart would break.'

Avain paused to wipe her eyes and her nose as well on one sleeve. 'Avain wants to see the dragons.'

'Well, mayhap later you can go across and see them.'

Avain's eyes narrowed in thought. 'The dragon, he be not my da. Mama did make me stay here.' With that she began sobbing again.

'Branna?' Dalla said. 'I doubt me if she understands what you mean by "later". Time is a hard thing for such as her to comprehend.'

'So I see.' Branna hesitated, then smiled. 'I'll fetch Wynni. I'll wager she knows what to tell her.'

The elder dweomermasters stood helplessly around as Branna trotted back in the direction of the manse and the kitchen hut. In the soft summer breeze the overhanging willow branches rustled softly, as if commiserating with the poor girl. Dallandra noticed Grallezar studying Avain with half-lidded eyes.

'Avain?' Grallezar said suddenly. 'Be it that you wish you were a dragon?'

Avain looked up with snot smearing her upper lip. 'Avain wants to fly.' She paused to wipe her nose on her sleeve again. 'Avain dreams about dragons.'

Dallandra became suddenly aware of Avain's green eyes, lashless, round, and slit vertically. She opened her sight and immediately saw what Grallezar had seen: Avain's etheric double, a faint dragon-shape hovering around her. *Tonight the moon will be dark*, Dalla thought. *Rori's true form will be dominant, so why not Avain's as well?* The three dweomer women exchanged glances, but no one spoke until Branna returned with Berwynna.

Wynni immediately went to Avain and threw an arm around her sister's broad shoulders. She spoke in Dwarvish, a soft murmur of words that soothed Avain the way a soft voice and stroking will soothe a nervous horse.

'I'll coax her back to her tower,' Wynni said. 'My thanks for fetching me, Branna.'

To please Wynni – and upon the promise of apple cake – Avain stopped weeping. She stood up and let her sister lead her away down the path toward the manse and tower. Grallezar set her hands on her hips and watched them till they disappeared among the apple trees.

'Well, well,' Grallezar said. 'I think me we now know what we might do with that excess of etheric substance. It wraps Rori up like a pit in a peach, and truly, I did have doubts we could earth all of it after we stripped it away.'

'Indeed,' Dalla said. 'I see what you mean – if we can keep from killing both of them.'

Grallezar smiled with a show of fang. 'Too true, but still, I do count this as one problem solved.'

There remained the problem of the dragon book, or to be precise, the problem of reading it. Dallandra sat down on the bench astride, as if she were on horseback, so that she could lay the book down in front of her. Branna hunkered down at the far end of the bench to watch. Both Valandario and Grallezar preferred to stand and keep their feet upon solid ground after their experience of sailing through the sky.

Valandario handed Dallandra the black crystal. A quick glance into it confirmed what Laz had told her, that the white one lay at the bottom of the lake.

'I hope the black will work by itself,' Dallandra said. 'Wish me luck!'

First Dalla tried looking at one of the pages through the crystal with no particular result. When she set it down on the page, nothing changed. She tried placing it upon the front cover, the back cover, on each page, in different areas of each page – still nothing. Finally she picked the crystal up, holding it without thinking close to her face.

'You wretched book!' she snapped. 'Will you unlock, or shall I burn you?'

The book shimmered like the reflection of a book upon water. Dallandra nearly dropped the crystal in surprise as the illusion disintegrated. The front cover vanished first, then the back. The pages began to peel away, one at a time, and fade into air. In a startling gleam of silver light the last page but one followed the others into nothingness. A single piece of parchment, slightly singed around the edges, lay on the bench.

'Ye gods!' Branna whispered.

'He always did like to make a gaudy display,' Dallandra said. 'Evandar, I mean, when he worked dweomer, no matter how much dweomer force he wasted doing it.'

Valandario quirked an eyebrow in her direction.

'Let's see what this thing says.' Dallandra handed the crystal back to Val. 'I know what you're thinking, and no doubt you're right. Does it matter? He's gone now.'

'That's very true,' Val said. 'I shan't mention it again.'

When Dalla picked up the parchment, she was relieved to see that the writing had turned into simple Elvish. As she read, she translated the words into Deverrian for the sake of Branna and Grallezar.

'If the man's shadow survives, then he will survive,' it began. 'If his shadow has died, then he will die unless he remain a beast. Fear not the dark of the moon but its full. Unweaving the dweomer is much like unpicking a length of cloth. Unravelling the threads is a simple task, but without a spindle upon which to wind them, they tangle and are lost. If you lack a spindle, then he will be lost. If the threads fall into water, they will drain the man's life. If they fall upon the ground, they will strangle the one who attempts the unweaving. If they come loose and waft through the air, they will destroy the spindle.'

Dallandra looked up to find her listeners nodding in understanding.

'Well and good, then,' Dalla said in Deverrian. 'At last! Somewhat that's perfectly clear.'

'True spoken,' Val said. 'But you do realize, don't you, that he just copied that out of the *Pseudo-Iamblichos Scroll*?'

'Now, now,' Grallezar broke in before Dallandra could make an angry reply. 'He did copy a bit here, a bit there, but he did put together a new sense out of the bits. And here, did he not point to the source with the picture upon the cover of the book?'

'Of course!' Dallandra said. 'That's why it's the opposite of the picture on Laz's copy of the *Scroll*.'

'That's very true,' Val said. 'I wonder if he saw Laz's book somewhere, but it doesn't matter any more. We have the information we need.'

Branna looked so stricken that Dallandra could practically hear her thinking, 'We do?' Grallezar gave her apprentice an indulgent smile.

'I shall tell you the answers to these riddles before the night does fall,' Grallezar said. 'But for now, I think me that Dalla's part of this work lies with Avain. Think you her mother will agree to what we have in mind?'

'I don't know. I'm going to go ask Wynni first.'

'What about Avain?' Val said. 'We should be asking her.'

Dallandra laughed, one startled bark. 'True spoken! But I think me Arzosah can convince her.' She swung her leg free of the bench and stood up. 'Val, if you'd call Arzosah over? I'll just be talking with Wynni in the kitchen.'

Although she never would have claimed that she understood the dweomer in Evandar's book, Branna did have some vague idea about the meaning of its instructions. She merely had no idea of how the elder dweomermasters were going to carry them out. One thing had come clear to her, however, the reason that Laz would remain in raven form for the rest of his life. His 'shadow', his human etheric double, had indeed died. Trying to unwind the raven form would kill him.

When Dallandra went to the kitchen, Branna followed the others down to the pier and the lakeshore. They could see both dragons, Rori lounging in the grass, with the two small figures of Angmar and Mara beside him, and Arzosah, lying a good distance away with her back firmly toward the group. When Valandario cupped her hands around her mouth and called out the dragon's name, Arzosah roared in answer, then took to the air. With a few beats of her enormous wings and a glide she crossed the lake and landed nearby on the sandy fringe of beach.

Out in deep water a beast rose to the surface and lifted its head to stare at the dragon. Branna could see a fine row of needle teeth as it opened its mouth, but it came no closer.

'It's trying to smell us,' Arzosah remarked. 'They have another nose, as it were, deep in their throats.'

'These beasts never lived in this lake before,' Valandario said. 'So they must have arrived with Haen Marn. Do you know what they are?'

'Water beasts is what I've always called them. A few live up in the Northlands. They're really quite stupid, just animals if huge ones.' Arzosah rustled her wings in a shrug. 'Their race, though, is even older than wyrmkind. I'm surprised that any are left.'

A second beast rose out of the water to stare. Arzosah swung her head toward them and roared so loudly that the sound echoed back and forth across the surrounding hills. Both beasts dived with a splash and disappeared into the rippling water with a flick of their long skinny tails.

'Ai!' Branna said. 'My poor ears!'

'My apologies, but sometimes a lady just has to relieve her feelings.' Arzosah turned toward Valandario. 'Now, why did you fetch me?'

'There's a person here we very much want you to see.' Val paused and glanced back at the manse. 'We need your opinion about – Ah, here she is, in fact, with Wynni and Dalla.'

Avain saw the dragon, broke into a grin, and came skipping down the path ahead of her two companions. Arzosah's lower jaw sagged open. She shut it with a snap of fangs, then shook her head.

'The poor soul!' the dragon muttered. 'Trapped in that nasty pink skin.' She raised her voice. 'Little hatchling, come here!'

Avain ran the rest of the way. She threw her arms around Arzosah's neck as far as they could reach while the dragon murmured to her in a soothing flow of incomprehensible words – Dragonish words, Branna assumed. When Avain let Arzosah go and stepped back, the dragon licked her face with just the very tip of a surprisingly gentle tongue. Avain laughed and clapped her hands together.

'You agree, then?' Val said. 'That she's a dragon in her soul?'

'Of course she is,' Arzosah said. 'Will her mother let her fly free, or will she insist on snatching her away like she's snatched Rori?'

'Mam will do what be best for Avain,' Berwynna said. 'And truly, that would be letting her go. But, Step-mother, there be a need on you to know that my sister does have her troubles. Never has she had keen wits.'

Arzosah snorted and rolled her eyes. 'She's very young, is all – for a dragon. Fear not, once we restore her to her true self, her mind will begin to blossom.'

'Well and good, then,' Grallezar put in. 'You do know more of such things than we do.'

'Of course I do.' Arzosah snorted again. 'I suppose Evandar had somewhat to do with this poor child's misery.'

'He did not,' Dallandra snapped. 'And you're a fine one to talk! You're the one who insisted Rhodry become a dragon in the first place, aren't you?'

Arzosah glowered but held her enormous tongue.

Distantly the boat's gong began to ring. Berwynna shaded her eyes with one hand and looked across the lake.

'Here they do come,' Wynni said, 'Mam and Mara, that be. Let me speak to my mother straightaway about Avain.'

'Avain wants to fly.' The subject of this discussion spoke up at last. 'But Avain loves Mam and Wynni and Mara.'

'We all shall talk about this.' Wynni caught her sister's huge hand in both of hers. 'See you Mam? She be on the boat, and the boat, it does come toward the pier.'

'We'll let you all make this decision in private,' Dallandra said. 'We need to go plan things out.'

'Will you be joining us for the evening meal?' Wynni said.

'We won't. We all have to fast, and truly, Avain should as well, if you can explain it to her.'

'That be no hard task. She does eat oddly little, and often but once a day.'

'Good. We'll wait at the bench under the willow. If you could let us know what your mother –'

'Of course! I know not how long I'll be.'

Dallandra glanced at the sky. 'We have a long while till sunset. If your mother will agree to releasing Avain, we'll go across the lake to speak to Rori. Otherwise – well, otherwise I don't know what we'll do.'

'Naught, I should think,' Grallezar said. 'Lest we slay the man we do try to save.'

Berwynna gave her a sharp look, began to speak, then turned to Avain. 'See you the boat?' she said. 'Go you now to the pier and wait for them.'

Avain trotted off, humming a little tune under her breath. Berwynna set her hands on her hips and considered Grallezar for a moment.

'Be you telling me,' Wynni said at last, 'that my sister be the price of my father's return?'

'Not a price that we demand,' Grallezar said, 'but no great dweomer comes without great price.'

'Never did I think that it were you who did demand it.' Wynni caught her lower lip between her teeth and thought for a long moment. 'I'll be telling Mam that. It be a hard choice.'

'Oh come now,' Arzosah said. 'She can always fly your way and visit.'

'As a dragon, not as Avain, and never will she be able to fly across the lake again to join us in the manse.' Wynni turned away. 'The boat, it be docking.' She strode off, heading for the pier.

'Come along,' Dallandra said to her flock of dweomerfolk. 'We can't influence their decision either way. Arzosah, that means you too!'

Grumbling under her breath, the dragon waddled after them as they walked away.

While Berwynna helped her mother and Mara climb onto the pier, Avain kept up a constant flow of chatter in Dwarvish about the black dragon. Berwynna had never seen her sister so happy, her smile so broad, her eyes so bright with life. Her words, too, made better sense than Wynni had ever heard her make. When, however, they turned to leave the pier, Avain realized that Arzosah had gone, and she burst into tears.

'Here, here!' Wynni spoke in Dwarvish as well. 'She's just gone round to the willow tree. She's still on the island, Avain.'

The tears stopped, and the bright smile returned.

'Well now,' Angmar said. 'I see that Avain has a new friend.'

'More than a friend, Mam,' Berwynna said. 'Come inside, and let's sit down, and I'll tell you what's happened. I'm not sure how much she understands.'

Although Avain disliked being inside the manse, for this occasion she did come in with them. She refused, however, to sit down at the table. Instead she wandered around the great hall, looking at the carvings on the walls, glancing out the windows, while the rest of the family discussed a wyrd she could barely understand.

Angmar spoke not at all when Wynni told her of the price of Rori's return. Mara had a few questions, but it seemed obvious to Wynni that the sort of dweomer Dallandra and Grallezar wanted to work lay well beyond her sister's knowledge. Finally Angmar shook her head and sighed.

'I don't understand everything,' Angmar said. 'But I've always understood the price that Haen Marn demands for its dweomers. It exacted the fee of my whole life when it brought me here. It demanded that Avain's father marry a half-breed woman he'd never seen. It took me away from my Rori when he was a man, and it took him away from me by turning him into the silver wyrm. Why would I be surprised that it would demand such a great price for giving him back?'

Mara and Berwynna exchanged a glance. Berwynna noticed with some surprise that her sister's eyes were full of tears. *I never truly knew her before,* she thought. *Her heart's not stone after all!*

'Avain,' Angmar said, 'darling, come here. Tell Mam this one thing. Do you want to fly?'

'Yes.' Avain smiled at her. 'Avain truly wants to fly.'

'Do you want to fly away with your new friend, the black dragon?'

'Yes, but Avain will come back. Avain loves Mam and Mara and Wynni.'

'Very well, then. Learning to fly is dangerous. You could fall from the sky and die.'

Avain considered this for a long moment. Berwynna wondered if she understood what death meant.

'If you die,' Wynni said, 'it will be like sleep, but you'll never wake up. You'll be gone. It will be dark, but you won't see the dark. You'll see naught.'

Avain frowned down at the floor while she thought this through.

Her lips moved as she repeated to herself the things Berwynna had said.

'Avain is frightened,' Avain said at last. 'But Avain will try to fly. Avain truly wants to fly, Mam.'

'Very well, then. Tonight the black dragon will help you grow wings.'

Avain threw both arms in the air and began to dance, a clumsy jigging of her body, an awkward thrust of her massive hips to one side and then the other. *She doesn't belong on the ground*, Berwynna thought.

'I'll go tell the others.' Berwynna stood up from the table. 'If you're sure, Mam?'

'Oh yes.' Angmar was fighting back tears. 'But I'll have you know that it's for her sake, not my own, even though I long to have Rori back above anything in the world.'

'I never thought otherwise, Mam,' Berwynna said.

'No more did I,' Mara said. 'I think me this is the moment when the dweomer gives back some of that fee you paid it, Mam. I truly do.'

Close to sunset, Branna, Dallandra, Grallezar, and Valandario went down to the pier. Arzosah carried Avain across on her back, but Lon and his crew of boatmen rowed the women across. Rori waited for them at the verge of the pine forest. The boatmen backed water and turned the boat into the shallows to let the women splash ashore. Branna carried a sack of cloaks as well as the implement she'd use for the ritual. Once she'd got the sack safe and dry onto the land, Branna turned back to watch the dragon boat gliding away. Mist rose from the water, just a few curls and tendrils as the evening breeze blew cool after the heat of the day.

Dallandra used her consecrated sword to cut a circle, some thirty yards in diameter, in the grass near the forest verge.

'We'd better mark out the circle now,' Dalla said, 'while there's still a little light.'

Valandario had brought several sacks of ashes from Haen Marn's hearths. She began to walk the circle, trickling ashes between her fingers as she went. When she'd marked out about two-thirds of the figure, she paused.

'Rori,' she called out. 'Come take your place.'

The silver dragon got up and shook himself, spreading his wings as if he would fly away, then folding them tightly against his back and sides. Head held high, he walked over to Valandario, ducked his head as if bowing to her, and walked into the ritual space, all without saying a word.

Dallandra placed Rori in the northern-western quarter, facing the centre, and Arzosah, facing him, in the south-eastern. The dragons lay with legs tucked under and tails wrapped around them, a posture that left just enough space for Avain to sit between them. The lass was so excited that she could barely sit still until Arzosah chanted a tuneless sort of lullaby under her breath. Branna found it irritating, but Avain smiled and grew calm, a mood that lasted even after the chant stopped.

Valandario took her second sack of ashes and finished the circle. She put the sack down, wiped her hands on her leather leggings, and picked up her sword. Grallezar had already taken up her ritual falcata. Branna, as a mere apprentice, held only a wooden staff.

'They are enclosed,' Val called out. 'It's time to begin.'

The dweomerworkers lined up behind Dallandra, then walked around the outside of the circle deosil. They made one full circumambulation, then began another. As they reached each directional point, the woman whose station it was stopped there. Once everyone was in place, Dallandra nodded Branna's way as a signal to begin.

'I stand in the north,' Branna said, 'the station of Earth and darkness.'

'I stand in the south,' Grallezar said, 'the station of Fire and light.'

'I stand in the west,' Valandario said, 'the station of Water and the setting of the sun.'

'And I stand in the east,' Dallandra said, 'the station of Air and the rising of the sun.'

'And I,' Arzosah rumbled, 'represent the Aethyr and the Portion of Wyrd.'

Dallandra raised her sword high. 'May the Kings of the Elements lend us strength, for we come in the name of the Light that shines behind all the gods. We would set right errors made in its name.' She lowered the sword and pointed it at the ground.

Although the sun had long since gone behind the western hills, the light within the circle suddenly brightened, a pale blue light that glittered on the dragons' scales and turned Avain's face a pasty white. The Kings had heard and agreed.

'All powers, you have my thanks.' Dallandra walked into the circle and laid the flat of her sword upon Rori's neck. 'The unwinding begins.'

Branna, Grallezar, and Valandario all knelt to conserve their energies. Besides the maintaining of the ritual circle, their primary task was to lend Dallandra some of their own life force should the senior mage require it. Branna summoned her dweomer sight and saw the auras of the three within the circle: Arzosah's strong dragon etheric double, Avain's weak one, and Rori's human form, hovering uncertainly above him.

Dallandra sent a pulse of blue light along her sword that burrowed into the dragon's body just at the joining of his spine with his skull. A line of light sprang out from the space just above and between his eyes in answer, a tendril like that of a vine seeking purchase on a wall, waving back and forth, reaching for Dallandra's aura. She held up the sword and caught it, then turned and tossed it Arzosah's way.

The dragon caught it on a line of light emanating from her own aura. The two began to tangle, but Arzosah's dweomer had vast strength behind it. As Branna watched the two tendrils separated again and floated downward toward Avain. Arzosah used a spear of light from her own aura to manipulate the thread from Rori's aura and fasten it to Avain's solar plexus.

'Now!' Dallandra called out. She used the sword to describe a sigil in the air above Rori's head. The line of light thickened and began to pulse, unwinding just like the thread of Evandar's chosen imagery. It flowed to Avain and began to wrap her round, while Arzosah guided it, carefully, patiently, spinning the thread around her just as, indeed, a spindle collects the spun thread from a spinning wheel. Standing beside Rori, Dallandra used her sword, flicking it this way and that, guiding the thread free of the dragon's body in front of her, to allow Arzosah to catch and claim it for Avain's etheric double that slowly, ever so slowly, began to take shape and size.

Thanks to the flying threads, the glittering blue light, and the mists of etheric substance flowing and forming between the two dweomer-masters, Westfolk and Wyrmish, Branna couldn't see either of the two physical bodies they worked upon, not even Rori's massive frame. She planted the end of her staff on the ground in front of her and clutched it with both hands.

When she glanced at Grallezar, she saw golden light pulsing in bursts from her falcata and travelling across the circle to Dallandra's aura, lending it power and strength. Valandario stood ready to do the same should the Gel da'Thae master tire. Branna would be the last resort, the apprentice who could offer little but who stood ready to give all she could if called upon.

On and on the working continued, unwinding from one, winding again around the other. Branna's back ached, and her knees as well, but she kept herself unmoving, watching, ready to join the battle in front of her. Once she did glance up at the sky and noticed that the wheel of stars had moved to mark the half-way point of the night. When she brought her gaze back to the working, she saw that Valandario had taken over from Grallezar, who'd laid her falcata down in front of her and now merely watched.

I'm ready, Branna thought, *ready to fulfil the vow Jill made.* Yet in the end, the only aid she needed to offer had nothing about it of the great and mighty act she wanted. Several hours before dawn, Dallandra suddenly stepped back and lowered her sword.

'It is finished!' she cried out.

From the sky came three great knocks, booming out over Haen Marn's lake, echoing back and forth from the hills. The blue etheric glow faded, plunging the circle into darkness. Branna flung up her staff and made a golden dweomer light upon it. She staggered to her feet and saw with her normal vision a young dragon, mottled blue and silver, crouching in front of Arzosah. A man with silver hair lay on the ground, sprawled out, naked, and shivering with cold.

Branna tossed her glowing staff to Valandario and grabbed the sack she'd brought across with her. She pulled out a cloak and darted forward to lay it over Rhodry, then brought another for Dallandra, who'd fallen, exhausted, to her knees.

'Val, the silver horn,' Dallandra said. 'We've got to get him into a warm bed.'

Valandario sounded the silver horn while Branna and Grallezar wrapped the unconscious Rhodry in a second cloak as well. The young dragon, slender enough to walk gracefully, came over to them and bowed her head.

'My thanks,' she said. 'Avain wants to fly now.'

'I'll take her back to my clutch.' Arzosah waddled over and looked at the man lying wrapped on the ground. 'Will he live?'

'I hope so,' Dallandra said. 'After all of this effort, he'd better!'

Arzosah rumbled in laughter, then touched Rhodry gently with her massive nose. 'Sleep well, Rhodry Dragonfriend,' she said. 'Soon you'll see me again, and our young son will have a mate, once he's grown.'

Ye gods! Branna thought, *she's as bad as Aunt Galla!*

Avain followed as Arzosah waddled some distance away. They spread their wings, then leapt into the air and flew, heading north and west to rejoin the royal alar. As their wingbeats died away, Branna heard the bronze gong as the dragon boat glided up to the shore.

The three elder dweomermasters picked up Rhodry and carried him out to the boat. Branna watched as Lon helped them lay him down in the bow. The three women knelt around Rhodry as with a

shout the rowers turned the boat and bent to the oars. Branna watched
them as they glided into the mists that shrouded the island and disappeared.

Even though Valandario would be contacting Salamander and Niffa
to tell them, and thus the royal alar, how things had gone with the
working, Branna decided that she wanted to tell Neb herself. She'd
stayed behind since she lacked the skill to contact him through Haen
Marn's vortex. When she sent her mind out to Neb, she found him
awake. His image, bright with candlelight, built up fast, floating on
the dark waters.

'We've done it,' she said. 'Rori's Rhodry again, and we've all survived.'

'That gladdens my heart,' Neb said, 'but not half as much as seeing
you unharmed gladdens it. Are you truly well?'

'I am, just tired.' She stifled a yawn. 'Well, exhausted, actually.
Where are you?'

'Still some miles from the Melyn. You know how alarli travel, and the
Cerr Cawnen folk are worse. Still, we'll be there soon, by my reckoning.'

'I'll join you there. It's only been a few days, but I've missed you
so much!'

'I've missed you, too. And worried as well. I managed to see a bit
of the ritual, you see, by scrying. It went on for a truly long time. I
hate to admit this, but I finally fell asleep.'

Branna laughed, and she could feel his laughter join hers.

'One thing,' Neb said. 'That child they were turning into a dragon.
Did she survive?'

'She did, and truly, she must have been a dragon in her soul, because
she leapt into the air and flew. She was born to the air, I swear it!'

'Splendid! You can tell me more when we're together. But I need
to ask, is it truly all right with you, that we'll be spending the winter
with the Cerr Cawnen folk?'

'It is. Dalla told me that we can learn much from their dweomer-
woman and their spirit talker.'

'That gladdens my heart! I hated to think we'd have to stop our
studies.'

'So did I. And I'm looking forward to getting to know them all, the
folk from the town, that is. It was their land, after all, before our folk
came here. Somehow that seems truly important to me, that we all
understand what our people did, even if it was ever so long ago.'

They spoke for a while more, mostly about how much they loved
and missed each other. Exhaustion finally got the better of Branna,
though, and she broke the link.

She blew the silver horn to summon Lon and the dragon boat, then walked down to the shore. She could hear the gong answering the horn's call, coming closer and closer, and the splash of oars in the water. Far off to the east a thin silver line appeared in the sky as the sun announced that it was intending to rise. *I'm free of him*, she thought, *of Rhodry and everything he meant to me*. Although she didn't know how she knew, she did know, and that, she decided, would have to do for now.

With the morning light Rhodry woke and realized that he was lying in Angmar's chamber on Haen Marn. The wide window across from the foot of the bed stood open. He could see the figure of a woman sitting on the window ledge, silhouetted against the brightening sunshine. Angmar, was it? His dreams still clung to him, confused images of flying among dragons, of pillars of smoke reaching to the sky, and ruined towers and vast caves inside fire mountains. He sat up and remembered that the Horsekin were marching upon Cengarn.

'Raena, the mazrak,' he said in Elvish, 'and that cursed false goddess of hers! I've got to get to Cengarn.'

The woman by the window stood up fast, as if she were alarmed.

'Don't I?' Rhodry went on. 'I've fetched the dragon like Jill told me –' He remembered suddenly that Jill was long dead. 'Or, no, wait, that all happened years ago.'

'Over forty years ago, truly,' Dallandra said. 'Rhodry, do you recognize me?'

'Of course I do! Ye gods, Dalla, I had the strangest dreams last night . . .' He let his voice trail away. 'Not dreams.'

'No. Not dreams at all.' She stood by the edge of the bed. 'You've been ensorcelled for a very long time. It's going to take you months to get everything clear in your mind. You've got Angmar and your daughters to help you. Do you remember meeting your daughters?'

'Yes, and I never forgot Angmar.'

'I know, and that's what saved you.'

'So it did. Where is she?'

'Just outside the door, waiting to come in.' Dallandra turned away and started toward the door in question.

'Wait!' Rhodry said. 'There's one thing I have to ask you first. Cerr Cawnen. Is it true, that the town's been destroyed?'

'It is, and the Horsekin army with it. Don't you remember?'

'I was hoping it was a dream, a nightmare more like.'

'What? Why?'

'There were slaves there, innocent souls. I saw them so I know.

What choice did they have? Why didn't I see that before? Why couldn't I remember my shame over Slaith? Why couldn't I see that –'

'Hush!' Dalla laid her hand over his mouth. 'Because you weren't a man at that moment, Rhodry. Because you were on your way to becoming somewhat cold and cruel. Soon you wouldn't have been a man at all.' She took her hand away. 'We brought you back just in time, before you became a dragon in your soul.'

'So you did.'

At that moment Rhodry couldn't bear to look at her. He covered his face with his hands as if he could physically block out the memory of the earth's blood boiling up and the screams of men dying in agony. He heard Dallandra moving away, heard the door open and the murmur of Angmar's voice. The door shut again. He lowered his hands, thinking he was alone, but Angmar stood quietly, leaning against the closed door and holding a small cloth-wrapped bundle in both hands.

'Be it that you want me to leave?' she said.

'Never,' he said. 'If you'll forgive me for the things I've done.'

'I care not, Rori.' She walked over, laid the bundle down beside him, then perched on the edge of the bed. 'Whatever it be that makes your heart feel shamed, it's naught to me now.'

'Truly?' He held out his hand.

'Truly.' She caught it in both of hers.

'Then I never want you to leave again, and even less do I want to leave you.'

'Well and good, then. I do feel the same, and all be as well as ever it can be.' She glanced at the bundle, then let go his hand. 'Dallandra, she did bring somewhat for you.'

Rhodry picked up the bundle and unwrapped it to reveal his silver dagger. Someone – Cal, he suspected – had rewrapped the hilt with fresh leather.

'It gladdens my heart to see this,' he said, 'not that I'll be riding the long road again.'

'You won't, truly,' Angmar said. 'You'll be taking my hire and none others.'

He looked up and saw her smiling at him. He laid the dagger down and caught her by the shoulders.

'So I will,' he said.

And with their long waiting over, he kissed her.

EPILOGUE

The Westlands
Autumn, 1160

Your soul does not sit in your body like a nut in a shell. It forms the etheric double, which interpenetrates the flesh. Indeed, the soul creates the body for its own purposes.

The Secret Book of Cadwallon the Druid

The royal alar reached the trading grounds near the seacoast shortly before the autumnal equinox. Several other alarli had already gathered there, and a few last traders from Eldidd lingered for the inevitable feasting and celebrations as well. The news spread quickly, that Prince Daralanteriel had established new farm-lands and planned to found a city up north along the river that men called the Melyn but elves, Cantariel, though the name means 'honey-coloured' in both languages.

News of a quieter sort arrived when Medea flew into camp, carrying messages and a passenger. The bards immediately dubbed Prince Dar 'Dragonfriend', an epithet that Medea graciously acknowledged.

'He's certainly my friend,' she told Dallandra, 'so your people can call him that if they'd like.'

The passenger, Pol, whom Laz had freed from slavery, stood quietly beside the young dragon and looked at the trading ground with wide eyes. Contrary to Laz's descriptions of him, Dallandra decided, he wasn't so much obese as oddly formed, thanks to the barbarous prac-tice among the Horsekin of turning young boys into eunuchs. He'd continued to grow long past the usual age, so that he was nearly seven feet tall with an abnormally large ribcage and long spindly arms. When he finally spoke, his voice was high-pitched but strong.

'I have messages for the prince.' Pol laid a hand on the leather pouch he carried. 'From the Red Wolf dun.'

'Excellent!' Dallandra said. 'Am I remembering this correctly? You're a scribe?'

'Yes, I am, but I'm just learning the syllabary. I can write in Deverrian and Gel da'Thae, though.'

'You'll pick up the Elvish script fast enough. The prince needs a scribe. The last one left his retinue to settle in the new town up north. Come with me.'

As Pol accompanied her through the camp, Dallandra noticed the other Westfolk doing their best not to stare at him, and he grimly kept his gaze fixed ahead. When they reached Dar's tent, however, painted with red roses in memory of the Far West, the sight of the flowers made him smile. He reached out and touched one of the images.

'We have these at home,' he remarked, 'in the seacoast villages. The legend runs that the People brought them from the old cities.'

'Do you?' Dallandra said. 'So something of the Vale of Roses survived. That's lovely.'

At Dallandra's urging, Daralanteriel took Pol on as his new scribe. When he read the messages out, Dallandra heard what she'd been waiting for. Lady Solla had been safely delivered of a fine healthy son. Gerran and his wife and heir would spend the winter with Tieryn Cadryc, then move out to the Melyn valley with the spring.

'That's splendid,' Dallandra remarked to Valandario later. 'The Gold Falcon clan's off to a good start.'

'So it is. Gerran will make a decent lord, I think.'

'If he doesn't, Dar will take him in hand.'

Valandario nodded and pulled her cloak a little tighter around her shoulders. They were sitting in front of Dallandra's tent and nursing a tiny fire against the chilly evening breeze. Around them swirled the normal sounds of a night camp: children crying, dogs barking, harp music, singing, and the occasional angry quarrel followed by soothing words.

'Summer's almost gone,' Dallandra said. 'Will you be going back to Mandra for the winter?'

'I don't know,' Valandario said. 'I'm too comfortable there.'

'What? There's naught wrong with being warm and dry.'

'That's not what I meant. Comfortable in my soul, with my gems and the books all around me. How long has it been since I truly worked dweomer?'

'When you evoked the spirit of Hanmara.'

'Oh, that was just a typical evocation. I wouldn't call it a real accomplishment.'

'Well, your scrying system is certainly valuable.'

'I know, I know, but once Sidro gets it written up from her notes, anyone with the smallest dweomer gift will be able to use it. I mean real dweomer, something to stretch my mind and soul, something with risks, even.' Val paused to add another patty of dry horse dung to the campfire in front of them. 'Ever since I approved Ebañy's plan to go live in that tower, I've felt guilty. I was always badgering him to do more with his dweomer gifts, but I wasn't using mine fully either.'

'I wouldn't say that.'

'But I would.' Val smiled at her. 'I've been looking back over my life. When Jav died I retreated from it, life that is. I've been living in a jewel-encrusted shell, Dalla. I've forgotten that I'm still young, and I've been a coward.'

'Here! I wouldn't call you that.'

'Thank you, but I would. I can't even make up my mind whether to destroy the black stone, can I?'

'Why should you, really?'

'It caused a murder, and Evandar meddled with it.'

'That's true.' Dallandra hesitated, then decided against saying anything. She badly wanted the crystal, she realized, wanted to cherish it as the last token of her love for Evandar. *It's Val's*, she reminded herself, *not yours to have or destroy.* She concentrated on watching the salamanders basking in the tiny flames. For their sake she added a few sticks to the fire.

'I'm going to ride out tomorrow,' Val said eventually. 'I want to take the black crystal back to the place where Jav found it, the ruins of that tower. I have the feeling that I'll know what to do with it once I'm there.'

'But the tower fell nearly two hundred years ago. There won't be much left. You probably won't even be able to find the place.'

'He said the broken stones were huge. The tide won't have washed them away.'

'Ah, I see. Who's going to go with you?'

'No one. I'm going alone.'

'What? That's dangerous!'

'I don't care.'

'Val! You can't!'

'I've made up my mind.' Val rose from her seat. 'I'm leaving on the morrow.'

When the morrow came, Dallandra continued arguing the point while Valandario loaded supplies onto her pack mule and saddled up her riding horse. Val merely smiled, refusing to answer. Eventually Dallandra ran out of words.

'If I get into trouble,' Val said, 'I'll call to you mind to mind. Besides, if you're truly this worried, you can always scry me out.'

'That's true,' Dallandra said. 'Very well, I'll hold my nagging tongue. The truth is, I keep wanting to beg you for the crystal. It's the last thing of Evandar's that I have.'

'I know you loved him, but it's time to put his schemes to rest.'

'So it is.' Dallandra hesitated, then forced out a smile. 'Take it and give it to the Lords of Aethyr then, should they want it. It's time, indeed, for me to let Evandar go.'

Over the next few days, as she rode west Valandario was aware now and then of the touch of Dallandra's anxious mind, watching over her.

At first Val found it annoying, but by the end of an eightnight, she began to welcome it. The grasslands stretched out empty to the north; to the south lay only the sea, muttering on its rocky beach. For company she had only the seabirds, wheeling and mewling over the green swells and the dark water that stretched to the southern horizon.

Although she'd brought a canvas shelter with her, most nights she left it tied in a bundle. She lay out in the grass near her tethered horse and mule and watched the wheel of stars while the sea murmured and sang nearby. On nights when the fog came in thickly over land and sea, she gathered driftwood for a fire. She watched the flames, burning blue from the salt crusted on the wood, for half the night. At times she saw strange images among them, of tall towers of stone amid the streets of ancient cities.

On the twelfth day she reached the ruins of the old guard tower. A half-circle of broken walls stood on the edge of a cliff. On the beach below, the corners of huge stones emerged from nearly two hundred years' worth of sand and driftwood as if they were swimmers just coming up from a dive. Jav had found the box with the obsidian crystal somewhere among them when they lay clean and exposed to the open air. If any dweomer objects lay in the sand now, they were too well-buried for her to sense. The remains of the tower wall, however, still stood on the cliff edge.

Some hundred yards west Valandario found a rivulet of fresh water digging itself a channel through the grass. It slithered rather than cascaded down the cliff face, then lost itself in the sand, but up on top it ran deep and clean enough for drinking. She unloaded her stock, watered them, and set them out to graze, then walked over to the tower. The half-circle of wall, grey stone mottled here and there with green moss, stood to a height of about ten feet.

Ancient, broken, gutted by time and sea storms – still the remaining stones gave out a peculiar energy. Val felt it as a tingling in the air and smelled it as the clean sharp aftermath of lightning. Someone had worked dweomer in this tower, someone powerful enough that the traces had lingered for over a thousand years. She ran her fingers along one flat stone, about five feet above the ground and set next to what seemed to have been a doorway. Under the moss she felt deep-carved runes, still readable by touch.

'Lords of Aethyr!' she called out. 'Grant me your protection in your temple!'

She felt their answer as a cold ripple down her back. The lightning-scent intensified around her. She stepped through the doorway and looked down. The grassy ground fell away some ten feet from the threshold. How far it would be safe to go was debatable.

'Lords of Aethyr! My thanks to you!'

Valandario turned and walked back out to ordinary ground. That evening she took one of the long sticks from her canvas lean-to and consecrated it as a ritual staff. She wanted to test the footing before she trusted her weight to the cliff edge.

In the morning, once the tide of Aethyr ran strong out on the etheric, Valandario stuffed the black crystal down the front of her tunic. She took her sword in her left hand and the staff in her right and walked back to the tower door. After a brief invocation to the powers of Aethyr, she stepped over the threshold and felt the etheric forces gathering around her. By tapping with the staff, she determined that she could safely walk some three feet in.

She laid the staff down and with the sword slashed a circle out of the tall grass, just a small one, perhaps two feet across. She took the black crystal and placed it in the centre, then picked up her staff again. She'd barely begun the ritual invocations when she saw a glimmering point of turquoise light appear above it.

'Be welcome in the name of the Light!'

The point expanded to a circle and changed to a pale lavender. The circle extended itself into a shimmering silver cylinder, some ten feet tall. Within the smoke-like interior another turquoise point appeared and gleamed, then swelled itself into a vaguely man-like shape, glowing with white light. The King of Aethyr himself had deigned to appear.

With a swing of her arm, Valandario used the staff to sketch out the sigils of Aethyr. The sword she laid cross-wise at her feet. The King acknowledged her with a nod.

'Have you brought this crystal back to us?' The thought came to her mind as a chorus of voices, not a single voice, even though a single figure floated inside the pillar.

'I have,' Val said. 'I believe it has been consecrated in your name.'

'You are correct in that. We shall retrieve the shadow, for that is what this black stone is, and reunite it with its true self. Child of Air, break the circle!'

Val laid the staff down across the edge of the circle in the grass. The spirit stone began to glow, first with its usual dark fire, then with a brighter, cleaner light. It shone grey, turned silver, and with a sound like a pair of hands slapping a drum it rose from the earth. It hovered some three feet above the grass for a few heartbeats, then began to spin, slowly at first, then faster, ever faster until with a burst of light as blinding as a lightning flash, it disappeared. From the sky above came three booming knocks of no natural thunder.

'The crystal has gone to its true home!' the King's voice echoed the thunder. 'The Great Ones approve.'

'The working is done,' Val called out. She knocked the butt of her staff three times on the ground. 'May any spirits bound by this ceremony go free.'

'It is finished, in truth and deed.' The silver King of Aethyr began to fade within his pillar. His voice rustled like wind in distant grass. 'Farewell, Child of Air! You have done well this day.'

His image swirled, faded into a beam of sunlight, then disappeared altogether. Val picked up her sword and slapped it against the grass to earth any lingering forces within it, then retrieved her staff. With a long sigh of exhaustion, she walked across the threshold and out into the ordinary world of the grasslands, the sea, and the sky, where the dawn had brightened into day.

When she lay down in her blankets that morning, Valandario fell asleep almost before she could pull them up to her chin. She found herself in the Gatelands of Sleep, which her mind conceptualized as a green lawn stretching out in front of a garden of roses. By the gate into the garden Aderyn stood, smiling at her, in the form of the silver-haired teacher she remembered so well.

'Val, Val,' he said. 'It's time you laid aside your long grief.'

'I know,' she said. 'And I will.'

'I must ask you an enormous favour. It's time for me to be reborn. Will you be my mother?'

'I never wanted a child!' Val was startled into truthfulness.

'I know that. Never would the Lords of Wyrd force a child upon a woman dead-set against it. Why do you think I'm asking? It's your choice, Val, your free choice.'

Valandario hesitated, remembering herself as little more than a child, orphaned by a flash flood that had swept away her parents and half their alar. Aderyn had taken her in, raised her with his own son, so patiently and so well, perhaps because she wasn't his bloodkin, and thus her success or failure had been less important to him than Loddlaen's. He was watching her patiently now, his face carefully composed to show no emotion that might influence her choice.

'For you I will,' Valandario said. 'I would be honoured.'

He did smile, then, a flicker of relief.

'But you know,' Val went on. 'I'm going to have a difficult time conceiving on my own.'

Aderyn laughed, so heartily that she knew his astral self had already turned toward life once again. 'So you would,' he said. 'Meet the ships coming from the Southern Isles. Remember that: meet the ships.'

With a glint of light like sun on water, he vanished. She woke, sitting up in the grass, seeing the long shadows of late afternoon, and wondering if the dream had been true or just some odd fancy. Perhaps she was merely lonely, envious of Dallandra, nursing her child, and of Sidro, so elated to be pregnant again at last. Yet his last words stayed with her: meet the ships.

On a day when a warm wind drove away the rain clouds, Valandario returned to Mandra to find the town preparing for a festival. Down by the harbour they'd set up long tables and dug pits, where several sheep were roasting for the meal ahead. Musicians sat on the grass and tuned their instruments or practiced bits and pieces of songs.

When Val arrived at their house, Lara and Jin greeted her with delight, and as they were carrying her goods up to her old chamber, Lara explained.

'Ships are coming from the Southern Isles,' Lara said. 'We've got a lookout on the roof of the new temple, and he saw them this morning. If this wind keeps up, they should make landfall tonight.'

'Wonderful!' Val said. She was thinking that she'd arrived just in time. 'New temple?'

'The town built it this summer. It's not very splendid yet, but it does have a few statues of gods inside.'

Just at sunset, the town crier went running through the streets. Four ships were pulling into the harbour under oars. As Valandario walked down with Lara and Jin, she felt oddly calm. She'd convinced herself, she realized, that she'd merely dreamt about Aderyn and his messages. Surely they couldn't be real, surely they could have nothing to do with Jav.

But he arrived in the first boat, a sailor with jet-black hair and golden eyes. Valandario was watching from the beach when she spotted him, leaping onto the wooden pier. A shipmate threw him a rope, which he hitched around the nearest bollard. With the knot secure he walked a few steps down the pier, hooked his thumbs into his leather belt, and stood looking wide-eyed at his new homeland. Or his old homeland, to which he'd returned – when he glanced her way, Valandario recognized him. *Jav!* she thought. *Oh Jav, do you remember me?*

Not, of course, that he would know that he did. Still, he took a few more steps, staring at her, smiling. She climbed the steps up to the pier, and as she walked toward the ship, he came to meet her with the rolling walk of a man who still expected his footing to rise and fall under him.

'Good morrow,' he said in a soft, dark voice. 'I seem to have come to the most beautiful spot in the world.'

'I –' Val could feel her face burning, and he laughed.

'Forgive me,' he said. 'My name is Braelindar. What's yours?'

'Valandario Gemscryer.'

'The wise one!' It was his turn for the blush. 'Meranaldar told us about –' He dropped to one knee and looked down. 'Forgive me, Wise One! I didn't mean to be so forward. I –'

'It's perfectly all right. I'm not in the least insulted.'

'You're sure?' Brae raised his head to look into her eyes.

'Very sure.' She smiled at him. 'Oh, do get up! It's not like I'm royalty or some such thing.'

He did as she asked, then grinned at her. 'Things are truly different here,' he said. 'They warned us, but I don't think I realized just how different they'd be. Back in the islands I'd never have dared speak to you, much less – uh well.'

'Uh well what?'

He laughed, she joined him, and they stood smiling at each other while the rest of the shipload of immigrants hurried past down the pier to their new homes on the land.

In the Hall of Light, they spoke to him of the work ahead.

They stood in pillars of crystal, pale lavender or mottled silver. They themselves appeared as shafts of light, glinting inside their crystal towers. He himself was but a glimmer of light, a beam of sun, perhaps, glinting on a stream, flickering, uncertain. Yet he heard them.

'They have all been born,' they said in a thousand voices that were yet one voice, 'those twisted souls you once failed, they who are called changelings. They have left behind the world of images, and they must learn now to live in the world of flesh, as children of the Westfolk, Children of Air. It is your task to help them learn. Will you remember?'

In the Hall of Light there are no lies.

'I will try to remember,' he said. 'I will strive to remember.'

'You will be helped to remember. Aderyn your name was once. You will learn to fly again.'

In the midst of the light a lack of light appeared, a shapeless thing, not a true darkness, for there can be no darkness in the Halls of Light, but still, it opened. He stepped to its edge. Among the crystal pillars a tiny flame of gold burned, quivering. He could hear its cry of pain.

'You'll follow me, Evandar,' he said. 'In due time you will follow me, and I shall father you a body. Dallandra's child will be your mother, and she will cherish you. They have promised.'

'So we have,' they said. 'Farewell and remember!'

He took one more step and fell, soaring, spiralling down and down through indigo light until he floated above a pair of golden auras that marked elven bodies. He recognized Valandario even in his disembodied state, because once she'd been his pupil in the dweomer. Deep within her body he perceived a dark knot of unensouled flesh, his body to come. For a moment he hesitated, remembering the freedoms of the Halls of Light. *Courage!* he told himself.

With a wrench of will he surrendered to the pull of the flesh. He sank down into the dark prison and slept.

AUTHOR'S NOTE

I understand that some few things will vex readers if I leave them untold. Once Avain had flown free to her true home, Laz moved into her old tower, his refuge for the rest of his days as he unwound the evil wyrd his life as Alastyr had given him. Kov and Mara married and had the children the island demanded of them. And, speaking of offspring, during his meditations in the tower at Dragon Meadow, Salamander did remember that Hwilli had once been his mother and Rhodorix his father, all those long years before.

As for Angmar and Rhodry, they lived peaceably on their island for some years more, then died within a few days of each other. Kov and Marnmara laid them in each other's arms on the same funeral pyre, so that their spirits could rise free of the dead flesh together. No doubt they were reborn at some time and place, but I for one know naught of what happened next, so you'd best not be asking me.

For so my saga ends. Of the souls who have formed its core, there is little more to be said, though many a fine tale about other souls lives in the archives here on this priestly island. Whether or not I will someday write about them, only Time knows, and as usual, Time isn't telling. So, farewell, dear Reader, and may you stay forever young in your heart!

Cadda Cerrmor
Wmmglaedd
in the 1,794th year after the founding of the Holy City

Received and translated from the Deverrian by Katharine Kerr

GLOSSARY

Alar (Elvish) A group of elves, who may or may not be bloodkin, who choose to travel together for some indefinite period of time.

Alardan (Elv.) The meeting of several alarli, usually the occasion for a drunken party.

Astral The plane of existence directly 'above' or 'within' the etheric (q.v.). In other systems of magic, often referred to as the Akashic Record or the Treasure House of Images.

Avro (Dwarvish) A warleader, roughly equivalent to cadvridoc and banadar, but possessing more absolute command than either.

Banadar (Elv.) A warleader, equivalent to the Deverrian cadvridoc.

Blue Light Another name for the etheric plane (q.v.).

Body of Light An artificial thought-form constructed by a dweomer-master to allow him or her to travel through the inner planes.

Cadvridoc (Dev.) A war leader. Not a general in the modern sense, the cadvridoc is supposed to take the advice and counsel of the noble-born lords under him, but his is the right of final decision.

Captain (Dev. pendaely.) The second in command, after the lord himself, of a noble's warband. An interesting point is that the word taely (the root or unmutated form of daely,) can mean either a warband or a family depending on context.

Deosil The direction in which the sun moves through the sky, clockwise. Most dweomer operations that involve a circular movement move deosil. The opposite, *widdershins*, is considered a sign of the dark dweomer and of the debased varieties of witchcraft.

Dweomer (trans. of Dev. dwunddaevad.) In its strict sense, a system of magic aimed at personal enlightenment through harmony with the natural universe in all its planes and manifestations; in the popular sense, magic, sorcery. Pronounced dway-OH-mer.

Egregore A body of knowledge that has been bound by astral forces and 'stored' on some higher plane. An egregore may be read by a person who knows the symbols necessary to 'unlock' it.

Ensorcel To produce an effect similar to hypnosis by direct manipulation of a person's aura. (True hypnosis manipulates the victim's consciousness only and thus is more easily resisted.)

Etheric The plane of existence directly 'above' the physical. With its magnetic substance and currents, it holds physical matter in an invisible matrix and is the true source of what we call 'life'.

Etheric Double The true being of a person for a single lifetime, the electromagnetic structure that holds the body together and that is the actual seat of consciousness.

Falcata (Latin) A curved and weighted sabre derived from the earlier falx – an ancient weapon, carried in our world by Hispanic tribes of the second and third centuries BC, independently reinvented by Gel da'Thae swordsmiths.

Gerthddyn (Dev.) Literally, a 'music man', a wandering minstrel and entertainer of much lower status than a true bard.

Gwerbret (Dev. The name derives from the Gaulish vergobretes.) The highest rank of nobility below the royal family itself. Gwerbrets (Dev. gwerbretion) function as the chief magistrates of their regions, and even kings hesitate to override their decisions because of their many ancient prerogatives.

Lwdd (Dev.) A blood-price; differs from wergild in that the amount of lwdd is negotiable in some circumstances, rather than being irrevocably set by law.

Malover (Dev.) A full, formal court of law with both a priest of Bel and either a gwerbret or a tieryn in attendance.

Mach-fala (Horsekin) A mother-clan, the basic extended family of Gel da'Thae culture.

Mazrak (Horsekin) A shape-changer.

Rakzan (Horsekin) The highest ranking military officer among the Gel da'Thae regiments, a position that bestows high honour on the mach-fala of the man holding it.

Rhan (Dev.) A political unit of land; thus, gwerbretrhyn, tierynrhyn, the area under the control of a given gwerbret or tieryn. The size of the various rhans (Dev. rhannau) varies widely, depending on the vagaries of inheritance and the fortunes of war rather than some legal definition.

Scrying The art of seeing distant people and places by magic.

Sigil An abstract magical figure, usually representing either a particular spirit or a particular kind of energy or power. These figures, which look a lot like geometrical scribbles, are derived by various rules from secret magical diagrams.

Tieryn (Dev., from Gaulish tigerinos) An intermediate rank of the noble-born, below a gwerbret but above an ordinary lord (Dev. arcloedd.)

Wyrd (trans. of Dev. tingedd.) Fate, destiny; the inescapable problems carried over from a sentient being's last incarnation.

Wyrd, Portion of, also known as the Pars Fortunae or Caput Draconis, in the Greggyn system, an astrological term for the position of the Earth within a horoscope; in the Elvish system it represents Aethyr. Deverrian astrologers have conflated the two meanings over the years.

A NOTE ON DATING

Year One of the Deverry calendar is the founding of the Holy City, or, to be more accurate, the year that King Bran saw the omen of the white sow that instructed him where to build his capital. It corresponds roughly to 76 C.E.